Faulks, Sebastian.
A fool's alphabet.

$19.95

BAKER & TAYLOR BOOKS

A FOOL'S ALPHABET

By the same author

A Trick of the Light
The Girl at the Lion d'Or

A FOOL'S ALPHABET

A NOVEL BY

SEBASTIAN FAULKS

Little, Brown and Company

Boston Toronto London

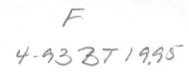

First U.S. Edition

The characters and events in this book are fictitious. Any
similarity to real persons, living or dead, is coincidental and
not intended by the author.

Library of Congress Cataloging-in-Publication Data
Faulks, Sebastian.
    A fool's alphabet : a novel / by Sebastian Faulks. — 1st
U.S. ed.
        p.   cm.
    ISBN 0-316-27547-6
    I. Title.
PR6056.A89F66   1992
823'.914 — dc20   92-23408

10   9   8   7   6   5   4   3   2   1

RRD–VA

Printed in the United States of America

FOR VERONICA

There is only one alphabet, which has spread over almost all of the world.

A. C. Moorhouse, *Writing and the Alphabet*

When you're a married man, Samivel, you'll understand a good many things as you don't understand now; but vether it's worth while goin' through so much to learn so little, as the charity boy said ven he got to the end of the alphabet, is a matter of taste.

Mr Weller, *Pickwick Papers*, Chapter 27

All letters form absence.

Edmond Jabès, *Livre des Questions*

A FOOL'S ALPHABET

ANZIO

aaaaaaaaaaaaaaaaaaaaaaaaaaaaaaaaaaaaaaaaaaaaaaaaaaaaaaaaaaaaaaaaaaaaaaaaaaaaaaaaaaaaaaaaaaaaaaaaaaaaaaa

Italy 1944

VESUVIUS was erupting. The trembling of the ground which was common in the Campania district was intensified so that cars would not remain still, even on level ground, but began to shudder and bolt like frightened horses. The sea in the Bay of Naples was being sucked back from the beach and swallowed by the ocean, leaving driftwood and stranded creatures on the suddenly revealed sand. Inland from the volcano a huge black cloud hung steadily until it was ripped by thick and wavering lengths of flame, which were like forks of magnified lightning. After a time the cloud began to sink down and cover the sea, obscuring the promontory and removing the island of Capri from sight.

In the streets of Sorrento, on the other side of the bay, the people ran to their houses. There was the sound of car engines being revved and rubber tyres squeezed against the roads by sudden acceleration. Shutters were brought together with a wooden thud before the iron arms descended to bolt them. The dense black cloud that hung across the bay seemed also to have loomed behind them, covering and flooding the hills. The flames remained distant, but ashes began to fall in the streets in dense showers.

Safe behind the glass doors of the balcony on the first floor of the convalescent hotel, Corporal Raymond Russell tapped a cigarette against the side of the packet, revolved it slowly between his fingers and poked it into the corner of his mouth.

'On your way tomorrow, then,' the medical officer had told him that morning. 'Got your orders?'

'Yes. Back to A Company,' said Russell.

The doctor briefly examined the healed shell wound in his left shoulder. 'Shouldn't give you any more trouble,' he said. He looked out of the window. 'It would be nice to spend the summer in Rome.'

'I'll do my best,' said Russell.

He had passed the day listening to the rumbling from across the bay, smoking cigarettes and thinking what still awaited him at Anzio. Vesuvius had taken his mind off it for a time, though the noise and violence of the eruption also reminded him of the forward positions in the beachhead.

He slept well, despite the volcano. In the morning he rose at seven, packed his kitbag and made his way downstairs in the old hotel that the Red Cross had taken over. There was a smell of coffee and the sound of Italian women talking and laughing in the kitchens. He felt caught in a trap of time, neither soldier nor civilian. He liked the sound of the women's voices and the everyday life they represented. He wanted this quite ordinary world of airy rooms, new bread, curtains, children. He forced the thought from his mind as he pushed open the swing doors of the hotel. His loyalty was with Sugden, Bell, Padgett, the Major and the other men in the icy slit trenches. He reconciled himself to the thought of further weeks of their undrinkable distilled alcohol, their sexual frustration and the slow hours of boredom punctuated by minutes of extreme terror.

The sun was out on the streets of Sorrento. As he began to walk downhill he passed a magnificent sign in which the iron was wrought like arthritic fingers to read 'Pasticceria' and hammered into a pink wall on the corner of a street. Under his feet the pavements were ankle-deep in grey dust from the volcano.

*

FOUR weeks earlier he had been jammed in between Bell and Padgett in the small landing craft that cast off from the mother ship in the Bay of Anzio. Bell's face was close to his, and he was breathing fast.

'Gallipoli,' he said, his eyes showing white through his blackened face. 'That's what our general thinks. Another bloody rat-trap. What do we want a Yank general for anyway?'

Russell felt the bevelled edge of the craft's iron rail beneath his hand. Next to him Padgett was praying with a rapid mumbling sound. It was a beautiful winter night, star-pocked, calm and mild. There had been cases of seasickness when they headed south towards Africa in some cumbersome diversionary move, but since the ships had swung round towards their true destination, carving a mile-wide circle of foam through the Tyrrhenian sea, the wind had died and the groaning had ceased.

Russell could see the dark outline of Anzio to their right. It looked a charming place: he imagined holidays and fishing. He had never been abroad until the war. Although in four years he had seen Holland, France and more of North Africa than he wanted, he was still excited by the sight of the small Italian coastal town and was disappointed that their craft would take them to the north of it.

'All right, you men?' The Major came to check morale. 'Nice little town, isn't it? Used to be a pirates' haven, you know.'

That was all he had time for as the craft surged on towards the beach.

'They sent out a group of men to test the texture of the sand,' muttered Bell. 'Never came back. Taken prisoner by the Jerries. They're waiting for us. Jesus Christ.'

The landing craft hit solid ground and Russell was thrown against Padgett, who dropped a box of ammunition on the deck. They heard the sound of 'Move', but they didn't need to be told. The waist-high water and yielding sand made it difficult to get going; with cursing and splashing, they managed to keep their packs and guns above the sea until they could move into a run. In his mind Russell heard the opening salvo of German machine-gun fire, the disdainful ripple of automatic weapons plied by men who had time to choose their targets; he was almost deafened by the expected thumping of entrenched artillery.

Nothing happened. Only Padgett's swearing and sloshing and the distant cries of encouragement from the landing craft came to his ears. They made the beach and ran for the tree line, weapons prodding the dark air, poised in the readiness of fear.

The landing was on a huge scale. The ships had come in from a measureless sea to disgorge men through the towns of Nettuno and Anzio, on up the coast to the furthest point of Peter beach, six miles to the north west. Their war had moved from Africa to Europe, yet they saw only the quadrant of darkness in front of their eyes.

Russell lay prone, the sand of Anzio in his nostrils where the force of his fall had driven it. Nobody moved or spoke. Their ears were bursting with expectation. Behind them they could hear more men splashing ashore. They willed them on, praying the gunfire would not start till they were covered. Other craft were landing further to their left. They began to lift their heads and look sideways. The beach was crawling with dark figures, hunched and labouring forwards under the weight of huge combat packs and boxes of ammunition. They were starting to pour into the scrub at the back of the beach and the pine trees beyond.

Still there was no sound, no shot.

The Major came to give them their orders. 'Get your men up there, Russell. Keep them out of sight.' He found it hard to keep the elation out of his voice.

'I don't bloody believe this,' said Bell. 'I just don't believe it.'

'Come on, Bell,' said Padgett, who was almost hysterical with relief. 'We'll get the action soon enough. It won't be like Pantelleria, you know.' He started giggling.

'At least we got the bloody craft the right way round this time,' said Bell.

After intensive practice, the company had landed the previous summer at the small island of Pantelleria, the first toehold gained in Europe by the Allied armies. A capricious wind had turned the craft around at the last minute so that the vanguard consisted of the medics, the caterers and the brigadier's car. It had not mattered. No shots had been fired, and the mayor had been pleased to see them. He kept giving Nazi salutes, then remembering himself, apologising and shaking hands.

'I liked Pantelleria,' said Russell, hoisting up his pack. 'I wish we could have stayed there longer. Come on then, let's get this kit up there.'

They moved rapidly inland – the heart of Italy at last – in the course of the night. From the town they could hear sporadic gunfire, but nothing that alarmed them. By dawn they had established radio contact with the Americans in Anzio. There had been hardly any fighting. A German car with four drunken officers on board had driven into the open mouth of a beached landing craft, mistaking it for a garage. It was, in Padgett's words, a piece of duff.

Two weeks later they had made no perceptible progress. They were penned into the beachhead by a continuous German bombardment that rattled and shook the fabric of their makeshift shelters and made the further landing of troops and supplies on the beach a job as hazardous as that undertaken by the men at the front. Russell's company had been pushed forward into a salient that stuck out, as many of the men remarked, like a sore thumb from the otherwise regular perimeter of the beachhead. The commanding officer had come to visit them. A tall man with a red, fleshy face, he managed to appear well dressed and relaxed even when stepping over the winter mud of the Italian plain with German shells landing a hundred yards away. He told them they were the best prepared group of fighting men in the British army. Their morale was high, their experience was unmatched and their company commanders were inspirational. He wanted them to show their courage, push forward when instructed and remember the glorious history of their regiment, a history which he himself appeared to have memorised down to the last details of the disposition of each platoon at Omdurman.

His talk went on at some length, but the Major had advised him that the men would not mind what he said or how long he took, provided they had been given permission to smoke. Much of what he said was in any case only a little exaggerated. The battalion was full of soldiers who had learned resilience under fire. Three of the four company commanders had been decorated. The Major in command of A Company had almost single-handedly secured the route to Tunis in a day of ferocious counterattack the previous spring.

That afternoon they dug slit trenches at the front. They could not delve too deep into the sandy soil of the plain or the water would have rushed in, though within a day even the shallowest were up to the men's calves with rain. Padgett's self-protective instincts had made him an inspired builder. He had the knack of finding old doors from shelled houses which he would cover with dirt to make roofs on their dug-outs.

At night the noise of bombardment made sleep impossible. The artillery barrage on both sides was almost constant, but the men soon learned to pick out other sounds. There was the rippling crackle of the spandau and the steadier bren. The mortars provided a background cough against which the high-pitched sound of a single bullet was still occasionally discernible.

Russell sat up smoking. He had begun the war as a private but had been promoted the previous year as a reward, according to the Major, for making the radio work. Although this was not now his responsibility, he liked to look over the equipment at night. Only two immutable rules seemed to have emerged from the war so far: that in preliminary fighting the artillery would kill more of their own men than the enemy's, and that once battle had been properly joined the 38 set from platoon to company headquarters would break down. The 38 set's principal function appeared to be picking up German propaganda broadcasts by an unconvincing temptress called Sally. The 18 set, by which the company communicated with battalion HQ, was more robust.

Some wireless experts built their own sets on which they were able to receive broadcasts from the BBC in London.

Sometimes at night, on the rare occasions of calm, Russell would make contact with an American in the 509th Parachute Infantry. This man, called Olsen, was an insomniac from Brooklyn. He told Russell about his family and about New York. The men in his regiment came from all over America. He would tell Russell about them. 'Then there's Washinsky, he's from Pennsylvania, you'd like him, he's real funny. And Bunny Wilson, he's from Minneapolis – you know, the twin towns, out there in the Midwest. It's great country there, farms that stretch as far as you can see. And let's see, there's Rossi, he's from Brooklyn too, and Williams and Lynch, they're both from Cleveland, and Eagleton, he's from – I guess he's from Nebraska someplace.' This was the voice of America calling; down the airwaves over the Italian plain.

Russell thought how strange it must be for these men to be here in this unforgiving marsh behind a seaside resort. Few of them, presumably, had known each other before; perhaps they had never visited one another's states. Nebraska must be as far from Brooklyn as Italy was from England. So this was their first experience of Europe. The randomness of it was peculiar. It had to be somewhere, so why not at Anzio? But the more interesting question was why? Why this unremarkable swamp which successive people had tried to reclaim and build on? He could feel as the days went on that newspapers, and then historians of the war, would talk about the invasion and the battle and that then it would become a name in history that would grow familiar and dulled. It didn't feel like that to him or, he was sure, to Olsen and his friends. It felt very particular, very ordinary and haphazard. The brutality of the fighting did not seem to change that, to make it worthy in some way of its place in history. It just seemed to make it more puzzling. Meanwhile it was hardly stretching a point to say that it was only here, in Italy, that Olsen's colleagues had become aware of their own country. Wilson from Minneapolis would never otherwise have met Rossi from

Brooklyn. The fragile idea of a nation only became real as they lay together, huddled in their wet trench.

THE next day they attacked. The artillery fired for an hour and then the Major gave the signal. In the clearing smoke and the mist they ran forward in the direction of a wood. Before they had gone twenty yards the field in front of them came alive. Shells from the German artillery bombardment had carved holes in the sodden grass, so that the residual green was brown with turned earth. The air was dense with machine-gun bullets. From all sides they heard the sound of fire, as though every piece of metal in the Fatherland had been melted down and forged and was now being fired at high velocity into the field they were attempting to cross. Flat on their faces, the mud of the malarial marsh in their eyes and noses, they edged towards the cover of a ditch which was not really a protection, more of a shadow on the ground. For three hours they attempted to return fire and retrieve what casualties they could. They spent the night in their exposed position, unable to get back to their lines.

For two days they attempted to regroup, advance or at least protect their flanks from the continuing counterattack. The radio had blown on the first day, both radio operators were dead and the shelling had not stopped at any time. 'These are the times that try men's souls,' Russell said to Padgett, who was lying beside him.

Bell flinched as a shell-burst sent mud and shock waves over them. 'This is not Gallipoli,' he said, 'this is the bloody Somme.'

Eventually a message reached them from the commanding officer. They were to withdraw to their original positions, but no further. Any German counterattack must be stopped at that line. As Russell stood up to relay the news to the seven men who remained in his section, a fragment of shell pierced his left shoulder.

IN hospital in Naples and later, recovering in Sorrento, he had time to reflect on the country he found himself in. How different

8

Anzio had looked from the sea. How different had the country-side around appeared when they took their first tentative steps into it. Up to the north-east were the Alban Hills, the alleged gateway to Rome that they were supposed to have taken by now. On the raised ground the Germans could look down on them and focus their bombardment with continuing accuracy.

The countryside had seemed quite pleasant at first, with a number of small farms just inland and the unconcerned shepherds taking their flocks to pasture. The lorries had rolled forward, with loud cries of 'Left hand down, chum', over the duckboards and through the woods, following routes devised by the dapper adjutant. Most of the scrub was burned by the end of April. What remained was blackened and charred, with clumps of uptorn roots. The good thing was that it no longer provided adequate cover for German patrols. In the early days many of the senior officers stood together on the overpass that crossed the main Anzio–Albano road, pleased with what they had achieved, and confident of progress. The overpass was now pitted and wrecked, with the remains of burned-out tanks beneath it.

In hospital Russell heard that the 8th Army's attack on Cassino had also failed. Despite flattening the monastery on top of the hill with bombs, the Allied armies had been repulsed and there was thus no prospect of their coming to the help of those at Anzio.

He had time to think about the people back in England, something he had not done much before. The house in Nottingham where he had been brought up had been ordinary in every way; it had not inspired much contemplation. From the view-point of Naples, his family, their friends and their houses seemed, if not dull, then at least unremarkable. He had no real sense of England as a place, either in geography or character. It was just where life happened. It was hard to reconcile that feeling with the suspicion that life might be as natural and as easily accepted in Pennsylvania, wherever that was, for Washinsky of the 509th Parachutes.

He had not expected to travel much, though he was surprised by how much he liked it. The aim of most people in his platoon seemed to be to minimise any differences they found between where they were stationed and what they knew in England. Insulated by the structure of the army, it was easy enough. The bully beef in the tins tasted the same in Italy as in Tunisia. But in various billets and on leave you could have some idea of the country you were in. The differences were a source of ridicule to most of the men: they saw any divergence from English customs as failure. It occurred to Russell, even as he laughed with them, that England would seem as strange to a visitor. He hardly knew his own country at all because he had nothing with which to compare it; perhaps the aspects of it he took as standard would seem as curious to a foreigner as those things in North Africa which made Sugden and Padgett guffaw. He regretted that he would never be able to see England through those dispassionate eyes.

His wounds, though slight, would in normal circumstances have entitled him to a period of rest. His battalion had by now, however, sustained serious losses and it was very much a question, as the Major put it, of 'all hands to the pump'. Russell didn't mind. He was fatalistic about whether he would die, and he felt uncomfortable being brought food in bed while the others were still under fire.

When he rejoined them, he found that they had retreated. The Germans were in the middle of a sustained counterattack which Hitler himself had ordered to drive the Allies back into the sea. The town of Anzio was forlorn. On the naval ship that brought Russell in from Naples the men took bets on whether various buildings would still be standing; between each of their regular supply runs another substantial landmark would disappear. Russell walked through the shattered streets where sections of elaborate cornicework, blown from impressive villas, lay in the more general debris. Some of the sturdier houses had walls or parts of them intact, though the roofs had gone. Most of the houses had been reduced to rubble, however; the rubble was then ground to powder by further bombardment.

Back with his company Russell found the men grumbling but

determined. The major of B Company, who was thought to be invulnerable, had been wounded. Having brushed aside shells and grenades, he had finally been hit by a sniper while he stood outside a recently captured farmhouse. Sugden had been blown up in the air by a shell during an attempted advance, but on landing had continued walking; Bell had seen it with his own eyes. Padgett had reported sick with trench foot. The medics had put the offending part in water, but it had not swelled up in the prescribed way, so he had been sent back to the front. Another member of Russell's platoon had had an attack of the shakes, or Anzio anxiety as the others called it, and had been ordered to rest. It was said that a man in D Company had been carried away screaming, strapped to a stretcher. Others had been killed or wounded. Nothing much had changed.

Russell's section was occupying one of the farmhouses they had taken from the Germans. It had a concrete oven in the courtyard which gave ideal protection to a machine gunner, and the half-broken walls provided cover for the others. As billets went, it was an improvement, and Padgett had been able to earth and sandbag the vulnerable points with his usual skill. It was only a temporary shelter, however, en route to another trench from which they were supposed to attack.

'We're lucky here, mate,' said Bell, who was brewing up that night. 'A couple of days and it'll be back to bloody Passchendaele.'

Russell was trying to play cards with Sugden. 'How do you know so much about the Great War, Frank?' he said.

'My dad was in it. Yes. What a show that was. The Somme. Ypres. He saw the lot. Come back with lungs full of gas. You should have heard him cough.'

Sugden looked up. 'There's some Yankee chap out on the Mussolini canal, he's got this new trick. When one of the Jerries slips out of his trench to go for a piss, this bloke picks him off.'

Bell ignored him. 'To tell the truth,' he said, 'I don't mind where we go or what happens provided we never inherit another trench from the Sherwood Foresters. Blimey.'

Sugden came from Yorkshire. He objected to the way Bell, a Londoner, was always grumbling. It was true that the Sherwood Foresters were known for leaving a mess. And it was not that he was so cheerful himself. It was more that he was suspicious of the fibre of a southerner and therefore resented his complaints. A half-hearted argument began to rumble between the two men, which ended when Bell produced the food.

'My brother-in-law's got a fish shop in Halifax,' said Sugden. 'Best fish and chips for miles.'

The men looked down dumbly at their plates.

'I could do with a nice cod and chips right now,' said Russell.

'Not cod,' said Sugden. 'We never have cod. That's a dirty fish. We have haddock.'

The officer in charge of the platoon had gone back to company headquarters excited by the prospect of the drink ration that would have accumulated for him since he had been up the line. He was an excitable but tenacious character of, it appeared to Russell, about sixteen years old. His absence meant that Sergeant Quinn, a thin, melancholy man from somewhere in the northwest, was in charge.

Quinn was an expert in body disposal. He appeared not to mind the stench of the corpses the previous platoon had been too hurried or too crazed to bury. He was also a sound organiser who made sure that the men's water bottles were full and that they remained shaved and passably clean. He had a number of theories about Bell's snoring, though none of his proposed remedies had yet proved effective.

That night Russell tried to call up his American friend Olsen, but there was no luck. Maybe Olsen was dead, or the radio smashed. As the German artillery started up again, Russell missed his voice. They had swapped addresses and agreed to meet one day, when the war was over. That night as he listened to the sinister rustling of shells in the air above them, he missed the voice of America intoning the names of those distant towns.

★

THE German offensive was in its last spasm. Goaded by the Führer, who spoke from the safety of Berchtesgaden, the exhausted infantry came forward once more. The Major was ordered to take his company up in the late afternoon to counterattack. In a ten-acre field ahead of the front trenches they ran into well-stocked German positions. The air again seemed to turn to metal and the men began to fall in numbers.

Sugden, who was advancing twenty yards to Russell's left, was lifted from his feet by a shell. This time he did not come down. The Major himself fell backwards with a bullet through the helmet. Crouched in a shell hole, serving as a pit for two bren, Russell was firing vainly towards the German lines when he felt the air taken from his lungs as though his ribcage had been crushed. Then he felt no pain, but was aware that the top of his battledress was filled with hot liquid. He fell forward in the mud. He had not heard the sound of the shell.

It was dark when he regained consciousness and the firing had stopped. He heard a British voice calling out for help, about twenty yards to his left. He tried to move, but found that the shell had not only pierced his chest but a second splinter appeared to have broken his right leg. Once more his cheek was against the wet earth as he struggled to stay conscious. He concentrated on calling out for help, though for all he knew it might just as well attract German sniper fire as medical aid.

For hours he lay shouting as loudly as his damaged chest would allow. The other man fell silent. Towards dawn he heard an urgent British voice from fifty yards away. It was a search party, with a doctor, who had heard his cries. As they came towards him, machine-gun fire started from the woods, and they dropped to their fronts. It took them a quarter of an hour to reach him. The doctor gave him morphine and bandaged his leg. Russell directed them towards the second voice. Two of them then lugged him towards a ditch at the side of the field. A Very light fired from the German lines showed them suddenly bright against the dark landscape, and as the firing began they bundled him into the ditch. They covered the hundred yards back to the trenches in slow dragging bursts. The top of the ditch was continuously strafed and Russell felt the two halves of his tibia rub together. Back in the dug-out he was given a second dose of morphine; the main supply was with the doctor, and he was still on his stomach in the field searching for the second survivor.

The next day Russell was removed to the tented hospital by the shoreline. Half conscious by now, he was only mildly upset when the German artillery shells began to land in the hospital area, smashing the wooden struts and planks that held the stretched canvas in a semblance of roofs and floors, killing medics and wounded alike.

That night he was on a naval ship that steamed slowly out of Anzio, south towards Naples and Castellammare, and this time there would be no quick return. Castellammare, he said to himself as he lay sweating in his bunk. A castle on the sea. Castellammare . . .

The town of Anzio, once the summer haunt of the Emperor Nero, receded from view astern of the plodding ship, its villas in ruins, its whitewashed cottages reduced to their constituent mortar, sand and brick, as though their existence as houses had been no more than a playful and temporary escape from the enduring facts of powder and earth. The water of the bay erupted with turbulent belches where the stray shells continued to fall from the night sky.

In Capua, some twenty miles north of Naples, the spring was unusually warm. From his farmhouse bedroom Russell could see the flocks of birds wheeling in the uncultivated foothills of the Caserta mountains to the north and watch the farm-workers busying themselves in the moist coastal plain to the south and west.

He had been sent to recuperate with an Italian family after being discharged from hospital; his wounds were not as serious as had at first been thought. The doctors in the beach hospital had saved his lung on the first night, and the leg had been broken cleanly. What was prescribed now was rest. The Major had defied expectations by recovering from his head wound; he was anxious to rejoin his men, but had insisted that Russell take time off. The Red Cross, whose convalescent centres were full, had been able through its network of volunteers to place some wounded men with sympathetic families.

Russell's family consisted of a large bearded man who ran the farm, his wife, three even bigger sons, and their cousin, a nineteen-year-old girl called Francesca whose parents had sent her from Rome.

On his arrival Russell, still struggling to overcome a fever induced by an infection in his leg, had slept for three days. He awoke to an unaccustomed sight. His eyes were used to a view of Bell's socks hung out to dry first thing in the morning, or to Padgett's naked back as he went through his rudimentary ablutions. He was aware of a knocking on the door, and footsteps on the bare boards. Shutters were opened on rusting hinges and a draught of air filled the room. He looked up and into the almost black eyes of a dark-haired girl, who took his hand and moved it to one side so she could lay a small tray containing bread and coffee on the bedcovers. Her face shone with concern, though in her eyes there was also a hint of shyness, as if all her sympathy could not overcome a feeling that he would not want her there.

Russell had a rough grasp of Italian and was able to thank the girl, Francesca. She had studied English to a modest level and was able to ask him how he felt. 'Much better, *molto bene*,' he replied. And it was true; the fever was gone, the constriction in his ribs was tolerable, the pain in his leg was less severe. He felt clear-headed at last, and hopeful.

After some exchanges about the weather, the town of Capua, and Francesca's family, an awkward silence fell.

Francesca stood up and smiled, then made as if to leave. Russell held up his hand. 'No, no. Please stay. *Voglio* . . . *Italiano* . . .' He could not think of the word for 'to learn'. '. . . *parlare*.'

Francesca laughed, a movement which caused her dark hair to

15

sway back from her white neck. She sat down on the edge of the bed, and the lesson began.

In the succeeding days Russell began to get out of bed and walk around the farm with the aid of a stick that the Red Cross had sent with him. He offered his help with the running of the farm, though there was not much that his physical state allowed him to do. He could manage to chop firewood for the range using a short-handled axe, sitting at one end of the cavernous kitchen. At the other end Francesca or her aunt would usually be cooking. Russell tried not to let them see how much he enjoyed watching them. He also liked to spend time in the uncle's workshop. He was able to mend an old wireless, and to do some simple woodwork, renovating window frames or planing new floorboards for the bedrooms. He liked everything about the place, from its position on the rising ground down to the rough linen sheets in which he slept. The quiet of the night, after the guns of Anzio, rolled over him.

His lessons with Francesca proceeded well. Soon he could speak enough Italian to converse with the family, though their accents seemed different from the one Francesca taught him. Although he was supposed to be the pupil, it became clear after a week that Francesca was in fact learning more English than he was Italian. Her mind was as quick as her movements, though as reluctant to draw attention to itself; when he pointed out what had happened she chided him and told him he must in that case try harder. He couldn't help noticing that she did so in English.

At nineteen she was seven years younger than him. She was also the gentlest creature he had ever met. He became aware after no more than a week that there was something in her character which transcended anything to do with the way she looked or the things she said; it was as if this part of her had been made for him alone. He was surprised in some way by this, because it had never occurred to him before that such a process could have taken place in a foreign country.

One day Francesca came running up the stairs to his room with a newspaper. Monte Cassino had fallen to the Poles, the

British had broken through to the east, and the Americans were driving up the middle. At Anzio they had broken out of the beachhead at last. 'We're shooting the works,' the American general had assured the British. The two armies would meet, and Rome would be theirs within days. Francesca's eyes were shining in excitement. They pored over the newspaper together. Russell felt disappointed at having missed the action.

A week later he had a letter from the Major, forwarded from a poste restante at Naples. The break-out had been sudden, bloody and determined. Many more men had died. The Major did not have space for detail, but in the savage fighting it appeared that Bell had, in the parlance of the company, gone berserk, going on a one-man charge, taking out two machine-gun nests and providing cover for a dangerous advance by his platoon. He was to be recommended for a medal.

Russell was expected to report to the Infantry Reinforcements Training Depot, a no man's land for the recovering wounded.

As the time grew near for his departure, Russell wondered what he could say to Francesca. The day he was due to leave he went for a walk in the scrubby orchard at the rear of the house. He was able to move with freedom and expected the medical officer's report in Naples to be positive. It was an intense summer's day, with the southern Italian sun softened by only the faintest westerly breeze. Russell felt the grass of the orchard already dry and long beneath his feet.

He tried to think of the life he would resume, but it was impossible. Nottingham. England. Sunday afternoons, buses, work. The beer in the pubs, the expectations of friends and colleagues. Would his Italian adventure seem insane when he looked at it from this perspective? Without the habit of self-examination, he had only instinct on which to rely. When he saw Francesca in the courtyard, filling a bucket from a pump, he took her by the arm and led her back into the orchard.

'I have to go tomorrow, Francesca,' he said.

'I know.'

17

He stood still and looked at her closely. Her normal vitality seemed to have left her when he brought up the subject of his leaving, but this might have been no more than politeness.

'And then I won't see you again,' he said.

'No, maybe not.' She was looking down at the ground.

'I shall go back and fight and then when the war is over I shall return to England, to the house I told you about.'

Francesca said nothing, but remained with her eyes fixed on the ground. Russell felt he had missed a chance. He had had no rehearsal for this kind of thing.

Francesca suddenly looked up. 'Tomorrow I will come with you to Naples, yes? I can take you to the station. I will make some food to take.'

Her eyes were wide and shining up into his. He felt grateful for the way she had saved him from his own silence. Spurred by the feeling of gratitude, he reached out to her with both arms. She laid her head on his chest and squeezed his waist tightly.

SHE did not in the end make a picnic but accompanied him to the station, where he left his kitbag, and then went with him to a restaurant for lunch. They ate fish and salad and drank white wine that tasted of herbs.

'You will wait for me, won't you?' he said. 'Even when I've gone back to England?'

'Ah,' she said, half mocking and then with growing concern, 'it is you who must wait for me. First until I am twenty-one and then until the war is over.'

'I will.'

Resting his elbow on the table, he reached out and took her hand. He could see from the intensity of her look and of her movements that for her the passing of time would be difficult. For him another month or two would make little difference; he had in any case to negotiate his own survival.

'And we will marry in my parents' village?' she said.

'If that's what you would like.'

He looked at his watch and felt the pressing anguish of his

departure. He drained his coffee cup. Francesca cried all the way to the station. He forbade her to come on to the platform. Even as he was kissing her goodbye she kept making him repeat his promises. 'You will write each week. And as soon as the war is finished you will visit. And you won't mind about my grand-mother at the wedding?'

As the train slid from the station he could still hear her voice in his head. 'And then we will live in the countryside. And the child, the child?'

BACKLEY

bbbbbbbbbbbbbbbbbbbbbbbbbbbbbbbbbbbbbbbbbbbbbbbbbbbbbbbbbbbbbbbbbbbbbbbbbbbbbbbbbbbbbbbbbbbbbbbbbbbbbbbbbbbb

England 1950

THE boy was born in the bathroom of his parents' house on the edge of Berkshire, where the Downs look one way into Wiltshire and another towards Oxford. The doctor, a shy man from Swindon, told Francesca Russell to move the bed into the bathroom to be closer to the hot running water. With hands prone to shake at the memory of night-time bombing missions over Germany, the doctor had no stomach for blood and was alarmed by the female body. Although he had delivered half a dozen babies before the war, he could no longer really remember what all that hot water was supposed to be for. He entrusted the close work to the local midwife, an efficient woman from Wantage.

Francesca Russell underwent terrible pain as she gave birth. It being the middle of the day, her husband was at work and she had only the midwife to ask later why the human body was so inconsiderately designed. Her son was not in fact particularly large. He was damp and red with a smear of gingerish hair across his scalp.

Pietro Thomas Russell, as he was later christened in the Catholic church, was one of the few children in the district not to have been declared a prodigy by his parents at the age of six months. He liked to sleep. Not necessarily at night, or only at night; but after meals, before bed and throughout the morning. His mother fed him lovingly and sang to him while he opened his mouth. He took the food with a steady unembarrassed zeal. Francesca, proud of his appetite, wondered if she should be boiling and drying quite so many nappies every day. When she cut down on the amount she gave him to eat, the baby began to sleep less and to show at last some interest in the waking world.

Raymond Russell was pleased with his son and didn't mind that Francesca wanted him to be a Catholic. His own version of Anglicanism was vague. Its central mood seemed to be one of apology. It was natural for it to defer to another brand of Christianity even if it mildly disapproved of some of its rituals. It would have been wrong and un-English for his religion to push itself forward or make its own claims. He assumed he would have his say when it came to the more material aspects of his son's education.

Soon after Pietro had learned to walk Francesca bought him a dressing gown that was several sizes too large and covered his feet from view. His tottering, erratic spurts about the room consequently looked as though they were propelled on hidden castors. He lacked concentration. When Francesca gave all her charm and skill to interest him in some highly coloured game, his eyes would glaze over and he would rush from the room to point with solemn interest at a milk bottle or a stone. When for the eighth time he ignored her warning about the steepness of the steps outside the kitchen door, she pretended to have no sympathy and told him that his bleeding lip would teach him a lesson. Then she picked him up and held him, seeing his blood on the front of her cotton shirt. For a moment he stopped wailing, but it was only so he could fill his lungs for a still greater effort. Francesca tried to believe that the lapse between the inhalation of breath and the final expulsion of the sob was not a true indicator of his distress.

The lightening of his solipsistic world came like a long-awaited dawn on a dark sea. First there was his evident love for his mother. Then there came a grudging but appreciable change of outlook in his other attitudes. He managed to listen to whole sentences uttered by his parents without tossing his head in impatience or frank disbelief. He formed an unprompted friendship with a surly boxer puppy that his father had bought from a local farmer. He took a fierce interest in the lives of various animal characters in the comic strips his mother read to him. At last, when some large-eyed bear was separated from its family, Pietro shed his first tears on behalf of another.

Francesca was relieved by the evidence of altruism. There had been moments in the long night of his infancy when she wondered if her son would ever look beyond the immediate desires of his body. Now she felt ashamed of such doubts. She wasn't yet ready to proclaim him a genius or a saint, but she was content that he would be a good boy, like his father, and like her own father back in Rome.

The pain of Pietro's birth, however, had not been merely the price of motherhood. There were minor abnormalities in Francesca which persuaded the doctor to refer her to a specialist who in turn told her that she should not consider having other children for the time being. He said she should come and see him at intervals and he would tell her when it was safe for her to begin again. Russell was more disappointed than his wife by the news. He saw himself as the head of a family of three or four children at least.

Francesca herself, brought up in the idea of large and extended families, felt the strangeness of her intimacy with Pietro. With no one else in the house, he was her friend and the recipient of her confidences. When she taught him to speak she felt as though she were entering a private conspiracy with him. She taught him Italian words as well as English. When something upset or worried her she told him about it, even though she knew he could barely understand the words and would have no conception of the feelings. Gradually he became more interested in what she said. Most of his utterances were demands for information, for the names of animals and objects. He always wanted to know what things were for. There came the day, however, when he asked his first personal questions of her; when he wanted to know about some aspect of her life.

The days passed in a long helpless slide as the boy was two or three or five years old. A new quality began to grow in him. It started with the way in which he mouthed the words he spoke. The first time he uttered a new word it was with a gentle awe that made it sound unspoken until that moment, as though his child's palate had just minted it. But it was not just the inexperience of the very young; although he was stern towards himself and others, there was also some gentleness in him, which showed in the way he spoke to animals or the puzzled manner in which he would hold a flower up for his mother's inspection and then put it back in its vase. He seemed impressed by the natural world, pointing in wordless wonder to the trees and hills near where they lived. There was often alarm in his voice when he first noticed something, particularly a new place, but he could be reassured by Francesca and would then become protective towards the thing he had seen. She thought of this gentleness as in some way connected to his Italian side. She told him he had her father's eyes and thought they were in some way the witness of his inheritance.

Though she was still almost a girl herself, Francesca felt the weight of adulthood when she looked at the unprotected innocence of the boy. It made her frightened when she thought of the masculinity he would rapidly and eagerly acquire. Then he would be taken away from her. Even in his innocence, which was really neither boy's nor girl's, only human, she was aware of the pattern of manhood waiting to emerge. When they talked and played together, Francesca felt strange in the protective role of her femininity towards his childish maleness. She held him in her arms and prayed, one thing: that her son would not, like her brother, die in war.

RAYMOND Russell hired a woman from the village to come and help his wife with the house. Mrs Graham was a large, uncompromising person who was used to being obeyed. She introduced a routine which had previously been lacking. Until then Francesca's start to the day had been three cups of coffee and a hurried breakfast with her husband before going to the garden gate and waving as his grey Humber Hawk disappeared from view. Then she went to play the gramophone or the radio, tucked her hair up into a scarf and zipped round the house with a duster. There was no pattern or purpose to her cleaning until Mrs Graham insisted on doing different rooms properly on selected days.

Pietro by this time was at school, where he was frustrated by his inability to do things. He could see in his mind the pictures he wanted to paint and was disappointed by the blotches he produced on the paper. Once he poured the coloured water in his jam jar over the girl sitting next to him. The headmistress of the school said he was not a naughty boy but that he needed bringing out of himself. Francesca used to go to collect him before lunch and put him on a seat on the back of her bicycle. He told her there were Red Indians following them.

Francesca Russell loved her son and she loved her husband. He wasn't an exciting or romantic man and, though she was undemanding, even Francesca noticed that he had an aversion to parting with money. He also, however, had an extreme modesty of aspiration. He had twice rejected the offer of further promotion in the army; he was grateful to have come through the war alive. To have married such a woman and to be a father was as much as he asked. Once a colleague at work hinted that he was a lucky devil to have a glamorous young Italian wife. Russell didn't know how to respond. His admiration of Francesca was at odds with his belief that nothing he himself had won or achieved could be worth having. He looked flustered and confused, and none of his colleagues raised the subject again.

When her husband had gone to work Francesca sometimes used to turn on the radio in the sitting room. She listened to *Housewives' Choice* or any programme that played tuneful music. When Pietro was very small she sometimes danced with him, going down on her knees so she was on the same level. When the music stopped she would speak to him, her cheeks a little pink from the exertion, her breath hot on his face.

He liked this moment in particular, and it came to be one of his first clear memories. Her breath sometimes had a faint residual smell of roast coffee, sometimes of violets, but usually it was just warm air which he felt was all the better for having come from inside her. When she talked to him she would hold the front of his shirt in her hands and then bring her wrists together so he would be trussed. There was no reason he could ever see for his mother doing this, but it was a good sign in her, like the way she made him lift up his arms when she belted him into his macintosh.

Although Pietro felt a fierce attachment to his parents and the place in which he lived, he always kept in his mind the possibility of Italy as a long-term destination. Encouraged by stories his mother told him, he had visions of a village by the sea where he would one day arrive and be happy. His Italy was a figment of his mother's imagination. Pietro, who had no means of verifying what she told him, imagined a large country where the sun always shone, even though it was never too hot. People did very little work and he had an idea that they sang to each other instead of speaking. Everyone, he believed, drove a Maserati. In a geography lesson at school they had been given blank maps of the world and asked to name the countries they knew. Pietro wrote 'Italy' diagonally across the continent of Africa because it looked the largest, most central and best shaped country. He was at first incredulous when told that Italy was only the jagged afterthought on the rim of Europe.

He loved the shapes of countries on the school globe and joined in the loud competitions to name the capitals. The relative sizes were perplexing. Britain seemed shamefully small compared to Africa or South America, to say nothing of Russia, which stretched on and on over the top of the world. But what happened there? You never seemed to hear of anything. Presumably boys like him went to school in these funny places and learned the same things. He could not help feeling a bit sorry for them, as though they had missed out on something. He tried to imagine what it would be like if he had been born in Egypt or Uruguay or Australia. Then his father would be an Egyptian. And his mother . . . It was not possible to imagine this, because obviously he would be a different person if he had been born somewhere else. This seemed to him an important thing to understand.

Now that he was at a school with proper lessons he saw less of his mother. He turned his eye cautiously on his fellow pupils. Most of the lessons were organised as competitions, with the winners announced and given paper stars to stick against their names on the notice board. Pietro at once joined in, certain he could master this game by determination. His tongue stuck vertically from the corner of his mouth as he covered his exercise books in heavy black pencil. When he gave in his work he at last allowed his eyebrows to relax and resume their normal shape. He sat back, waiting for his due reward, and couldn't believe it when his name appeared towards the bottom of the class. He redoubled his concentration, but found that effort was no substitute for ability.

Once a year the school had a football match against a rival school ten miles further along the edge of the Downs. Although Pietro's school taught thrift and modesty it made an exception for the match. The chosen eleven boys were given coloured shirts with numbers, which they were allowed to keep. After the game the teams had a cooked tea which had become the subject of myth over the years. The boys competed through the winter for the honour of being chosen. Pietro practised with his friend Stephen Brown after school, kicking a football backwards and forwards, bouncing it off the wall at the back of the playground. They were too small for selection in the first year but had hopes for the second.

Pietro's parents also liked the area in which they had chosen to live. His father was pleased by its remoteness and by the fact that he had managed to buy the house for a reasonable price. Francesca was so absorbed in her son and in the world of her imagination that she barely noticed where she was. Sometimes she looked at the grey, stripped hill through the fading light of a December afternoon and felt an ache in her muscles for the sun of Italy, but her temperament was so naturally high-spirited that she felt no real discontent. They made some friends in the district, though seeing them was always a planned and formal operation. There were cocktail parties where men, unsure of American fashion, made potent mixtures in chromium shakers, and women became light-headed and flirtatious. At one party Francesca was present in the kitchen when the host took a bottle of gin, drank a couple of inches straight from it, filled it up with grapefruit juice, shook it and served the result over small cubes of ice. Two people were sick in the garden.

One day when Pietro was on his school holidays Francesca suggested that in the afternoon they go for a walk to the old barn. They had macaroni cheese for lunch and Pietro looked at his mother suspiciously, wondering why she had not only given him his favourite food but was then taking him to the place he liked best.

Pietro stood outside the house watching his breath make trails in the air while Francesca went to fetch Rusty, the dog. The first time he had noticed the hot clouds people made with their mouths was when his mother had sung to him. They had been walking and he was complaining of being tired. She told him to carry on, because it was good for him. When he was almost asleep on his feet she took his hand and burst out laughing: 'Your little hand's so cold.' When she realised what she had said, she laughed some more and began to sing, 'Your little hand is frozen'. She had picked him up and carried him and he could feel the rise and fall of her chest as she breathed. He thought the vapour clouds that trailed from her lips were something to do with singing.

He was too big to be carried now, though he hadn't lost his dislike of walking. The road up from the village was the road of all his childhood. There were houses at first, then only trees and fields. The trees were bareish and dark with angular branches. The earth was turned and often muddy. The colours were grey and watery green. At the top of the road was a path through the wood which was so waterlogged that Pietro could sink deep enough to let the water in over the top of his boots.

They didn't take that track on this occasion, but where the road from the village petered out they took a short walk uphill to the broken-down barn. Francesca sat and watched while Pietro balanced on fallen beams and climbed up a ladder to a platform where he hid from her. She pretended she could never tell where he was, despite his excited gurglings. He made her laugh, though he was never sure then or later if she was laughing at his game or whether it was because he seemed such a fool to her.

When she had allowed him just two more minutes at least three times, they finally left the barn and walked to the top of the hill. Here there was a long, bending track which disappeared into dense green woods at the far end. On either side the fields fell away steeply. Here you could feel at peace. This narrow, pitted roadway, with its strip of grass along the middle where the tractors and the carts hadn't worn it down, was like a ridge or spine that joined two things: at one end, the friendly barn and the village below, and at the other, the dense and alarming woods. To the right were falling fields; to the left, on the horizon, were the first evening lights of the town. Rusty, the dog, was running flat out in the distance. Some yards ahead of him a brown shape popped up and down, switching direction in mid-leap, so that Rusty was always swerving and checking in his pursuit.

'Come here, mister. I want to tell you something.' Francesca was sitting on a stile. 'Come here and sit on my knee.' Pietro looked up into her face. Her cheeks were pink from the air but her dark eyes didn't have their usual sparkle. 'Your mama's going into the hospital tomorrow for a tiny operation. I'm going to be out again in three days' time. It's nothing at all serious, just a thing lots of women have. But I want you to be a good boy while I'm away.'

Pietro could hardly believe she was serious. Nothing could express his horror of that big alien building with its doctors and death and strangers in a huge room. The thought of his mother in such a place was unbearable, and he began to cry, as she had guessed he would.

'Don't be silly. It's a tiny operation. I promise you. My little boy, would I lie to you, would I?'

Pietro didn't know what to say. He saw that he had been silly and that his mother was telling the truth, but it was too late to stop crying now.

They held hands as they walked down the hill back towards the village. When he got in from work Raymond Russell gave Pietro a talk in the sitting room, saying he would have to learn to cook and be like a wife to him while his mother was away. Pietro went along with the idea, though they both knew Mrs Graham would come and do the work. His father wasn't good at moments like these and tended to assign people roles in the hope that some sort of discipline would do the trick.

'Come on, Ginger,' said Mrs Graham, who had already moved in, 'time you were in bed.' His father called him 'Pietro' or 'old man', his mother called him 'mister' or 'my little boy'. It was only Mrs Graham who sometimes called him 'Ginger'. His hair still had some red in it but was more noticeable for being stiff and unruly. He didn't mind being called Ginger, however, because it meant Mrs Graham was in a good mood with him.

When he came back from school the next day he was told that his mother had gone to hospital. He went and had a talk with his father, thinking he wouldn't know how to pass the time without his wife. Russell was smoking a cigarette and looking through some reference books. He seemed quite cheerful. Mrs Graham had cooked the tea and sent Pietro off to have a bath afterwards. Everyone seemed so normal that he forgot to worry.

The next day at school the football team was announced for the annual fixture against the local rivals. Pietro and Stephen Brown were both in it. Football was only allowed under supervision in the afternoons. During the morning break between lessons they went and played their own game in a neighbouring field. One gang had possession of a large fallen tree. A second, smaller gang based itself on the rooted stump and tried to push the members of the bigger gang off the trunk without losing control of their own camp.

After tea that day Pietro went round to Stephen's house for tea. He was aware dimly that Mrs Brown was trying to be very nice to him. Later on, Stephen's father, who was a policeman, rode up on his bike. The dynamo used to falter on the hill leading to his house, so the light was always feeble in the darkness. He was very jolly that afternoon and let Pietro try on his policeman's helmet. He had a cup of tea with the rest of them while the laundry hung on wooden clothes-horses and washing-lines around the kitchen.

Two days later, just as she had promised, Francesca returned from hospital. Pietro was sitting at the kitchen table with Mrs Graham, sick with excitement. When he heard the familiar rumble of the Humber Hawk in the road outside, he leapt from his chair. He felt Mrs Graham's hand on his shoulder. 'Remember what your father said. She may be weak.' Pietro tried hard to restrain himself as he ran down to the garden gate. He was partly successful, arriving against his mother's ribs with the subdued thump he might have reserved for a not very important football tackle. His eyes scanned her face to see if she was still the same. To his shame he heard himself say something like, 'Don't ever go away again.'

Things returned to normal. After some days of rest Francesca was up and about again, moving round the house with her hair escaping from her scarf. She had taken to wearing slacks with small slits at the ankle, like Doris Day, and her husband had given her, as a get-well present, a pink plastic transistor radio from America. There wasn't much change in her day except after lunch when Mrs Graham would sometimes order her up to bed for a rest. She went reluctantly, clutching the radio beneath her arm.

After he had come back from school Pietro would sometimes insist on reading to his mother. He read in a halting, loud voice, like an East European trade unionist determined to deliver in English a fraternal greeting to delegates. Eventually, to put an end to the agony of the slowly moving forefinger and the harsh, plosive delivery, Francesca would have to read to him instead. He would go and stand by her chair and try to read with her. Then if he was tired, he would rest his head on her shoulder so that her hair trailed across his cheek, enfolding his head, and in these moments Francesca felt a deep tranquillity.

At the weekends Pietro sometimes went out with his father in the Humber and urged him to drive it faster. He said there was a boy at school called Jeremy Wingate, who was the best footballer, and his father had a car that could go a hundred miles an hour. His father smiled patiently and explained about speed limits and fuel conservation. He didn't talk much. He smoked a good deal and gave off a generally obliging air.

The countryside they drove through didn't have the evergreens of Surrey or the ragged beauty of the north with its drystone walls and open countryside. The grass was light green, and sometimes the trees looked ashen, greyish against the hills. The land wasn't farmed heavily and there were no fields of yellow corn or fat cattle. There were discoloured sheep and regular, anaemic crops. The earth had a certain character, however; it had a dry, ancient feel, as though it had been there, unregarded, for a long time.

ONE morning at school there was a development on the tree trunk. For the first time ever the small gang from the stump took control of the entire fallen tree. Half a dozen small boys, Pietro among them, stood on it taunting the others. During the skirmish that followed a fat boy with glasses, called Nicholas Worrall, fell from the trunk and tore the sleeve off his shirt. He also lost the skin from the bridge of his nose. The bell rang before the main gang could regain control and the boys went back into the school.

There was an immediate row about Nicholas Worrall's shirt and bloodied nose. The teachers wanted to know who was responsible. Pietro, said somebody. Pietro, silently proud of his part in repelling invaders, didn't deny it, but assumed the others

31

would also claim their part in victory. None of them came forward. In a swift change of mood, Pietro was wrong-footed. From having been one of the heroes of the moment, he suddenly became the object of remarks like 'Typical Pietro' and 'Pietro does it again'. The headmaster took him outside and lectured him on respect for property and violence towards other boys. The punishment was that Pietro was dropped from the football team for the match on Friday.

Incredulous, he returned to class, where, by an effort of will, he prevented himself from crying. When the bus dropped him off and he ran up the lane that afternoon he could no longer keep his indignation inside him. He found his mother in the garden and hurled himself against her. At first she laughed as he tried unsuccessfully to explain his distress. His voice came in broken whoops and explosions of compressed air.

Francesca stopped smiling and soothed him till he could tell her the story of his great injustice. From the narrative that came out, back to front, still broken up by sobs and indignation, she eventually pieced together what had happened.

Then she folded him in her arms and laid his head against her shoulder. 'My little boy,' she said, 'my little boy.' She talked to him and stroked his head until at last he was calm. When he had stopped sobbing and allowed himself to be soothed by his mother's words of reassurance, he gradually came to see that there was nothing she could do to set right what had gone wrong. She could offer only comfort; she was not, after all, omnipotent.

COLOMBO

Sri Lanka 1980

PIETRO Russell was the only passenger to leave the plane
when it stopped at Colombo on its way from Hong Kong
to the Middle East. Hong Kong to Colombo is a strange
trip to make. A few Chinese businessmen might reluctantly
leave the Crown colony and inspect some business project in
up-country Sri Lanka to see if it is worth the investment of a few
million dollars. Or some unusually adventurous Sinhalese
businessman might be returning after an attempt to raise capital
in Hong Kong for a scheme in his native island. But these things
are rare, and when Pietro came down the steps of the Boeing 747,
there was only him to feel the heavy night air that blew in from
the palm trees round the airport.

It was a luxurious sensation. He was the only man to offer a
passport to the smiling immigration clerk, the only man to see
his suitcases carried in by the equally smiling porter. There was
none of the usual feeling of displacement. There was hardly
anyone there at all.

Pietro wondered how the thin porter could carry his heavy
cases outside to the taxi and tipped him an amount which in
Hong Kong might have passed for normal but which in
Colombo seemed to render the porter speechless. Soon the taxi
driver was telling him how the Sri Lankan cricket team was as

good as any in the world. He drove a Morris Oxford in a high gear in the middle of the road, turning round frequently to emphasise his claims for the skill of Gehan Mendis or Ravi Ratnayake. He used the horn to move the night-time bicyclists and bullock carts, but never touched the brakes. His style of driving, one-geared, one-paced, was like that of a New York cab driver on Fifth Avenue when he gets a good run of lights late at night, though his conversation, not being a paranoid creole from behind bulletproof glass, was more enjoyable.

The night was exotically warm. The air was soft, though occasionally there would come a blast like that from an air extractor in the kitchen of an Indian restaurant. Pietro lay back against the seat, unable to help out further on the problem of the island's shortage of quick bowlers. He watched the palm trees and wooden roadside shacks trail out behind them.

He had booked a hotel on the south side of town that had been recommended to him as cheap but reliably clean. The rooms were ranged round a courtyard in the middle of which was an elderly swimming pool. A soft-footed room-boy in an orange tunic carried his cases into a large, bare room in which an air-conditioning unit rumbled against the wall. The light was dim and the furniture old. The floors were tiled. No rumour of corporate chain identity, of plastic-sealed lavatory seats or built-in radios had penetrated the hotel. A mosquito coil sat on the windowsill waiting for a match.

The room-boy sat down and stared at Pietro as he unpacked. He asked him about the country he came from, if he was married, and how many brothers and sisters he had. Pietro piled his clothes into a 1950s walnut chest of drawers that might have come from a Bexhill boarding house. When he came back from the bathroom, the room-boy was still sitting on the chair. By now he had stopped talking and seemed to want only to stare at Pietro's European face and rough mousy hair.

It was one o'clock in the morning and Pietro wanted to sleep. He gave the boy some money. Unlike the porters in Hong Kong, the boy didn't at once inspect it, then disappear swiftly in the hope of making more. He smiled his thanks without looking down at his hand. By the time Pietro managed to ease him out of the room the boy was still unaware of how much was in his palm.

Pietro placed his large camera bag on the table by the air conditioner. From a side pocket in the case he pulled out a number of prints made at different times. The top one was about eight years old. It showed a young, fair-haired woman with brown eyes and a bright vermilion sweater. The picture had been taken somewhere in the United States, perhaps New England. The tail-end of a station wagon was visible to one side bearing a Vermont registration number. Half a woolly dog disappeared from the other side of the imitation-leather frame. Composition had at that stage been low on Pietro's list of priorities. He had learned a good deal in the meantime – about the girl in the picture and about photography. At the time he had been anxious just to catch her likeness.

He took a sleeping pill – two, *nocte*, the pharmacist's instructions read, for benefit of Latin speakers – and lit the mosquito coil. He turned his transistor radio to the World Service and lay back under the sheet. A few minutes later he felt the sleeping pill reach out and gently uncouple the connections in his brain.

HE took breakfast beneath a roughly constructed porch by the pool. By daylight he could see the broken tiles on the inner roofs and the rough masonry of the hotel walls. He also saw a rat which was the size of a small dog. It was strolling along the flowerbed beyond the pool. A waiter told him not to worry. 'Is bandicoot, sir. Friend to man.' It was hard to see how a giant rat could be friend to man, but Pietro trusted the local knowledge. The boiled egg he had ordered arrived after forty-five minutes, and he ate it with a wary eye on the flowerbed.

Later that morning he drove up into the hills in a Japanese car he had hired in Colombo. As the road snaked through the tea plantations small children tried to sell him flowers. While the car took the gradual ascent round the edge of the hill the children ran up the escarpment and were ready at the next corner. Finally he stopped and took the photograph of a small girl. She handed him a ready-written piece of paper with her name and address on it. He promised to send her a print.

The man he was due to meet lived in an old plantation house near Kandy. It had a veranda with wickerwork chairs and a gloomy sitting room in which an electric fan, suspended from the ceiling, turned with an unoiled click at each grudging rotation.

Mr de Silva was a small, bald man in his fifties with a round face and tortoiseshell glasses.

'Will you take beer?' he asked Pietro.

'Thank you.' Pietro stretched out his legs on the veranda and clasped the beer bottle. It was marginally below room temperature. Mr de Silva filled his own glass with gin and water.

Pietro explained that he had come to take pictures to accompany a newspaper article. Mr de Silva knew this; the journalist had already done the interview, which was to form part of a series on new politicians of the Third World. Pietro said he would like to take some shots that would show his subject looking urgent, or wise, or leaderly.

Mr de Silva nodded. 'Tell me about this newspaper. Is it as good as the old *Times*? By God, that was a paper. The "Thunderer". I used to read it for the law reports.'

It turned out that Mr de Silva had once been a barrister in London. He asked Pietro for news of his contemporaries, many of whom were now judges. He was on first-name terms with most of the law lords.

'And Simpson's in the Strand. You could have a good blow-out there. Not that I could often afford it in those days.'

Pietro brought him up to date with Lyons Corner Houses, the Boat Race, various West End theatres, and, so far as he could, the results of the county cricket competition. He asked him about Sri Lankan politics.

Mr de Silva grinned, his jaw falling to reveal discoloured teeth. 'It's not an occupation for a gentleman. I like to think I've done my bit, but I only do it from a sense of duty. I am what W. B. Yeats called "a smiling public man". I don't think your journalist chappie really understood that. It isn't like Westminster, you know.'

Pietro fiddled with some film and a light meter. 'We'll be having lunch in a minute,' said Mr de Silva. 'Leave your box of tricks over there till later.'

A woman servant placed various dishes on the table beneath the electric fan. Mr de Silva drank another gin and water and smoked a thin cigar. Towards the end of lunch he became confidential.

'I loved that country, you know. To me it was wonderful to have travelled from the other side of the world and taken dinner in the Inns of Court. I felt sorry for my compatriots who were resentful. Eventually I had to return because I thought it was my duty. I think a part of me is still there, though. Just by St Paul's, where David Copperfield worked in Doctor's Commons. No, not there. I left my heart in the Middle Temple garden.' He laughed. 'That's a pretty rum thing to say, isn't it?' He spooned some boiled rice and vegetable curry on to his plate as he spoke.

Pietro smiled. He watched the drip of condensation run down the side of the beer bottle and listened to the grinding of the fan.

He said, 'Do you feel in some way bound or restricted by England and its culture?'

'Not bound. Enriched.'

'Don't you feel that it stopped you developing and enjoying the culture of your own people?'

Mr de Silva laughed. 'Our civilisation is connected with yours. It is not subservient. This is a matter of history and there is no point in denying it. I don't feel my people are diminished by this. What is remarkable really is how little has changed in this island. When you look at us here, do you think to yourself: this is just like Guildford? Or Sheffield?'

Pietro smiled. 'Of course not. But you speak very good English and –'

'I was a barrister!'

'I know. But everyone does, that's what I mean. No one in England speaks Sinhalese. I just feel how odd it is, when it could so easily have been the other way around. Suppose Sri Lanka, or Ceylon, had first stumbled on the steam engine, had built up its navy, had done the half-dozen things that were necessary. Then I might just as well have been brought up speaking Sinhalese as well as English.'

'Exactly!' Mr de Silva laughed. 'Now you've got it. It's a matter of chance. Pure chance. But there is also choice involved. We have chosen to keep and adapt certain things we learned from the British, but the choice was freely made. In some ways we should have kept more.'

'And why did you come back?'

'I told you. Because this is where I am from.'

After lunch Pietro took the photographs of Mr de Silva seated at his desk, apparently examining the economic problems of Sri Lanka. When the photographs were later developed he noticed that the shelf behind contained a complete set of Wisden's cricket almanac.

Before Pietro left, Mr de Silva told him about the Tamil people and their difficulties with the Sinhalese. 'Who the bloody hell do we think we are?' he said. 'Who are we but people who came from India some thousands of years ago? Nobody can deny you the right to live where you choose. It's better if it's the same place as your ancestors, but sometimes history isn't kind and people can't be too damn choosy. As long as you don't forget your manners you should be made welcome.'

When Pietro said goodbye he took various messages of good will, including one to the Lord Chief Justice. 'It's not impossible,' said Pietro. 'I might have to take a picture of him one day.' They shook hands and surveyed the tropical fertility that tumbled away from the edge of Mr de Silva's garden. 'It is the most beautiful island on earth,' said Mr de Silva, answering the question Pietro had been asking himself. 'If only it had the Inns of Court!' They both laughed as Pietro loaded his camera bag into the back of the car. On the way back he took two films of pictures trying to capture something of the landscape.

THE following night he sat by the pool in Colombo, drinking a glass of arrack, the local spirit, diluted with Coca-Cola. Mr de Silva had seemed to him to be the prisoner of another country's culture. 'Prisoner' was perhaps the wrong word for a man who seemed so happy in his condition. A willing captive, perhaps; or some other more colloquial phrase which Mr de Silva himself would have been able to produce. Even in de Silva's historical contentment there was a trace of sadness, Pietro thought. A man cannot have everything.

It was very late when a porter on his routine round shone his torch about the edges of the courtyard. Pietro, who was gazing up at the hot stars, asked him about the bandicoot and the man settled down to explain the habits of the creature and in what way, precisely, such a beast could be considered 'friend to man'. They drank some whisky that Pietro fetched from his room, and the local man went into detail about the eating habits of the bandicoot's close relation, something which was apparently called a 'hotampoor'. He, it appeared from the porter's excited narrative, was a redneck country cousin of the bandicoot. He lived off eggs and chickens and made a nuisance of himself to farmers and smallholders. The streetwise bandicoot, by contrast, lived only in the city where he liked nothing more than killing snakes. But more than this, his particularly prized meal was the one poisonous snake in Sri Lanka. They drank a toast to the bandicoot, truly friend to man, then refilled their glasses, the porter because he had seldom tasted whisky before, Pietro because he was anxious about lying down to sleep.

DORKING
ddddddddddddddddddddddddddddddddddddddddddddddddddddddddddddddddddddddddddddddddddddddddddddddddddddddddddddddddddd
England 1963

RAYMOND Russell's flat was in a mansion block off Baker Street. It had large, elegant rooms kept at a stifling temperature by the furnace in the basement of the block. None of the apartments had their own heating controls, and the previous tenants, a thin-blooded old couple, had sealed the windows in the sitting room. There were long corridors with mauve carpets leading from the front door. The proportions stifled noise. Laughter was swallowed in the vacuum of the airless spaces and silence could never be driven back more than an inch or two before it seeped in again like the warmed air from the boiling radiators behind the curtains.

Russell had been transferred, at his own request, by the Civil Service. His steady record and occasional ability to solve problems that had perplexed his superiors had been appreciated. In the evenings he had begun to cultivate a new hobby. A planning application he had been supervising in Swindon turned on the addition to a listed building of something the owner described as a penthouse. Russell was familiar with the word only from American films and, like the rest of his department, was unclear exactly what it was. According to the applicant, a penthouse was another name for a top floor, usually with a good view and a built-in cocktail bar. Some discussion followed, and

Russell called in at the library on the way back from work and
looked the word up in the full Oxford English Dictionary. He
was surprised and oddly interested to see that it had nothing to do
with houses – or pents, for that matter – at all. It was a corruption
of the French word *appentis*, from the Latin *appendicium*, meaning
an appendage. At the next meeting of the committee he told
them this and asked if it didn't shed a new light on the
application. The feeling of the meeting was that it didn't, but
Russell's interest was kindled. He bought a couple of second-
hand books on the subject of etymology and put an advertise-
ment in the local paper asking if anyone wanted to sell a complete
second-hand set of the twelve-volume Oxford English
Dictionary. He had no replies, so set about tracking it down bit
by bit at jumble sales and auctions. After five years and various
forays in his car, sometimes as far away as Nottingham, he had
all the volumes except 'V to Z'.

Studying them brought a slight but noticeable change to
Raymond Russell. He became briefer, even briefer, in his speech. If
he knew the root of a word and used it in a way that was close to
that root, he thought he had expressed himself unimprovably. It
didn't matter if no one else was aware of that meaning or if it wasn't
the most current one; Russell went for the oldest and purest
instance in the book. 'I've got this chronic pain in my leg where
this boy kicked me during the match yesterday,' complained
Pietro. 'If you received the injury yesterday, it can't be chronic,'
said his father, not with spite or irritation, but with calm satisfaction
as he seemed to feel the word and its true meaning fall upon each
other like blissfully congruent triangles. 'What?' said Pietro.

Raymond Russell frequently tried to interest Pietro in his
hobbies because Pietro seemed to have none of his own. The boy
seemed withdrawn, and his father could not think what else to
talk to him about.

He came back one day from a disappointing search in the
Charing Cross Road for the missing volume of the dictionary.

'I think I shall have to advertise again,' he told Pietro, as he
hung up his coat in the hall.

'Why is this one so important?'

'Because it's the one I haven't got. Once I've got "V to Z" I'll have the whole set.'

Pietro followed his father into the sitting room. He seemed to make an effort to carry on the conversation, as though for his father's sake. 'Do you think it's rarer than the others because it's near the end of the alphabet and fewer people bought it?'

'It doesn't matter where it comes in the alphabet. I won't be fixed up until I've got it.'

Pietro said, 'Is it towards the end of the alphabet because it's less important?'

'No. The order of the letters is just random. It could equally start RJN, I suppose.'

'And who decided the order?'

'I don't know,' said Raymond Russell, delighted with Pietro's apparent interest. 'But do you remember learning your ABC at school?' Pietro nodded. 'I can still remember the day I mastered it at the village school,' his father went on. 'I went through all the pictures on the wall from apple to zebra and the teacher said to me, "Now you've got the whole world at your feet." '

Pietro was staring out of the window. His father was not sure if he was listening. He said cheerily, 'Do you know the Fool's Alphabet?'

'What's that?'

'A for 'orses, B for mutton, C for yourself, D for dumb, E for brick, F for vescence, G for police, H for 'imself, I for Novello, J for oranges, K for restaurant, L for leather, M for sis, N for a penny, O for the wings of a dove, P for comfort, Q for a ticket, R for mo, S for Williams, T for two, U for me, V for la France, W for money, X for breakfast, Y for mistr – er, husband, Z for breezes.'

Pietro smiled. 'It's good. But why is it the *fool*'s alphabet? It sounds quite clever to me.'

'It's just a phrase,' said his father. 'It's called that because it's funny, not because it's stupid. It's like saying the Beginner's Alphabet, or One Man's Alphabet. Anyone can have his own version.'

'I see,' said Pietro, and resumed his long stare from the window.

'When we were in North Africa during the war, a chap in my platoon called Padgett, who'd never been out of Yorkshire before, he noticed what funny names the places had. He said he wanted to spend a night in a place beginning with every letter of the alphabet before he died.'

'And did he?'

'I shouldn't think so. There weren't many XYZs in Yorkshire.'

BEFORE the move to London there had been a period in which Raymond Russell wanted Pietro to go to boarding school. With the money from an uncle's legacy he thought he could afford the fees and he had investigated some possible places. He drove Pietro to Dorking, near which was a place whose soft, bucolic name – Brockwood, as it turned out, though it might have been Greenglades, Mossbank or something equally misleading – gave no hint of the crazed routine and discipline behind its ivied walls. Pietro watched his father depart, then sat in his cubicle until it was time for bed.

In the morning an adolescent boy with a quavering voice called out the passing of each minute to wake the others. Twelve past, thirteen past, fourteen past. Breakfast was at seven-thirty, served from a battered trough by a paroled lunatic with shaking hands. New boys scrubbed the tables, the cookers, the floors, and anything else that was greasy. There was PT in white vests with a retired but still vigorous sergeant major. The showers that followed were cold through some official negligence. The books were old and scribbled over. Latin primers had failed to inspire pupils to anything more than drawing phallic diagrams in the margin. The brittle measure of the first declension, the moody grandeur of the subjunctive slumbered on for ever undiscovered by generations of Brockwood boys. Small pieces of chalk, flicked by muscular men with hairy ears, came through the air like tracer fire. By the end of trigonometry, the rows of desks were dug in like a front-line trench at Ypres. The boys, with bulging thighs pressed into grey shorts, took interest only in bodily functions, their dug-out world deep beneath a cloud of fart and morning breath, their talk of dicks and spots and spunk. Plastic dustbins with sliced loaves of white bread and margarine were manhandled up to the dormitories at mid-morning by the new boys. Six or eight slices went down each adolescent throat. Then came the scrubbing of the tables, removal of margarine from walls and floors by cold water and an unaired cloth that left more stench than it removed. Back in class was the tedium of physics which spawned competitions to see who could hold his breath longest. Light-headed and purple in the face, the boys staggered on to chemistry and the slim chance of making someone suck sulphuric acid through a pipette. There was a constant anguish at having failed to do the prep properly and of dreading the tests, which were incomprehensible. No boy dared ask the chemistry master, a Scottish cruiserweight with homoerotic leanings, to explain his indecipherable marks on the blackboard for fear of exciting his wrath, or worse. Lunch and the waiting at table, carrying the food from the metal troughs up to the senior boys, serving the whole table in turn, left no time for a new boy to eat, even if he could have stomached it. Then there was rugby and the twitch of the knotted string of the referee's whistle about the back of mottled thighs. The showers this time were optional, though still cold, and the afternoon dispatch of bread and margarine could be improved by chocolate or ice cream from the food shop. The shop, like everything else, had a name, coined with affection by some Victorian patriarch but used now in unthinking tradition. No boy would have found the name outdated. No boy had a view on anything.

Every morning was the struggle with books, each lesson requiring perhaps four or five, so that the boys walked invisible down the colonnades behind piles of textbooks and bursting briefcases lifted with both hands. It was good training for the runs, which culminated in a school race, six miles up and down hills, over the rifle ranges, through woods and, when their legs were buckling, across a broad lake and uphill to the finishing line. The white-haired head of history liked to show how easy the course was by running it without a vest before breakfast. He could be seen one morning jogging up the front drive with shards of ice clinging to the snowy hair of his chest, and blood running down his abdomen where he had forged through the lake's ice.

Pietro had no idea what it was all about. At first he tried to like the place. He imagined what kind of man had first thought of the quaint names for things. Where had it all gone wrong? He saw that the older boys were bent only on self-preservation. He copied them and said nothing unless he was spoken to; he gave up trying to puzzle out the philosophy of the school and kept his thoughts to himself. The good thing was that he never had time on his own. Only briefly at night on the hard iron bedstead, which he grew used to after a time, did he think about the changes in his life. But he was too tired to stay awake for long. The evening drill of supervised work, some more chores for the younger boys and the humping of the final dustbin-load of bread and margarine left him exhausted.

THE school, oddly enough, was expensive and enjoyed a high reputation. Parents in the Dorking district spoke well of it, without really enquiring what went on there. The boys never described it to them and, in any case, would have had little with which to compare it. An unplanned conspiracy of ignorance thus kept the school's reputation intact, and allowed the Dorking parents to say things like, 'It's not as smart as one of the famous public schools, of course, but it's jolly good in its way'; or, 'They teach them to stand on their own two feet'.

When they went for runs in the surrounding district, Pietro looked with pity at the houses there. He wondered why any normal person would want to live near such a place; he felt sorry for the children whose lives were darkened by their parents' inexplicable decision to live in the shadow of the institution. Later in his life he drove through the leafy roads of Colney Hatch and spent a day in the pleasant little town of Verdun. They were decent places in their way, but you wouldn't want to live near somewhere so blighted by association.

At the start of each term he would watch the boys arrive in old cars driven by their parents. They emerged from the Surrey woods, the sandy soil still on the wheels of their shooting-brakes. The women wore a cowed, defeated look, the fathers seemed embarrassed as they shook hands with their sons. The cars withdrew in procession through lines of rhododendrons and took slowly to the roads, through long forests of conifers and patches of land wired off by the Ministry of Defence. Then they dispersed, each to its minor road, which took it past numerous golf courses, through the occasional village with an unpatronised pub, then down the final sodden lanes with laurels and dripping evergreens back to an unheated house and the welcome of an ageing Labrador.

Take me away from this, Pietro prayed, as he once more fell back silently into the prescribed routine. Take me back to London, take me to Italy, but take me away from Dorking. He was sure his mother wouldn't have wanted him to be in such a place. The trouble was, she had never expressed an opinion. If only he had known how ill she was, he could have got her to tell his father what she wanted for him. When his father said, 'Your mother's going into hospital again,' he thought it would be like the first time and she would be back in a few days' time. When he had been taken to see her after a week he thought it was odd how hard she hugged him when he left. He quickly rubbed the memory from his mind as he left the hospital, and turned his thoughts to the football game he would be playing that afternoon. Then a few days later he was taken to see her again and he thought she looked peculiar, rather yellow in the face. At the age of twelve he didn't often notice these things, or attach much importance to them: he could never understand how his mother was always saying to his father, 'You look very well', or 'You look awfully tired', when the old man always looked the same.

Then she was discharged from hospital anyway, so he assumed she was better. She spent the time in bed, it was true, but he remembered how Mrs Graham was always telling her to run along to bed after the first time she'd been in hospital. After another week he asked his father what the matter was. He said it was the same trouble as before – nothing serious, just a little thing lots of women have, but now she'd got a bit of a complication. He didn't sound upset. In fact the cancer had run out of control. Pietro went and sat on his mother's bed and talked to her after the shy doctor had been and gone. She wanted him to read to her.

'I thought you hated it when I read to you,' he said.

'That was when you were little, silly! Not now.'

So he read her some pages from the book by her bed and she fell asleep, her black hair splayed about the pillow, her face very pale. Pietro looked at her in puzzlement, his dark eyebrows knotting as he studied her slightly open mouth. Why was she so tired?

The following day when he returned from school Mrs Graham was looking very grim. 'Don't go upstairs,' she said, as Pietro put his foot on the bottom step. 'Come into the sitting room.'

He expected his father to be there, but in fact it was the doctor. He clasped his hands nervously and coughed a few times. 'Now listen, Pietro. Your mother's not at all well, you know.'

He did it, for all the anguish it cost him, exactly as you are supposed to do it. He broke the news in stages, and, as he talked, Pietro seemed to see his mother grow iller by the second, until he knew how it was going to end.

'She died this morning.' The doctor seemed so overwrought that Pietro wanted to assure him he knew it wasn't his fault. He tried to say something to that effect, but it came out as 'Thank you'. What he wanted to know was why no one had told him. Then at least he might have said goodbye properly.

And as for Dorking, she would never have allowed it. It occurred to him that perhaps his father had sent him there *because* his mother was dead. Perhaps he thought it would be better for him to live away from all the memories of her. This wasn't what

Pietro himself thought at all. Surely now was the time for him to be with his father, and perhaps be a comfort to him. He knew Mrs Graham had moved in and did all the work, but she wasn't like his mother.

Raymond Russell didn't ask Pietro about Brockwood, and Pietro didn't tell him. Russell was happy to accept the good word of other parents. One thing did arouse his interest, however, and that was the bill. The school announced that it was putting up its fees the following year, and he had a close look at what was charged.

That first night of his fourth term, as Pietro fell asleep in the hated Surrey countryside, his father came across an entry in the bill for 'Piano tuition: £25.' It was too much.

EVANSTON

Illinois USA 1985

P IETRO sat in the rosy darkness of a restaurant on the edge of Chicago looking at a photograph he had pulled from his wallet. It showed a two-year-old girl, Mary Francesca, with a shy, determined smile and a disregard for danger that made her parents despair.

'That your kid?' It was an English voice. 'I hope you don't mind. I heard you speak to the waiter. It was strange to hear another English voice out here.'

Pietro looked up from his solitary reverie. Sometimes alone in a foreign country he felt overpowered by the place. In London he barely noticed the pavements and buildings because he impressed his own will on them. Leicester Square was merely a connection between him and his destination; by hurrying through it, thinking only of where he was going, he was oblivious of it and could not have described it to a stranger. Some cinemas certainly; souvenirs on trays, clockwork tumbling puppies with nylon fur, plastic London bobbies' helmets and Union Jacks; a few trees and benches; a smell of onions and a sticky feeling underfoot from wet leaves, abandoned fast-food cartons and a suspicion of dog. But he could have given no architectural detail or description of shape and colour; no history or analysis of purpose. He had not noticed that from the first storey upward the buildings were still quite dignified. Like most places in London it was to him only a connection between other tube stations, an inconvenience between his starting point and the place where his real life awaited him in the greeting of work or friends.

Abroad it was the opposite. His eyes would drain each shop sign or building feature of its unintended significance; he was so anxious to orientate himself that he would take from each café, street or apartment block a weight of history and meaning that would have amazed its indifferent owners. The more alone he was, the more receptive, sometimes morbidly so, he became to the signals of place. It was possible for him to be overwhelmed, so that it was not he who printed himself on the place, but the place which subsumed him in its greater identity.

The presence of someone he knew could halt this process by restoring his perspective. Through his affectionate dealings with other people, he could resume an equilibrium that left him still animated by the sense of where he was, but not overpowered by it. When he was abroad alone, and starting to lose himself, he longed for the sound of his name spoken by someone who knew him. The conversation of the waiter or shopkeeper was better than silence, but was no substitute for the greeting of a friend, of a human voice whose inflexion carried the knowledge of his identity. In a simple greeting such a voice could convey a reassurance that he was valued or familiar in a proper scale of things.

When he looked up at the sound of the English voice, he was therefore inclined to talk. He saw a man in his early forties, dark, with thick glasses. He wore a soft flannel suit and glowed with self-confidence.

'My name's Paul Coleman. Are you from London?'

Pietro pushed back a chair in invitation and poured some wine. 'Yes. I'm here on business in Chicago. A friend of mine has relations here in Evanston who've lent me their house. They're back next week. And you?'

'Business, business. Always business.' Coleman smiled, his

narrow eyes sparkling behind the glasses. He had thick, wavy dark hair and a swarthy skin.

'Pork belly futures?'

'There are other things in Chicago. Been out on the lake?'

'Not yet.'

'What's your line of business?'

'I have a company in London. We deal in photographic equipment,' said Pietro. 'My real interest is colour origination and printing.'

'Picture books, part works, that kind of thing?'

'Yes.' Pietro wished Coleman would stop smiling when he spoke. It made him feel nervous. He steered the subject on to families and found that Coleman lived in Hertfordshire. He spoke of his wife and of his daughters. He was generous with information and frank about himself, but seemed to be engaged in something tactical. Pietro couldn't say what.

'I'd suggest going to a bar,' said Coleman, 'but this is the one town in America you can't, because there aren't any. It's the home of the Women's Christian Temperance Union, founders of Prohibition. Right here in Evanston. But they let you drink in restaurants, so I suggest we have another bottle of wine.'

By the time they left the restaurant Pierto felt that he had revealed more than he had at first intended, but it didn't seem to matter. He walked the streets in a happy glow as he searched for the house he had been lent: along the lake front with its spacious mansions and their commanding views, then back into the ordered rows of houses beneath the soft glow of the street lamps, their big cars pulled up off the street, the tended lawns and the occasional smudge of curtained light. To the east was the pleasant oak-lined stretch of Lake Shore Drive, to the west the raised interchanges of the Kennedy Expressway. You could be happy here, he thought – big city, small town, whatever you wanted it to be.

I am going to die, he thought. It seemed a shameful response to the news of impending parenthood. He lay flat on his back, with

51

the sound of Hannah asleep beside him, staring into the darkness. He felt as though his body was shaking with the closeness of death. He heard the rattle in his lungs as he breathed, and regretted each cigarette that might have contributed. He felt the delicate tissue of his flesh and imagined the blood vessels starting to swell and seize, their fantastic intricacy unregarded by him until it was too late. He pictured the big organs of his body, the liver, the kidney, things he had treated with disdain, beginning to buckle and rot. More than anything he felt the pressure of darkness, a fear of being turned off like a light.

This was not what he had expected to feel when Hannah had emerged from the bathroom that morning bearing a flat plastic tube about the length of a thermometer, in which were cut two small windows. Across the dead centre of each one were two firm blue lines.

She passed the tube to him without comment.

'What does this mean?' he said.

'It's positive. I'm definitely pregnant.'

'Shouldn't you have it confirmed by a doctor?'

'I could, but the doctors can't tell any more accurately than these tests.'

After the celebrations and the hasty planning about who should be told and where they should live, he felt only like death. It was as if he had never previously thought himself subject to termination; as though he believed that when death came he would be unavailable, too young, or somewhere else at the time.

He looked down at Hannah's brown hair against the blue cotton pillowcase. She seemed by contrast invigorated; not dying but reanimated.

He got out of bed and walked into the sitting room of their London flat. He lit a cigarette – a suicidal gesture – and pulled back the curtain. There was a drone of traffic from the arterial road going north, then a car starting and revving angrily a few streets away. The driver kept his foot down on the accelerator, pumping and pumping the stationary car for three or four minutes before he clutchlessly engaged first gear and moved off. There was a whistle of Victorian plumbing behind the plastered walls and then the half-silence of the city night again.

Lately involved either in dealing with cash flow and share ownership or with the equally abstract and delicate negotiation of his marriage, he was surprised by the primitive fear that held him. This was the same puzzled terror with which savages had looked down at the corpses of their friends or mates. Now here was he, a sentient man in a European world of complex futures and medical research, and he had never even contemplated death.

He turned his mind to Hannah and the invisible embryo inside her that represented some fatal intertwining of genetic codes, even now locked into a determined course.

Then he felt an equally primitive emotion, one of fierce protectiveness towards this invisible fusion and its mother, something the least threat might have provoked to violence. Then his own fear of death began to wane.

PIETRO went out with Coleman in his boat. He was intrigued by him and his strange accent, which stumbled on easy consonants, as though he had some East European past. Everything else about him was overpoweringly British, in idiom and reference.

He wondered what his best friend Harry Freeman would make of him. At the age of thirty-three Harry was already on his third successful career and had an enviable ability to sum people up on first meeting them. He and his wife Martha returned to the house in Evanston the following week. It belonged to some cousins of Martha's who had taken a year out. Coleman invited them all over to his place for dinner. Pietro explained that Hannah would just have arrived from London, but Coleman insisted she should come too.

Pietro went to pick her up from the airport. She was five months pregnant and had found the flight uncomfortable. She was also worried about Mary, whom she had left with a friend in London. However, it was the first time for a year that she and Pietro had been away together, and her spirits quickly lifted after she had telephoned London and been reassured that Mary was all right. 'To be honest,' she told Pietro, with a glint in her eye, 'it's not Mary I'm worried about. I feel sorry for Jane having to look after her.'

They drove past the stately campus of Northwestern University and got to Coleman's house at seven-thirty, as instructed. It was large and imposing, with two huge oak trees either side of the damp front lawn. They could see the wire cage of a tennis court behind one side of the substantial building.

Harry and Martha were already being given drinks in the front room with its fat, pink-upholstered sofas. Two girls, aged about eight and ten, opened the door to Pietro and Hannah. Both wore dresses with sashes at the waist and black patent leather sandals.

Coleman gave them large drinks and sat them down in front of a glass-topped table that held small bowls of nuts and pretzels. His wife had reddish-brown curly hair. She was tall and had a baffled air that was increased by some defect in her eye which made her focusing uncertain. Coleman called her Pet or Petal, so they weren't sure if she had another Christian name.

She sat Martha, Harry's wife, next to her and talked to her about children. Martha had a leaping vitality of movement and speech which was reined in by East Coast manners. Occasionally she would throw her head to one side and smile at the whole room, as though the single conversation couldn't contain her delight. Her legs were drawn up neatly beneath a beige wool dress as she sat sideways on the edge of the sofa.

They went through sliding doors into a heavily carpeted dining room. Rows of cutlery flanked the place mats on the teak table. Coleman moved around with a bottle of wine while an unsmiling Spanish woman in a blue pinafore brought in a tray of food.

'Now I want to talk to you guys about a little proposition,' said Coleman.

'Not now, Paul,' said Mrs Coleman in a dull voice.

'Ah, come on, I'm just going to float a little idea. Just so they can think about it. They can hammer out the details later.' When he talked about business, Coleman's stumbling consonants became smoother as his voice took on an American burr.

Pietro looked at Hannah, who was sitting opposite him. She glanced sideways at the melon that was being served to her and gave a momentary and conspiratorial grimace. Hannah's habitually stern expression could be altered by the smallest dilation of her eyes into a look of pity or flirtation or suppressed humour. She reached up to take the proffered serving spoons.

'. . . and with Pietro's visual experience and know-how, with your publishing experience, Harry, I think it would be a cinch. We'd be looking at a modest turnover to begin with: not more than half a million in the first year, but after that . . .' Coleman pursed his lips and shrugged suggestively.

'We'd probably get a grant,' said Pietro.

'Christ, they're falling over themselves to give you money,' said Coleman.

'That's enough now,' said Mrs Coleman. 'You can finish later.'

She couldn't have timed the interruption better if she had planned it with her husband. Pietro looked at Harry and could see him rubbing at his chin with the first two fingers of his left hand. It meant he was interested.

'I want to know how you all met each other,' Mrs Coleman went on.

'We'll talk later,' Coleman said to Pietro.

'Are you from these parts?' Mrs Coleman said to Martha.

'Oh no. I'm from New York. At least, I was raised in Boston, but I was working in New York when I met Harry. But I keep in touch with my cousins. We're a close family. When Harry mentioned Pietro was going to Chicago, it seemed a good idea he should go see them.'

Martha's voice had the softness of an expensive education; even when she was exuberant there was a degree of consideration in her tone. As she began to talk about her childhood, prompted by her hostess's questions, Pietro noticed how Coleman stopped eating to watch her. His eyes fixed on her with an avaricious stare. Martha's face glowed with the recollection of school and college, or summers at Cape Cod or travelling with friends. Harry had met her on vacation in Jerusalem. She was working for a law firm on Park Avenue.

Dinner moved slowly onwards. After the melon there was fish, prepared in some Spanish way that left the bones scattered hazardously through the tomato-coloured sauce, and then chicken in cream and mushrooms with very white boiled rice, a choice of lemon, coffee or raspberry mousse, cheese and biscuits and coffee from a thermos flask that doubled as a jug. Mrs Coleman pushed glass dishes of chocolates round the table. She seemed to have imported English cuisine to the Midwest.

Afterwards in his study Coleman gave Pietro and Harry more details about his business plan. He wanted to produce a new series of street maps and guides, beginning with London, but going on to other large cities. They would be aimed principally at foreign visitors and would be in various languages.

'Look at what there is at the moment,' he said. 'Dull maps printed on toilet paper. We start with new maps. We print in colour. We fill the books with historical information and help for tourists. Addresses, phone numbers, cinemas, museums and so on. It's a market monopolised by one player at the moment. We can take them apart.'

He had prepared a printed synopsis which he intended to show to potential investors. He told them he had a certain amount of capital of his own to put into the project; it would be one of several he was financing. Harry began to question him. Coleman poured brandy from a crystal decanter. Pietro listened. Coleman drained four glasses in ten minutes. The deal proposed by Coleman was more far-reaching for Pietro than it would be for Harry. For some reason it would involve his own company becoming nominally at least a subsidiary of Coleman's, while he himself would have to work in Coleman's office. 'Tax advantages all round,' Coleman said. He poured more brandy. His speech became slurred but his confidence was overpowering. He had finished in Chicago and was headed back to London. The evidence of his material success was all around him.

FULHAM

London England 1964

Pietro took the tube from Baker Street and got to his new school early. He wore his blazer and school tie and braced himself for some arcane initiation rite in which someone would hold his head down the lavatory or swab his private parts with red paint. He asked a matronly woman the way to the lower fifth classroom and went in, ready to keep low. A couple of girls aged about twenty-two were sitting on a desk, gossiping. They ignored him. A large American boy in sneakers and an open-neck shirt hurled his bag across the room and patted one of the girls familiarly on the backside. Pietro, confused, asked him where the lower fifth classroom was. 'Right here,' said the American.

By nine o'clock the class was assembled. Of the fourteen pupils there were only two others Pietro thought looked like schoolboys. A couple of Arab girls looked no more than sixteen, and the two Japanese were ageless; the rest, who were principally American, were not only physically large but had a loud self-confidence. They wore T-shirts with the names of towns that Pietro had never heard of or initials like UCLA. The teacher, a woman with an indeterminate European accent, treated them as if they were children. They responded with contempt. Pietro introduced himself to the only other normal-looking boy during

57

the break between lessons. He was called Harry Freeman and Pietro liked him because he wore the school blazer and he looked uneasy. 'Don't believe half the stuff they say,' he said. 'Dave hasn't really got a Harley Davidson, though I think he's once ridden his brother's.' 'What about that girl who said she'd done some modelling?' 'Yeah, I'm afraid that *is* true. Her sister was in this film with Steve McQueen.' Pietro hardly knew what to tell his father when he returned that evening to the suffocating calm of the Baker Street flat.

One thing he had to say for the school was that he didn't have to scrub the floors or dish out the school food. At lunchtime most people disappeared to nearby shops or cafés. Harry and Pietro ate the sandwiches provided by the canteen and then went for a walk in the small park nearby. Harry gave him the lowdown. Weiner and Gupta, he said, had the academic side of things sewn up. Weiner was a tall, thin boy who could speak German and French; he also seemed to understand history and English and could write essays that were not just a semi-animated list of dates. Gupta, who was Indian, sometimes beat Weiner and sometimes came second. He had formidable concentration in all subjects, only occasionally turning round to give a reproving look to Gloria Katz and Laura Heasman, the two chattering girls in their twenties, who turned out to be fourteen.

'Gloria's a cow,' said Harry. 'Laura's all right, but all the guys in the sixth are chasing her.' Gloria was forced by her mother to acknowledge Harry because they were both Jewish, but she was embarrassed by the fact that he looked like a schoolboy. Laura was different. Although she gossiped all through the lesson she seemed able to absorb everything the teacher said. When he came over to tick her off he would look down at her exercise book and find she had somehow taken down all the notes. She would swivel her brown eyes up from beneath her blonde fringe and turn them on him in an expression of hurt innocence; he would retreat to the blackboard.

Gloria used to get Harry to run messages for her and carry her books. Harry used to make an effort not to, and put on an exaggerated Jewish manner. 'Don't make me *do* it, Gloria, don't make me *do* it. If it was up to me of *course* I would. But listen . . .' He ended up doing it anyway. Laura used to laugh and didn't herself ask Harry or Pietro to do anything for her. When Gloria made them carry both her and Laura's bags, however, Laura didn't object. Gloria and Laura called them the Blazers, because they were the only two who bothered with the uniform.

Pietro liked being in London. Sometimes after school he would go to a coffee bar and look in the record shops with Harry or with one of the other boys. Harry's father ran a chain of bookmakers and once a week would ease from his pocket a densely packed round of banknotes, from which he would peel four or five to give to Harry without making any appreciable change to the size of the bundle. Pietro went to their house in Highgate for tea. It was a big, noisy place, with the telephone ringing and people shouting up and down stairs. Harry was quite different there. Although he was frightened of his father and his elder brother, he answered back to his mother and swaggered around, testing out his strength. Pietro dreaded the return tube journey. Mr Freeman dropped him in his Jaguar at Hampstead station, and on the Northern Line he thought of the airless corridors of the Baker Street flat and the starchy supper the German daily help would have left for him and his father.

In the course of two years Pietro came to know the shops and cafés of the Fulham Road. The street was in a spasm of self-importance. Hairdressers and restaurant managers enjoyed unexpected status if a singer or actress had recently called. People who couldn't get a reservation in the King's Road happily came a block further north where more record shops, hamburger bars and unisex coiffeurs opened up for them. Pietro and Harry, now sixteen, sat in cafés after school, their ties loosened, their blazers concealed beneath the seat, and watched the people come and go. The young men and women had a look of innocent urgency – the girls with their black-rimmed eyes and the men with their flowing hair and waistcoats, as though no generation had ever understood before the inspired responsibility of being young.

From the moment Pietro arrived in London he felt at ease there. It was the first place he had lived where he felt the character of it had eluded the inhabitants. Because it was so amorphous it could not be described or comprehended; therefore it could not be oppressive or limiting. London had been seriously mis-represented, he felt, by visitors and by people who lived there. The double-decker buses, Piccadilly and the Mall were all there, sure enough, but they accounted for less than a hundredth of what the city was about. It was so ugly, to begin with. It was comical, this hideousness, when you compared it with other capitals, yet it was also an unacknowledged deformity. No one mentioned the thousands of Archway Roads; they must have closed their eyes and kept them shut except for fleeting moments in Regent's Park. Who talked about Green Lanes, Old Street, Shadwell or North End Road, which were not marginal suburbs but central, typical parts of the city? This huge con trick made Pietro like Londoners more. It was like the way some women loved their husbands when they were bald and overweight and set in their dull opinions: they looked at them still with bright, loyal eyes, amazed that anyone might see in them anything other than a paragon of virile life.

For somewhere so ugly and so important, London seemed also strangely calm. Perhaps it was so large that people could lose themselves in its quiet pockets; it did not have the cohesion to be daunting. Foreign students in the bedsits and hotels of Bayswater seemed to like it; they gathered on the steps of their language schools or ate American hamburgers in the rubbish of Leicester Square with no visible sense of disappointment. They didn't mind that in the middle of town there were long streets of residential houses with no shops, cafés or dry-cleaners. They accepted that they needed to walk, and that even then the place would probably be closed.

The best thing about London, Pietro felt, was discovering it for yourself. Some of the more blasé of the students at the US Collegiate made disparaging remarks about how early the clubs seemed to close, but he doubted whether they had found the unadvertised parts of the city. At the very least in London you could be sure you were not missing anything; no town in England was likely to offer more.

IN the summer came O levels and then the long holidays. Pietro went to stay with his grandfather in Nottingham and then with his father for a week at the seaside. He was glad when term started again and Heathrow was busy welcoming back the children of the Collegiate school from Washington, Tokyo, Rome, Beirut – still the garden capital of the Middle East – and New York City.

The teachers read the roll call with difficulty at the start of the term when children with complicated Oriental or Middle Eastern names had arrived at all levels of the school. Those who couldn't speak English went to language classes; those who could were given an education that was English in the exams it addressed, American in the structure of the discipline, and stateless in the way the teachers tried not to stress the claims of one culture over another. The imperatives of Chanukah, Ramadan or Thanksgiving were given the same respect as those of Easter.

Arab and Israeli children, whose parents' mutual hatred had extended in some cases to bearing arms, sat next to one another. Their antipathy was stilled in the muggy air of their London classroom under the inflexions of an American teacher. For the duration of the lesson the children meekly conceded that the need to learn about inert gases or punctuation was all-important: they borrowed books from one another, competed in tests, copied each other's exercises. Released from class they still had tenuously common interests in sport or music, shared sexual anguish or urgent new enthusiasms. But as they left the school at dusk Jewish boys made disdainful comments about the Arabs; girls from Lebanon looked back in soft incomprehension as old allegiances re-formed.

In their uncertainty most of the children preferred to carry with them an idea of the place they had come from and to take

61

their identity from that. Pietro sometimes wondered whether they would not be happier if they were more enthusiastic about their adoptive city; but their parents were sometimes strict, retaining in the service apartments of Marylebone and St John's Wood the settlement or enclave of a distant country, which London was too big and too indifferent to break down.

The O level results were not good. Weiner hadn't done himself justice. A certain middle-European largesse had caused him to write too much on single questions and to show a highbrow disregard for the examiners who wanted only pellets of schoolboy information fired back legibly and to length. Gupta had scored, as far as anyone could see, one hundred per cent in maths and physics, but some retentiveness had made him finish only half the questions in the other subjects, as if his one perfect answer would excuse him the rest. The best results were Laura Heasman's. Somehow her absurd calmness and instinctive knowledge of what was needed had satisfied the examiners. Pietro had managed three – a scatter of art, physics and Italian – which left his proposed course of study as a scientist in doubt.

Laura had become even more beautiful, he thought, during the holiday. The school's navy-blue skirt clung to her hips and her perfectly shaped legs moved beneath it encased in shimmering grey. Even when she wore the tiny skirt the girls were given for games, the skin of her bare legs was so smooth it looked as though she was wearing some fine powder or an exquisite invisible covering. She sometimes seemed embarrassed by this physical perfection, especially next to the lumpish Gloria, but after turning aside the boys' comments with a blushing puzzlement, she was able to forget them in the intrigue of gossip.

Pietro shook his head in anguish. The whole class would meet in the morning for roll call in the lower sixth common room. This was a large room on the first floor, littered with old coffee cups, Coca-Cola bottles, footballs and books. Pietro's locker, as luck would have it, was next to Laura's and it was inevitable that he would remove his books from it at the same time as she did each morning. Then they might be in different classes, but Pietro got to know her timetable so he was always able to be passing in the corridor when Laura emerged from her lesson. At the end of the day he would naturally be packing up at the same time as her and would watch with anguished eyes as she disappeared with Gloria or a group of boys from the upper sixth.

The pleasure of being close to her was enough. In the lessons they shared he simply gazed at her, incredulous that anyone could be so perfect. Even when her legs were tucked away beneath the desk there was her choice of tops, which were within the regulations prescribed by the school but with a button or two undone or a raffish black cardigan instead of the navy-blue pullover. The sunlight shone through the dusty window and into her hair. Pietro laid his head on his folded arms and with one eye still partially open gazed at an oblique angle, so no one could see what he was doing, at Laura's enflamed golden head. Her brown eyes were alternately sparkling as she talked to Gloria or capable of a brimming look of injured innocence when addressed by the teacher. She had a short, slightly upturned nose, full lips and small white teeth. Her face was never in repose for long enough for Pietro to say if her natural expression was innocent or wicked. Sometimes when he couldn't bear to gaze at her any more he would force his eyes to the blackboard.

Harry Freeman was slowly making ground. He had bought some new clothes, had got himself four or five O levels. He had rumbled the Americans. 'They can't write,' he told Pietro. 'I know I'm no one to talk, but you should see that Dave Snyder's essays. He's got handwriting like a five-year-old!' 'And a Harley Davidson.' 'OK, and a Harley Davidson. But I tell you, they're thick, those guys.' 'I know,' said Pietro, 'but who's going to tell Laura that?'

Two weeks before the end of term a notice was pinned on the main notice board announcing a school skiing trip to France. Pupils over fourteen were invited to put their names down. There was a wait while everyone consulted their friends; then cliques of two or three signed up. When it was known which teachers were going, more people signed. Pietro and Harry watched the notice board. Finally the sixth form condescended. Dave Snyder said he was going skiing in Colorado and wouldn't mind a warm-up. He made the Alps sound very small.

Eventually Laura signed, and so did Pietro and Harry, their urgent signatures piercing the paper.

GHENT

Belgium 1981

'MARY, Mary, Mary,' said Hannah. 'When are you ever going to learn to be sensible?'

The four-year-old girl looked up from the floor of the kitchen, where she was making a sculpture from potato peelings, her younger brother's water bottle and the electric flex of the washing machine, which she had disconnected from the wall.

Hannah viewed herself, above all else, as capable. If she had had to give a one-word description of her character she would have chosen either that one or the related 'realistic'. Yet Mary's perversity and lack of any apparent sense of self-preservation taxed her more than she could have predicted. Each day she had to stop, keep calm, and try to find some deeper reserve of patience inside her. It was not that she didn't love Mary; on the contrary, her devotion to her made the worry more acute. The trouble was that she found that the little girl's irresponsibility wore down her own natural good humour. She never seemed to have time to talk with Pietro as she had in the old days. With Anton as well, now two years old and in the first exuberance of discovering his voice, she could never complete a conversation, or a book, or even a newspaper article. She often felt as though the person she had been would be lost; that when, in ten or more years' time, she attempted to resume an ordinary life she would find her ability to concentrate had left her, that the world had moved on irrevocably during her decade's sabbatical, and that she was unable to reconnect with the calm adult pleasures of other people's lives.

She had stopped working when she moved to England with Pietro. She had been a director of her father's import-export business in Antwerp. Now she did occasional translations for companies that needed expertise in French, Dutch, Flemish and English. Her father was from Holland, her mother from northern Belgium; Hannah was therefore, according to Pietro, 'very Flemish, whichever way you look at it', though she herself was not much concerned with nationality. She liked Paris and had had no difficulty settling in London.

Nothing had surprised her as much as the depression that shook her after Mary's birth. It was uncharacteristic and it made her feel guilty. She had wanted a child; always, from as long ago as she could remember, she had wanted a child. She had seen no conflict between being a mother and any other activities she wanted to pursue; she did not think it would compromise or limit her but make her, if anything, more happy and complete. The depression passed, helped by her determination. The storm of physical imbalance blew over, but it left an impact.

In the utter frankness of her character she told Pietro of all her emotions. She saw nothing to be ashamed of and hoped that by sharing them with him, she might more easily dispel the gloom or anger. In any event, she saw it as his function or duty to help her. He often looked perplexed by her honesty, but evidently tried to help in his own oblique way.

Her good humour reasserted itself, though the birth of their children did change things between them. Usually Hannah saw the change as a deepening of their affection through their involvement in a common task. Occasionally, however, she saw the feeling that existed between them as if it were a third person, an organic thing in its own right, and she worried that it had become hardened or sclerotic with all the strain it had had to take.

'Come outside,' she said to Mary. 'Go and play with Anton.'

Mary made off meekly enough into the garden of their rented house near Avignon.

'Is everything all right?' said Martha Freeman, coming into the kitchen with a breakfast tray from the terrace.

Hannah smiled. 'Yes, thank you. I do worry about that girl, though. She never seems to learn. She sticks her fingers in electric sockets. She kisses stray dogs.'

Martha said, 'I'm going to put Jonathan to sleep in a minute. What time are we due in Uzès?'

'Not till one. I expect they'll be late too. It's quite a long way over to Bédoin.'

'If we can get the kids to have a nap,' said Martha, 'why don't you tell me that story you always promised. About how you and Pietro met?'

'Must I?'

'Yes, Hannah, you promised me.'

'All right. I'll keep it short.'

'No, no. I want all the details. Absolutely everything. Clothes, who said what and when. What the houses looked like. Everything.'

'All right,' Hannah laughed. 'I'll make some more coffee and see you out on the terrace.'

I was living in one of the nicer parts of Ghent, in an apartment block. It had beautiful wrought-iron balconies and windows with long slatted shutters.

My parents were from Antwerp but I had come to look after my uncle, who was very unwell. My aunt was dead and there was no one else to look after him. He owned the top two apartments in the block. He lived in the lower one; the top one was not as good because it was right under the eaves and you had to walk up a little wooden staircase to get to it. They used to let it out to young men, often doctors who were still studying. It was also smaller than my uncle's flat, which was one of those huge apartments where the rooms seem to keep opening off each other for ever.

One night I was awoken by a tremendous banging from upstairs. The floors in the top apartment had only one or two thin rugs and we relied on the tenants to be very quiet at night. I could hear loud voices and laughter and the words of what sounded like English songs. There was a deafening crash, as though someone had pushed over a huge wardrobe, and I heard my uncle calling for me from along the corridor. From upstairs I could hear the sound of muffled laughter and of people trying to move very quietly, but without much success. They sounded clumsy.

I rushed naked to the bathroom (I had never worn anything in bed) but could find only my uncle's old dressing gown, which was much too big for me. I rolled the sleeves up and put it on, tying the belt tightly. I prepared to go upstairs and tell them off. I wasn't worried about speaking English, if that was what was necessary, because we had been brought up to speak it in Antwerp.

I went to make sure that my uncle was all right and then I went and hammered on the door at the top of the wooden stairs. There was a sound of surprised laughter inside and eventually the door opened straight on to the sitting room.

Wilfred, the young doctor who rented the apartment, attempted to introduce me. He was very drunk. He could barely get the words out. I was angry, but felt at a disadvantage because of my uncle's dressing gown. There were two girls in the room, and a young man with dishevelled hair I had never seen before. One of the girls was called Kitty. I had seen her around and knew she had a bad reputation. I didn't know the other one. All four of them were finding it hard to control their laughter.

The second man – not Wilfred – had an Italian-sounding name and he had a wild look in his eyes. He was thin and looked quite young.

'What sort of way is this to behave, Wilfred?' I said. 'You know very well my uncle's ill. And do you know what time it is?'

Wilfred shook his head slowly. He looked very pale. The two girls on the sofa were sitting close together. Kitty was gripping the other one's arm, though whether this was to stop herself laughing or because she was frightened of me I couldn't say. Wilfred made a broad gesture with his arm from me towards his friend, as if he were trying to introduce us. Then he tried to speak, gagged, and brushed past me on his way to the bathroom from where we could hear the sound of retching.

The other man stood up and walked towards me. He said with great charm – rather theatrical in fact: 'My friend is lucky to have such a charming neighbour.'

'Landlady,' I snapped back.

I was rude, and I thought he would be offended, but the drink seemed to have given him some sort of fluency.

'I should have guessed, I can see that you're wearing your rent collector's gown.'

'My uncle is very ill and you have woken him up with your noise and your singing. It's very unfair to a sick man.'

Wilfred's friend came and stood close to me. He took my hand and looked into my eyes. His own, though sparkling with all the effort of his charm, were very sad. 'I would be pleased to be nursed by someone like you,' he said. 'I wouldn't mind what kind of sickness I had.'

One of the girls sniggered.

I was feeling slightly at a loss because I hadn't managed to provoke any apology. I pulled my hand away. The awful truth was that I felt suddenly aroused. The young man's eyes followed me and I pulled the dressing gown more tightly across me.

'Will you please go to bed now?' I said loudly, trying to regain my composure.

'Stay and dance,' he said. 'Wilfred was going to find a record. He said he had some champagne as well.'

'This is not a time for dancing,' I said, looking across at the two girls on the sofa. I had meant to show my contempt for them all, but the man seemed to think I was indicating that it was only the girls' presence that was a problem.

'I can get rid of them,' he hissed.

'Don't be ridiculous,' I said. 'Now please be quiet, all of you,

69

or I shall call the police. I think you had all better go and let Wilfred get some sleep. Come on, now. All of you!'

The two girls, rather to my surprise, stood up and gathered their bags and coats.

The man stood closer to me. 'Don't change from your man's clothes. You look beautiful,' he said.

I suppose he must have been very drunk to have spoken like that, and yet he seemed quite calm. At that moment Wilfred reappeared from the bathroom. He was sweating a little on the upper lip, but looked better than before.

'We're leaving, Wilfred,' said the other man. 'Thank you for your hospitality.' The girls went past me and he took my hand again in the doorway. Then I did something which I still don't understand. I said: 'My name is Hannah van Duren.' I was on the verge of saying 'You can come and see me', but I could tell from his eyes that he understood. He kissed my hand, and began to go unevenly down the stairs, two or three at a time.

I heard his voice coming up the stairwell. 'And be wearing your tweed suit,' he was calling, 'and your bow tie.'

THE next day I felt ashamed of myself. I'd never behaved like that before towards a man. But not that ashamed. After all, I'd only told him my name. During the morning I stayed indoors with my uncle, hoping he would call. The telephone was silent. About midday there was a ring at the door, but it was only the postman.

After lunch I had to go out and do some shopping. I got the caretaker's daughter to come and sit in our flat while I was out. I went to the market and then to the pharmacy to pick up a prescription for my uncle. All the time I was turning over the events of the night before in my mind. My boyfriend had left Antwerp for a job in Paris about a year before. I was glad. We had begun to irritate each other. Although he was a kind man, and of course I was fond of him, I no longer felt passionate about him. He was confused by me in return. I think he was secretly pleased that we now just kept in touch by letter. He told me I was staid and middle-aged, but I wasn't. The truth was that I no longer found him romantic.

I hurried around the shops and I don't know what I bought. I got it all wrong, as far as I remember, so it was difficult to cook dinner that night. I'd bought prawns to go with beef, or something like that. I was excited. Do you know Ghent? It's a boring place. Bourgeois. The word could have been made for it. Not like Antwerp, which I like. But that afternoon I thought it looked magical, it was quite different. You know how it is when you see things suddenly in a different light, in a new light, as though you were a traveller who has just arrived.

I didn't stop to ask myself why I was so excited, or what it was about this man – a man whom I'd in any case only seen for a few minutes. Maybe it was just that physical thing. You can never underestimate that – though it felt like something much more. I wanted to take his head in my hands and hold his poor ragged hair against my chest. But I didn't feel sorry for him. Well, a little bit maybe. I felt more in awe of him, really.

When I got back to the block I hurried through the hall because I didn't want to be detained by the caretaker who always wanted to talk for hours. But it was no use: he was waiting beside the lift with his horrible dog. 'There's some flowers for you,' he said, in a way that was supposed to make me feel guilty. But I didn't. I just said, 'Good. Where are they?' 'Which ones do you mean?' he said. 'Which ones do *you* mean?' I said. He was always playing silly games like this. 'Well, there's been three lots, haven't there?'

I took the lift up to the apartment and found my uncle in his dressing gown, walking up and down in the hall. He wasn't supposed to be out of bed, and I told him he'd catch a chill. He was muttering about flowers. There were three bunches on the table in the hall.

'These ones came first,' he said, picking up some yellow roses. 'Then when I was going off to sleep again, the girl came up with this bunch of – whatever they are, irises. And then just before you got in, the bell rang and it was the boy from the florist's shop who brought this huge bunch here. There was a note.'

My uncle looked perturbed. He couldn't make out what was going on. Often he could go for a month with no one ringing the bell at all. He looked at me over his glasses a bit crossly, and I told him to get back to bed. I pretended I was annoyed with him. I opened the note, which said: 'I am sorry about last night. Please come down to the street at 9 p.m. I will ring the bell.' The handwriting was rather spluttery. All three bunches were from Pietro.

I didn't want him to be too sorry. I went downstairs again to ask the girl if she would come and keep an eye on my uncle. I knew it would be all right with him, because he went to sleep straight after dinner, which he liked at about seven anyway. Then I thought about what I would wear. I supposed I should wear something very feminine, so it wouldn't look as though I was just playing his game. So I looked through the clothes I had, and there was a black dress which I _could_ wear. Then I thought maybe he would only take me to a bar for a drink and I would feel overdressed. I spent a long time in my room. Perhaps I should continue the game and borrow one of my uncle's tweed jackets. Then suddenly I wondered if it was wise to go out at all with this man I hardly knew. I went upstairs to speak to Wilfred, to ask him about his friend, but he wasn't there. In the end I settled on a black skirt and a white top, with a spotted bow tie of my uncle's. It was very loose, and I had to tie it myself, or try to.

I went running down to the street when the bell rang. He was standing in the doorway, trying to keep out of the rain, with the collar of his mac turned up. He took my hand and said something about the bow tie, and I was glad because it showed he wasn't going to spend the evening apologising. He rushed me over to a car on the other side of the street and said he was going to take me to see the city. He sounded a bit unconvinced, as though he wasn't sure that there was much of Ghent to see. But in Belgium there is always a square or two, and the façades of the big buildings are often gilded, which looks good in the rain. The city is built on various waterways with bridges. There is an old castle, a huge cathedral and some lovely guild houses. He pretended he was navigating, and I let him know where to go without puncturing that illusion. He was very kind. He laughed at his own driving, though not as much as he laughed at the Belgian driving.

I loved showing him around. It made me look at the place properly and appreciate it. It also made me think about the life I lived there as I looked at it through his eyes. We got into a big brasserie in the end, with bright lights and wooden stalls. It was all right. He was drenched, because he'd held his mac up for me when we ran over from the car. He pushed his hand through his hair a lot to begin with, but then he seemed to give up. He offered me a cigarette and I began to look at him properly for the first time. I just liked his face. I don't know why. You wouldn't say Pietro's really handsome, I suppose, but it was a kind face. I liked his narrow eyes and he had a lovely mouth which moved in a very seductive way when he talked. But he was frightened. I could tell that almost straight away. He wasn't at peace with himself.

We had dinner. He had mussels, I remember. He was struck by how many mussels people ate. He wanted them with mustard, because he'd seen someone in Mons or Charleroi or somewhere eating them like that. I told him it was very bourgeois, like talking about dogs and football. He said that was all right with him and he teased me a bit for what I ordered. I can't remember what it was now. The truth was, he thought I was a really solid landlady, a bossy woman with just a bit of sparkle in her eye. I think that was what he wanted from me in some funny way. I didn't mind.

He had been doing business in the south and had been driving back to catch the ferry at Ostend when he decided to pull off the motorway. Apparently he had fallen in with Wilfred in some bar. So they'd drunk a lot, and Wilfred had introduced him to Belgian beer. There's some stuff they pour in a glass bowl which is held up by a wooden stand. You have to grasp the wooden bit to drink it. It tastes like beer, but it's as strong as wine.

So the usual thing had happened. They'd drunk a lot of these, and then they'd met these two girls and Wilfred asked them back

73

and so on. He told me all this in a very straightforward way. Then he asked me a lot about what I did, and about my family. He seemed fascinated that I spoke such good English. I explained all about the country and how people in the south spoke French and so on and he was very interested in all that.

'Do you mean to say,' he said, 'that people in the same country have different names for the same places?'

I said, 'Yes, that's right.'

He seemed amazed, and I suppose it must seem peculiar to an outsider. It's something we were brought up with, though even so I suppose we are a bit sensitive about it. I explained how every political party had a Flemish-speaking and a French-speaking wing, how the whole place was split in two in every way, except Brussels which was more like an island. I said that when we were at school our teacher had told us that in Yugoslavia they were even worse off. Half of them wrote in Greek letters because they followed the Greek Orthodox Church and half of them wrote like us. So it wasn't just different names but different letters.

He asked about my education, and when I told him he said something like, 'Belgian schoolgirls. Belgian schoolgirls on a bridge. My grandfather would have liked that.' I hadn't a clue what he meant.

I wanted to know about him. He told me all the jobs he'd had. Some of them were very strange. In America he'd worked as a garage mechanic and then he'd spent one summer on a chicken farm, catching them by their legs for vaccination. In Italy he said he'd worked a ski lift. He spent a whole winter there. But then he'd discovered photography. He explained to me how you develop and print pictures; he sounded quite entranced by it. All the time he was telling me these stories I was wondering why he'd never really settled on one thing. He told me he was settled now, that he'd got a little company in London and this was what he was going to do. But I looked at him then, and there was something wild in him, it seemed to me. I don't know what it was – something that made him restless, that wouldn't let him be. I wanted it to be all right for him. I felt he could still be caught just in time, but this was the last chance. So I held his hand across the table. He was moved by this, and I couldn't believe he could be so soft after all the things he'd been telling me.

I let him kiss me that night. I let him kiss me as much as he wanted. He had a beautiful soft mouth. He stayed for days and days in Ghent, and I never let him do more than kiss me. But I think I knew from that first evening we spent together that I wanted to marry him.

HOUCHES, LES

hhhhhhhhhhhhhhhhhhhhhhhhhhhhhhhhhhhhhhhhhhhhhhhhhhhhhhhhhhhhhhhhhhhhhhhhhhhhhhhhhhhhhhhhhhhh

France 1967

PIETRO gazed at his twenty-five-year-old face in the mirror of his small wood-lined room in the mountains. It was still the same wire-brush hair and his blue eyes looking rather sunk today, little lines of black beneath them. He had not shaved for three days and there was a spiky shadow on his upper lip and an irritation beneath his chin. His face was tanned a reddish, peasant brown, but the skin was tight back against the skull, and he was thin.

He pulled the cover over the bed and opened the window. The blast of Dolomite air tasted good. It was like the best detoxifying agent ever invented. He filled his sinuses with the rarefied icy gas and felt a shiver of health, despite himself. The fighter pilots training for the Mercury space programme used to cure their hangovers with draughts of oxygen in the morning as they stumbled to the plane. The trouble with the mountain air was that it was so effective Pietro was tempted to use it as a cure every day. He drank too much. After a day in the mountains he needed to warm himself though, and the people he had fallen in with – local men who worked with their hands – had big thirsts in the evening. Drinking as much as they did was the price he had to pay for their company.

He dressed and made himself some coffee. He always felt good

76

in the mountains. People said one resort was where all the smart people went, another was only for barbarians, but in Pietro's experience this wasn't true. There were extreme examples, certainly. In Gstaad, for instance, no one seemed to ski at all – perhaps because there was hardly any skiing to be done. He had stopped there in his car and seemed to be the only person who looked dressed for sport. People in fur coats with leather skin and vacant eyes stared at him curiously. Then again, he had been once to an Italian resort derided for being full of British trippers – the Blackpool of the slopes, they called it. If you put yourself in the Andy Capp bar at midnight then it was certainly true that you could tell you were not in Gstaad. But apart from these extremes, most mountain villages had more in common than they had apart. In all the resorts he had visited Pietro found he felt the same. His body felt clean and alert. His digestion changed on the day he arrived so that his saliva tasted different and he required different foods – dried ham, beef and cheese. Was it the drinking water that made this fundamental change, or was it the air?

He worked on a ski lift halfway up the mountain. It was a job that was in the gift of the German-speaking South Tyrolean businessman who ran the village. A vicious cartel was operated by a family whose roots in the village long pre-dated the rise of Italian nationalism and who had never therefore bothered to learn more than a few words of the language. Their loyalty was first to the Tyrol and second to Austria. This was another way places could be deceptive, Pietro thought. On the map it said the village was in Italy, but it had about as much in common with Milan as it had with Okayama, Japan, or with Green Bay, Wisconsin.

After three months working as a waiter in a big hotel he had fallen in one night in a bar with a man called Enrico, a muscular, battered forty-year-old with fingers like salamis. Enrico was the Italian face of the German-speaking cartel; he was in charge of the main cable car from the village and the subsidiary lifts on the slope above. He talked to Pietro about Italy and Austria and he seemed to like the stories Pietro told about England. Pietro spoke a slightly accented and incomplete Italian; but then so did Enrico.

He was impressed by Pietro's knowledge of the mountain, which he had gained by skiing every day for three months when he could escape from his waiter's duties. Now, towards the end of the season, Enrico had offered him a job looking after a sunless chair lift in a remote angle of the mountains. Pietro accepted at once. When he discovered how much the job paid he arranged to do some shifts as a barman at the hotel in the evenings as well.

He took the cable car up as soon as it opened and reached his workplace by a number of different drag lifts. The skiing he did between them was all he managed until the end of the day when he was required to ski down slowly, making sure the pistes were empty. He had a radio for speaking to Enrico, or someone in the office back in the village, and for contacting the men with the bloodwagon.

Once installed in his wooden cabin, he waited for the first skiers to arrive. His lift was not much used; it was a link into a system of three runs which were steep and often icy. He had a transistor radio in the cabin and a thermos of coffee. When skiers approached he slowed the mechanism of the lift. If he felt well disposed he held the seat so it wouldn't smack them too hard behind the knees. He looked at their passes and nodded them through. He hardly ever spoke, even when people said something friendly to him. He felt alone in the mountain, he felt close to the rock and earth beneath the snow. He wanted very much to feel part of it, to feel something solid beneath his feet. There had been times in the last year when he had doubted the existence of any solid earth at all.

The chairs gave soft, metallic bumps as the wheel at the end of the cable span them round and pointed them once more up the mountain. Apart from that, it was quiet. When Pietro felt the silence of the mountain coming on, he turned off the squawking transistor and tried to feel the massive peace of the world under his feet. The air was alive in the sunlight with tiny particles of ice. I am a poor boy, he thought, a wretched, ragged man with no significance. Let me find some security, some sense of what I am from these mountains and the tranquillity around me.

At midday one of the other lift operators brought him a loaf of bread with salami and a small bottle of local spirit. Pietro thanked him and ate hungrily in the greasy atmosphere of the cabin where the oil fire smoked and spluttered. People came and went in their brightly coloured clothes, laughing to one another, and Pietro drained the last of his drink in silence. He went out again into the air and nodded to the next skier. He felt good again; for a moment he felt fine.

When he had first gone skiing, eight years earlier in the small French resort of les Houches, the job of ski-lift attendant was not one he envisaged doing. The men who did it looked red-faced and inbred; they made jokes in impenetrable local dialects, and when they laughed you could see how many of their teeth were missing.

But some bitter determination had entered Pietro's mind in the course of his first trip to the mountains, as a seventeen-year-old schoolboy. This curious figure he now cut, lonely and silent as he tended the chair lift, was not the cheerful boy who had squeezed into the early-morning train to Gatwick. After the tearful farewell of Gloria Katz's mother ('How many suitcases is Gloria *bringing*?' said Harry) there had been too much bustle at the airport and too little room on the plane for him to see who was there and what it was all going to be like. Then the coach took the damp motorway from Geneva. It was not until darkness fell and they began to climb that some of the children fell asleep. Pietro, his nerves sizzling from Harry Freeman's cigarettes, went down the swaying bus, clinging to the seats as he passed. Dave Snyder reluctantly offered him a pull from his duty-free bourbon. He was sitting with his new friend Kurt Boshof, a burly, fair-haired American who had apparently skied every mountain in the United States. The two boys had overseen the loading of their own skis on to the plane, causing Pietro a moment's panic. Was he the only person without skis? He had assumed dimly that you were given them when you got there.

An address on the coach microphone by the teacher in charge, Mr Maxwell, had reassured him.

Next to Kurt and Dave, across the gangway, Gloria sat plumply asleep, exhausted by the travel, by Dave's bourbon and her mother's solicitude. Her head lay on Laura Heasman's shoulder. Pietro had never seen Laura out of school before and he was at first slightly disappointed. Her legs were covered by long leather boots and a full denim skirt. She looked at him with her electrifying but ambiguous smile over Gloria's shoulder. As they climbed, it grew colder in the bus and Laura huddled up to Gloria for warmth. Pietro offered her his jacket as he stood in the gangway, watching the eddies of snow that fell from the trees by the black, onrushing road. She smiled sleepily as she took it.

There was a fight for rooms at the hotel, with Mr Maxwell, an Englishman in his late twenties, trying to keep the children at bay while he found the best room for himself and his colleague. It was too late. Dave Snyder was already on the first-floor landing, where he and Kurt had set up camp in the largest room, overlooking the mountain. There were screeches and recriminations as the others made their claims. Harry Freeman secured a cosy twin-bedder with its own bath at the back of the hotel, while Pietro brought up their baggage. Ten minutes later Laura came in to say that she and Gloria had been given a room with two fourteen-year-old Iranian boys, but they refused to move out, unless . . . By some logic, the only solution was for her and Gloria to have Harry and Pietro's room. Harry refused. Laura seemed upset; her lower lip trembled. Then she laughed and teased them. They still refused. Then she pleaded with all the power of her almost-womanhood, and five minutes later Pietro and Harry were bunked down with the two Iranian boys.

The next morning there was skiing. On Harry's advice Pietro had brought his own boots made by a company called Gauner. They were dark blue with red fastenings and gave a certain pain across the instep which Pietro assumed was normal. He and Harry were in the beginners' group, where they spent most of the morning trying to get their skis on. A laconic Frenchman called Bernard gave instruction. 'Knees,' he said to Pietro. 'What does he mean, "knees"?' said Pietro as he unplugged the snow from his ears.

It was slow and tiring work. They sweated beneath their anoraks – a gardening jacket belonging to his father in Pietro's case, an Italian style bought at discount from the trade in Harry's. At lunch they took the cable car up the mountain and sat outside a café. There they could see the distant figures of people skiing at impossible speeds. One man came down with his skis glued together, making only the tiniest sway of his hips as he plunged over moguls, skirted a narrow icy patch and, scorning the prepared piste, finished the run in the virgin snow beneath the chair lift. It turned out to be Dave Snyder.

Released from Bernard's gnomic instruction, they were free in the afternoons to go where they chose. The only good thing, as Pietro remarked, was that they spent much more time coming down than going up. Dave Snyder and Kurt Boshof came down so fast each time that they spent most of their day queuing for lifts. Harry and Pietro only needed two short ascents in the whole of the afternoon. As they were clinging tight to a drag lift whose main purpose was apparently to cause bruising to the soft areas between the legs, Pietro saw an all-in-one pink ski suit coming slowly but gracefully down the mountain. He knew at once that it was Laura.

'Has anyone seen Gloria?' she called out as she glided past.

'She's still in the café,' he called back.

'Typical,' laughed Laura.

'Yes, typical,' called Pietro, though she was already out of earshot.

That night he and Harry counted their bruises. It wasn't the sodomy of the drag lift or the pain from hip bones blue from sudden impact on the ice so much as the fierce ache in the calves that bothered them. The showers were cold. Harry, for the first time, looked defeated.

'I know,' said Pietro. 'We could ask Laura and Gloria if they'd let us use their bath.'

Gloria answered the door in her dressing gown, her hair up in a scarf. She wasn't pleased to see them. 'The Blazers want to use the tub,' she called out to Laura. She hadn't called them that for a long time. 'I'm so tired,' said Gloria. 'Maybe tomorrow, OK?'

'Tired? But you sat in the café all day,' said Harry.

Pietro didn't think this was the right way to get round Gloria. 'Please, Laura,' he called out. 'Remember we did let you have the room.' He thought that if he could get past the presence of Gloria in the doorway Laura's better nature would be vulnerable. It worked, and he was able to climb into the small but hot bathtub a few minutes later.

It seemed impolite not to linger a little while and take a drink with them afterwards; he didn't want to use them like a hotel. The next evening he took some salami and some peanuts to go with Gloria's gin and orange. From then on the routine became established. Gloria eventually put down her book and listened to the exaggerated stories they told of what had happened during the day. Pietro sat at the foot of Laura's bed while Laura sat tucked under the duvet, smiling seraphically as she swallowed tumblers full of gin.

On the third day things came to a head with the Gauner skiing boots. For some time Pietro had wondered whether their inventor, Herr Dr Gauner, had not been a defendant at the Nuremberg trials. As he limped down the main road of Les Houches he hid them under an old blue Peugeot and prayed never to see them again. With some hired boots and a padding of thick socks over the Gauner-inflicted weals, he made progress. By the fifth day he and Harry could navigate slopes of medium difficulty. After lunch on the terrace of the restaurant, washed down with wine from Dôle, they joined a large party of skiers that included Laura, Dave and Kurt. Harry said it was foolhardy, but Pietro reckoned the boys would have to slow down a little for the girls. Grim-faced, they exchanged curt nods and set off, leaving Gloria Katz sunbathing on the terrace.

Laura skied with minimal effort. She said she was afraid and she didn't go fast, but on narrow tracks she could keep on turning from side to side just by swivelling her skis, which remained parallel; she never seemed to do any of the knee-bending, trunk-twisting or ankle-flexing recommended by Bernard. Luckily Rania, a slim Saudi Arabian girl with brown eyes, fell over twice, and while Kurt and Dave were fussing over her bindings and dusting the snow from her thighs, Harry and Pietro came over the horizon, heads down, in a hectic *schuss* that brought them up alongside.

At the bottom, Laura looked at the pair of them panting and grimacing. 'Look, you're all hot,' she laughed, not unkindly. Pietro vowed that he would one day ski with his skis so close together that not even a razor blade could be slid between them.

It was the late-afternoon hour at the bottom of the slope. The sun had gone off the mountain and the skiers were heading into cafés for tea and chocolate. Mothers stood anxiously in the fading light, calling to their errant children. The mountains, no longer a sunny playground, had begun to look cold and menacing. Pietro hoisted his skis once more on to shoulders sore from carrying them and trudged off up the village street. He breathed in the atmosphere of bustle underlaid by Alpine calm; he saw the lights coming on in the shops and chalets and thought of the hot bath and the excitement of the cocktail hour that awaited him.

On the way back to the hotel he stopped in a supermarket and bought some black olives and some cashew nuts. As he left the shop he noticed that the road was called the Chemin des Anes. Opposite his hotel he had already seen a cul-de-sac called the Impasse du Désir. What strange names these places had. 'Dear Dad,' he would start a postcard, 'I am having a lovely time. I am in Thwarted Desire, Asses Way, France. Love to all. PS Would your army friend collect this place under L or H?'

Now, eight years later, when he banged his hands together in the cold and nodded silently to the skiers as they showed their passes, he thought of the extraordinary mixture they had then felt of real anguish and continuing hilarity. He remembered Harry's generosity and the way he had laughed things away.

The mountains guarded the valley. To the west was the Marmalada, a slope with a single swooping run served by three vertiginous cable cars. The mountains merged imperceptibly across the top of Italy into the Alps; so according to the maps, the place he stood was part of the same upthrust formation as the hills that underlay les Houches.

He was connected to his former schoolboy self by a geological feature as well as by memory. In his solitary distress, he reminded himself of such physical connections. He needed to believe that places were joined to each other; that they formed one continuous world, not distinct universes. Then he might be able to believe that he had not lost touch with his former life and with himself.

IBIZA

Balearic Islands 1966

'I do appreciate it,' said Pietro. It was hard to thank his father warmly enough for taking him on holiday without sounding surprised that he had agreed to it. He hadn't yet mastered the subtle falsities of tact. 'It's marvellous,' he gushed, 'I mean it.'

'Of course you do,' said his father kindly.

The package to Ibiza left from Gatwick. When Pietro had gone to Italy with his mother they had flown from Heathrow, so this was the first time he had seen the thronging families of uncertain Britons preparing for abroad. He liked it much better than Heathrow. There were pretty girls of about his age, slightly over-made-up, peering out from beneath the wings of their harassed families. Their fathers gave orders in loud voices to show they weren't nervous and their mothers talked about the price of refreshments, the whereabouts of toilets and tickets, the closeness of the hand baggage. The girls tried by their looks to disown their parents as they would later be able to on the beach and in the discothèques; Pietro felt at an advantage having only a father to shrug off.

They were in an apartment in a new block about two hundred

yards back from the beach. Pietro was sharing a room with his father, which had its drawbacks for both of them. The old man's idea of a good morning was to go to the beach early to get a favourable spot, erect a sunshade and read a book on etymology. Pietro found getting up before ten was a torture. He liked to go to the beach about eleven with a book recommended by Mr Maxwell at the US Collegiate, sunbathe for an hour, swim vigorously, open the book and close his eyes. He looked enviously at the Spanish men in their twenties with their hairy chests. He noticed how the English girls fluttered towards them and didn't seem to mind that all the men could say was 'Bobby Charlton, very good, Bobby Moore, very good, ha, ha.'

He was happy nevertheless. He liked not only the hot beach with its pointless games but also the town, which was responding to its northern visitors. The white buildings were cool and exotic, the people in the bars spoke little English and the beer was still *cerveza*. But small handcraft stalls had started to appear beneath awnings at the side of the sloping streets; local traders consulted young Europeans with tangled hair and six-string wooden guitars. They collaborated in the making of primitive jewellery with pliers, beads and strips of leather. Pietro liked the steamy shade of an outdoor restaurant at lunchtime when all the muscles were relaxed by heat and the willing waiter brought sangria and then pans full of paella which seemed indulgently sophisticated with its greasy mixture of shellfish and chicken. He smiled at his father, who nodded back over the melon.

One day Pietro got into a five-a-side game of football on the beach. A boy called Tony suggested that he come along to the discothèque that night. It was a little way out of town in a whitewashed building with stuccoed arches and red tile floors. It played mostly Spanish songs with the occasional British or American pop record. Whatever they played, it was loud enough and fast enough to pack the floor. With a pack of local cigarettes in his shirt pocket and a bottle of red wine under his belt, Pietro danced until the place closed, and still they weren't tired.

'Dear Harry,' he wrote, 'this place is great. I danced with a girl called Marsha who comes from Birmingham. Her favourite singer is Cliff Richard!! Got into a great football match against the locals. We lost 1–4. Guess who scored our goal? There are a lot of girls here. Hope you had a good time in France. I will be a changed man by next term. Tanned, suave. You won't recognise me. Nor will Laura. Must dash. P.'

'Dear Laura, this place is a bit crowded (package trips!) but I quite like it. Sun, sand and so on. Hope you're having fun in California. So much discoing here I'm exhausted! See you in September. Love, Pietro.'

AFTER dinner that night Pietro and his father walked back up the hill to the block they were staying in. It had been decided that visits to the discothèque should not be a nightly event.

Pietro undressed in the hot bedroom while his father cleaned his teeth in the slit of a bathroom at the side. The room was too small for two people and their belongings. Pietro sat on the bed, waiting for his turn in the bathroom. When he came back he found his father in bed reading a book. He climbed into his own bed, pulled up the sheet and turned off his light. He wished his father would do the same. He found their physical proximity almost unbearable. His father continued to read, the sound of regularly turning pages the only noise in the room. Outside there was a ragged sound of cicadas and dimly audible beyond that the intermittent thump of the discothèque. Another page turned. Pietro wondered what sort of earthquake or natural disaster it would take to make his father turn his light out. Please, he silently begged, just reach out your hand, just a small pressure of the fingers on the switch . . .

JERUSALEM

Israel 1982

I<small>N</small> the *sherut*, a shared taxi, through the surprisingly dumb and threatening suburbs of Tel Aviv, usually characterised as international city, Hilton-sur-mer, and out into the Sharon Plain, invisible under darkness except for vague swellings, no hint of abandoned tank or other mementoes left to mark the millennial argument, regular as a heartbeat, over the dry soil.

The twinkling dining room of the Jerusalem hotel, full of visitors, tourists, Americans, Germans, a few British. Someone says a *kiddush* and Harry places a napkin on Pietro's head. They watch the soup growing cold on the table as other diners intone 'Amen'. They eat the bland food and go up to their room. Although both are tired, they find it hard to sleep. Guests are advised to leave all valuables in the hotel safe.

In the morning Daoud, the Israeli guide, arrives at the hotel. He is a man in his late forties, thickset, balding, who wears an open-neck shirt, sandals and aviator shades. He has an air of world-weariness and a deep mocking laugh that rises from his chest. He carries a leather key-fob with a metal flap that he flicks back and forth in place of worry beads. As they walk towards the old city, Daoud says, 'OK, you want a history lesson first?'

'Sure.'

'How many different peoples do you think have controlled Jerusalem?'

'I don't know,' says Harry. 'Four or five.'

'I don't know either,' says Daoud. 'I can give you maybe ten to think about before we start. Babylonians, Persians, Greeks, Egyptians, Syrians, Romans, Idumeans – Herod was one of them – the Christians, the Byzantine empire, the Moslems, the Turks.'

They are at the start of the via Dolorosa, the Lions' Gate, or Stephen's Gate, as the Christians prefer.

'And what about the Jews?' says Pietro.

'I'd almost forgotten them,' Daoud says drily. 'And of course the Jordanians.'

Along the stations of the Cross are lamps, beads, relics, Coca-Cola, crosses, camera films, hats, pardons.

'Hey,' says Daoud, 'I can fix you an egg from The Cock That Crowed.'

Beneath the Ecce Homo arch, past the second station of the Cross, Daoud explains that it was named after Pilate's scornful words of dismissal when the captive Christ was brought to him. Under the assault of souvenir sellers and the lit signs saying 'Gifts', Pietro pictures the slow progress of the man beneath the heavy cross, his bare feet pressed where they now stand.

'Then the archaeologists discovered the arch didn't even exist in Christ's time.' Daoud laughs as he leads them on.

Harry takes notes of the facts that Daoud gives them. Pietro tries to form pictures in his mind of what happened.

At the Church of the Holy Sepulchre they find that the place where the Christian God died is guarded by Moslem Arabs. At the top of a marble staircase a Greek priest yawns by the spot where the cross was raised. Cheap icons and lamps surround it; similar lighting, a sort of Middle-East kitsch, glows over the sepulchre where he lay. Pietro fights a feeling of distaste, which he guiltily ascribes to vestigial snobbery, Englishness, un-acknowledged racial prejudice.

'The place was discovered by Queen Helena in the year 326,'

Daoud recites. 'Three crosses of mysteriously preserved wood were in the crypt. She was guided by an angel.' He flaps his key-fob. 'Your English General Gordon didn't believe her. He couldn't stand the place. Do you know why?'

Pietro feels himself addressed. He shrugs.

Daoud laughs. 'Because it's so Arab! So he decided Jesus was buried in the Garden Tomb because he said burials were always outside the city walls in those days.'

'So it couldn't have been here?'

Daoud shrugs. 'Might have been. The city walls moved. Gordon was wrong. This place was probably inside them in Christ's time.'

They wander in the streets of the old city, Harry and Pietro occasionally questioning, Daoud telling stories with a smile that sometimes looks like condescension.

They go through the process of disillusionment that every tourist experiences. Daoud doesn't mind. He will show them something more interesting later on.

They can hear the frequent tap and scraping of chisels, the rattle of hammers as the archaeologists hunt for history through the layers of the city. Beneath the covered streets Pietro feels that he and Harry and Daoud are part of another stratum in an unresolved search; future generations will question their existence.

The lanes are muddy, full of eggshells and orange peel, with commerce spurting from the fronts of dwellings; donkeys led from indoors, trays of souvenirs slung from ropes and awnings, tailors pumping sewing machines with their feet, potters working with their doors open.

At the Dome of the Rock, Daoud at last becomes enthusiastic. He gestures towards the golden cupola. 'This is beautiful,' he says. 'Built on the site where the temples of Solomon and Herod once stood. The place where Abraham prepared to sacrifice his son and where Mohammed rose to heaven on his horse.'

'Both?' says Pietro. 'In the same place?'

'It's a small city. A very small city.'

'I'm surprised the Christians didn't muscle in too,' Harry says beneath his breath.

Daoud overhears him. 'They did. The Caliph used Byzantine architects. Good, isn't it?'

Inside, they see the rock where Isaac lay beneath his father's upraised arm. Pietro is surprised to see it revered by Moslems, almost as much as a box next to it that contains some hairs from the Prophet's beard. 'Doesn't it confuse you?' he asks. 'Doesn't it tax your faith, seeing all these conflicting claims? It makes me inclined to disbelieve all religions.'

'It's simple enough,' says Daoud. 'Jerusalem is a holy city. The Moslem faith grew from a Jew – from Abraham. They have a respect for Jewish history. In any case, why should I mind?' The key-fob flicks. 'I'm a Christian.'

HARRY and Pietro arrive ten minutes early for dinner in the restaurant and order beer.

'What does your friend David do?' Pietro asks.

'He teaches. We knew his family in London. He came here a few years ago, when he married.'

'And his wife?'

Sarah turns out to be American, a quiet, determined woman with searching eyes. David is fair, bespectacled, with a shirt that hangs loosely from his slightly concave chest. They have brought with them a friend, Shimon, also bespectacled, with a soft black beard. After the introductions David smiles broadly and spreads his arms. 'So, Harry, you're a journalist! What on earth made you do that?'

Harry smiles sheepishly. 'I can't think. My family have never forgiven me.'

'Don't worry,' says Sarah. 'We're used to it. There are more of them to the square foot in this city than anywhere else on earth.'

There are some enquiries about Harry's family, followed by a short pause. Then, as though the preliminaries have been properly concluded, Sarah begins: 'Did you see the article,

Harry? Did you see it? What is he thinking of, that man? Does he
know what it's like?'

There is no need to ask what article she means. They have
already heard it mentioned. A visiting writer, an ironist of the
aristocratic Anglo-American school, has written a magazine
essay that includes the reflection that it was arguably unwise of
the Jews to have assembled in one place, in case by some cruel
paradox they made the task of genocide easier for a second
aggressor. He has also enlisted the 'lessons of history' to predict
that the present ownership of the land is unlikely to be more
enduring than any of the dozens that preceded it.

'What does he mean, "another short-term tenancy"?' Sarah
wants to know. 'Has he read no history? Doesn't he understand
about a land promised by God and by man? I wanted to write to
him and say, "Excuse me, but it's not the Jews who have been
inflexible. When the original partition plan was drawn up in 1947
it included a separate state for the Arabs and we said, Yes, go
right ahead. It was they who didn't want it. They wanted all of
the land; they wanted to drive us into the sea." This man doesn't
understand that at all. We attracted Arabs from other countries
because we were so good at cultivating the land and making it
work – something they'd never managed. That's why there are
so many of them. Not because they came from here but because
the Jews made it such a good place to live! And what are these
countries they come from anyway? Jordan is a line in the sand.
Syria, Saudi Arabia . . . Good heavens! All these places suddenly
so proud of themselves when they were just bits left over,
unwanted by the Europeans from what was left of earlier
empires. And the Palestinians, don't put me on. They have a
homeland if they want it. It's called Jordan. They want to stay
here, of course. Who can blame them? Who would want to live
in Jordan? But if they stay they must remember this is our
country. What did that writer say – "Just another passing
phase"? And that old story about how the Jews had been offered
Uganda? He doesn't understand. He should talk to these people.
They won't let us live. They want to kill us, all of us.'

Pietro feels uneasy that the conversation has already reached such fundamental questions. In a gesture of what he thinks of as tact, he gives vent to his curiosity about some of the more superficial aspects of life in Jerusalem. With the menu in his hand, he remarks on the amount of chicken and asks what else people eat.

'A lot of salad, and hummus – you know hummus?' says Sarah. 'And sweet things. People here eat a lot of cake and sweets.'

Harry says, 'It's mostly chicken though, isn't it? Chicken and eggs.' He laughs sociably.

Shimon leans forward and runs his fingers through his beard. 'We eat anything.' There is a wry, defensive note in his voice. 'We don't have human sacrifices, you know.'

'I just . . .'

'Sarah's right,' says Shimon, taking some bread. 'It was the Arab nations who resisted the idea of partition put forward by the UN. What's more, they went on to persuade world opinion – even Americans – that the Jews had descended on Palestine after the Second World War and evicted the Palestinians by force. Nothing could be further from the truth. During the conflict that followed the Arab refusal of partition, Palestinian society – which had never really taken root here – began to fall apart. This is not just my view, this is the account of their own historians. The big families left to find peace in Egypt, Syria or Lebanon. They left behind the peasants and villagers. They were frightened, they fell apart. If anyone displaced the Palestinians it was themselves.'

Shimon speaks English with only the slightest accent, though there is a certain thickening of passion in his voice. Pietro wonders how many times he has rehearsed these events, how often he has been believed or disbelieved. He does not spare them, or hold back; he is ready with the full argument, facts, history, assertion. When the waiter brings meat he does not check his urgent version of events. It is as though each reiteration makes it more certain, makes the defence more unbreachable.

David, a mild man, smiles at Harry and Pietro, and makes sure they have what they want to eat. When there is a moment he asks them about their hotel and how they have spent the day. He still has the English habit of drinking alcohol and becomes effusive as the meal wears on.

'Your first visit to Jerusalem, Pietro? Isn't it a wonderful city? I lived here once when I was a student and then I made the mistake of going back to London. It was hard to return to Jerusalem. If once you leave her, she doesn't easily take you back. Now I'm so happy here. It's the centre of the world. This tiny little city. Yes, I believe that, I really do. Everything that happens here has significance for the rest of the world. Even the bad things.'

Pietro nods in agreement. In a way this is what he has already begun to feel: that the intensity of dispute gives a charged atmosphere to the place, though this seems to him unfortunate rather than marvellous.

'And it's so beautiful,' says David. 'If you look towards the Dead Sea, there is something in the light. It is very ancient, yet glowing. And the powder and dust under your feet is that of history, lived by people who have given their lives for what they believe in, all here, here in this one tiny place – this place out of all the places in the world. Sometimes even the air seems magical. Invigorating.' He smiles.

Their guide had taken them to the edge of the city that afternoon and swept his arm towards the landscape of the Judaean hills, inviting them to look and form their own view of the promised land. They had driven towards the Arab town of Bethlehem. The land looked white and bleached bare, with knots and hillocks formed as though by bones; later there were olive groves, but here it was like an ossuary created by a conceptual artist of a zealous cult: no lichens, moss or weed softened the death-white, leprous bubbles and crags; it was as though petrification had squeezed organic life, even decay, from the blankness of the hillsides. Yet within that landscape were people whose lives drew the gaze of the world. It was strange that their struggles, so heavily contemplated, so vital that the participants and most onlookers were convinced that of all such struggles they were sure one day to be labelled 'history', were enacted in this shroud of white dust. It gave a ghostly quality to the present, with all its guns and passion, as though it were already powdered with futile antiquity.

'Come back to my house,' says Shimon when dinner is finished. 'Come and have some tea.'

'Thank you,' says Harry, looking interrogatively at Pietro.

'Sure,' he nods.

'It's not as if we have a busy schedule tomorrow,' says Harry. 'We're meeting the guide at ten.'

Harry walks with David and Sarah, while Pietro goes on ahead with Shimon.

'Were you born here?' he asks.

'Yes. My parents escaped from Hitler. My grandparents were all killed. I was brought up here in Jerusalem. I fought in the Six Day War when we liberated East Jerusalem. In some ways that was the greatest time of my life, except that I lost many friends. I was only twenty years old.'

They climb some stairs to Shimon's apartment and he goes to the kitchen to make tea.

When they are all sitting down, ranged around the sofas of Shimon's room, each within reach of tea or cigarettes, Shimon says, 'You know, one thing annoys me more than anything about people like that journalist. It's not necessarily what he believes or what he sees. It's the way they come to Israel for moral recreation. People expect Israel to be better than other countries, to have to prove its right to exist by constantly being more just. This is absurd. It is a country, a nation like any other, there can be no argument about that. By continually accepting the need to set some sort of world example we tacitly accept also that we have not yet been granted automatic right to nationhood. This must stop. We don't need to prove that we are "better" than Syria or Iraq. God, that would not be difficult. We need to be smarter or stronger. That's all. I don't want people to feel sorry for us, to view us with special concern. I want them to be frightened of us.'

Sarah is nodding her head in agreement. 'That's what your

journalist friend will never understand. There will be no more Hitler, no more pogroms. It is a matter of life or death. I feel sorry for someone who cannot see that.'

Occasionally David asks to differ on some particular from his wife and friend, but he looks tired, and slumps back further in his chair as the talk rolls on. Shimon and Sarah both want to redefine themselves, to set things straight. Pietro suspects this is a daily process, but they go through it with enthusiasm. They hold nothing back. There is no sense of fatigue, no sense of going over familiar ground. Any alternative opinion, even David's, is swept aside with the certainty of truth. Words like 'genocide' are the unembarrassed currency of their talk.

Pietro and Harry leave at one in the morning to walk back to their hotel. Pietro's head is throbbing with the effort he has made to try to follow the facts that have poured out. Life and death, the right to exist. He can't think of anything else to say to Harry as they go up to their room; it would seem frivolous.

'I suppose what I remember best about my time on the kibbutz,' said Harry, as they drove northwards the following day, 'was the amount of sex. All these young women in the army, toting their big guns around, the feeling that you were smack up against life and death.'

Harry's lightly freckled face lit up with pleasure at the memory. His large brown eyes took on a mischievous look.

'I thought you were in charge of watering the avocados,' said Pietro.

'That too. I wasn't personally in uniform, you understand. But if all boys and girls are in the army from the age of eighteen, it puts things in perspective.'

Sarah, who had decided to accompany them and was sitting in the front with Daoud, the guide, laughed out loud. 'Do you remember nothing else about the kibbutz, Harry?'

'Marijuana. Getting up very early. Working hard. Most of us went home thinking small communes were the best way to run society. I don't know if that was what was intended. Mostly I just remember this overpoweringly erotic atmosphere.'

They stopped at the Jewish settlement of Ofra, where Sarah, a keen amateur archaeologist, wanted them to see some pipes from the Nablus-Samaria aqueduct. Daoud watched in pantomimed amazement as she explained how the Jewish settlers in the West Bank, pioneers whose camps were considered provocative even by many fellow-Jews, investigated the historical antiquity of the area.

Then they looped back through Ramallah. It was empty. Figures occasionally ran along the walls, like shadows. Eventually they arrived at a settlement that Sarah had wanted them to visit. It looked at first like a defensive fortification, concrete boxes and wire netting, the kind of thing breached by the Germans in the Ardennes in 1940. There were also cheap apartment buildings, unweathered, lacking in the accretions of community life. Children buzzed around the forecourts, unaware of the millions of deaths on which the positioning of their playground was premissed. The desert sky was empty towards Jordan and north to the Lebanese border – ten minutes away by fighter jet. The settlement was like a bunkered provocation in the dense, mad air.

An armed guard let them through the gates. An older man, with a khaki shirt and a large belly, shook Sarah warmly by the hand and took them through into a building that looked like some communal centre or school. There was a circle of small chairs and a table with a slide projector. He and Sarah talked in Hebrew for a time until she remembered the others and asked him to speak English. Like most of the people they had met, he spoke fluently with a thick accent. He had been in the middle of explaining some building programme to her, but when he heard Harry was a journalist he was anxious to know about the crosswords in the various London newspapers. The papers came late, if at all, and he was worried that his prize entries were not reaching the judges.

It was not long before a chance enquiry brought him back to

the subject of survival. 'It's not so terrible, is it, to build houses on the land we have won? I tell you, if we can have a few more years of peaceful building the question will be over for all time. Some of these Peace people in Jerusalem, some of the journalists who come, they ask me: do I hate the Arabs who live here? Of course not. Do I want to kick them out? Of course not. There are a similar number living in the Galilee and no one suggests we give that to them and stop building there. No. But I tell you, I think they should stay if they like, but since this is our country they should take citizenship of another country. Maybe Jordan. Let them live where they like, but be citizens of another country. I can't see what's wrong with that.'

A young American came in. He was introduced as Michael. He wore jeans and an army shirt with the sleeves rolled up to reveal muscular forearms under silky black hair. He was clear-eyed and restless, bouncing round from one handshake to the next. Unlike Shimon and David in Jerusalem, he looked like an athlete, a fighter.

With no prompting he told them how he had come. 'I was in a bar in Trenton. It's near where I was raised. Why do we always end up in places like Jersey?' He laughed. 'A few of us were talking about the war in '73. I'd been a bad student. I'd had bad grades and everything. What was I doing drinking in a bar in any case? I should have been home. We got to talking about Israel and how proud we felt of the army, what they'd done, how they'd resisted. This friend of mine Mischa said it made him want to live there and a lot of the guys said, No, it wasn't much of a place, Tel Aviv was like Florida. And Mischa said, No, he wanted to be a settler – someone who went up and made his life in the land we'd won, the land that was rightfully ours. He began to talk about the pioneers in America going West. He said it was a great American tradition, and some other guy pointed out most of us had come from Poland.'

Michael laughed again, briefly, showing even white teeth.

'I saw the only way for me was through the Bible, through study. I started going to class properly and after a year I told my parents I felt ready. You know, I thought they'd be proud and I thought they'd be relieved because they'd never really learned to speak English properly themselves. But they were sad I was leaving. I told them it was the way of God. America was not for us with its modern ways, its lack of faith. But God is great, and he brought me here to this beautiful land. We have been weak for too long. I don't blame people like my parents. But the Jews in Eastern Europe were passive for too long, they always wanted more time to think. Now we have a duty to take this land and to keep it, because God gave it to us. To go some place there was danger, to me that was part of the pioneering spirit, too. We hear so much these days from people in Tel Aviv and Jerusalem who talk about "peace" and how we should not be here in Samaria. I think we should talk to them. They're wrong, but they're not past a point where we can discuss things. I think it's a phase and I think it's coming to an end. They will see the simple truth sooner or later. Someone even mentioned the words "civil war" to me the other day. Ridiculous! They would never be that foolish. I pray for them. Did you hear that? I pray for my enemies! Maybe I'm becoming a Christian!'

He beamed at them all with the healthy certainty of faith. There was a brief pause, interrupted by Daoud clearing his throat, before the older man went to get drinks.

BACK in the car, negotiating the rocky driveway back to the road, Daoud said, 'I think you guys should see Nablus.'

'What happens there?' said Pietro.

'It's the Palestinian stronghold in the West Bank,' said Sarah. 'It's an awful place.'

Daoud laughed. 'It's beautiful. I have friends there.'

'Would we be welcome?' said Pietro.

'Of course,' said Daoud. 'They are decent people. You mustn't believe everything these others tell you.' He jerked his head back in the direction of the settlement.

They drove on through the empty roads of Samaria. Pietro found that his first impression of the bone-white hills of Judaea had been corrected or altered. There was after all something desirable in this barren land, particularly when you thought of the yearning with which it had been regarded by poor people in the *shtetl* of Eastern Europe, or by pressed and persecuted immigrants in the big cities of America. When a man lay down to sleep with his wife in the ghetto in Warsaw, had he dreamed of a promised land that would look like this? Perhaps when his body ached with the work of the city he had thought of a whitewashed house with a vineyard, a little grove with fruit trees, animals; a tiled roof, a shady tree, bougainvillaea, and grandchildren running in to be caressed and petted at his knee. How his soul must have longed for it, under the hammer of city labour, broken, beaten, among hard buildings in a foreign land.

The detested author of the magazine article had pointed out another irony: that the olive trees, the fig trees, the cultivation of the land, the trailing trellises of grapes, the sheep on the hills, the gentle flow of water through tiled cisterns, the essence of the landscape that had so inflamed the early Zionists could best be summed up in one word: Arab. In the occupation of Samaria, the Jews had built with pre-stressed concrete, steel and plastic tiles; in taking possession, they had built over their loved biblical landscape so that the promised land was, by some further irony, withheld from them in the moment of fulfilment, as it had been withheld from Moses.

To a foreigner, a Gentile, the land looked neither especially Arab nor Jewish nor promised. More than anything else, it looked frightening: the object of too much desire.

IT was a cloudy day in Nablus. The people went about their business overlooked by a large hill whose massive physical indifference made their swarming lives look aimless. Pietro took photographs. Here it was impossible for the camera not to be full of people; yet the men and women added a particular force to the images of place, because part of the reason for their existence was simply to be there. What they did was less important than the fact that they did it there, in that spot, and by their occupation laid claim to it.

It was a close, grey afternoon. They went into a café and a waiter brought them tea with mint and sugar. A table of four elderly men played backgammon. The town seemed mortally depressed, slouched in torpor. Yet in the streets there was the anxious and frenetic activity that accompanies poverty. Young men ran and shouted in the alleys; women elbowed their way through the crowds. The result of these contrasting moods – the languor with the activity, the passionate sense of possession in a place that no one could be proud of – was a sense of threat. The missing factor in the equation could have been violence.

Two men came in and greeted Daoud. They sat down at the same table and after cursory introductions fell into conversation.

'That doesn't sound like Hebrew,' said Sarah.

Daoud broke off. 'You're right. It's Arabic. Excuse me. I'd forgotten for a moment.'

He said something to the two men and they talked in a mixture of Hebrew, Arabic and English. Daoud was the only one who understood everything. It seemed to amuse him. His eyes narrowed as if in amusement at some grand joke that none of the others were quite equipped to understand.

'My friend here,' he said, touching one of the men on the arm, 'says he would like you to know that he and most of his friends concede that the Jews have a rightful claim to live in Israel. He says his dream is that there should be one state in which people live together peacefully, like brothers, but given what is happening here in Nablus, with terrorist bombs, and what has happened elsewhere he thinks this is not likely. So he says there must be two states, one for each of the two peoples. He says he regrets very much that many Jews think his people are not worth considering, that they think of them as . . . dirt. But he says the Palestinians and the Jews are similar peoples and they must work out their destiny together. It is like a difficult marriage. You would not have chosen this partner, but you are stuck with her.

You can fight for ever, or you can decide to live in peace. He does not like it, but he has accepted it.'

Sarah smiled. 'That is a very reasonable view.'

Daoud said, 'If you doubt my translation, you can ask him to repeat it in Hebrew.'

'Not at all.' Sarah looked embarrassed under Daoud's mocking gaze.

The older of the two Arab men lit a cigarette and asked Daoud a question in Arabic.

'He wants to know if you have noticed about the street-cleaners,' said Daoud. 'The garbage men, the labourers, the shit-gatherers.'

Pietro and Harry nodded. Daoud turned back to his friend.

'And do you know why they are all Arabs?' he asked Harry. Harry shrugged.

'My friend says it is because his people are not permitted proper citizenship of this country, this model society.'

Sarah said, 'Ask him why his people don't unite with their friends in Jordan or Syria.'

Daoud didn't ask him. He said, 'It's because they must first have their own independence like any other state. They must first have their own land and their own city.'

'You mean Jerusalem?' said Sarah.

'Why not?'

'Oh God.' Sarah rolled her eyes heavenward.

THEY were due to spend the evening in Tel Aviv, with a family who were friends of Harry's mother. As they walked back to the car, Pietro said to Sarah, 'How come Daoud speaks Arabic so well?'

'Because he's an Arab,' she said. 'Couldn't you tell?'

'It hadn't occurred to me,' said Pietro, glancing back to where Daoud was walking with Harry. 'He told me he was a Christian yesterday.'

'There are quite a number of Arab Christians in fact.'

'And yet by nationality he's Israeli. Perhaps that helps him see all sides of the question.'

'I don't think so,' said Sarah.

It was growing dark as they emerged from Nablus. Pietro thought of the good Samaritan as they drove through the rocky hills. A man had fallen among thieves in just such a place. Then he remembered that this was wrong: the Samaritan had come from here, but the robbery had been elsewhere. And the Samaritans, had they been Jews, a lost tribe? Or were they Arabs? Or Gentile? He had heard it said that the Palestinians themselves were initially Jewish, more authentically the children of Abraham than those who had remained in the faith.

They were on a narrow motorway with headlights bending towards them and the tarmac road lit by the chemical splash of sodium overhead. With the snaking red tail-lights of the cars ahead, the scene might have been from any busy highway at dusk: the rush hour from Seattle out to what its residents called the 'burbs'; the packed *périphérique* at Lyon; the drab slip roads from Runcorn and Liverpool. The world was bounded by the red velour of the car seats, the smell of the ashtray, the lit instrument panel on the dashboard and the swish of cars passing in the opposite direction. In their moving capsules no one at this moment cared about the ownership of the terrain they crossed; their aim, like that of any traveller, was only to be somewhere else.

BACK in the lobby of their hotel in Jerusalem the next day, Pietro saw a photograph which excited him more than the arguments he had heard. It showed four Israeli soldiers arriving for the first time at the Wailing Wall after the capture of East Jerusalem from the Jordanians in 1967. It looked quite familiar – perhaps he had seen it in a newspaper – but its eloquence had survived. Three men stood in the foreground, close up to the camera. The photographer had knelt with his back to the Wall, facing the soldiers. One had his eyes raised beneath the rim of his helmet, looking up and to the right, his eyes scanning what he saw, but watchfully, as though still expecting resistance. On the right was a slightly older man, also helmeted, his face in shadow, unshaven, looking up and straight ahead in the passionless expression of a trained soldier. And in the middle was a younger man, fairer, perhaps not more than twenty years old, who had his helmet in his hands, as though, contrary to Jewish custom, he had doffed it in reverence. Of the three, only he had quite given way to personal emotion, and in his face, half frowning, half turned, there was a look of concerned wonder, of excitement barely contained by the discipline of arms. The arrangement of the three figures close to the camera gave a sense of movement. It was as though they still quivered with the momentum of arrival; this was clearly the actual instant of awe and of possession. Then they would be gone, succeeded by other soldiers, whose helmets and faces were already edging into the background of the picture. Then they too would be replaced; on and on.

Pietro had doubted all the words he had heard in Israel because he did not know enough to check them, but he could not doubt the evidence of this picture.

He parted company with Harry and the guide, and went to visit the Garden Tomb, in the spot selected by General Gordon because the Holy Sepulchre was 'too Arab'. Aware of everything that argued against it, Pietro still privately hoped that this might be the place; that if he sat quietly enough and watched, something might reveal itself to him. He encountered a problem. It was something he could not quite express, but it meant that he came away like most tourists and pilgrims, feeling uneasy. What was said to have happened, resurrection, seemed too important to have happened here, in this particular place. He tried to work out why. Was it again some kind of snobbery? Was it the inscription – 'He is not here. He is risen' – which instead of sounding numinous, seemed bathetic? Was it the ripe scepticism of the local people? Certainly the proximity of the East Jerusalem bus station at the foot of the slope was unfortunate. But then Christ had been born in a manger. Did these difficult sur-roundings in fact not constitute exactly the kind of paradoxical test of faith He would have wanted? The Son of God, born in a barn with animals; buried among trinkets and diesel fumes . . . It was not really that either. It was a problem of believing that an event of such universal magnitude could have had such a specific location – this stone, this blade of grass, these atoms. He wondered whether that made him an atheist; if not here, then where? It was more complicated than that too, he told himself, though he could no longer find the words to frame the thought.

He did, however, have his camera. With this he took several photographs of Arab children playing in the bus station with the skull-shaped hill behind them.

Harry had been to the Wailing Wall with Daoud, and they reunited at lunchtime. Daoud sat eating falafel and drinking Fanta. He had brought a friend with him he thought Harry and Pietro ought to meet, a dark-skinned, smiling man who told them his parents had come from Morocco. They were observant Jews and forceful in their Zionist beliefs, but he was not so happy.

They ordered beer and talked about the climate in Tel Aviv compared to Jerusalem, then about whether military conscription made young people more sexually active. The small talk lasted about two minutes before, as Pietro had expected, Daoud's friend began to define himself and his beliefs. Though not religious like his parents, he was a keen Zionist and believer in Mr Begin. His hatred was not for the Palestinians or even the Jordanians, but for the effete Ashkenazi Jews who toyed with the idea of giving back parts of the West Bank to the Arabs, who despised and abused Sephardic people like himself, employing them only in menial jobs the Arabs could not be made to take on.

Pietro had begun to feel light-headed on his way back from the Garden Tomb and now felt a thin sweat breaking out on his back. He imagined he had caught some chill or flu. He watched the dark-skinned, earnest face arguing, but because he felt slightly removed from the world around him found it difficult to take in more than occasional phrases. This was a new development as far as he was concerned – intra-Zionist bitterness – and he wanted to understand it. But the phrases that stuck in his mind seemed too colourful or exaggerated to be worth trusting. 'Our parents imported to be slaves . . . like blacks in Mississippi or South Africa . . . I would be arrested as a suspicious character if I showed up where they live . . . What chance for my children if they let the Arabs have their own land? We will become the slaves again, even people like me who've pulled ourselves up.'

He was more difficult to follow than some of the people they had met. He did not use the smooth English of political debate that was polished by practice and repetition; but he was quite as angry, just as certain of his right to survival on his own terms and no one else's. In childhood Pietro had liked to choose a side to support in any debate, even if it turned out to be the 'wrong' one – the Roundheads, the Southern States, Sonny Liston, even, when he was older, George McGovern. When a combination of experience and laziness showed him there were seldom easy solutions, he relied on balance as a substitute for commitment.

He began to be depressed in Israel because there seemed to be no ground available for compromise, no logical way in which all the parties could be even partially right. So whose experience counted for most?

IN the schedule of visits Harry had arranged before leaving London there was a stop for tea at the home of a woman he had met when he was on his kibbutz. She welcomed them to her small apartment in a modern block on the edge of Jerusalem and gave them tea and cake. When Pietro thanked her for her hospitality as they were leaving she turned his thanks abruptly away. Life was too urgent for such matters as thanks, she implied; there was no time for anything but the truth and the question of survival.

As they walked back to the hotel, Pietro said to Harry, 'Don't tell me; I don't understand. You're the only person who hasn't said that to me yet.'

'You don't understand,' said Harry.

'Of course I don't. And sometimes I feel my attempts to understand just make people more annoyed. My ignorance is like a sore to them. My questions are distrusted as though they're not only ignorant but in some odd way prejudiced as well.'

Harry laughed.

'And do you understand?' said Pietro.

'Good God, no.'

IT is the evening. It is their last night and they are back again with David and Sarah, Harry's friends. This time they are in their flat, and a couple of other guests are expected.

Pietro is sweating under his shirt. He can feel a film crawling over his back, like traces of fixer clinging to a photographic print. His head feels hot and stuffed up. The sensation is not altogether unpleasant; he also feels insulated and secure. The problem is that his brain feels as clogged as his sinuses; his thoughts are as impaired as his breathing. He drinks beer and takes some nuts from a little dish on the coffee table.

David and Sarah's son, a small boy called Ben, totters round the room. He has black curly hair and a slightly hectoring manner when he calls out to his parents. Pietro thinks briefly about the boy's upbringing. No doubts for him about where to live. His parents have made the decision. This land is natural to him. Soon he will be in the army, preparing to fight for it.

The doorbell rings and Pietro feels a start of disappointment, for which he guiltily corrects himself, to see that the guest is Shimon, the man whose political certainties he had found close to remorseless on their second night in Jerusalem.

Shimon sits next to him on the 1950s sofa, drinking canned orangeade. Pietro talks to him about pictures, and Shimon lends half his attention, with a patient, quizzical air, as though to a child's presentation before the main event.

The doorbell rings again and Sarah bustles out to answer it on stocky denimed legs, her hips brushing the armchair in which Harry is sitting with a vacant expression while Ben loudly explains to him some aspect of his school.

She returns with a woman who looks quite out of place.

'This is Martha, an old friend of mine from school.'

Martha is dressed in loose-fitting beige wool. Her chestnut-coloured hair is caught up at the back and falls in artless but rather exact waves to her shoulders. Her wide-set eyes are of a bright, candid blue enhanced by discreet make-up.

David pads over, pushes his grey-framed spectacles up towards his tangle of curly hair 'Would you like a drink?' he says. 'We have beer, orange juice, wine . . . some whisky.'

Harry has lost the vacant expression. He is unconsciously smoothing down his hair at the back as he begins to tell the story of their visit to the Jewish settlement. '. . . on the very edge of enemy territory, armed to the teeth, and he wants to know who sets the crosswords!'

His body is facing Shimon, but his eyes are looking at Martha. She laughs in a carefree manner. It is a sound they have heard from no one else for three days.

'. . . in Boston,' she is saying, in reply to some query. 'I knew Sarah in school. We were like best friends for a while.' Her voice has a slight interrogative lilt, as though she is seeking confirmation from Shimon, or Pietro, or Harry for these episodes in her past. 'We were like best friends for a while? Then I met this guy?'

She has an uninhibited laugh, which she tries to restrain, apparently from a sense of good manners. When she moves her hands to take something from her handbag or to replace her drink on the table, there is a certainty and elegance in her action.

Pietro wonders if he is going to make it through the evening. When he stands up to go to the dinner table his stomach feels weak. Hummus appears on his plate, with olives and cucumber salad. He is not sure what he is hearing, or what he is seeing. Why is this woman who seems to have stepped out of a Park Avenue elevator sitting next to this bearded man with his thick rubber-soled shoes?

Can this man really, already, be saying this: 'I don't mind the Arabs. Let them stay and live here with us if they want to. But they must understand their place. Most of them do. Deep down, they are not really a military people. They know this land is ours. Even their own books tell them that. If they want to stay as hewers of wood and drawers of water, then we should allow them to. The danger is among people who want to deal with them, to treat with them and give them land.'

Pietro shakes his head to clear it. Shimon is leaning forward at the table, stroking his beard. 'If some deal is offered we have to say no. We have to start a war if necessary so the weak-minded among us don't fall for that trick.'

Harry is countering with his experience at the Wailing Wall. He has been approached by a Hassidic man wanting him to go to a school to examine the Talmud so he can learn about his true roots. 'This *yeshiva* business . . . it sounded appalling. He said if I went along he'd give me a free bed for as long as I was in Jerusalem. Frankly I'd rather share with Pietro. You get used to habits after a time.'

The food comes. Martha explains that she has long promised to visit Sarah. She is on a week's vacation. She hopes to go to Eilat for some swimming and sunbathing. She is pleased to have visited Jerusalem but she wants to relax.

Harry is inventing new holiday plans as he goes along. 'No, no,' he says, 'we're very flexible on time. We were thinking of spending a few days at a resort ourselves.'

'Sure,' says Pietro, feeling the dated airline ticket for the next day in his pocket.

David is not tired tonight. At home and in control, he is forceful in his views. 'It seems to me that the settlers and people like them are in for a surprise. Old-fashioned people like me are not going to sit back. They despise us because they think we will give in, but they don't realise that we have a different idea of Zionism. It is an older one. It is we who were at the sharp end of the movement until they started running around with their machine guns. We are not giving in to anyone – least of all to them. Their attitude has made it impossible to have a proper debate, they have reduced it to a slanging match. But they will find that when it comes to words we are better prepared than they are. That's one war we won't flinch from.'

Pietro is now finding it difficult to concentrate at all. Sarah interrupts her husband. Ben comes in wearing pyjamas. He cannot sleep. Shimon lays down his knife and fork to make his point more clearly to Martha, who has accidentally strayed into his path, like a car pulling timidly off the hard shoulder of the motorway into the line of a truck at full speed. Harry is trying to deflect him with humorous asides.

As the meal wears on, Pietro comes close to delirium. But the voice he hears and the words he remembers are those of David. He is almost shouting to make himself heard. 'I find myself summoned to show my solidarity ten times a day. After every newscast. Of course I give my loyalty. But when you are part of history at each moment, when is there time to sit on your own and talk to your child? When will it be possible for us ever again to put the simple human feelings of love and family back where they ought to be – at the centre of the world?'

Through disagreement from his wife and derision from Shimon, he persists, flushed and loud: 'We can't live in a place outside time, in a way prescribed thousands of years ago. The diaspora taught us many things. Our encounter with Europe has enriched us, not weakened us. We can never shed what we learned of humanism in Europe and nor should we want to. I'm proud of what we have assimilated and it is my right to retain that heritage, even within this old-fashioned idea of a nation state. Our battle now is not to keep everyone at a political fever pitch all the time, but to depoliticise people. One day I will sit by the well with my little son and he will tell me not that he loves his country, but that he loves his mother or that he loves a girl from the next town. And his own feelings and sufferings, his individual life will be the one important thing. That is the aim of good art, I think, and that should be the aim of our lives too. When Mandelstam was exiled and dying at the ends of the earth he read out his *poems!*'

Pietro feels like offering hallucinatory applause. Shimon laughs harshly. The evening dissolves for Pietro into unconnected fragments.

'The greatest threat to Israel is not from the Arabs but from the disagreements between the Jews themselves . . .'

'Why don't we get a bus down together? Which hotel are you staying in?'

'They came here after the Six Day War and the boy was born during Sadat's visit . . .'

'At the Yad Veshem memorial they will have a darkened hall lit by candles in which a tape-recorded voice will read out on an eternal loop the names of the one and a half million children who were slaughtered by the Nazis.'

THAT night Pietro sweated out his chill. He removed the soaked sheets from his bed at four in the morning, found a T-shirt and clean, dry blankets in the cupboard. In the morning he awoke clear-headed and purged. He went for a walk while Harry slept in.

He watched the changes of light on the rich-coloured stone of the city as the sun was momentarily obscured by cloud. Jerusalem, the city of peace. Temporary structures leaned against the ancient walls: much of the building was dilapidated and unrepaired, much of it carefully removed and set aside by archaeologists. In the shifting light, the masonry itself seemed to change allegiance, from one colour to another, while new evidence to be debated rose from the excavated dust.

On the plane back to London he read an article in the *Jerusalem Post* about how the Greeks and Coptic Christians were in dispute about who owned which part of the nave of the Church of the Holy Sepulchre.

IN the evening he went to a pub in Maida Vale and fell into conversation with the landlord, whom he knew. 'What was Jerusalem like?' he asked. 'How was the weather?' It was a friendly question.

Later he watched a debate on television between two British politicians in which each accused the other of inconsistency in his attitude towards the problem of inflation. Then there was an item about class divisions, in which the reporter went to Henley in a straw hat.

KOWLOON

Hong Kong 1980

O N the plane from Hong Kong to Colombo, Pietro took out a pad of paper and began to write down his impressions of the colony for the benefit of Harry, who was supplying the text for a book about it. He had spent a week there taking photographs and was glad to be leaving. He had disliked the place, even though he had enjoyed his visit. This puzzled him.

The principal problem, it seemed to him, was the people. One of the English guests at dinner the night before had explained at length how he was going to take his car with him on his new posting in Singapore. By some complicated manœuvring, it would remain on his company's books yet he would be able to sell it.

'That's not really the spirit of the law, is it?' said Pietro, perhaps, he now conceded, naïvely.

The man looked up, his young, fleshy face suddenly still. 'Law?'

'Well, the spirit of the game, if you prefer,' said Pietro, not wanting to accuse him of impropriety.

The young Englishman was shocked. 'Game?' he said. 'It's not a *game*. It's *life*. It's about maximising profits.'

Perhaps that was why another man there owned three

Ferraris, even though the speed limit on the island was 40 m.p.h. There was a market in them, he explained. He imported, finessed the paperwork, sold on expectation, reinvested. He didn't drive. Well, sometimes at weekends. What was the point, with a 40 m.p.h. speed limit?

Pietro began to write.

'DEAR Harry

Here are the notes for the Hong Kong book. I have kept them very personal and anecdotal, as requested. I hope you can make something of them for your text. I'm not sure what I saw is really much good for the "Last Outpost" theme of the series, but I hope the pictures will be all right anyway.

Obviously you'll throw away some of the purely anecdotal stuff, but I haven't had time to sift through it all myself because I'll have to post this from Colombo in the morning. I still think you ought really to have visited Hong Kong yourself before you write it. But I leave that to you.

I went up inside a glass bubble on a monorail lift. We looked down into the atrium with its gravelled gardens and silver fountains. The bellboy was a very small Chinese who called me sir every second word and wouldn't let me help him with the cases. On the top floor we went into another vast lounge and he put the cases down. I assumed he was tired. He said "Sitting room, sir." I said, "Yes, but where's my room?" He said, "This your room, sir. This your sitting room. Bedroom upstairs." This place I thought was some sort of public lounge turned out to be my own sitting room. Upstairs was a vast bedroom. The place is ridiculous. It has two bathrooms, a bar and a dressing room. It is about twice the size of my entire flat in London. There are two televisions, two stereos and God knows what. The long windows overlook the harbour, and there is Hong Kong island on the other side, a sort of greyish pile with advertising signs illuminated on top of the skyscrapers. SEIKO. It is both exotic and rather prosaic. Which travel company gave you this? It is extraordinary.

In the afternoon a young Chinese woman called Polly came round. She is very helpful, so helpful in fact that it's difficult to concentrate. She's pretty in a traditional way, though with quite large eyes. Some European ancestry? She was keen to show me all the other hotels and all the shopping. I couldn't see the point of this but didn't want to seem churlish. So we looked at lots of other places. None of them are as flash as this one.

The next day I told Polly I had to go off on my own. I hired a car and drove up from Kowloon through the New Territories to the Chinese border. There's a British military post there and I introduced myself to the man in charge, a major. He took me up the tower, to the top of the observation post, and we gazed over into China. It looked green. Watery green. Temperate, distant, large. The hills make you think of bamboo shoots and pandas. It's pale and insipid, a bit like Cantonese cooking. There was a light mist over the trees. The temperature was cool but sticky, like an April day in England. Maybe if I hadn't known it was China it wouldn't have looked so exotic. I took a lot of pictures, some of them with the major, who had a limp, in the foreground.

He seemed a bit bashful and made a few excuses about not having his "best bib and tucker" on, but he didn't seem to mind. He spends a lot of time trying to keep Chinese illegal immigrants from crossing the border. It seems a bit of a game. They just round up the odd one or two and throw them back. This is not a high-security job. In fact he just sits there staring into China. He spoke very respectfully of the Chinese government and the Governor-General of Hong Kong. I offered to take him out to dinner in Hong Kong and he agreed.

It was odd to see this man here, on the rim of China. Those Scotsmen in the nineteenth century who decided to come over here in the first place. That was a strange move. From Motherwell to the South China Sea. It must have seemed a daunting distance in those days. I admire their daring. I suppose many were already out here, running drugs out of China et cetera.

The next day I persuaded Polly that I had seen enough shopping arcades and hotel bedrooms. I asked her to show me what she thought was the worst side of life here. She took me to the camps where the refugees from Vietnam were kept. It reminded me of the time I worked on a chicken farm in Wisconsin. They were like hen runs, nailed up with wire netting, cardboard and bottle tops. It was a parody of a village. No work, no economy, no jobs. Feed shoved into cages, people lying almost on top of each other. It was worse than somewhere like Madras where people just lie in the street. At least there you feel they could walk away, they can beg, they have freedom of movement, even if they are starving. But these people were also imprisoned. The camps are policed by officers of the Correctional Services Department. I don't know how people remain human when what separates them from animals is taken away.

We went to a restaurant on the way to some water project in the New Territories. It was like a vast canteen with surly Chinese (they aren't at all friendly) wheeling trolleys round with battered metal dishes. You didn't know what was inside, there was no menu. I just had what Polly picked off for me. It was disgusting. But I couldn't complain. I'd asked her to show me the other side of life; but the odd thing was that although the refugee camp was supposed to be the worst, I don't think the restaurant was part of the low-life excursion.

She insisted I go shopping for radios and cameras and electronic things. Each shop is like the floor of a stock exchange, people shouting and trading. They have no embarrassment about greed. I tried to bargain over a camera, but he wouldn't let me try it out and I thought I'd rather wait and get one back in London where I might pay more but at least I'd know what I was getting. I did buy you a little portable cassette thing, on the other hand. I'll bring it back with me. I don't know if I can resist the temptation of using it myself in the mean time. The thing that strikes you about Hong Kong is how naked the pursuit of money is. I suppose it's prudish to object. A little hypocrisy wouldn't be out of place, though. The Chinese are amazing. They work very hard for it. And the British and the businessmen, it's all they talk about. Whether it's multi-million deals and bonds or twenty-quid cameras, it's just barter and push all the time.

Relations between the nationalities. There are none, as far as I can see. The English are completely ignorant of Chinese culture and languages and see nothing odd in this. The Chinese ignore the foreign devils. I walked through the roughest, most Chinese parts of Kowloon, down dark side streets, and no one paid me the slightest attention. You could send a tribe of Zulu albinos down here and no one would look up from their work unless they represented a business opportunity. The English and the Chinese are bonded by mutual disregard. It is odd. They are brothers in money.

I was introduced to a Scotsman who is organising the forthcoming arts festival. I asked him about local artists and he hummed and hahed for a time. Eventually he said, "Well, there's a local jewellery designer. She's a bit unstable, I think. But her designs have become very popular. I believe she is beginning to penetrate world markets."

Your friend Jerry was tied up but he put me in touch with some lawyers. We went to a restaurant and met a lot of other young Englishmen. They all called each other by their surnames and shouted at the waiters, who didn't seem to mind. We ate dim sum, which is bits of feet and head and bladder. They liked it a lot and made jokes about things called "sick bags" which are flabby parcels that you prong with your chopstick. They were all very friendly and insisted I drank beer and whisky with them. I wondered how many of them would have done so well "back in UK", as they say. They have an odd way of talking about it. They are very dismissive, talk about strikes and the inflation and how you can't afford a decent house. Yet I think they are also a bit in awe of it.

That night I insisted Polly let me take her out. She wanted her company to take me to another of its international cuisine restaurants, but I was firm. She brought a lot of brochures about a new building development in the middle of central Hong Kong island. I don't know how they are going to manage to slip another building in. It'll have to be about three feet wide and a mile high. I think she was a bit worried about having shown me the refugee places, so she was finishing off with a strong emphasis on the good life.

I tried to get her off the subjects of hotels and service. I asked about her family and her life and if she had a boyfriend. She wasn't affronted by this question but gave me to understand that a young woman must put her career first and there was not much chance of that with the dead weight of a boyfriend in the background.

We went to a Szechuan restaurant recommended by the major. I teased her a bit about her seriousness and her English name. Afterwards we went to a bar I'd been to with the major where women with no tops on sit in the middle of tables to serve drinks. It was very unerotic. It must be the best-known tourist trap in the place, I suppose, but Polly wanted to go there. The light was dingy and the women all looked old and uninterested. It was as if they had just taken their tops off for a medical.

The red-light district used to be in Wan Chai, though this is very tame now. Everyone mentions a film about a Wan Chai prostitute called Suzie Wong, though no one seems to have seen it. It is brought up with a certain local pride. In fact there is a bit of a local newspaper subculture here altogether. The Hong Kong *Tatler*, an exact imitation of the London one, seems somehow unreal. There is that feeling of the place pushing itself, so that an aircrash in which three hundred people died might be reported as "Hong Kong man injured in air disaster". This cultural thing is odd when you come to think how dauntingly big and important the place is financially. It could treat itself more grandly, less parochially, as the equal of the other great financial centres. Then again you could say that American papers are inward-looking also.

Anyway, the red-light action is now centred, as luck would have it, near my hotel in Kowloon. On Nathan Road the signs advertising sex shows run one after the other up the hill. No moving lights are permitted in Hong Kong because they would confuse the aircraft, which come in to land on a narrow causeway perilously close to the residential area. So, just as the big signs on top of the skyscrapers in Hong Kong Central are still, so the signs in the Nathan Road saying "Strip Show" or "Live Sex" are also motionless. There is something odd about looking at a sign saying 'Live Sex' that does not flash or glitter. It makes it seem a cool and prosaic transaction. I took a photograph of it, though I'm not sure the reason for this will be clear in the finished print.'

PIETRO put down his pen and pad as the air stewardess brought drinks. He rummaged through the pocket of his jacket and pulled out a notebook in which he kept a record of the pictures he had taken for purposes of identification. Against the number of the film and the number of each exposure he wrote a date, time and place. He had been too often frustrated by not being able to identify exactly people or places in pictures he wanted to use.

HE had begun to take photographs when he was living in New York seven years earlier. There seemed to him something about the city that had not been caught by people who talked about its frenzy and pace. He tried to fix this quality by taking pictures on snowy Sunday mornings, when the office buildings stood empty and the older New York of brownstones and 1930s fittings was more visible. He tried going to parts of the city not so often photographed. He particularly liked the warehouse buildings of the Lower West Side on which the sign-written names of enterprising importers had all but faded through the soot and wear of successive owners. From his first view of Manhattan there seemed to him something poignant in the city that had not been expressed. The amount of endeavour that had been poured into this small island by people lonely, far from their native lands, gave it an atmosphere more heroic and more tender than the

119

usual descriptive phrases allowed. The trouble was that his pictures just showed tall buildings.

He read some manuals on photography and went to a few lectures. He became convinced that if he could have access to development and printing he could make his photographs more accurately convey what he had in mind. Through a friend in SoHo he was allowed into a small commercial darkroom where he was shown the various steps of the process. After three visits they said he could take in his own film and see it right through.

It was frustratingly slow. He loaded the film easily and poured in the developer. The lab technician, an easy-going man called Max, smacked a clock on the table and told Pietro when to agitate the tank. After the stop bath and the fixer Pietro was anxious to see the results, but Max made him wash the film for half an hour before directing him to a drying cabinet. Pietro had no idea it would take such a long time, or that so many precautions were necessary: even the sponge tongs with which he cleaned moisture from the film had themselves to be cleaned first. Still, in the smell of the chemicals and the gloomy atmosphere of the darkroom, he could feel his excitement beginning to mount.

They examined the dry negatives and Max was able to predict merely from the degrees of contrast already visible what the print would look like. Further precautions followed before the enlarger was turned on and Pietro was shown how to make a contact sheet. There were pictures at last, but he restrained himself from peering too closely at the first positive sight of his camerawork. Under Max's instruction he turned the crank on the column of the enlarger until the image exactly fitted the frame on the easel.

'You should do some test strips now,' said Max, 'so you can see what the best exposure time is. We won't bother with that today because I can guess from the negative what they need.'

He slid a blank piece of paper under the easel, then stuck his hand under the lens of the enlarger. After a few seconds he whisked it away and smacked the clock with the other hand.

Max tilted the developing tray slightly away from him as he slid in the exposed print, then lowered it so a wave of developer sloshed back over it. 'OK,' he grinned at Pietro, 'here she comes.'

Through the colourless fluid Pietro saw the first markings appear like smudges on the white paper. He was beginning to see some shape occur: the darkness was of a building – no, some steps; the scuffed edge of something feathery was a cloud, a sidewalk tree. At this moment Max flipped the print over with some tongs which he then handed to Pietro. 'When I tell you, take the print out, let it drain for a moment and put it face up in the stop bath.' The ticking of the clock stopped and Max said, 'Right.'

Pietro grasped the print with the tongs and lifted it dripping from the bath. He turned it round so the printed image faced him. It was magnificent. The blank paper had filled with pulsing tones and shadows; the buildings were no longer just tall, but sad and purposeful. Something had happened in the transference of the street, via chemical baths and exposure to a piece of paper: a part of himself had entered into it.

From that day he became obsessed with what could be achieved in the acrid air of the darkroom. He could see potential in things that were technically mistakes. An underexposed negative, with its poor contrast and lack of shadow detail, could sometimes be made to give a more interesting print than a negative with a correct range of tones. By changing the developer or merely extending the time, a different spectrum of contrasts could be brought in. Max showed him the simple trick of push-processing, which Pietro then used even when it was not necessitated by poor light. The over-grainy prints that resulted did not worry him.

He spent Sundays, when the darkroom was closed for business, experimenting with this new world. He liked to overdevelop and print on hard paper then burn in highlights with his hands. He quickly learned all the elementary variations of the darkroom in an attempt to give his pictures depth and surprise.

He was as unartistic, as mechanical as it was feasible for a photographer to be. His ability to see what he wanted to photograph came only after he was confident that he could manipulate the image at a later stage. The problem was that the moving world so seldom offered a correlative for what he felt. He often thought that this was in any case an improper search; that the task of the photographer was to record what he saw, not to project on to random scenes some counterpart of his own inner feelings. He was therefore encouraged when he read an exhibition catalogue in which Stieglitz recalled photographing some cab horses soon after his return to America from his student days in Germany. Stieglitz felt bereft in his native country and experienced a yearning to be back in Europe. Opposite the old Astor House in 1891 he saw a driver in a rubber coat watering some steaming horses. 'There seemed to be something closely related,' Stieglitz had written, 'to my deepest feeling in what I saw, and I decided to photograph what was within me.' Those words, particularly taken in conjunction with the affecting photograph that had resulted, seemed to Pietro to legitimise his own ambition. Stieglitz was quite emphatic. 'I felt how fortunate the horses were to have at least a human being to give them the water they needed. What made me see the watering of the horses as I did was my own loneliness.'

With the confidence that his darkroom ability gave him, Pietro became bolder and more relaxed in what he chose to photograph. He went through the customary phases of looking for new angles, of photographing the crowd rather than the incident, the supporting actor not the star, and so on. But he quickly returned to the main event, and photographed people and scenes head-on. Some visual flair was lacking. He compared his pictures to those of the great photographers and could see that his ability was limited by his eye; he did not have that instinctive feeling for a moment or a composition. However, he did know what scenes could yield something of what he felt, and he also knew as soon as the shutter had fired what tricks of processing, if any, would be necessary to bring out further what he had intended.

He continued to take photographs in every country he visited, but he did not consider trying to make a living from it until he was twenty-seven. He had had enough of odd jobs, the last of which had been in a school laboratory in Oxford. He sent some pictures to a newspaper in London and they commissioned some freelance work from him. With work for magazines and illustrations for books, he almost made a living. When he visited Rome and saw how badly his pictures were reproduced in the subsequent publication, he became interested in colour origination and the way mass printing could be improved.

Parallel to the uncertain life of a travelling photographer, he continued to cultivate his interest in the technical side of reproduction. By the time he met Paul Coleman in Evanston he was ready to leave the closing of the shutter to others while he exercised his control of origination and a new-found interest in what computers could be made to do, but for eight years he tried to make a living by taking photographs of the world he saw. His pictures of Hong Kong were adequate for the purpose, though there were aspects of the place he felt unable to capture.

HE took up his pad again. He wrote:

'I think I have conveyed a negative impression of Hong Kong. This is not fair. It is certainly not somewhere you would want to come if you were feeling timid or unsure. Nor would you want to be too morally scrupulous. The colony was founded on the profits of drug-trafficking and has been kept going by greedy expatriates, many of whom would not have made the grade 'back in UK'. It has stuck to a creed of profit and personal gain while the rest of the world has turned away – though I suppose it might come back into line.

And yet it has incredible bravura. It is narrow – but not small-minded. They pay themselves more but they work harder. There is a phenomenon here that you never see in England: greed satisfied. The people are happy. They live at the limit of their capacities. They like it here. They are not bored, they are not defeated or depressed. What they call the "quality of life" is high, and if you only have one life I suppose you can't altogether ignore the simple question: are you enjoying it?'

LYNDONVILLE

Vermont USA 1971

THE train slunk from Grand Central Station in the early
evening. Pietro glanced round the compartment as they
left the outskirts of the city: people were slumped in their
books or gazing, like him, at the flashing landscape. He dozed
intermittently during the night and woke finally when the train
jolted into a station. For the last half-hour of the journey he
rehearsed what he would say to Laura when they met.

It was still dark when he arrived at White River Junction and
humped his luggage out of the train. A tall man with a tweed
jacket and black hair was visible dimly in the yellow light of the
ticket hall. 'Hi, you must be Pietro. I'm Laura's father,' he said,
shaking hands and taking one of the cases. 'Laura's gone out with
her mother but she'll be back later.'

He threw Pietro's bags into the back of a station wagon. It was
a long drive up the interstate before they turned off north of St
Johnsbury. The mountains of Vermont were white, the
evergreens obliterated by the sticky snow and the grey swirling
fog that lifted off the road. Pietro had washed and changed on the
train but still had the taste of tiredness and the alternate clarity
and fuzziness of vision that follow a night of too little sleep.
Eventually they reached Lyndonville, where Mr Heasman
parked the car and went into a hardware store on Depot

Street to buy a new shovel. Pietro looked up and down the main street of the little town. His eye was caught by a stately building called the Darling Inn Apartments. What a place for an afternoon tryst, he thought.

The Heasmans' house was in an exposed position on a hillside, backing into thick pine woods. It was a substantial place with white clapboard walls and a standing-seam metal roof designed to shrug off snow. Its position gave it something of the feeling of a settler's or pioneer's cabin; although it was good-looking, it wasn't built for style but to withstand the elements.

Pietro's bedroom was under the eaves. There was a large springy bed with a harsh white cover and a fat eiderdown. The sheets were so clean they were almost painful. As he unpacked he could smell a variety of different culinary scents drifting up the stairs. The window opened on a cumbersome contraption operated by a rotating handle. He watched the snow falling over the huge garden below. Beyond were fields, and the mountains he had seen on his way up in the car. He turned the handle so the window closed, and felt the warm air circulate again in the insulated room. There was a hint of paint and dried herbs.

He waited downstairs, drinking a Catamount beer Mr Heasman had given him before vanishing on some further outdoor errand. He picked up a local paper and read the main story, which was headed 'Covered Bridge Snag Corrected'. Then he read another piece with the headline 'Sparks Fly Over Traffic Lights'. He was deep into an account of the local council's renaming of a road when he heard the sound of women's voices outside. Laura burst into the room and hugged him enthusiastic-ally. He went through some of the words he had practised for the meeting. Most of them had to do with trains and being on time or late so had lost much of their impact. 'You must come into the kitchen,' said Laura, taking him by the arm.

The kitchen looked as though the household was preparing for a winter siege. Mrs Heasman, curiously unremarkable-looking, Pietro thought, for the mother of such a creature, shook hands over the scrubbed table and Pietro said hello to Laura's younger sister Sally. A big woman with red cheeks and grey hair in a bun looked up from where she was peeling a sinkful of potatoes. Mrs Heasman went to stir a pot of soup, the one whose smell had reached Pietro's bedroom. There were also on the table several plastic butcher's bags, two geese, and deep bowls of cod, mussels and prawns. The women talked across each other in the bright electric light of the kitchen. Clusters of dried and painted corncobs hung on the wooden beams around the cooker.

At dinner that night Mrs Heasman's sister and her husband and their two children came to join them. It seemed that almost everything they ate had been grown or killed by the family. No wild goose ventured unmolested over the neighbouring woods; no square inch of the vegetable garden was not silently toiling, even as they ate, to yield up more knotty tubers or fibrous greenery. Mrs Heasman had made her own wine from berries and assorted flowers, though Pietro, having taken a glass out of politeness, yielded to Mr Heasman's advice and drank some Californian wine with the duck. Laura looked about her, slightly flushed, as she chattered to her family and recounted some exploits she and Pietro had been involved in at school. She managed to make it sound a long time ago without disowning it. She was now about the age Pietro had first thought her when he went into the lower fifth classroom and saw her swinging her legs from the side of the desk.

Christmas was more English in Vermont than in London. Instead of big adolescent boys singing one verse of a carol out of tune on the doorstep and extorting money with unspoken threats, they had choirs of a dozen people, mostly female, who knew all the words and raised large sums for charity. Instead of the weather being rainy and what the man on television called 'unseasonably close', it snowed at night and was bright and cold during the day. Mr Heasman had grown his own Christmas tree, a ten-foot beast from the edge of the encroaching forest.

One morning a few days before Christmas Pietro lay awake in his bed, looking up to where the sloping rafters met in a white point. He had reached a decision. His hankering after Laura had become ridiculous. It was time to do something about it. Nothing in him was going to change so that he suddenly became more attractive to her; nothing would reduce her suddenly to his level. He just had to face the facts as he found them. So he would . . . what?

He had no experience of what he ought to do. He was twenty-one years old. He got up and went to the washbasin, which he filled with scalding water. He wetted his face and squeezed a worm of shaving cream on to his fingertips. He had been made so serious by his fixation on Laura that he had felt old, weighed down with worldly understanding. The truth was, he reluctantly admitted, that he had no experience at all; he was making it up as he went along.

Laura suggested they go into St Johnsbury – St J, as she called it – to do some shopping; she wanted to buy one or two extra things for Christmas, and the stores in Lyndonville were limited. Pietro stood outside, waving directions as she reversed the station wagon past a visiting propane tanker and down the icy drive. Once on the road, she drove the car in surges, fighting with the unfamiliar manual shift.

'Maybe you should get another couple of cows from the butcher,' he said, 'just to be on the safe side.'

Laura looked across from the steering wheel with a slight pout. 'Didn't you like your breakfast?'

'I did. I liked it a lot. But I can't remember when I've eaten so much.'

Mrs Heasman and her silent helper had handed him a plate with fried eggs, muffins, bacon, cheese, tomato and a blueberry pancake. Mrs Heasman kept telling him to put more food on to it. 'Have some pumpkin butter. You haven't got any maple syrup on that, have you? Here, let me. Why don't you have some fruit with it? Laura, pass Pietro the sour cream.' Out of politeness he ate everything that was offered, forcing down the fresh pineapple and peanut butter with the fried egg. 'Have a banana,' Mrs Heasman had suddenly suggested. And when he had finished she said, 'Perhaps you'd like an ordinary English muffin with marmalade?' in a hurt but helpful tone of voice as though he had pushed away the plate untouched.

Laura said, 'That's what people do here. They don't eat much for lunch, though.' She fought to find the gear as they passed the snow-covered bandstand in the park.

'Why don't you pull in and let me drive?'

'Do you have a driver's licence?'

'Sure. It's a British one, but it's all right. At least I learned on a car with gears.'

They changed sides, but before he restarted the car, he put both hands on the steering wheel. 'Laura, I've got to tell you something.'

'What?'

'I'm crazy about you. You know that, don't you? Right from the start I have been. The first day I walked into the classroom and saw you I thought you were the most wonderful thing I'd ever seen. You did know that, didn't you?'

Laura looked confused.

'You don't have to pretend with me. And you don't have to worry. I won't embarrass you. Don't look so crestfallen. It can't be the first time a boy has fallen in love with you.'

Laura's confusion of modesty and embarrassment resolved itself in indignant laughter. 'No. Of course it isn't. Of course it isn't.'

'Well then.' He started the car. He found that by being a little aggressive he could in some way stay on top of the conversation. He located the gear and let the clutch in violently, so that the car shot forward. 'But you needn't worry. I won't get heavy about it. I'll never mention it again. I just wanted you to know.'

'That's fine,' she said. 'Right-hand side of the road.'

'Good. Right-hand side. No problem.'

They drove together most days, the station wagon rattling through covered wooden bridges and up snowy roads beside which at regular intervals was the bleak announcement: 'Frost Heaves'. Laura did not like to be shut in the house for too long, and showing Pietro around gave her an excuse to be out. She enjoyed his pleasure when he saw things that were familiar to her, like a shop in some remote village that sold Guns, Clocks and Music Boxes. 'Hey son, you got a licence for that music box?' she muttered as Pietro pointed out the sign.

On Christmas morning they gave each other presents, then went to the Congregational church in Lyndonville. Afterwards Pietro was told to go for a walk with Sally, Laura's sister, as their help was not required in preparing dinner. Sally talked enthusiastically about the college she would be going to the following year. The air was brilliant and alive as they walked up into the hills. It seemed strange that this so lavishly favoured countryside had been known in the West for so short a time. Yet it was also well suited to its present inhabitants: it seemed to need its telegraph poles, its railway lines and its discreet automobiles hidden by the side of the houses. However much the people lived from the land and allowed the wilderness to lower over them, its beauty profited from the closeness of modern life.

On their return Pietro went to fetch some logs for the fire. He had to walk across a snow-covered yard to a white door indicated by Laura's father. The floor was plain concrete, illuminated by an unshaded bulb. All round the walls the logs were neatly stacked. Each armful was dry and fragrant. Pietro noticed two long radiators on the wall. A centrally heated wood store, he thought; not much was left to chance. He returned to the main house through the double back doors. The inner glass door gave a pneumatic hiss as it sealed the interior.

Mr Heasman offered them drinks – beer or Bloody Mary or punch. Pietro, who wanted a Bloody Mary, asked for punch, in the way that he always asked for coffee mousse at dinner because everyone preferred orange. He didn't realise when he accepted a second glass that they wouldn't have lunch until four o'clock. By the time they sat down to a milky fish soup, in which a wave of crustaceans lapped against the brim, he was irrepressible. Mr Heasman carved two geese while his wife fussed over the different kinds of stuffing and the gravy, which was Laura's contribution. Everyone therefore pretended not to want any, though no one dared tease the large woman with the bun when she piled their plates with vegetables.

LAURA had not shown much emotion when she left the school. She hugged Pietro, and Harry, and, unfortunately, Dave Snyder, and she cried a little as they all separated on the last day, but she didn't swear devotion and give out signed photographs as Gloria Katz did. She had submitted herself to the final exams in her own way. Unrevised and garrulous, she was rebuked by the invigilator for talking to Gloria, but on the strength of her results she was offered a place at Harvard, her father's old university. His spell in London had ended and he was returning to New York; he had been anxious for Laura to find a place at an American college, and for once she had done what he told her.

Laura wrote to Pietro telling him she was having a good time at Harvard. He scanned the letters for any hints about men. It was hard to tell. There were phrases like 'a few of us went to a movie', or 'I'm going to Boston with a couple of guys', but no names and no way of telling what they were like. He worried that she was rushing ahead. Things seemed to happen so easily for her. University wouldn't be dull or disappointing or hard work; it would be a breeze and she would at once take to her fellow students. By the time he next saw her she would have outgrown him again, just when he had at last begun to catch up.

She sent Christmas cards and postcards ('We're on vacation in Mexico. The food is disgusting') and always answered his long and elaborate letters, in which he tried to make his own life, a science course in London, sound romantic, as he teased out the laws of the universe. 'When are you going to come and visit me?' Laura wrote at the end of most of her letters. One day. When I've saved up the money, Pietro thought. 'As soon as I can afford it,' he wrote back. 'But aren't you coming to London some time?' Pietro made friends with his contemporaries, but felt his mind was always in America.

Laura stayed another year at Harvard and Pietro finally saved the money he needed for the flight. 'Come for Christmas,' she at once replied, when he told her he was free. 'Come and stay with my family in Lyndonville.'

HE stayed on until the New Year and returned to London in January. London. What was the problem with it? For once, the answer was obvious. After all, Harry Freeman was enjoying it enough. He had been to New York, Chicago, Rome and Tokyo, but he reckoned London was the best of all. He had a job as a reporter on a radio station. He had borrowed a large sum of money and bought himself a flat in Bayswater; he had become a hero of the discothèques and late-night bars. The last trace of blazerdom had left him.

In April Pietro had a letter from Laura asking him if he would like to go over again and stay for a couple of weeks in the summer. She would have graduated by then and would be spending some time in Vermont. Pietro pored over her letter like a biblical exegete at work on a hermetic text. What were the implications of her asking him? Was the relaxed fluency of her prose (no wonder she had got all those exam passes) indicative of a new beginning in her feelings? Was the invitation a statement of intent, or just an invitation? And how much did she mean by 'lots of love'?

He worked nights in a restaurant to save up enough money for the air fare. This time he flew from New York to Lebanon, the nearest airport, just over the border in New Hampshire, and this time Laura was there to meet him.

Vermont in summer was as well provided as Vermont at Christmas. When it had been cold, the central heating had pumped thermal currents through the rooms; now it was hot, the fridge produced ice by the sack. If there was a big game on, they didn't make you wait until the next day to see it on television. They didn't seem ashamed of gratifying their desires. Pietro would have felt guilty if he could have gone into a shop in London and found everything he wanted.

Laura took all this for granted, but she wasn't spoiled. She was a model daughter in some ways: Pietro saw her father look at her proudly and listened to him tell his friends how Laura was going to choose between a number of jobs she'd been offered. But she was also untamed and hard to understand. Pietro hated to think what her father would have said if he could have heard some of the stories not granted a certificate of parental suitability.

One night they sat up late talking seriously in her room, drinking beer. She told him that she wasn't seeing Al at all any more. Pietro nodded calmly and asked why not.

'He got kind of possessive. Even after we'd stopped going out together.' She grimaced, then laughed. 'He got to be a real pain. I can't think what I saw in him in the first place.'

She rolled back on the bed and laughed as if a burden had been taken off her. Pietro, who had prepared himself to be earnest and sympathetic about Al was wrong-footed by Laura's change of mood. He laughed gamely, but not too much, for fear of tempting providence.

IT grew very hot the following week.

'This is kind of unusual,' said Jack, the yard man, who was a weather expert. He drove a heavy pick-up truck which had a variety of guns stuffed down by the handbrake, like clubs in a disorganised golf bag. You couldn't be sure, as Pietro remarked, whether he was going to change gear or blow the roof off. He spent much of the winter digging people's cars out of snowdrifts. In the summer he had more time for hunting.

'It's as hot as the Mediterranean,' said Pietro.

Jack looked at him suspiciously. 'I ain't been there,' he said. 'I'm going to Maine in the fall. Apart from that, I don't leave the state.'

'Have you never been abroad?'

'Yeah. I went once. Never again.'

'Where was that?'

'Vietnam. Never again. Boy, was that place scary.'

'But you could try somewhere else, like –'

'Picked you up and put you down out of some goddamn plane. Didn't know where the hell you were.'

'But maybe somewhere in Europe . . .'

'No, sir, that was enough for me.' Jack looked up at the sky. 'Reckon this weather's come all the way up from Virginia.'

They arranged to go swimming in a nearby lake with two friends of Laura's. There was a man called Steve who had a moustache that came out of his nostrils and covered both his lips, and a waif-like girl of about nineteen called Jesse, with tousled hair and old, patched jeans cut off at the thigh. She said she knew of a good spot where no one ever disturbed you. Maybe they could catch some fish for lunch and build a fire. No day in Vermont, it seemed, was complete without taking life.

They found a clearing in the forest with a still, cold lake in the middle of it. Someone had left a rowing boat pulled up by the water's edge near a wooden hut. After some discussion about the propriety of borrowing the boat without the owner's permission, Steve and Laura went fishing in it while Pietro and Jesse, who were supposed to build a fire, drank some beer and sunbathed in a patch of chequered light.

'Are you in love with Laura or what?' said Jesse conversationally.

Pietro looked up from his book. Jesse had taken off her shirt and was wearing only her cut-off jeans. She had small, pointed breasts with quite large, brownish nipples, around each of which were half a dozen brown hairs.

'Yes,' he said, 'I suppose I am.'

'OK,' said Jesse.

'What about you and Steve?' said Pietro.

'Steve? No, Steve's just a friend. Wanna cigarette?'

Eventually they decided to gather the wood for the fire. Even if the fishing trip was unsuccessful there was plenty of food in the car. Pietro had watched Mrs Heasman chopping Spanish onions and putting them with vast, orange yolks of egg and minced steak for hamburgers. Steve and Laura returned with one small trout and a long story from Laura about how it had been caught. Steve nodded a few times. He didn't talk much. While Laura chattered over lunch, he nodded some more and wiped a few bits of food from his moustache. At one stage he said, 'I really love pawsta.' 'What?' said Pietro. 'Pawsta. You know, fettucine, linguine.' 'Oh, I see. Yes.' 'Pietro's half Italian,' said Laura. 'Right,' said Steve.

Laura was wearing a white cotton shirt and scarlet earrings. Her hair lay coiled on her shoulders where the shirt was loose at the top. She looked up at Pietro and smiled over half a hamburger she had burned on the fire. He smiled back, opened another beer, and settled back on the pine-needle floor against the bole of a tree.

The atmosphere closed in and thick clouds formed above the forest. They finished the beer, put out the fire, and lay down to sleep for a while. Jesse smoked a cigarette and read her book. She hadn't put her shirt on again.

Pietro was awoken by the sound of thunder, rolling in from behind the mountains. He sat up and looked over to where Laura was lying. She stretched her arms in the air and yawned. Fat drops of rain began to pierce the canopy of trees.

'Shit,' said Steve.

Jesse stood up and stubbed out her cigarette beneath her bare heel. 'I'm going for a swim,' she said, and peeled down her denim shorts. She stood naked in front of the others, like a witch doctor or a guardian spirit. She had bony hips and a big tuft of brown pubic hair. 'Come on, you guys,' she called out and started laughing. 'Shit,' said Steve, 'I'm going back to the car.'

Laura Heasman stood up, and with her back to Pietro and Steve, undid the waistband of her skirt. She dropped it to her ankles, revealing a pair of white underpants. Then she pulled off her shirt and unhooked her bra. Finally she peeled the white pants slowly down her legs, kicked them away with her foot and ran after Jesse into the water. Pietro's head was blowing fuses, as though the pathways in his brain had been incorrectly wired and now the rain was getting in. He began to pull and tear at his clothes, his hands snagging on the buttons and the zips. At last he was down to his underpants. He paused for a moment, then whipped them off and sprinted for the lake, not feeling the pine needles, sticks and small stones that scored the soles of his feet.

The rain pelted on to the surface of the lake so it looked like a grey milkshake. Jesse, who swam like an eel, wriggled and dived some way ahead. Laura was standing waist-high in the water shouting to her and laughing. Pietro put down his head and drove forward in a big Australian crawl. He turned round and looked back towards the shore. There was no sign of Steve.

Laura laughed and splashed water at him. They both swam on to where Jesse was plunging up and down and banging her chest like a Red Indian. Laura dived and caught her legs under the water. They both disappeared. Pietro saw two white backsides periodically appear above the water, then vanish again, until both girls emerged spluttering. 'Let's get him,' said Jesse, and Pietro felt her slippery body winding round his legs while Laura heaved herself on to his shoulders from behind. The thunder rumbled above them as though someone were shifting trunks in a giant lumber room. Jesse called out and danced in the water.

When they were exhausted, Laura headed for the shore. Pietro and Jesse swam along behind. It was still raining hard as they emerged on to the muddy land. Laura shook her head like a dog, and Pietro smoothed back his hair with both hands. 'OK,' said Jesse, 'catch me then!' And she ran off through the woods. Laura looked after her, started for a moment, then stopped. Then she began to walk along by the side of the lake and Pietro watched the swing of her hips and legs and the white divide of her buttocks. When she reached the wooden hut she turned and called out, 'Come in here and dry off.' Pietro went with deliberate steps up into the cabin. Laura stood in front of him, and he was overwhelmed by the sight of this girl, whom he loved, holding out her arms to him. But he made no mistakes. He kissed her on the lips and felt them part and the hot flutter of her tongue inside his mouth. He took her head between his hands and stroked the enflamed golden hair he had gazed at for so long. It was wet and flat against her head, but it felt beautiful under his square hands. He dropped to his knees so he could touch the legs that had tormented him, all the way from the ankle to the hip, stroking and holding them both. The perfection of their shape was as he had known it would be. Then he stood up and held her tightly in his arms. She squeezed him in return, pulled back her head and smiled at him, allowing the full force of her eyes to beam into his narrowed, concentrating gaze. Still he kept his head. Her hand trailed down his stomach and she seemed to give a small sigh of pleasure as she tugged at him. He put his hand on hers and she knelt on the floor of the hut, which was made from rough wooden boards. Then she lay back on the floor, circled his neck with her hands and pulled him on to her. When he entered her he felt the last icy drops of lake water give way to something scalding hot and smooth. Gradually, fearful of splinters, he manœuvred both their bodies into place and closed his eyes.

To make love to an American girl was to occupy some of that endless country for himself. He inhaled the smell of her body, and from somewhere unknown the words Pasadena Rose Parade formed in his mind.

He had the feeling he had sometimes had before when making love, though never as strongly as this, that he was in the right place; that this was the one spot on the turning globe that he was supposed to be. Although the nerve-endings of his body were crackling with delight, he felt a calmer sense of his proper location. Once, as he tried to contain the rising pleasure, he opened his eyes and found a wooden knot in the floor gazing back at him from an inch or so away. Laura squirmed beneath him and called him some name, some soft, endearing name that, in his passion for her, he didn't register. He kissed her upturned face in which the brown eyes were closed as if in concentration, the wet lashes flat against her cheeks, and thanked whatever providence or deity had, against all the odds, allowed him this moment.

STEVE looked at them suspiciously when they sauntered back to the car where he had been listening to the radio while it rained.

When Jesse returned and got dressed she looked at Pietro with big, interrogative eyebrows.

For the next two weeks Pietro lived in a fever of desire. When he and Laura went for walks they could hardly wait until they were out of sight of the house before they would be kissing and fumbling at each other. As soon as Mrs Heasman left the house they were in each other's arms, in her bedroom, in his bedroom, on the veranda and once on a kitchen chair when they heard the sound of the car unexpectedly returning.

For the rest of the summer they were barely apart. They flew to Detroit and drove to the small town of Kalamazoo where Laura had a cousin called Cathy, who was at university. She had stayed on to do an extra course during the summer. She hated the place, with its stick-like telegraph poles on the bare streets, the campus on the hill with its bogus Tyrolean bar and big impersonal supermarket, closed for the vacation. Pietro spent an hour or so in a record shop on the main drag while Laura and her cousin talked family matters. He thought the place had an agreeable air.

One thing he couldn't puzzle out – one thing he could never puzzle out – was what the place meant. What was Kalamazoo? Why live there? He looked hard at the wooden porches on the weatherboard houses and thought of the subatomic particles that made them. At some stage they had taken on a physical form, at some early organic stage in the life of the tree, prefigured by their life as seed or sap. It took an element of human will, though, to cut and saw and plane and build.

What worried Pietro was that he couldn't see at what point the geographical position of a place on the earth's surface influenced the character of the human activity that took place on it. Could you really say that it was only human beings who chose, by cutting trees and making bricks, to force something unnatural on a wilderness? The human will itself, which was the decisive factor, could hardly be called inorganic. It wasn't enough, he thought, to say that people built cities on the estuaries of rivers, or towns on trade routes or villages in the most secluded spots.

Some relation, more than that of climate or finance, existed between a site and a people.

Meanwhile, he liked this middle America, the butt of satire and derision. He had been momentarily put out when he once heard Harry talking about what he called James Dean America – 'all that drive-in diner and cherry-pie bullshit'. But he believed that what excited him about the country was more than nostalgia for 1950s film sets. Places like Duluth and Milwaukee were to him not just placid but inspiring. He supposed this was partly because he was moved by the thought of a migrant people inventing a nation and then imposing it on the mind of the world. In the ancient city of Rome they had been taught through books and films to accept the myth of small-time Milwaukee, a mockable, low-rolling town, not just for now, but as if the character and tradition of the place were as old as those of the Palatine Hill. This was a heroic feat of imaginative enforcement.

Yet he liked the places, too, not for some sort of mythic quality, but because they were calm and self-assured in their industrial or residential identity. It did not occur to him that his appreciation of them was coloured by his emotional condition. When he took the wheel of the hire car, he felt they couldn't come at him fast enough: Rockford, Madison, La Crosse, and on up to the airport at the twin towns of Minneapolis-St Paul.

MONS

〃〃〃

Belgium 1914

THERE were two reasons Pietro dreaded going to see his grandfather in Nottingham. The first was Bobby, a woolly-coated terrier who lay in front of the fire letting off staccato noises, the loudest of which made him stand up and sniff in an accusing way, as though someone else were responsible. The other reason was the old man's conversation, which ran along lines which were familiar and uninteresting to a sixteen-year-old boy. Later, when his grandfather was dead, he wished he had listened harder. At the time, the stories seemed all part of the atmosphere of dog and sealed windows and stifling gas fire.

'And where is it this year?' said old Russell, settling ominously back in his chair.'

'Ibiza,' said Pietro.

'And where's that then?'

'It's in the Mediterranean.' It sounded promising enough, with cheap food and wine and young English people. Girls.

'Everyone goes abroad these days, don't they?'

'I suppose so. It's become cheaper, hasn't it? And the weather. It always seems to rain in England.'

Pietro expected a homily on the virtues of the English seaside. He had been instructed by his father to spend the afternoon with the old man but was to be allowed out to go to the cinema on his own in the evening.

What his grandfather was in fact saying was, 'Those places we went to every now and again on the east coast, like Skegness, they were bloody terrible. You were always so cold. I couldn't wait to go abroad. That's why I joined up in the first place on the seven and five. It was the only way you could afford it, if someone else was paying.'

Pietro glanced at the clock on the mantelpiece. It was a quarter past three. The other side of the river, at Trent Bridge, the test match was midway through the afternoon session. They would have tea at five in the hot little house, supervised by a friendly neighbour. He let his mind drift into neutral, as for a divinity lesson at school, and settled back to let his grandfather talk. He was not yet eighty; he had a full head of hair and no physical disability, but to Pietro he seemed to have lived in an era he had mentally filed under 'history'. His conversation always looked to the past, and what he said therefore went unregarded.

'. . . so of course it was a big excitement when you got the telegram, or when you heard in the pub or whatever you were doing. I packed up the shop there and then and told Watkins he'd have to look after it while I was away. And you can't say we weren't well looked after then, either. They gave you a warrant if I remember rightly in the post office, just a little ticket sort of thing, and you took that to the station and they gave you a free ride to your headquarters. It was full of reservists when we got there and some of the regulars didn't like it at all. But they had to put up with it, because without us there wouldn't have been an army at all.

'It was a lovely summer, too. There was a bank holiday just about this time and some people were annoyed because they cancelled all the trains so they could move the troops, but most people didn't give a damn. It was better than a holiday really, there was such an air of celebration about the whole place. I must say some of the reservists weren't quite as fit as they should have been. Chap in our unit ran a pub and he'd got so fat they couldn't find the trousers to go on him. There was a bit of a scrum for food as well, but it was all pretty good-natured. Belgium was where we were going, though some of the men didn't know where Belgium was. Somehow we got down to Southampton. My God, there were crowds there. The number of trains coming in, the people come to see us off, the docks were swarming with them. I watched some cavalry people trying to get their horses on board. The animals hated it, being winched up in the air like that. Some of them had heart attacks, some of them kicked their way out of the slings they were in.

'We had a good party on board, too. Some fellow had got some wine and they didn't fuss about smoking. Later on they changed the orders about tobacco, because officially you weren't supposed to smoke when you were on duty. But they changed that temporarily. They didn't know it would go on for four years, though.

'We felt proud of the way we could just sail across like that too. Tom Swarbrick said it was because we had the whole Channel cleared and they didn't dare come near us. It was wonderful when we arrived. Boulogne. It was the first time most of us had been to Europe, and I thought it was the best thing that had ever happened. There were banners out, there was a band on the quay. Most of the chaps in my unit, they couldn't believe their luck. We had to listen to a speech by the mayor. I couldn't understand a word, but there was a young captain with us – only about twenty, but he was very well educated, was killed on the Somme, poor fellow – and he translated. The mayor was saying how pleased he was to have the gallant British troops arrive, how amazed he was by the speed with which we'd got there and so on.

'I think we were all a bit amazed, to tell the truth, but what we were surprised at was that we were on the same side as the French! It was the first time, and it took a bit of getting used to. There were plenty of men in our unit who said they'd rather be fighting against them, but I just thought it was a job and it didn't make much odds who the enemy were. We'd all had a message from the commander-in-chief, or some bigwig anyway, saying we weren't to fraternise with French women, if you see what I mean. That was easier said than done, because they were pretty friendly, I can tell you.'

He paused for a moment, and Pietro, who had been half listening, as though to a radio playing in another room, blinked and thought of a question. 'It must have been terrible,' he said. 'Did you –'

'Terrible? It wasn't terrible at all. We were having the time of our lives. The marching was a bit tough, I suppose. I hadn't worn boots for two or three years, and these places in France they all seemed to have cobbled streets. It was hard on the feet and that's where the regulars scored over us. But we didn't make a big fuss. Every little place you went through there would be crowds of French people cheering you on and the girls asking for souvenirs. They wanted your cap badge or your buttons or something like that. By the time we got to Amiens there were chaps in our unit could barely keep their uniforms done up, they just had bits of twine instead of buttons.

'The officers were good, though. They let us have beer to drink, if you had the money. I remember sitting by a big corn field. It was harvest time and one or two men had said they'd help. It was hot work, I can tell you, and I don't know what they got in return, though I can have a pretty good guess, knowing Tom Swarbrick, who was a handsome fellow. There was a big lorry pulled in across the road from the Army and Navy stores, and I'd seen another one from Selfridges. They'd all come to help transport the kit, but it made it feel like a big outing.

'It was so hot that night that we didn't bother with the bivvy. We slept out under the stars. I was with Swarbrick and Simpson and a chap called Reynolds and we all agreed this was the best thing we'd seen yet. We had a smoke and plenty of tea to drink and apart from a few blisters we were as happy as sandboys.

'Then it must have been the next day I think we got on the train. That wasn't quite so good. Some bright spark had had the idea that if you could transport all the kit and all the horses in animal trucks, you could do the same with the men. The officers were allowed in proper carriages, first class I shouldn't wonder, but we all went standing up in these cattle wagons. It was pretty ripe in there, I don't mind telling you. But we didn't care, because we thought we were just going to give these Germans a lesson. Our spirits were that high. And the journey wasn't all that long anyway. We got a bit of a rest the other end, then we had a talk from the company commander. He said we had to get a move on then. We were to go up to the left flank of the French and so stretch their line out. They were already fighting, you see. We had to head for this place in Belgium pretty sharpish. What we didn't know was the Germans had made the same plan, like a rendezvous.

'It was a nice town when we got there. We sat in the square and the rations were dished out to us. You just got a tin, didn't know what was in it. I had a tin of herring and some bread. I should think it had been in the stores since the Crimea but we were so hungry it didn't matter. Then the people from the town, they started giving us bunches of fruit, then someone else came along with some loaves still hot from the baker's, and cheese and bits of ham. All we needed was some beer, and lo and behold a barkeeper said we could have a big jug of that too. We ate all this stuff just sitting on the cobbles in the shade. You didn't want to sit in the sun, not after marching with all that kit.'

Pietro, who found his interest had lifted a little at the mention of food, said, 'So you quite liked the town then?'

'Oh yes, it was grand.'

'But what about the . . . you know, the battlefield? That must have been awful.'

'Not really. It was like I was used to it, to tell the truth. You've seen the mines round here, haven't you? It was like that.'

'But what about the trenches?'

'We didn't have trenches there, not like the ones we had later on. No, we tried to dig a bit, but we were fighting in a town really, in a what do you call it, a built-up area. The artillery couldn't get their field of fire because the place was full of slagheaps. If it wasn't slagheaps, it was railway cuttings and little villages all along the side of the canal. And in the morning you could see all the miners clocking on for work, just like a shift in one of the Nottingham coalfields. They waved at us as they went into the pits. Funny people, the Belgians. The first thing we heard was that a cavalry officer had met some Germans on the road and had gone chasing after them with his section. He'd run his man through and come back with blood on his sword. You wouldn't think we'd be killing with machine guns and howitzers in a few months. The French army we'd seen in Amiens were wearing scarlet trousers. They'd just gone off across the fields to the south of us and walked into it.

'It was hazy in the morning, I remember. Tom Swarbrick said it was going to rain, but it soon cleared. We'd been pushed into a salient north of the town.'

'What's a salient?' said Pietro.

'A bit that sticks out. I remember that morning. We knew something was coming, but most of us didn't worry a bit. We knew we'd cop it in the salient if they did attack, but we thought we'd get the better of it. I remember the smell of burning coming off the canal. The engineers had set fire to all the barges in case the Germans used them as bridges to get across. They'd stuck charges on the proper bridges. When the firing began it was a relief. When you're stuck there under attack you don't know what's going on. We didn't discover till later they'd had six divisions to our two. All morning we just kept firing as we'd been trained. We got off so many rounds they thought we were using machine guns. And then we all had to stop because there was a group of Belgian schoolgirls on the bridge.'

'Schoolgirls?'

'Don't ask me how they'd got there, but we all had to stop while their mistress took them to safety. I'll never forget that sight. I used to think about it later in the war, when we'd been stuck underground in mud for weeks on end. I used to think of the way we all stopped firing.'

'I thought it was supposed to have been a terrible battle.'

145

'Well, it got very hot again. We were thirsty all the time and we were under fire for six hours in there.'

'For six hours? That must have been awful.'

'It was a bit unexpected.'

Pietro couldn't reconcile what he'd learned in history lessons with his grandfather's memory of the war. The old man looked down and poked at the sleeping dog with his foot.

'To tell you the truth, it did get a bit rough towards the end of the day. The fire was very heavy and we had a job getting out of that salient. In the evening, when we'd pulled back, some of the lads were shaken. We didn't know the war was going to be like this. At night when we were digging into our new positions, the young captain I told you about, he came round to see us. I remember him saying something like, "Congratulations, gentlemen. You have just shaken hands with the twentieth century." What was that supposed to mean? We hadn't a clue what he was talking about, but I did think of it again when we buried him two years later.'

'So did you lose the battle?' said Pietro.

'We withdrew, that's what it was called. We withdrew to new positions. But we lived to fight again. It was tough getting out of there, holding the bridges while they got the kit out. There were three VCs won on that first day, I think, chaps who hung on under the bridges, wiring them up, covering the retreat. It started to rain again that night. Simpson, I remember, he took his shirt off and let the rain get on his back where he'd got burned when he'd been digging. It made the ground slippery. It was hard to march on when you were carrying all that clobber. The countryside of Belgium looked pretty odd. It was as though it had snowed, there was so much white dust from the shelled houses. And I remember the smell of all those men who hadn't washed, not to mention the dead bodies in that heat, because there hadn't been time to bury them. But we weren't down-hearted, not most of us. We'd shown that man for man we could take them on.'

'And what happened to Simpson?'

'He was killed at the Somme.'

'Like the captain?'

'Yes.'

'And Reynolds?'

'The next year.'

'And your friend, Tom . . .'

'Swarbrick? Passchendaele, towards the end.'

'Didn't any of your friends make it all the way through?'

'Not really. All the officers in our company were dead by Christmas. I got it in the leg from one of our own shells. Bloody artillery, the Drop 'em Shorts, we called them. I was out for a year and a half. They sent me back again though. To the Somme. I rejoined my old unit and some old man came up and shook my hand. I thought, "Who's this old bugger calling me by my first name?" And he said, "Don't you remember your old pal Tom?" It was Tom Swarbrick. He'd been somewhere called the White City. That's what they called it. They gave these places nicknames from England. I didn't recognise him.'

NEW YORK

USA 1983

T HE speech had been the difficult part. What to say about someone he had known for almost twenty years, and then how to say it. He took instructions from Harry. No smut, not too long, try to make it accessible to Americans as well as British, no jokes about being a goy. Then he sat down one Sunday afternoon with the sound of the six-month-old Mary occasionally penetrating the closed door of the sitting room. He could hear Hannah's solicitous footsteps going to calm the baby and turned his mind back to an earlier age.

Harry had been a good friend to him, that was for sure. He wanted to say so in public. On the other hand, he didn't want to put himself too much into the story. Tell them what sort of a person Harry was. Anecdotes. Stories that would interest Americans who hadn't met him but which would not bore English people who had known him all his life. The time they had been to India and Harry had suffered from, of all things, constipation. Something nobler. The time they had raised money for a London charity by swimming hundreds of lengths of an over-chlorinated pool in Highbury. Too self-admiring. Perhaps Harry would best come alive if he talked about his family. But he didn't like his mother, and his sister had run off with someone unsuitable, possibly even a photographer.

★

148

IN the taxi from Kennedy airport he felt the shiny black cover of the seat beneath his left hand and the chrome of the door handle in his right. The bench was slippery and the driver pressed on in the New York fashion, using only the steering wheel to pilot them, as though the speed had been preset at an unvariable level. His photograph stared villainously from his ID card beside the meter. GOMEZ.

The wind was funnelled down the cross-street outside his hotel, and Pietro pulled his jacket tight around him as he hauled his suitcase inside. In only a few moments on the pavement his legs felt frozen. Inside the lobby, the heated air at once began to make his scalp sizzle. Up in his room he hurriedly unpacked and prepared for bed. His fatigue had vanished, however, and he felt impelled to go out for a nightcap. Within a few minutes, he was sitting in a chair at the bar, watching a football game through watery eyes on the mounted television, his right hand wrapped round a prodigious shot of bourbon. I must ring Hannah, he thought. Mary had developed a virus which at the last moment had prevented Hannah from coming with him to New York. She would be waiting for his call.

'WHERE's Barbara?'

'Anyone seen Nancy? She was supposed to be here.'

'The traffic's terrible on Lexington.'

'Have you seen Harry, Pietro?'

'A few minutes ago. He was in the aisle, or whatever.'

'Now listen, everyone. My name is Michael. I'm in charge. I want you all to take the places indicated on the chart here.'

The master of ceremonies looked harassed. Two of the bridesmaids were missing and the other four would not stop talking. People surged up and down the steps of the synagogue, looking for each other, being introduced, attempting to find their places in the order of the procession.

'You're walking in with Simon.'

'Surely I'm with Elliot? Look, it says right here.'

'He's right.' Elliot stepped forward. He was a neat American of about thirty-five who was one of the twenty people Pietro had been introduced to in the last quarter of an hour. Elliot had met a similar number of people from England. The difference was that he remembered all their names and repeated them with ostentatious ease.

'Richard's right. Pietro's with me,' he said. 'Simon should be walking in with Jonathan.'

There was a shriek from one of the bridesmaids. 'Nancy! How are you?'

A pretty, dark-haired girl came running up the steps in a navy-blue trench coat. 'Jesus, the traffic,' she said between kisses. 'I couldn't get a cab anywhere. Martha! You look fantastic!'

'Now where's Allie gone? We can't start without her. Simon, did you see Allie?'

'I thought she was with Nancy.'

'Pietro, I want you to meet my great-aunt,' said Martha.

A minute woman who looked like a bird with a single orange plume on her head held out her hand, then lifted up her powdery face to be kissed.

'Oh my,' she sighed, looking up at Pietro, 'how you've grown.'

Baffled, Pietro turned back to resume his place. Behind them was a glass-fronted display case in which were two huge scrolls and an ancient book, open to reveal some sacred Hebrew texts.

The rehearsal eventually took place. They were to process in pairs up what Pietro thought of as the aisle, then take their places on either side of the bride and groom, ushers on one side, bridesmaids on the other. After the complications of arrival and introduction, the main business seemed quite straightforward. All Pietro had to do was walk up with a friend of Martha's called, almost certainly, Richard and come down again with Nancy on his arm. His participation in the service was limited to shouting '*Mazel tov*' when Harry broke the glass beneath his foot.

★

150

HE took a dry martini, straight up, at 12.15 in a bar on Bleeker Street. His eyes watered slightly and his nose ran as the warmth of the bar, augmented by the almost neat gin, thawed his sinuses. Next he had a beer and a cheeseburger, which he ate at the bar. The meat was rare and loosely packed; the blood from the burger made the french fries furry at the edges. He reckoned a single glass of red wine would just make him sleepy enough to drop off for half an hour back at the hotel before he needed to think about getting ready for the wedding. Without ever quite adapting to the time change he found himself negotiating with his energy reserves, borrowing an hour and repaying it with snatched sleep later on. Having taken the subway on the journey down, he felt he owed himself a taxi back. The yellow cab pulled in and whisked him over the potholes at a fixed thirty-five miles an hour. BRODSKY, Ion.

THE familiar bleeping of the alarm came at 4.15 p.m. His reactions were all of London mornings, work, panic and Hannah as he reached out his hand and scrabbled frantically on the bedside table, banging down on keys, books, passport, aspirin until he mercifully quelled the noise. He lay back, his heart pounding, his head in deep fog, to see the noisy purple wallpaper of the hotel room, the white wood table and reading lamp, the blank grey screen of the television. New York. He checked the clock again. It was all right. He needed a cup of tea but the hotel couldn't oblige. He thought about finding the coffee shop that had given him breakfast but decided there was not enough time. He would have a bath instead.

He went into the bathroom and moved the slanted bakelite switch upward in its metal plate. The light came on and an extractor fan began to wind itself up in the ceiling. He bent over the bath and struggled with the faucet, a single stick that controlled temperature and speed. An icy stream pelted on to his head from the shower attachment above. Eventually the water ran from the tap at a reasonable temperature and with a force that made the tub thunder. He squeezed in a small plastic bottle of gel and whipped up the purple liquid with his hand until the surface of the water was covered with cool, slimy bubbles. He climbed in and lay back, staring at the cracked, ungrouted tiles that whispered 'cockroach'.

He tried to scoop off the gel and break it up with violent attacks of hot water from the tap, like a ship dispersing an oil slick at sea. Eventually the worst of it was gone and he relaxed, thinking of Harry and Martha. He had begged Harry not to go on to the club his American friends were suggesting the night before, but knew he had little chance. God knows what had happened. His own speech was going to be passable. He had written it out, learned it, then jotted a few words on a postcard to remind himself. Parents. School. Blazers. Paris . . . only ones who etc. Mr F, generosity . . . whole £5, what meant . . . H career. Radio, paper. French story . . . Martha. H's phone call re. Meets H's mother. Weekend with H in Lake District, won't mention her name . . . Bridesmaids: lovely etc. Laurie (?), Nancy, Allie esp. M's sisters × 2. All agree, Ladies and G, lucky man. Toast.

He wiped his hand across the misty mirror and shaved with care, inserting a new blade in the razor and scalding it beneath the tap every few seconds. He wetted his hair and roughed it up a bit, leaving any combing he thought necessary to the last minute. With time on his side, he dressed with care. New underwear, new black socks, old but clean white shirt, gold cufflinks. As he fitted these, he began to relax and look forward to the evening.

Thirty-three years old and it looked as though Harry and he were going to be all right. His own sense of salvation lay in his wife and daughter: it gave him pleasure to contemplate Hannah and Mary, their faces smiling (Hannah's anyway) from a photograph propped up against the bedside light. Presumably Martha would also have children after she and Harry were married. Pulling on his dinner jacket, Pietro went over to the white wood table and picked up the bottle of whisky he had bought at Heathrow. He poured some into a toothglass and diluted it with cloudy-looking water from the basin tap that eventually cleared as whatever had misted it sank or dispersed in the glass. He took a long pull and walked over to the window. He could see the ground eighteen floors below, the headlights surging up the cross-street in the dark. He lifted his glass in a silent toast to Harry, wherever he was now, wherever he would travel. Then he went downstairs, wrapping his coat tightly around him as he turned on to the avenue with its white-lit buildings roaring against the sky.

In the doorway of the synagogue stood one of Harry's English friends with a flat, open basket of yarmulkes, around which he had wrapped his arm like Nell Gwynne. Pietro stood at the other door, watching the guests climb up from the street, banging their hands together. There were so many fur coats at the height of the influx that it looked like a migration of wild animals, pouring in a soft, scented flock into the warmth.

Downstairs it had been pandemonium as the photographer tried to arrange the groups. Most of the bridesmaids were only half dressed, in expensive lingerie and heavy make-up, so the ushers, tuxedoed and with hair slicked back, stood around watching, sipping soft drinks and smoking. The bridesmaids ran around the hall, gossiping, adjusting their hair at a dressing table, and always evading the beseeching grasp of the photographer.

He had done his best, and with the guests all seated, the much-rehearsed procession was due to begin. The inside of the synagogue glowed in the candlelight. The ends of the pews were decorated with white lilies. Pietro walked at funereal pace, as directed, up the carpeted aisle. Ahead he could see Harry standing alone beneath the chuppah, a canopy that had been erected since the day before. As best man he should have been up there already, but the MC had insisted that he walk up the aisle as there would otherwise have been odd numbers.

An elderly rabbi began to read in Hebrew from the scriptures. To Pietro's ears it sounded primitive. He thought of the desert lands and Abraham's sacrifice of Isaac to the cruel god, Jahweh, foreign and remote. He looked down over the rows of faces, the

men in their white yarmulkes, the women hatless and smiling up
at the platform. Outside were the shops of Madison and
Lexington, Italian suits and wine merchants with wooden floors
and shelves designed to look like Montaigne's study near
Bordeaux. And on the pavements were pretzel sellers hunched
over braziers, the flash of burger restaurants and big American
cars barging through the gridlocked traffic. Inside the synagogue
the people spoke of a foreign land and an ancient God, with no
sense of paradox in their devotion. He thought of the web of the
diaspora, its filaments stretched around the earth, even to this,
the largest Jewish city in the world, which was still not their
own. The unimaginable histories of the families passed through
his mind: persecution and exile, immigration, labour and
patience, none of which was visible in their cultured New York
faces. He pictured the Great Hall at Ellis Island with its ambitious
tiled roof and little star-shaped windows around the inner
balcony; down on the floor the throngs had surged, a boat-ride
from the Battery, as though at the gates of heaven: tired,
bewildered travellers clutching their children and their bags,
feeling the press of hands on their elbows as members of Jewish
societies from Hester Street came with the offer of rooms. In the
sound of the rabbi's voice there was a sense of grandeur,
something more numinous than he had found in Christian
churches, but also something cold, a suggestion of a will that
would not relent.

Harry's face was contorted in what Pietro took to be
happiness. Twice he smiled broadly and seemed to be on the
verge of laughter. A younger rabbi gave an informal talk in
English. There was no singing, no prayers. Harry trod on the
glass with an enthusiastic stamp of the left heel, the congregation
shouted '*Mazel tov*', and the ceremony was over.

STILL it was calm on the streets, not like a megalopolis of the
future, gleaming and frenzied. There were only the rattling cabs
and the tall buildings with their quaint Thirties fittings. Harry
wanted a photograph of himself on the street with headlights

going past in a waving ribbon of red. Pietro squatted on the pavement as Harry and Martha finally cleared the crowds of well-wishers to stand by the door of their limousine. He aimed the camera at the lights of a yellow cab and fired. You want a cliché, he had told Harry, you can have it. Then all the guests at once were looking for taxis, so he decided to walk a few blocks on his own. He found that Elliot had materialised from the darkness and was walking alongside him over the big paving stones. Another usher with curly hair and round glasses suggested they stop for a drink on their way to the hotel. They were somewhere in the Fifties, quite far east, and suddenly the coloured awnings with their frequently Irish names, the glowing light from behind curtained windows that signified strong drink and warm air, were nowhere. Two blocks north, despairing, they pressed into the strip light of a burger chain outlet and found a staircase. Upstairs was a deep bar, fitted like a Victorian pub in London, with room enough to hold two hundred people, another world within a world. They drank bourbon, which tasted fine here, though never the same in England, and talked about Harry, feeling a touch of guilt that they were not already in the queue to shake hands.

HARRY, hoisted aloft in his chair, shaking the white traditional handkerchief with Martha, wore the look of terrified hilarity he had worn when Dave Snyder pointed the way back to the hotel from the top of an icy mogul field in les Houches sixteen years earlier. The guests stamped and clapped as he wobbled backwards and forwards, his seat precarious as the men holding his chair on their shoulders tried to keep him steady against the pull and tremble of the others.

Almost all of Martha's friends seemed to be on diets. The plates of salad, steak and vegetables, the piled dishes of dessert and extra, celebratory morsels of hors-d'œuvre or chocolate were carried back untouched by teams of skilful waiters, close-shaven in white tuxedos, with uncomplaining manners and neat hair.

The speeches came sporadically and some seemed unprepared. Eventually, between dances, there came a moment when Martha's father, a white-haired man who had been acting as master of ceremonies, called Pietro to the little wooden platform at the end of the room. Looking over the clustered tables of guests, their faces turned eagerly towards him, Pietro felt isolated. A space of polished dance floor separated him from the nearest humanity; it was no more than five or six yards, but it might have been the Delaware. He pulled out the piece of card and began. His eyes searched for some sympathetic face in the crowd, but he could fix only on a white-coated waiter who was standing assiduously still, as though not to interrupt important proceedings. Pietro found himself imagining the waiter's life. Brooklyn? Queens? Some outlying borough where no tourist went . . . He noticed that although his voice was steady his left leg was shaking. It had assumed some independent life he was powerless to control. He could see Martha's father look down quizzically at the trembling platform beneath his feet.

What he said sounded platitudinous to him, but he said it with conviction and he could tell that the guests were not in a critical mood. He kept it short, as instructed, and when he had negotiated the final stretch and found himself nearing the end, he began to relax his concentration.

'. . . and I'm sure all my fellow-guests from the other side of the Atlantic would agree with me that the hospitality laid on today by Martha's parents' – he swiftly consulted his postcard – 'Lee and Abigail has been absolutely overwhelming. It has been a wonderful experience for us to come over here and find such a warm welcome from people on the other side of the world – to find hotels booked for us, taxis ordered, flowers in the room and suggestions for how to pass the morning – to say nothing, of course, of this magnificent banquet here tonight. All this, all these people trusting and helping one another because of the occasion we are here to celebrate, the love and marriage of two people dear to all of us, Harry and Martha. And I hope you won't think I'm exaggerating if I say that I for one have never experienced such generosity and warmth as over the last twenty-four hours here in Jerusalem.'

He had begun the next and final paragraph, the toast itself, before he realised that the noise from the guests was not just encouragement, but a gasp and then laughter as well. He felt his dress shirt entirely filled with the beating of his heart. It had become instantly soaked. How could he have said it? It sounded anti-Semitic, snide, appalling. All the effort he had made and then to stumble like this, to spoil his friend's wedding at the critical moment . . .

Speechless, he gazed down at his card, on the words that should have led to his way out. He could not gauge whether the sound in the room was of mirth or anger or contempt. Somehow in the synagogue he must have become confused. All those speculations about New York, the biggest Jewish city in the world, and about what immigrants had thought when they arrived had muddled him. Brooklyn, Samaria, Hebron, Galilee, Queens . . . Christ. Jocular excuses half formed at the edge of his mind, but they all came to him in even more insulting shapes. Jerusalem, New York, what does it matter . . . No.

He took a long breath and grasped the microphone stand. 'I meant New York. I was confused into thinking about that beautiful city because . . . because that is where Harry and Martha met one evening when I was there!' He sensed a narrow exit from his shame. 'Jerusalem was where they fell in love, the city of peace. To fall in love in Jerusalem and to be married in New York . . . ladies and gentlemen, these are two people with a sense of style. To have conducted the most important incidents of their lives in what in my view are the two greatest cities in the world.'

It wasn't up to much, it sounded like a fashion magazine, but he was free and running for cover. A swell of generous agreement pushed him on his way. He went through the bridesmaids' names with disdainful precision, raised his glass and moved smartly back to his seat, lowering his head against the volume of forgiving applause. At the table he had time to drink deep of the wine he had till then avoided.

THE party didn't grow any bigger or more ragged at the edges, but as people danced it seemed to intensify, so that by the time Harry and Martha left all the guests were either laughing or shouting. By the doorway a red-faced Englishman was pushing a young American angrily in the chest.

Relieved that the wedding and his part in it were over, Pietro agreed to go on with half a dozen people to a club. He sat back in the taxi driven by an ancient cabbie on the dual carriageway of Park Avenue, heading downtown. The name was clear. OLSEN.

At three in the morning he found himself being regaled by a black cloakroom attendant about the merits of a man who had invented twenty different uses for the peanut. Because he was black, it was argued, he had never had the recognition he deserved; you never heard about him at all. The cloakroom attendant kept calling him sir as he politely put his case against the way American history had been written.

The temperature had taken one of its sudden freefall drops, losing what felt like ten or fifteen degrees in a couple of hours. Now alone, for a reason to do with someone needing to take the cab onwards, Pietro stood on the deserted sidewalk of Fifth Avenue. All around were the strong buildings of commerce and display; between them were the stark crenellations of St Patrick's Cathedral, white and clear against the night sky.

He looked up for the number of the cross-street, caught for a moment in this cold balance.

OXFORD

ooooooooooooooooooooooooooooooooooooooooooooooooooooooooooooooooooooooooooooooooooooooooooooooooooooooooooooooo

England 1976

I T was always *Start the Week* with Richard Baker on the radio
when Pietro drove up the Woodstock Road for his weekly
9.30 appointment at Dr Simon's. When you were off to talk
about what had gone wrong with your life, it made you feel
doubly isolated to hear others celebrating their successful and
coherent world. With skin still slightly tanned from his months
working the ski lift, Pietro had reached the nadir.

A theatre director was discussing new themes she had
discovered in *Othello* as he drove through the north Oxford
streets. Polstead Road, Rawlinson Road – he presumed they
were occupied by married dons with large families who played
and grew in those sturdy brick houses with their damp gardens
and rocketing values. If you got married, did your college pay
for you to live in one of them? he wondered. It would certainly
be a powerful incentive to get away from the quiet colleges
which, for all their beauty and historic dignity, had a trace of
Brockwood about them.

Pietro's contact with the university was confined to a couple of
research students he had met at a party, and a girl reading classics,
though she called it something else. How the colleges functioned
was therefore a matter of unhampered conjecture for him.

He was working at a school in Oxford where he had a job

somewhere between laboratory assistant and apprentice teacher. It had been arranged for him by Mr Maxwell, the young English teacher who had taken the pupils of the US Collegiate School to les Houches and now taught at an Oxford private school. Pietro had met him by chance in London shortly after his return from the Dolomites. Mr Maxwell, who had been half in love with Laura Heasman himself, had always liked Pietro and now, seeing him thin and troubled, had helped him find a job. Oxford would not have been his first choice of places to live, and the pay was poor, but Pietro was grateful for the chance and had worked hard.

Dr Simon stood back politely from her front door and showed Pietro through into a tiled hall off which her consulting room opened. Even though Pietro knew the way he didn't think he ought to go in first, so he waited while Dr Simon closed the front door and came down the hall. Then they would stand on the threshold of the consulting room urging each other in.

Sometimes at nine-thirty on a Monday morning Pietro didn't feel too bad. He sat down in the big chintz armchair and looked over at Dr Simon, who peered back with an expression of interested compassion through her tortoiseshell spectacles. Pietro would make conversation for a while, asking after Dr Simon and her husband, and whether she'd seen some interesting item in the papers or on television. Dr Simon answered briefly, politely, but with the unmistakable suggestion that something more urgent was preoccupying Pietro and that his conversational excursions were just a ruse to keep the subject bottled up.

Often this wasn't true, and after the opening exchange there would be a long silence. Dr Simon never spoke. It was one of the few things about which she was dogmatic. Although she occasionally asked a question, she would never break a silence. Pietro watched the minute hand of the walnut-cased clock move through two, three, four minutes at a time. To begin with he would laugh and Dr Simon would smile wanly back; then he grew used to the silences and was not embarrassed by them. Usually they made him feel sad, or at any rate introspective and this, presumably, was what Dr Simon wanted. Pietro stared every week at the same two book titles on the shelf: *A Textbook of Pathology* by J. M. Sykes, twelfth edition. *Sexual Deviation* by Barnes and Miller. He looked for hours at the fat, battered red spine of the former and the shiny jacket of the latter.

It had been easy to begin with. He had arrived in a state of rigid fear. Dr Simon asked a couple of questions about his family and his life. At the fourth question she asked, Pietro suddenly began to cry. Such successes were harder to come by in the ensuing months as Pietro opened up what was in his mind for the doctor's inspection. He was honest because he was desperate. Sometimes he had to wind himself up to make some particularly shaming admission, but Dr Simon always took it in her stride. If he had told her he was an arsonist, a pederast, a cannibal, Dr Simon would merely have nodded and tried to find out why. Sometimes Pietro grew tired of talking about himself, of looking again and again into the same areas of experience.

'Couldn't we talk about someone else?' he said. 'I'm so bored with this character.'

'Perhaps that's because you don't yet fully know him,' Dr Simon returned. These bleak responses discouraged frivolity, and in the end Pietro was grateful for them because he knew one of them had to keep at it.

'I think we ought to go back to the day in California,' said Dr Simon in one of her rare moments of intervention.

'Ah yes,' said Pietro, 'the fateful day. We've been over it before, haven't we? But I suppose I could tell you again.'

'You could tell me how you felt.'

This was one of Dr Simon's favourite lines. She made Pietro feel that his stories were all narrative with no emotion. The only solution was for him to go back and reverse the process: strip out the structure and coherence of the event and tell the story with colourful and inconsequential stress on his response. To his own ear he then sounded like a débutante on her return from holiday, but it seemed to be what Dr Simon wanted.

'I knew it was doomed. She was far above my station. I

suppose I shouldn't have tried. But I did. I was very young. I thought you could have everything. I didn't see how I could *not* try really. I never expected to be successful, but then when the first hints came my way of course I redoubled my efforts. Quite late on I remember still thinking that she was far too rarefied for me.'

'Yes, you always say this, but you can never explain in what way.'

'Too beautiful. Too exotic. Too clever. I can't think why she ever went out with me at all.'

'What do you imagine she might have wanted or needed from you?'

'I suppose she felt sorry for me or something. And there wasn't anyone else around at that time. I can't imagine.'

'You ought to try.'

'Try what?'

'To imagine. Someone like Laura wouldn't enter into a love affair with a man unless she felt some emotional need or pleasure.'

'Well.' Pietro scratched his head. 'I suppose she did like me. We did get on well. We laughed at things. I was quite good fun – especially then, when I was so happy. It probably made me seem more interesting than I really was, just because I was so happy and alive all the time.'

'What were your feelings when you first began to go out with her?'

'Gratitude.' Pietro laughed. 'And incomprehension. And, I suppose, a dull certainty that it couldn't last.'

'You keep on the same line all the time. It must have occurred to you to wonder why she chose you of all the men she knew and what you must have meant to her.'

'I find it very mysterious. I see what you mean – no woman would just enter into a passionate affair for no reason, unless there was something in it for her, as it were. But what that something was I've no idea. I couldn't begin to guess.'

'But that's exactly what you must do.'

'Why?'

'Because that something was you.'

Sometimes when Dr Simon completed these balletic turns of thought Pietro thought she was just a phoney who wanted to frame a nice paradox. He usually gave a snort of laughter or derision when they came out. Often, however, he found when he thought about them during the week that, hackneyed as they seemed, there was some particle of truth in them. The trouble was that they always turned on a contradiction, so they became predictable: the things he had thought about least were the most important; the days when he had felt nothing were the most significant; the people who made him most angry were the ones he truly loved, and so on.

After a while he could hear Dr Simon coming and would head her off before she had time to articulate the smart paradox. Dr Simon, irritatingly, wasn't irritated; she nodded and smiled as if to suggest that now Pietro was thinking in the right way. 'He who would save his life must lose it,' she once bafflingly added.

'How does it feel,' Pietro said one day after a long silence, 'to have a box of tissues as the principal tool of your trade?'

They looked at the item in question, a pack of man-size, or more accurately, handkerchief-size, Kleenex on the table between them.

'They're not the principal tool, they're –'

'I know. I'm sorry. I was being flippant.'

The box was regularly emptied and replaced, and Pietro wondered what it must be like to sit and listen while people pulled out of themselves their concealed miseries. He thought of the stories that had been told in this north Oxford room where poor overstrained students had brought their tensions on the point of snapping; where middle-European wives of dons came with their long tales of Hungarian fathers, abuse, disappointment, betrayal; where local Oxford people with no university connection tried to learn the academic art of applying rigorous examination to their feelings; and where others, poisoned by

163

illness, had feebly tried to find words for the indescribable assaults of schizophrenia.

He sometimes thought his own problems must seem trifling to Dr Simon, who quickly replied that it was how they felt to Pietro that mattered.

They felt bad. He had a sensation of being removed from the world by a veil or gauze, so that nothing around him seemed real. It was as though he had taken a drug which had a mild hallucinatory effect. In some circumstances it might have been almost pleasant; but when there seemed no end to it, it became a matter of panic. His nerves, stretched by unhappiness, caught hold of the panic and set him in a vicious circle in which fear of unreality and fear of fear chased each other round. To these he was able to add also the more straightforward symptoms of agoraphobia, sleeplessness and – unsurprisingly, in view of the rest of it – depression. There were other sensations his body experienced as though they were physically induced but which Dr Simon assured him sprang from the same causes. The doctor's name for the group of symptoms, ranging from vague unease to uncontrolled panic, was a phrase which struck Pietro as ridiculously genteel – 'unwanted feelings'.

It was in the hope of shifting these feelings that Pietro had gone to see Dr Simon. He had hoped it would be simple: a prescription, a trip to the chemist, and a couple of weeks off work. He hadn't expected they would spend so much time talking about his childhood, his parents, his girlfriends and so on.

Six months later they were still at it.

'I want you to think about something today,' said Dr Simon, polishing her glasses in a large oculist's cloth.

Pietro was glad not to have to find the subject for the monologue himself for a change. 'Fine,' he said.

'When you see a woman that you greatly admire and think of as what you call "above your station", how do you imagine she sees herself and the question of finding for herself a partner or companion?'

Pietro thought for a long time. 'I suppose I feel envious in that she seems to be above the competition and the compromise – she doesn't have to fight with the rest of us. She can have what she wants.'

Dr Simon said nothing. She looked a little quizzical.

'I know that can't be literally true, of course. No woman can actually say, "I'll have him or him or him", when the "him" might be spoken for. But I envy them.'

'Yet there's no reason to suppose they're happier.'

'I suppose not.'

There was a pause. Pietro said, 'Perhaps their beauty is in a way its own reward.'

'You think beauty is a form of goodness?' Dr Simon's scepticism had an abrasive edge.

'I know what you mean. It sounds ridiculous. It can't be true because all people are helpless, they're all just human. And you mustn't think I loved Laura only for the way she looked. It's just that I can't express her true qualities.'

There was a pause.

'What else do you value in these women?' said Dr Simon.

'Gentleness, I think, before anything else. And modesty.'

'Was Laura gentle?'

'Yes, I think so. She was wild, but she was gentle towards other people. And she had an innocence of nature. Even if she was doing something quite outrageous.'

'And modest?'

'Yes, she was modest. I once asked her if she knew how beautiful she was. She said that sometimes she could look in the mirror and think she looked all right that day, but that was all. She had to admit something, I suppose.'

'And all the women you've most admired or loved, do they have this thing in common?'

'There is something. I don't know what you'd call it. A femininity which is made of strength. Not just gentleness. Which is comforting as well as inflaming. Excuse me.' He reached for the maligned box of tissues.

'And yet you didn't trust it.'

'In Laura?'

'You've used words like "doomed".'

'You're trying to say it was a self-fulfilling prophecy?'

'Those are your words,' said Dr Simon and sat back in her chair.

Damn it, thought Pietro. He felt that he had, in some way he did not understand, walked into a trap.

'YOU'RE well travelled for someone of your age, aren't you?' said Dr Simon one day.

'Yes,' said Pietro, happy to expound on something apparently neutral. 'I've always liked it. Well, I mean I did until that episode I told you about – the thing that started all this off really.'

'In Guatemala?'

'Yes. Before then I'd always hoped that I would find somewhere I could feel was truly mine – somewhere I was supposed to be. I didn't feel myself to be wholly English and I didn't think of England as the right place.'

'Yet you speak very warmly of the village you lived in as a child.'

'But that was an episode. It ended when my mother died.'

'And her death ended your affection for the place?' Dr Simon's voice was compassionate but sceptical.

'Not completely. But it was over. The story was complete.'

There was a silence. The clock ticked. After a minute, Dr Simon crossed her legs. Pietro looked down. The silence filled the room again. Pietro tried to feel what he was supposed to feel, but he couldn't make the connections. Time, people, a place.

'I suppose,' he said, 'I felt I would be nearer if I kept moving. If I was static I would be lost. But you don't know what it's like. I didn't like that school I told you about. I didn't feel comfortable in my father's flat. Why should I?'

'He's your father.'

'Yes, but, you know, it wasn't right somehow. Anyway, I envied people, people like Harry, who's Jewish so he might feel his allegiances were elsewhere, but he was perfect there in London. He was made for it. I'm half Italian anyway.'

'Is that what makes you restless?'

'I don't know.' Pietro laughed. 'I suppose it's quite improbable, isn't it?'

Dr Simon gave one of her thin smiles and nodded very slightly.

At Dr Simon's suggestion, Pietro kept a note of the better interchanges in a book in his lodgings and looked back at them carefully. There were important things there, he was sure, if only he could puzzle them out.

On other days he felt he had simply wasted his time. He drove slowly back down the Woodstock Road into Oxford and looked at the young students hurrying along the streets on their bicycles or walking along wrapped up in their scarves. Why did students and old people always wear scarves, he wondered. Some of the different colours proclaimed a college allegiance, others were just for show. Even the young people with glasses and piles of books, however, seemed to look quite part of the town. Perhaps because it belonged to no one, then it was impossible for anyone to feel excluded. Presumably the dons looked with distaste at the migrant undergraduates. They were not worth befriending since they would only be there for three years. Yet it must have been difficult for the students, he thought, to decide when they arrived whether they would colonise Oxford and make it theirs for a short time, or whether they would skim over it and acknowledge that history had dispossessed them. The choice was especially hard when ownership of the place presumably entailed knowing all the antique nicknames of the colleges and streets as well as knowing which society, bar or party was to be recommended or gone to at any time. The thought of trying to keep abreast of it all was exhausting. Pietro had been to the required functions in London, but it had hardly been the same. Outside the lecture halls and assembly rooms the identity of the place was dissipated in the commercial town; academic purity lasted only a few footsteps down the pavement of a London street.

To cure his agoraphobia, Dr Simon suggested a simple solution. Pietro was to walk as far as he could from his lodgings before panic set in, then return. The first day he managed one hundred and fifty yards. In succeeding days, safe in the knowledge that he could get at least that far, he was to go a step or two further. By the end of the first week he had made it to Magdalen College where he touched the stonework before heading hurriedly back to his lodgings.

As the weeks went by he found himself inching up the High Street. One evening after work he reached the crossroads at Carfax. He turned and pressed his fearful legs a little further. It was like leaving the earth's atmosphere: he was out, beyond gravity, in a floating world.

He regarded the colleges not by reputation, of which he was in any case ignorant, or by architecture, but by their distance from his house. He believed they helped him on and he was grateful to the early landmark of All Souls, the approach of what a painted notice told him was St John's and the welcome of a neo-Gothic brick institution on the way out of town.

PARIS

ppppppppppppppppppppppppppppppppppppppppppppppppppppppppppppppppppppppppppppppppppppppppp

France 1979

THERE seemed to be a conspiracy among the French to prevent Pietro from understanding them. Shown a French newspaper, he could immediately tell what had happened. Given a French novel, he could not only follow the story but see if the writer was any good. But when they talked, he heard a continuous vowel burble in which it was not possible to say where one word ended and the next began. Some well-known expressions stuck out from the noise, so there would be a long ribbon of sound, then *cinéma*, more uncut ribbon, then *très bien*. There were enough spiky or unmissable words for him to have an idea of what was being said, but never enough for him to understand with a completeness that would have made the conversation worthwhile.

This was the first major failure Pietro had suffered for some time. He had been hopeless at school to begin with, it was true, but by the end he had belatedly come into his own. Hearing Laura talk about books had inspired him to read. He didn't read his first novel by Dickens until the age of twenty-three, but in a way it was more rewarding. He wasn't compelled to understand or enjoy books; if he didn't like them he didn't finish them, and at the age of twenty-six he could see better what Flaubert was driving at than he could have done at the age of fifteen when he

169

first declined to read the set text at school. He liked books of ideas rather than narratives of people's lives. His knowledge was patchy, but passionate in unexpected areas.

He stayed in a small hotel near the Gare du Nord where he was well placed to see the Americanisation of Paris. His nearest café was a burger bar where the waiter wore basketball boots which he called 'les basket'. People fulminated in the press against the corruption of language and the loss of culture, but Pietro was quite glad because each English word that took root in the vocabulary would reappear as a beacon in the otherwise incomprehensible Parisian burble. They had a way of trying to throw him even with their anglicisms: they liked to chuck in an extra 't', so the food was processed in a mixter, and someone at dinner asked him if he played squatsh.

HIS eye was caught by the giant advertisements in the Métro. Young women caught in a moment of lively hesitation on a windswept street, their skirts billowing to reveal their legs – three metres long on the hoarding, against a cream tiled wall with a tunnel in the background. Children, brightly dressed, leaping hugely above the platform, their health assured by some vital milk derivative. Films from which the dramatic stills were as large as a cinema screen and on which the lettering, across an empty track, was made bold and powerful. His camera fired.

The first time he had plunged into a hole in the pavement he had found a different world: not Paris, but an independent state with its own geography, climate and character. It was as rich and strange as any place he had visited. On the map were names like Barbès-Rochechouart, Solférino, Filles du Calvaire, Réaumur-Sébastopol. Some were imposing, like Châtelet, Nation or Défense, some sinister like Denfert-Rochereau, with its suggestion of hell, some obviously foreign like Wagram or George V, some baroque like Reuilly-Diderot, some weird like Iéna, and some lovely, like Mairie d'Issy, Mairie d'Ivry and the most beautiful of all, Mairie des Lilas.

On Vincennes-Neuilly, the straight east–west line, the

modern wagons rolled on their rubber wheels, chasing each other across the city with an eyeblink between them, their wire conductor brushes circling briskly against the charged rail. On other lines, such as Porte d'Orléans-Porte de Clignancourt, they still had rattling wagons on which the doors had to be opened by hand. Some of the stock that clanked away to remote areas like Eglise de Pantin looked as though it might have transported the wounded back from Verdun.

In the lettering of the names, the look of them on the maps in the carriages and the sound of them as Pietro repeated them wonderingly in his head, was a universe as complex as a microelectronic circuit, yet in its subterranean way as grand as a painting by Géricault. It bore no relation to Paris itself, to the streets he walked when he left the Métro. These were just variations on the theme laid down by Baron Haussmann: carved boulevards and squares, with narrow streets interlinking, the architecture of Napoleon III dominant. The Métro was its own world, more interesting because of the character of other places to which the names of its stations gave it access.

Rather than merely wonder at it uninformed, Pietro sought out articles and books. He became an expert in the subterranean country. From the aerial platform of Barbès-Rochechouart he peered down at the hectic street scene below, a big junction of the Boulevard de la Chapelle, where Zola had set his novel *L'Assommoir*. One founder was Armand Barbès, a revolutionary politician born in Guadeloupe, whose death sentence was commuted to imprisonment by the intercession of Victor Hugo. He was exiled on Belle Ile, a Breton island not unlike Cornwall, and later in Holland. The other was the Abbess Marguerite de Rochechouart, a redoubtable leader of the Abbey of Montmartre in the early eighteenth century. The station had seen the start of the worst ever Métro disaster. A carriage which had caught fire was sent back to the terminus in the belief that the flames had been extinguished. But the fire began again, asphyxiating eighty people in the station at Couronnes. Barbès-Rochechouart was also the site of one of the first acts of open armed resistance against the German occupation, when a Colonel Fabien (also known as Frédo) shot Alfonse Moser, a German officer, on 21 August 1941. Fabien, who blew himself and several other people up when wiring a mine near Mulhouse in 1944, was rewarded with his own Métro station: Colonel Fabien, which replaced the former name of Combat, which had been given because it was the scene of open-air fights in the eighteenth century between dogs, wild boar and sometimes tigers.

Combat fell victim to superior claims. Others became un-stations as history dictated: on the outbreak of war in 1914 Berlin became Liège, and Allemagne became Jaurès in honour of the great socialist leader assassinated by the incredibly named Raoul Villain. Jaurès had, in Pietro's view, the particular honour of being a *correspondance* with three other lines. To have a station named after you was one thing, but a triple *correspondance* . . .

He was not much interested in the trains themselves, only in the human dramas they joined. The haphazard, cruel nature of history was exactly reproduced in the station names. Here was no order of merit, but pure chance. Eleven French writers were honoured, but they did not include Molière, Racine, Balzac, Verlaine, Rimbaud or Baudelaire. They did include Edgar Quinet, author of the 1833 prose poem 'Alias verus', and the itinerant nineteenth-century Gascon poet Jasmin. No Flaubert. No Proust, though he had even lived on the boulevard named after the architect of Paris.

There was an impressive martial air in the Métro too. Partly this came from the names like Stalingrad, Austerlitz, Wagram, but also from the printed instructions regarding reserved seats. '1. Aux mutilés de guerre. 2. Aux aveugles civils.' Pietro could not help wondering how many war-wounded were left from 1914–18, and how in any event they could prove in an argument with an injured civilian fighting for the same seat that their wound had been sustained under fire. He was not aware that France had participated in later wars, apart from the Resistance movement. He was therefore surprised to read in a battered book he found in a second-hand barrow an entry on Bir Hakeim, a station whose name had caught his eye: 'This was a fortress in Libya where the French troops resisted heroically under General Koenig for almost three weeks against the tanks of Rommel's Afrika Corps in 1942. Their action permitted the British to retreat to El Alamein.' Pietro knew what had happened in Italy, but hadn't otherwise interested himself in the events of the war. What he knew came from his father. He had had the vague impression that the French had been on the other side. He also remembered that El Alamein had been the scene of a British victory. Perhaps that had been later. It was perplexing.

The Métro's attitude to foreign people and places showed the same element of chance as in its honouring of French writers. As well as the fort at Bir Hakeim, the country of Argentina and the little town of Campo Formio near Venice were selected. From all of human history the seven people chosen from 'abroad' were three revolutionary leaders, Bolivar, Garibaldi and the Greek Botzaris; one artist, Michelangelo; one American, Franklin D. Roosevelt, author of the New Deal (*Nouvelle Donne*); one king, George V; and an outdoor-concert sponsor, Lord Ranelagh. In his Chelsea garden the lord had installed a bandstand for daily public recitals. In 1772 the governor of the Château de la Muette gave permission for a similar building to be erected on the lawn of the castle, then just outside Paris to the west. It found favour with the court and was increased in size in 1779. Towards the middle of the nineteenth century, it disappeared. The area was absorbed into Paris, next to the noisy streets of Passy, whose thermal baths and rustic beauty once attracted Balzac, Lamartine and Victor Hugo. The Métro station still bears the name of Lord Ranelagh, unpronounceable even to the English.

'Reprenez votre billet' warned signs just after the barrier, but it was a point of pride among Parisians to drop them at once, causing drifts of yellow beneath the hurrying feet. Later would come the notice 'Au delà de cette limite votre billet n'est plus valide', with its implications that seemed to go beyond transport to something more sinister. The new carriages gave a gratifying pneumatic belch as the doors closed, then a jerk which could send unwary tourists flying down the carriage. Young men always raised the lever on the door while the train was still moving, taking advantage of the power-assisted mechanism to be on the platform before the train had stopped. Even on the cattle trucks in the dingiest, most strangely named stations, dark and deserted at unfashionable times of day, the trains offered first-class carriages in a demonstration of liberté if not égalité. In the rush hours, better named *heures d'affluence*, there was also fraternité: big men embraced smaller people of either sex who trembled on the threshold as the doors began to close; they wrapped their arms around them and brought them into the pack of coats and jammed bodies.

But much more than the street-wisdom of the Métro user, and almost as much as the names of the places, it was the smell that intoxicated him. From the moment he first inhaled it (Argentine, *direction* Château de Vincennes) he knew it would summon this infernal world to him with all its grief and history at the merest sniff. It was a mystery. It was not food or cleaning fluid, metal, or anything identifiably mechanical; nor did it vary from station to station or with the different rolling stock. There was something of rubber in it, perhaps, of soot . . . he couldn't say.

He wrote to a man whose name he found in a book about the Métro to ask him what he thought. He did not know. 'However,' he replied, 'I can tell you that an attempt was made just before the Second World War to deodorise the station of Châtelet-les Halles using a lemon-scented disinfectant. An earlier attempt was made at Père Lachaise in 1907, but since the practice did not become widespread, we have to assume that this was not a success either.'

A vegetable market and a cemetery . . . perhaps these two stations had special reasons for smelling, Pietro thought. He was glad in any event that the scheme had not worked. The smell was inimitable. He loved it, and could not be indifferent to any people for whom it must have brought powerful messages of nostalgia.

★

'You can't be serious!' said Harry when he telephoned him in London. 'You go to the most beautiful city with the most beautiful women in Europe, and you spend the whole time in the underground railway!'

It was the sort of thing that sometimes made him despair of Pietro.

'Not the whole time,' said Pietro. 'I went up in a plane too.'

He went to photograph a director of the Ariane space project. He lived in Neuilly, just west of Paris, and welcomed Pietro with a firm handshake and the clear-eyed look of a man to whom the expression 'hangover' would be unfamiliar. With his sandy hair and open manner, he seemed a little American.

They talked for some time about the project so that Pietro could have an idea what his subject did and what the whole story was about. He had several other people he was supposed to photograph as well, but the magazine had told him that this was the man to give him the background.

Pietro's father had given him a question to ask, though it wasn't one Pietro felt he could introduce straight away into the conversation. His father, still involved with a personal archaeology of English, wanted to know whether Ariane would use the American term 'astronaut' or the Russian, 'cosmonaut'. The first, he explained to Pietro, would signify from its root 'star sailor', the second 'world sailor', though admittedly the word 'cosmos' now covered a greater space than the Greeks had first intended. So would they have star sailors or world sailors? To Raymond Russell, and perhaps two or three other people in the world, this was the principal question about the project.

Pietro asked about finance and the perils of manned flight, firing the camera as he did so. He liked to find an angle that brought out the structure of a face and was prepared to spend hours doing so if the assignment permitted; with some newspapers it was just a question of making sure the pictures were light enough and getting the film back on time.

He hadn't thought much about space flight before. He had a

vague picture of a capsule full of baffling instruments, crackling messages from mission control, and tumbling, weightless orbit. It was a job for the brain dead, he assumed, people with zero anxiety levels who could act as efficiently and inhumanly in the unnatural circumstances as a trained ape.

The pictures didn't seem to go well. The director had a bland face which Pietro found hard to set up and frame in an interesting way. He felt a lack of mutual sympathy. Each was professional and polite, but they seemed to be at cross-purposes.

Pietro said, 'I suppose you couldn't let me go up and take some pictures from the air? Maybe if we could get a plane going fast enough I could give some impression of what the earth looks like as you leave it.'

It took a week to arrange with the public relations people, but the director was not only passionate about publicising his project, he felt Pietro hadn't understood much about flight. The pictures he would take from a plane would have no relevance to the restricted view of an astronaut travelling at speed, but if he were to go high enough he might get some idea of the dimensions of the earth's atmosphere and of the sights beyond it.

They drove to a French air force base and Pietro was given a day's instruction in safety. He began to wonder what he had taken on and felt twinges of panic. The pilot laughingly assured him that they wouldn't be taking a civilian foreign photographer on anything dangerous; on the contrary, they were merely being extra cautious. Pietro felt he had hardly room for manœuvre when they set off. With oxygen and parachutes as well as his camera equipment, he felt it was going to be difficult to swivel around enough to take good pictures. The plane was a training version of a supersonic fighter, underpowered and roomy, with a cockpit full of computerised double-fail-safe lights and circuitry. Pietro felt the seat kick into the small of his back as the pilot, who spoke to him in English through his earpiece, opened the throttle on the runway.

Above the circular tracery of Paris he began to feel calmer, and as they headed west for Brittany and the sea there was a sense of creeping exhilaration. Pietro fitted his lenses and talked to the pilot. It was somehow reassuring to be so close and to be able to see exactly what he was doing. When Pietro gave the word, they went into a steep climb, the jet engines driving them up through the thinning air. Sickly, Pietro fired the camera at the receding earth.

For an hour they flew and Pietro wound in film after film. They reached heights he didn't think possible in a small aeroplane, where he could see the curvature of the earth. When they landed Pietro shook the pilot's hand and embraced him. He felt they had done something extraordinary together. The pilot smiled and winked at him without giving the impression that he had been much excited.

Pietro wound up his business in Paris and returned to London. He took the films to his usual darkroom in Waterloo where they didn't mind his supervising the development and printing. The images that emerged, as if by some slow alchemy, were alarming. The world seemed turned on its head, dislocated. Then, in later films, the shapes were more ordered and there was a better perspective. The different bands of colour that shot round the rim of the pictures made the earth look bizarre, like Saturn with its rings.

QUEZALTENANGO

Guatemala 1974

ROM Watsonville he drove south and reached Los Angeles in the evening. The plan had been to drive through the whole of central America to Panama City. He saw no reason why he should not stick to it.

He pulled off the Pacific Coast Highway at the petrol station at the foot of Sunset Boulevard. He got out of the car and walked stiffly around the forecourt. Just up the road was a sign that said 'Castellammare'.

He turned the name over in his head. Castellammare. As he paid for the petrol he asked the attendant what it meant. 'Castellammare Drive,' he said. 'It's the name of a street.'

The weather was soft and warm, a perpetual spring. Across the highway the Pacific lay sluggishly against the coast. Someone had done a good job of naming it. He drove onwards, his exhausted vision beginning to blur. He was on the Santa Monica Fwy, according to the overhead signs. Right Lane MUST Turn Right. His head ached as he sank his foot once more on the accelerator. The freeway and the city behind it took on a fuzzy, unreal look. Then he saw things with sudden clarity. The white rivets that held each white letter on the green-backed sign: Sepulveda Blvd. Sepulveda, Sepulveda. Right Lane MUST Turn Right.

In San Francisco he had found difficulty in sleeping and once, when he had smoked too much marijuana, he had experienced a feeling of dislocation. A doctor had prescribed some tranquillisers and he had thought little more about it. He was starting to lose a sense of his own identity.

IN the heat of the Mexican nights he smoked nothing and declined the magic mushrooms people offered him. He drank beer and looked at the stars. Towards midnight he would swallow one of the yellow pills and go inside to sleep.

He rose early in the morning so he could drive a hundred miles or so before it grew too hot. The car, an old Ford they had bought second-hand, rattled down the highway at a steady 70 m.p.h., only overheating in the towns. It took him two days to reach Mexico City. He felt sick and took to his bed in the hotel with a bottle of Immodium. He stayed for three days but felt no better. When he went for a walk his legs felt weak. He paid the bill and drove fast back towards the coast, hoping a loss of altitude would help. He wondered what she was doing. Perhaps she was listening to the same record back in the hills of Vermont. He thought of her driving down to the lake to swim and he imagined the taciturn Steve nodding as he slipped his arm round her shoulders. He didn't stop driving.

Somewhere down near the coast, past Oaxaca with its flower-filled courtyards glimpsed through stone arches, he began to feel lonely. The poor adobe houses, the infrequent towns and coarse landscape beneath the mountains no longer seemed to be full of opportunity or surprise. He wanted to talk to someone, to be called by his name.

That night he awoke in a sweat, thinking he was back in New York. He sat upright in bed, trembling, and it took him some time to shake off the dream. He walked round the hotel room, touching the furniture, the white cotton curtains, the slatted shutters, in an effort to reassure himself of his physical whereabouts. He poured a warm beer and spent some time staring at the label on the bottle. Corona Extra La Cerveza Mas Fina. There was some golden heraldic animal to the left of the blue lettering. He couldn't stop his hand from shaking.

There was another full day's driving, and on the morning of the third day the border with Guatemala came as a relief. By this time he had it in his head to keep on driving, as far as he could go. The immigration officer, more accurately a soldier with a rifle slung round his neck, asked him where he was from. The soldier had never heard of London and looked at him with blank eyes. It took an hour of paperwork before he was convinced that he was not importing the vehicle. He had been told that Lake Atitlan was a popular destination for American tourists and pointed the car in the direction of Guatemala City where he would rejoin the Pan-American highway. Quite early he took a wrong turning and found himself climbing. It had begun to rain. The burned brown of the hillsides was relieved in places by pale patches of planted maize; in the valleys the ground was pitted from the harshness of the summer drought. The Ford began to wheeze as he climbed. Remembering what he had been told about the continuing guerrilla war in the Indian villages of the north, he began to feel uneasy. He didn't really know where he was; he had crossed the border on the southern coast, it was true, but even there the presence of the military was inescapable. Every mile or so were road signs, saying 'Alto', Stop, relics of checkpoints from troubled days. They were the most successful army in Central America: critics of successive governments had been wiped out either in loud massacres and shrieking torture or in the silent way that gave birth to the soft-footed term, *los disaperecidos*.

The Ford was starting to make odd metallic noises, yet its temperature showed barely above normal. Finally, on a hillside bend, it made a loud grinding sound and the engine gave out. He pulled the freewheeling car over to the side of the road and clambered out into the rain. He lifted the bonnet but didn't know what he was looking for. The points were dry, the radiator was sealed. The usual amateur checks yielded nothing. He assumed the oil pump or big end had given up.

He walked for five miles with his suitcase. The landscape began to take on a surreal quality under the shifting curtains of rain. He came at last to a village where he sat down under the leaky awning of a roadside café. The first thing he had to do was to change as much money as he could afford. He showed his only hundred-dollar bill to a thin, yellow-skinned waiter who smiled and took him by the arm. They went into the café and downstairs to a small, airless room that smelt of frying and rank sweat. A fat woman drinking coffee took the bill and, after a rapid exchange with the still grinning waiter, handed him 140 Guatemalan quetzales.

In a mixture of Italian, Spanish, simplified English and creative gesturing, he extracted from the waiter the news that he could get something called a *camioneta* to a place named Quezaltenango, which was in the mountains, on the side of a lake. The waiter spoke fondly of it, but he, confused by the similarity between the currency and the name of the place, thought for some time he was asking him for more money. He suddenly thought of his father. If he ever got to this place he would send him a postcard for his old army friend who hadn't found a 'Q' in Yorkshire.

It was late afternoon when the *camioneta* arrived in the village. It was an old American school bus, and he had visions of high-school children chattering about their math test or their spelling bee as they rode to school. Since it had presumably been bought from one of the southern States, perhaps it had even been used in the derided 'bussing' programme that ferried children round town to force an equal ethnic mix on socially disparate areas.

The unpadded seats, designed for children, were squeezed close together. The conductor, a vigorous youth of no more than sixteen, was in perpetual motion, throwing the baggage of new passengers on to the roof, collecting money and shouting orders down the bus. Where normally he would have delighted in the strangeness of it, he found the bus journey disturbing. In his apprehension or perception of this place there was something like fear. He began to recognise that it came not from the country but from inside his head.

At one point they were required to leave the bus while a group of soldiers searched them. The male passengers had to lean against the side of the bus while big hands ran along their ribs and inner thighs. If their legs were not well enough spread, a helping boot was cracked into the ankle. He had no idea why they were being searched. Presumably a military state was continually at war with its citizens. From the bored faces of the soldiers, however, it looked more like a routine show of force.

Quezaltenango turned out to be a sedate, pompous town with an air of municipal permanence conferred by the grey stone buildings of the plaza. The neoclassical banks and official buildings looked politely at each other across the square. He found a room in a white plastered building in the Spanish colonial style. From his window he could see the brown mountains beneath the cloud. It was too late for a garage that night so he went in search of food. In a restaurant that seemed well patronised he ate chicken stew and tortillas, washed down with Cabro beer. He read a book between courses, determined not to brood. He decided he would get the car fixed, finish the journey to Panama City and fly back to New York. Although he had left his job, he still had a room in an apartment in the Village, and he had friends there. It would be all right. He kept his mind firmly away from the subject of Laura. Occasionally as he sat in the restaurant, watching the rotation of the greasy ceiling fan, hearing the excited conversations of his fellow diners, he found his mind wandering, as her brown-eyed smile and searching hands appeared in his memory. He shut them out with a slavish application. He felt that if he pondered them his head would explode. Before he left the restaurant he bought a bottle of a spirit called Quezalteca he had seen other people drinking.

On his way back to the hotel he was accosted by several children asking for money or food. He gave some small change to an old man smelling of drink who lurched at him from a doorway, and hurried on, clutching his own bottle. Back in his room he lay on the bed and poured himself half a toothglass of liquor. He put away the novel he had been reading at dinner and took from his case a history of Central America he had bought in San Diego.

His head was half filled with episodes of the country's history when he fell asleep. The imaginative role of the Dulles family and the intervention of the CIA to make sure Guatemala would remain a vast factory for the United Fruit Company; the extermination of the Indians by the Spanish conquistadors; the cruelty, murder and tortures of the successive 'strong men' who had presided over the place . . . These odd facts were like bricks that kept his mind temporarily dammed.

In the small hours of the morning, at about four o'clock, the dam burst and he awoke. Physically the symptoms were so slight as to be unnoticeable. His blood pressure had risen to a point where only a very litigation-conscious American doctor might have worried. His pulse rate had gone up from its usual sixty-five but only to a still reasonable eighty. His heartbeat was lumpish against the sternum, but not dangerous. There was a light sweat on the scalp, which was strange in the suddenly cold night. There was no rash, no broken bones, no bleeding, no symptom that would have given any doctor pause.

What was happening inside him was indescribable. When he later tried to find words for it, he could reach only for analogies, which seemed inappropriate. After he had awoken he continued to keep on waking up. It was as if having hit the normal level of morning consciousness, he exceeded it by the same distance of wakefulness again. Then again. By this time he was pacing round the room in an effort to shut off the sensations that were coming at him. He was seeing five times as much as normal, five times more clearly; he was hearing each whisper of wind, each bare footfall on the wooden boards with an aggressive clarity. More than the high definition, it was the speed with which everything was being sensed that was alarming.

In addition to this overload he felt unsure of his physical reality. He touched the things in the room in rapid succession, in the same way he had done in Mexico, but much faster. If he could convince himself, he thought, that the grain of the wooden table or the weave of the curtains was truly tangible, then he could somehow hold on.

He was also uncertain where he was. Bits of the Guatemalan history he had been reading came up through the channels of his memory. As they arrived in his already overcrowded brain he couldn't distinguish between history that had happened to other people long ago and the current experience of his own mind. At some moments, he felt as if he were an Indian peasant or a Spanish soldier. Sepulveda. MUST Turn Right.

He knelt on the floor and held his head in his hands, but he couldn't stop what was happening inside it. He went over to the wall mirror to try to reassure himself of his physical reality – that old familiar face, the hair with its last touch of red, the dark eyebrows, the eyes his mother had loved. But his skin looked translucent, like the wax overlay of a medical model that demonstrates the working of the nerves and arteries. He looked at himself and pleaded for the familiar picture to return. Nothing was there.

Unable to deal with the sensation, he stumbled on some instinctive stopgap. He took the bottle of Quezalteca and drank straight off what remained. With it he swallowed four of the yellow pills given to him by the doctor in California. There was a momentary respite as the liquor slowed his system. It was the first time since he had woken up that he was able to think. It hadn't occurred to him until this moment that there might be something mentally wrong with him; so powerfully physical were the symptoms that he assumed they had their origin in some violent bodily disease.

The relief was short-lived. As the effect of alcohol began to ebb, he felt that all the certainties and previously dependable facts of existence were in question. He didn't know where he was, who he was, or what he was. With an effort of will he held on to the wooden leg of the bed and pressed his face against the counterpane.

Let them exist, he prayed, let me live.

As the panic mounted in him he thought that when the last

thread that connected him to reality was worn away, he would go into an endless free fall. If he failed to hold on to himself, then he was going to go into meltdown, like a China syndrome of the personality.

THE brand-named Diazepam, manufactured in the tranquil country of Switzerland, was enough to knock out a person in a normal state of mind. It didn't make him sleepy, but it reduced the panic to controllable proportions.

It was dawn when he released the leg of the bed he had clasped to himself for the last half-hour and lifted his head from the covers. He was shaking like a leaf in an autumn storm as he walked slowly to the window.

It was arctically cold in the mountain air. He put on two spare shirts and a sweater, which were all he had. He pulled open the shutters and stepped on to the balcony.

He looked out across the lake to the brown hills, and then down at the sleeping town where he could hear a stray dog barking. He leant his damp, exhausted head against the white plastered wall. Good morning, Guatemala.

ROME

Italy 1978

I N the Protestant cemetery, overshadowed by a large pyramid, is a modest white tombstone beneath which is buried a stablekeeper's son from Finsbury, north London. It is dated Feb. 24th 1821 and has a carved lyre towards the top. The ground is covered with grass on which grows a riotous creeper. The trees between this modest white grave and the giant pyramid are semi-tropical. It is intensely hot. The cemetery, by its nature, is filled with foreigners, people from the northern lands of the Reformation who have ended their days exiled by choice or accident in this southern imperial city. This particular grave contains, in the words of the inscription, 'all that was mortal of a young English poet', John Keats, who a year and a half before his death, with no relevant training and little formal education, wrote, at the age of twenty-three and in the space of three weeks, four of the greatest lyric poems in English.

It is hard to sense from looking at the hot Roman grass what sudden comet must have flared that spring in north London, where he was living with his friend Charles Brown. Nothing, certainly, could have been done without hard apprenticeship; nothing without the reading and investigation of what others had written; but, with all the willed preparation, the carefully

186

settled domestic life and the encouragement of friends, there was something freakish in that cold burst of genius.

When Keats returned from the garden one morning in April he thrust some scraps of paper behind a row of books on a shelf to save them from the maid's over-zealous tidying. When his friend Brown asked him what they were, he said they were nothing. When Keats was out of the room, Brown fished them out and found that they in fact contained the 'Ode to a Nightingale', which Keats had written that morning beneath a plum tree in the garden. The previous day the poem had not existed.

Hampstead in those days was a long way from what was known as London. It was surrounded by fields and streams. A rainy stagecoach ride back from town produced a startling fever in the poet. Even at the height of that summer in 1819 he had already begun to cough with the tuberculosis that would shortly kill him.

The Roman room in which he died is much visited by tourists, particularly Americans. The visitors' book in the small apartment above the Spanish Steps contains many names written in the neat cursive handwriting of the American high school, expressing a sense of wonder or elation at what the room contains. 'A great experience', according to a woman from New Brunswick. 'You can feel him here', according to another from Santa Barbara. 'Well worth traveling to see', says a man from Sioux Falls, South Dakota. Rome with its citadels and seven hills is joined to the motels and luncheonettes of the Midwest by a dead twenty-five-year-old from Georgian London.

It is very quiet. On the wall is a picture of Keats sketched on his deathbed by his friend Joseph Severn who nursed him. The handwriting at the bottom says: '28 Janry 3 o'clock mng. Drawn to keep me awake, a deadly sweat was on him all this night'. It is all too easy to feel the presence of the man, the sight and smell of the night-sweat throughout the hot small hours with Severn nodding at the bedside. Although the room has been repainted, the original fireplace remains. It was here that Severn used to warm up meals he had been to fetch from the Osteria della Lepre in the nearby via dei Condotti: the restaurant is now part of the giant premises of an opulent jeweller called Bulgari.

Keats had come to Rome for the sake of a warm climate and managed to prolong his life by a few months. He had had little reason to travel before. Despite being ebulliently energetic – to the extent that his schoolmasters thought he would make a name for himself as a soldier – he found worlds open to him not through travel but through the cut pages of books. He did, it's true, spend a long time in the Isle of Wight, but that was so he could more quietly imagine the mythical landscape of *Endymion*. The exile and the poem over, he could begin his work in earnest; and even to Regency London, the Isle of Wight was not a daunting voyage.

Outside the death room, the Roman traffic roars. The shop next door, which sells shirts and socks, is called Byron. It is a loud, hot city and the small Cockney youth, weakened and dying, must have felt a long way from London. He wrote his own epitaph, 'Here lies one whose name was writ in water', to express the fear that his memory would evaporate beneath the Italian sky. Rome and Finsbury are twinned in the shade of a pyramid. Day after day it is burning hot in the Protestant cemetery and the trees are not those that grew along the muddy lanes that led from Edmonton.

When he left England to die in 1819 Keats hadn't the strength to write. He did revise a poem, however, as he lay in his bunk on the boat bound for the south. It was a sonnet beginning 'Bright star, would I were stedfast as thou art'. The poem, the last he completed, doesn't dwell on the sadness of exile, although it does take a detached view of the world, seeing it from above, from a star's point of view.

What Keats was concerned with at that point was not a place but a person. He would like to be as steadfast as the bright star, he said, but not alone, not a 'sleepless Eremite'. No; while sharing that fixity with the star, he wanted to be with another – to lie with his head pillowed for ever on his 'fair love's ripening breast'. The star may watch above as the waters of the earth wash the shores of the continents: the poet must be with his love – 'and so live ever – or else swoon to death'.

In the faces of Italian people Pietro saw the features of his mother. She had seemed exotic and unique to him as a child with her black hair and slightly accented English. He didn't like seeing all these people who were recognisably of the same kind; they seemed to threaten her uniqueness. Many had similar colouring, reminiscent gestures, or the same agile movement and sudden laughter. Yet he found also in this country, from Milan with its fashion-conscious women to the rough surliness of the south, that he was on a quest. If one woman should turn her face and prove to be Francesca, or her double, he might forgive her the trickery and the anguish it would cause him because it would show that in some way she was alive, or that she had lived. The beauty of Italian women was held by experts – Italian men in other words – to be a recent phenomenon. After the war the men had eyes only for the young American women who arrived by the boatload to study or sightsee in Perugia, Rome and Florence. Then suddenly, in the late 1950s, a spectacular change came over Italian women: their legs grew longer, their brows lost the last trace of autochthonous heaviness; they bloomed and flourished and became the most beautiful women in the world. So the story went.

Pietro's affection for Italy had not wavered since his first discovery of its actual position on the map. He succeeded in continuing to see it in double vision: the way it was and the way he had pictured it from his mother's description to him as a child. He liked the affability and flaring honesty of the people; and he liked the way the Moto Guzzis roared round the walled towns of Tuscany, the way hot modern engineering could coexist with the cool civilisations of Rome and the Renaissance. He could converse with the people who, unlike the French, seemed anxious to make comprehension as easy as possible. He had spoken Italian for too long still to be charmed by quixotically musical words like *ragazza*, but was still pleasantly surprised to find that the bat that kept him awake in an Umbrian farmhouse one night was a *pipistrello*. When he notified the police of his three-month visit, as the law obliged him, he saw the sloth and dishonesty of the public institutions. It took him three days with visits to four different departments to acquire the single document. He was obliged to produce eight passport photographs, the officer denying the existence of the first four. He was charged twice the regulation sum but was glad to end the procedure at any price.

In Keats's death room Pietro was trapped by his ignorance of the poet and thus of what he wanted to photograph. The whitewashed house in Hampstead had been easy enough, but this was different. There was something threatening in the air, the feeling generated by a man whose work had been dedicated to making time stand still at a particular moment and had succeeded in an unforeseen way, by dying.

The picture he eventually took could have been of any young Englishman's lodgings in a hot foreign capital, *circa* 1820. Perhaps because of this ordinariness, it was considered successful.

SORRENTO

Italy 1958

FRANCESCA'S hand lay flat on the table and the sun illuminated the lateral folds on the knuckles, the white half-moons at the base of the nails, even the minute diamond webs that make up the surface of the skin. Pietro reached out his hand to hers and twisted the gold ring on her finger. She smiled at him and laid her right hand on top of his.

The tablecloth was white linen. Between them was a glass jar of olive oil and one of vinegar in a silver holder with a curlicued grip. All of the table was in the light, a bright, even sunshine that washed over the red tiled floor and lay on the idle surface of the Mediterranean sea below them.

'Are you too hot?' said Francesca.

Pietro shook his head.

'What do you want to eat? Look, you can have spaghetti or soup and they've got fish and chicken and all sorts of things.'

'Macaroni cheese.'

'I don't think they have that. But you could have risotto.'

Pietro took his hand from his mother's to look at the scrolled print on the menu. It opened up like a book. There were two or three pages, and then a list of wines. It was hard to read some of the longer words; they hadn't featured in his Italian conversations with Francesca.

There was an old couple sitting by the cash desk, well inside the restaurant, in the shade. No one else was there. Perhaps it was still a little early, but Pietro had had that pallor only food could take away. The waiter, a tall, grey-haired man of resolute dignity, stood beside the table.

'Now what do you think?' said Francesca. 'The risotto? Then maybe chicken? You like chicken, don't you?'

Pietro nodded and smiled, an uncertain lifting of half his mouth, which, as Francesca described the roast chicken and how good it would taste, developed into a full and trusting illumination of his face. She asked the waiter to tell him what the food would be like.

He explained how they would make the risotto specially. He transferred the poised pen from his left hand to the right, where he clasped it against his pad. With his other hand he was then free to imitate the ladling in of the stock and to make his fingers explode like a star at the moment he mimed the first taste of the risotto. Pietro watched with puzzled eyes.

'And what would you like with the chicken?' the waiter asked. 'You like some salad?'

Pietro shook his head from side to side.

Francesca said, 'I think some potatoes. Some fried potatoes. Can you do that? And maybe some peas?'

Francesca ordered for herself and the waiter swept the menus away from them.

Pietro said, 'When you were young did you come to a place like this every day for lunch?'

'Oh no. We used to take something to school. Bread and ham, usually. On Sundays we often used to go out to a restaurant. Nonno would take all the family.'

'Every Sunday?'

'Not every Sunday, but very often.'

'And what did you have then?'

'Oh, lots of things. We often had fish. And I used to like veal. That was delicious. There was one restaurant we would go to where they made osso bucco, which is a bone of veal, which has jelly in the middle.'

'Jelly! That sounds horrible.'

'Not that kind of jelly. It's the jelly from the bone itself. It was a special treat.'

Pietro put his hand out to Francesca again and began to twist the ring. 'Mummy,' he said.

'Yes?'

'What was it like being in Italy?'

Francesca smiled. 'I don't know where to begin. It was lovely. I didn't think of it as anything special, it was just where we lived.'

The waiter brought some bean soup for Francesca and the risotto for Pietro. He put down a white bowl first, then took the lid from a steaming dish. There was a daunting mound of rice, which was disappointingly uniform in colour. He transferred some into Pietro's bowl, and webs of cheese clung to the spoon as he raised it once more to the dish.

Francesca poured some white wine from a small jug into Pietro's glass, then filled it with water. Another two tables in the restaurant were now taken, but it was still peaceful in their corner, overlooking the sea.

'What did you think of Daddy when you first met him?'

Francesca laughed. 'All these questions, mister. I thought he was a kind man. And he was very brave.'

'Because he'd been fighting in the war?'

'That's right. And he'd been hurt, but he didn't say anything about it.'

'And did you like him straight away?'

'I think so, yes. I was only nineteen. My aunt asked me to take up a tray of coffee to the English soldier. I was a bit frightened. I thought he might be like an animal that's been hurt when it's caught in a trap. But he was so gentle. He didn't want me to go, he wanted me to stay and teach him Italian.'

'You weren't frightened any more?'

'Not after that, no.'

'If you hadn't met Daddy would you have married an Italian man?'

'I suppose so. I don't know. Now leave some room for the chicken, won't you?'

Pietro nodded and put down his spoon. He refused to take extra cushions on his chair, so his head was always close to the table. He looked up at his mother's face, which had its customary expression of smiling solicitude. Her black hair was pulled back a little from her face, so he could see the corner of her jaw, beneath her white ear.

The waiter brought the chicken, ready served on to a plate. The peas came threaded with onion and had pieces of bacon at intervals among the green. Francesca had a grilled mullet, which let off a burst of vapour as she folded the white flesh back off the bone. Pietro began to saw at the chicken.

'Is that nice?' she said. 'Have some peas with it if it's too dry.'

He watched as Francesca took the vinegar bottle and plugged the end with her thumb so that only a few drops escaped when she shook it over her salad. Then she took the oil and poured three or four concentric circles gently over the leaves. She looked up in the act of rubbing salt and pepper between her fingers and saw his eyes on her. She laughed. 'This is how you make a salad dressing here.'

Pietro drank from the wine and water in his glass and looked out over the terrace and out to the sea beyond.

He began to dream of how he would one day come back to live here. He would be rich, he would probably be famous too, though it wouldn't matter how or what for. He would be married himself by then and his wife would be Italian. He would have a red sports car, an Alfa Romeo, and he would let his parents come and live here too.

Francesca watched him as he stared out of the window, the chicken now left abandoned. She rested her chin on her hand so that her mouth was concealed as she smiled indulgently at the boy. Anyone watching would therefore have seen only the subsequent expression of her eyes, which was one of fear, as though she doubted her ability to protect him.

The tall waiter took away their plates, scraping the

backbone of Francesca's mullet on to the remains of Pietro's chicken.

'What would you like now?' he asked. He offered them ice cream or fruit or tiramisu.

While he was fetching some chocolate ice cream, Pietro said, 'When are we going back to Nonno and Nonna's?'

'Not for three days. They have some people coming to see them so we're going to spend the time here, just the two of us.'

'And what are we going to do?'

'We're going to go swimming and play on the beach. We're going to go out in a boat and sail. Maybe we'll do some fishing. And then we'll take a bus somewhere. And you can come and look in the shops with me. And if you're very good you can stay up late enough to have dinner too. Would you like that?'

'Oh yes. And are we going to stay with someone here?'

'No. We'll be in a little hotel, something called a *pensione*. It's a nice one which Nonna's friend recommended.'

The waiter reappeared and laid down a glass bowl with two globes of ice cream in front of Pietro. It had a dry, dark taste which took a spoonful or two to get used to. Francesca drank coffee from a tiny white cup.

The room was nearly full. There was a table of young girls with bright voices who called out to a waiter with a moustache, telling him to hurry along with their food. There were some elderly people, the men in suits, the women in dark floral dresses as though they were all afraid of the sunlight. And there were more tourists, a table of English and some Americans.

A long-established resort, Sorrento had not suffered too badly in the aftermath of war. The hotels had begun to fill again, though the town had not yet had its first experiences of large-scale tourism from the United States and northern Europe.

The waiter attending the table of six Americans ran through a brief but obvious sequence of emotions. He began by being sympathetic and interested in their enquiries. They wanted to know what spaghetti alle vongole consisted of, and he was happy to explain. Then, as they discussed among themselves what they would like, his interest turned to boredom. When they began to describe how they wanted to drink not wine, but large cups of coffee with milk, his face showed only contempt.

They looked around them when he had gone back to the kitchen. They seemed irritated by the town.

One woman said, 'I feel like we're living in a place that's not the real world.' She did not sound enchanted. She went on, 'It ought to be *more like* the real world.'

Pietro, who had overheard, said, 'What does she mean, it's not the real world?'

'She means it's not like the place where she lives,' said Francesca.

'But it's real though, isn't it?'

'Yes, it's real,' said Francesca. 'Listen, when we've finished we'll go and find our *pensione* and we'll leave the suitcase. Then you can have a little sleep if you like. Then you'll be able to stay up for dinner tonight. Or if you're not sleepy we can go to the beach.'

The tall waiter brought them a bill. He laid his hand on Pietro's shoulder as Francesca sorted through a pile of banknotes.

'You liked it?' said the waiter. 'It was good. The chicken and the risotto. It was like I said?'

'Yes, thank you,' said Pietro. The waiter ruffled his hair and smiled at Francesca as he gestured the way to the door.

They were struck by the heat outside. Francesca put down the suitcase and pulled an address from her handbag. She went into a shop to ask the way, leaving Pietro to guard the bags. She emerged with a stick of chocolate which she gave him. 'All right, my little boy, it's up this way. It's not far.' She hoisted her bag over her shoulder and picked up the case. She held out her other hand to Pietro, who took hold of it.

They walked up a narrow street over large, pocked paving stones, away from the sea. Francesca asked an old man the way to their *pensione*. He told them to turn right in the Piazza Lauro.

'I'm sorry it's so steep,' said Francesca, as Pietro dragged his feet.

'Look,' he said, 'Piazza Lauro.'

As they continued uphill they passed a magnificent sign in which the iron was wrought like arthritic fingers to read 'Pasticceria' and hammered into a peeling pink wall on the corner of a street. Under their feet the pavements were damp and cool where the cleaning lorry had passed.

TERMINAL 5

1988

THERE was a stagy delay when he pressed the plastic switch in the armrest before the overhead light came on. It had been some time since he had flown and he had forgotten the details of the half-world he had entered. On the back of the seat in front was a hard plastic tray, secured with a rotating clip. The pocket beneath it had a concertinaed elastic top; inside were vinyl-covered safety instructions and an in-flight magazine with an article called 'The Magic of Malaya' by Robert Morley. The engine noise began to mount as the fuel tankers pulled away. The aircraft lurched briefly backwards as the wheels were freed. Reaching up, he twisted the ventilator nozzle and pointed it at his face. Some chemical researchers claim that the sweat of schizophrenic patients is distinguished by the fact that it contains trans-3-methyl-2 hexenoic acid, and that this substance, unscientifically described, is the smell of madness. By the same token, the smell of reconditioned air and jet fuel that filled the cabin from the ventilator was for him and a few others as they strapped themselves in, the distillation of fear.

From that moment on he had lost any connection with the wider, autonomous world and had become an item in transit. The process began in the terminal with the checking-in of the bag with all the personal connections it contained: clothes given as presents at various times that would fit no one else, a framed photograph, a sponge bag with prescribed ointments and pills. Feeling the marble floor of the building beneath his shoes, he walked over to the gate marked Departures and showed his ticket. He had half an hour before the flight was called, but once through the passport control he was already stateless. The only way he could re-establish his identity then was by surrendering to the prescribed journey, and emerging, some hours later, a foreigner.

He drank beer beneath an indoor parasol and looked at the people who worked in this place that was nowhere. At first he felt sorry for them, as he might have felt for people who lived in towns that had become famous to the world for some tragedy, like Aberfan, or Chernobyl. He had to admit, however, that the fat Spanish-looking barman and the cleaner with her turbaned hair and red lips seemed quite happy in their work. Day after day they caught the bus or train from a real street, a proper house, to come and work here. For them it was a particular location, it was work, the office. Presumably this suspended world of clattering departure boards and scarf shops was not an unmapped plain of hell but a place they knew, whose corridors and back entrances they could refind, and pass, and name.

Business, always business, as Paul Coleman had sighed with fake ennui to hide his excitement when they had met three years earlier. On his own now, without Coleman, Pietro echoed the words with genuine remorse.

He crossed the final no man's land of the check-in gate. At Logan airport in Boston you could buy live lobsters at this stage, their claws held together with a rubber band for safer transit. Just the thing you might need. As he set foot on the plane and met the unblinking smile of the stewardess, he noticed the simple construction of the doorway. These plates and rivets would shortly be under unimaginable pressure in a freezing empty world high above this one, he thought, as he trailed his finger over the metal. He folded, then shoved his overcoat into the locker above the seats, squeezing the two parts of the catch together to spring the door open. His was the aisle seat, as far as possible from the sights of the window. He leaned over the empty seat and pulled down the hard floral blind. Then he reached for the plastic switch in the armrest.

Take-off was not frightening. The increased engine noise was reassuring. It was only after ten minutes or so, when all trace of earth was gone and there was no doubt that the aircraft was unsupported in the air that his palms began to slip on the metal ends of the armrests where he had unconsciously clamped them. There were a number of different kinds of crash. The nose might shear off as the plane ran into a mountain. He imagined the sight of the rock, quite clear for a fraction of a second, that would appear to him from the other side of the cinema screen, behind the curtains of the business class section. It would be the last thing he would ever see: perpendicular granite. Or the wings could drop off. This was unlikely, but his fear was not a reasonable thing. The engines raged and died as the plane banked. It had once been explained to him that one engine had to turn faster than the other during this manoeuvre, but it surprised him that no one else seemed to notice. They continued with their crosswords, they talked calmly, they even slept. The most likely way to crash, it always seemed to him, was as a result of turbulence. No man-made structure could survive the buffeting an aircraft took when it unaccountably dropped in the sky. It would disintegrate eventually and it would spiral down into the sea, though he would be dead from decompression before it completed its fall. The calm of his fellow passengers when the plane plummeted was the most miraculous thing of all. Reason and experience might eventually persuade anyone that such turbulence was seldom dangerous, but surely any sentient being, any creature with the meanest instinct of survival, should be alarmed when the machine in which he was travelling at hundreds of miles an hour lurched into sudden freefall. But apparently it was his own reflexive grasp of the armrests that was morbid or misplaced; the normal human response was to fill in another crossword clue.

★

'AMONG those who died in the crash, the largest civilian disaster of its kind, was Pietro Russell, the famous . . .' There was always some problem at this point in the obituary. What he really hoped was that people would feel sorry for the dreadful way he had died and that their sympathy might in some way save him or bring him back to life.

He looked down the aisle where the drinks trolley was making irksomely slow progress towards him. The stewardesses wore royal-blue uniforms and tan tights of a peculiarly dense weave. He ordered a whisky and ginger ale, something he never normally drank, which came with a thin plastic stick and a small packet of dry-roasted peanuts which emitted a sharp little stench when he pulled the packet apart. He took the headset from the pocket of the seat in front, then from its plastic bag, and stuck the ends into his ears. He found himself listening to a rasping, singsong comic with storms of interference, possibly from audience laughter, which the flight guide identified as 'Nutter on the Bus by Jasper Carrott'. It conjured distant worlds. The television in the front room, London, a theatre, a Birmingham bus queue, terra firma. What a way to go down to your death, with so many references, with this thing playing in your ears.

AFTER five weeks in Los Angeles he had forgotten the flight, the fear, pretty much everything. The man came round to shampoo the dog in a white truck with the words 'Critter Cleaner' on the side, but he had no shame about this. It was a good job, it beat pumping gas, and he liked the weather though one day he'd go back to New York, he reckoned, he figured.

Inside, the movie on Channel 13 was *Big* with Tom Hanks. He played a child in a man's body, going wild in a toy store, which seemed like a good enough metaphor for the city and even the country. The kitchen had M & M chocolate beans in a glass jar and a can of spray-on butter, guaranteed dairy-free, and a giant pack of Twiglets and some herbal tea, but no bread. So breakfast was tea and peanuts and a drink from some Mexican bottle in the cupboard that said 'Mezcal con gusano Monte Alban Regional de Oaxaca' and that last word seemed to spell trouble. The label also said, 'with agave worm' – and there it was, a dead worm at the bottom of the bottle. Out in the garden, with the orange tree hanging over the wall from next door, the critter cleaner gave a squeeze to the avocados in the sunshine to see if they were ripe. By the french doors were tall plants that wilted only for a day before reblooming in the permanent spring.

And in five weeks things began to slide. He had lunch in Santa Monica. A Greek or perhaps Armenian café with tabouleh and hummus but also chicken sandwiches and Coke. The girl had even teeth and her legs were tan, though he couldn't see that much because the pants were mid-calf. She was going to play tennis with Gail because her boyfriend was out of town, then maybe she'd go to a movie. But she'd definitely call if she was free. She looked so healthy, her hair was shiny and her eyes were bright. She was drinking diet coke, eating diet burger.

Later he drove up Mulholland and wondered if he needed to buy a hummingbird feeder he had seen advertised. The creatures had been hovering that morning, minute things more like insects than birds, hanging between the orange tree and the oleander. In the end he was heading for the new cinema complex in Century City. He had all night ahead of him and all the next day and all of the day after that, and there was no impediment in view and no end to the even sunshine. He discovered there was an art to pleasure, that gratification requires hard work; and in that art and hard work, the absence of guilt became at first negligible, then imperceptible.

They sat over dinner one day at some new French place in Hollywood, West Hollywood, whatever. The valet parking had taken the car and parked it in back. 'What did you get for dinner?' she asked him. No longer confused by this question, he said, 'The endive salad and the grilled lamb.' The waiter had curly hair cut short up the sides and back, glistening with gel. He dealt deftly with questions about the regional Alsace cuisine, the *choucroute garnie*, the Strasbourg sausage and the Gewurztraminer by Hugel or Hartmann. Afterwards they drove down freeways, boulevards, underpasses, strips and highways, out towards Malibu, the hot wind in the palm trees by the road. The music for some reason was wrong, a Beethoven sonata on the cassette and rap on the radio, but she whistled the right song anyway through her teeth: 'Then she looks in my eyes / It makes me come alive / When she says / "Don't worry, baby, / Everything will turn out all right . . ." ' Nothing would happen between them.

Idling one morning in the kitchen, where the sunlight flagged the floor, he read an article about the Ligurian coast of Italy. The sights and only barely evoked atmosphere in the rudimentary travelogue, all olive oil and gnarled enchantment, seemed overpowering. Through the picture window the Pacific Ocean lay like a boundary that marked how far he was from England; yet being so absent made him also want to be elsewhere.

At other times his body quickened with a sense of loss and possibility. It was still feasible for him to change his life. He was being shown an existence that might have been his if he had made other choices. It was too late, but not quite too late. Without practice or testing, however, what could either choice mean? Where was the value in a blind decision with no appeal permitted?

SITTING in Los Angeles airport, Pietro ordered a gin and tonic at the cocktail bar.

It was over. LAX to LHR, the baggage label changed.

He thought of Hannah, and so powerful was his desire to see her that he could sense the cool touch of her skin, he could almost taste the peculiar fragrance of her neck and hair. He pictured her waiting at the barrier in London and how her body would feel when he wrapped his arms about it: the firm, flat waist, the soft tissue of the upper arm; the long slender legs said by Harry to be the most beautiful in the world. She would be holding James, their third child, now five months old, and he would take him from her. His arms could feel the boy's compact bulk, the weight of the buttocks resting on his own right forearm; he envisaged the toothless, twisted smile; he could smell the sweetness of the baby's hair over the unclosed fontanelle.

Tears stung his eyes as he raised his glass. His body was raging with a sense of mortal urgency. He could not be sure if this was caused by expectation of seeing those he loved, or by the abandonment of America and of the lives he had not led.

AT some strange time of night they crossed the Pole. He saw the VACANT sign on the cabin ahead and struggled from his seat. The light in the cubicle didn't come on until he slid the bolt in the door. There was a smell of liquid soap or perhaps the blue disinfectant that swirled in the metal bowl of the lavatory. He splashed water on his face. Since he could never sleep on planes he thought he might as well be as wakeful as possible. Soon they showed a film in which Michael Caine played an American with an English accent unremarked by the other characters. His daughter was sleeping with a man old enough to be her father. There was a thriller subplot with tropical locations, slow wisecracks and a glimpse of nudity.

When he lifted the plastic blind there was a sense of light outside. They had flown from day to premature night, and through the other side. The sky below was bleached and foaming with fatigue. Someone else's dawn was coming up.

A stewardess presented him with a tray, which was breakfast. His mouth furred by red wine and sleeplessness, he drank the orange juice and held out the thin plastic cup for coffee. His stomach churned with acid tiredness. Under a foil cover was a dense, overdone but still warm omelette, cooked light years ago by some hapless immigrant in San Diego. It would lie in his stomach on the back seat of the taxi on the M4 as it went past Hounslow.

UZES

France 1987

I t was dark when Pietro heard the theatrical whispering at his door. 'Wake up.' Harry's voice was urgent. 'It's half past five.'

This was a terrible way to begin a morning on holiday. Harry was standing fully dressed in the corridor outside. 'Come on,' he said. 'We're supposed to be in this village by six.'

They tumbled down the steps of the old hotel and out into the first signs of dawn. Harry switched on the headlights of the car. The top of the dashboard was crammed with suncream, dark glasses, postcards and other hot-weather holiday clutter that seemed out of place in the chill morning. They shivered in their shorts and sweaters as the engine started. Pietro stowed their picnic in the back. There was a smell of garlic from the terrine, though the soft cheese was as yet unnoticeable. Harry drove out of the square and found the road east towards Mont Ventoux.

They travelled in silence, each doing his best just to survive the unnatural earliness of the hour and the sense of injustice at having to spoil one of the valued few days of vacation.

In the main square at Bédoin there were signs of reluctant life. At the far end of the sandy expanse was an empty bandstand and a couple of locked pizza lorries. At the near end, where the road

205

bent round to the left, were some small cars, Renaults and Fiats, and a short Provençal man emerging from an alleyway with his arms full of baguettes which he began to distribute.

'Is this where we're supposed to be meeting them?' said Harry.

'I think so. Yes, look, there's Patrick.'

A man of about forty, bandy-legged, with black curly hair and a red face, came over and shook their hands. He slapped them on the back and said, 'Fait froid, hein?' several times, then took them over to a car where he introduced them to half a dozen other men, mostly in their twenties. 'Philippe, Jean-Pierre, Martin . . .' Hands were shaken, and one of the men handed Pietro a baguette.

'Alors, vous me suivez maintenant,' said Patrick, and got into his car, a white Simca with yellow fog lamps.

A small convoy trailed out of Bédoin, branching off through the second square and out into the foothills of Mont Ventoux. Pietro chatted to the two men he had been assigned to take. Harry, who could not speak French, looked moodily out of the window where the road began to mount through the scrub on a well-made surface with loose white chippings at the side. When they had climbed above the tree-line and were in sight of the summit one of the Frenchmen pointed excitedly to the side of the road and asked Pietro to stop. They went over to a small memorial stone erected to the memory of Tommy Simpson, a British cyclist who had died on his way to the top. Harry muttered about a similar fate awaiting the rest of them, but the two Frenchmen placed bicycle tyres over the memorial in a gesture of respect.

There were about twenty of them at the top. It was light, but there was no heat from the sun. The men stamped and hit themselves with their arms as they looked out over the whole spread of the Vaucluse down to the south and east.

'Worth coming, just for the view, wasn't it?' said Pietro.

'Listen,' said Harry, 'I'm thirty-seven. I haven't ridden a bicycle since I was twelve. Most of these guys look about twenty, don't they?'

'Yes, I should think that's about what they are. They're the local football team.'

'Thanks for telling me. So what's Patrick doing with them?'

'He's the coach.'

A long, open lorry was allowed on to the final peak by an official who guarded the road. On it were two rows of mountain bikes, which the men eagerly removed and began bouncing up and down on the road, testing for resilience and snap.

'Allez, 'arry.' Patrick took him by the shoulder and presented him with a bike, which Harry rode shakily up and down.

'It's like riding a bicycle,' said Pietro. 'Once you've –'

'La descente. Ça commence!' shouted one, then several, of the young men. There were cries and calls as they set off down the little road from the peak. 'C'est la descente,' Patrick confided. After a hundred yards the leaders suddenly veered off the road and on to an area of loose white chippings like those that lined the route on the way up.

'What's wrong with using the road?' called out Harry.

'Search me,' said Pietro.

The hill funnelled down into a narrow track between the trees. The gradient meant that both brakes had to be applied all the time and neither could be released more than half an inch. Pedalling was unnecessary, but the legs took almost as much strain as the arms as they held themselves rigid on the bike against the steep fall of the ground. The surface was made up of sharp white stones, packed into loose trails through the forest. They jarred the hands and wrists through the juddering of the handlebars. Occasionally a squeezing wheel caused one to fly backwards at eye level. Soon Pietro and Harry found their arms aching with the strain of supporting their weight against the sharply descending bikes. From time to time they lifted themselves from the saddles to ease the soreness, but this only increased the pressure on the wrists. After a particularly steep section they lost sight of the rest of the party and were relieved to find Patrick by the side of the track. He was mending a puncture inflicted by one of the pointed little stones. To their disappointment this took him about a minute and a half.

'When I was a kid,' said Harry, as they reluctantly set off again, 'that used to take me the whole morning.'

'How much would you pay not to be doing this?' said Pietro, the words shaken up by the impact of the bucking machine beneath him. The lever on the gear change had rubbed a patch of skin off his right hand. On the rare occasions that they came to a clearing and could see down the mountain, they appeared barely to have begun the descent.

The sun made spectacular paths and patterns on the forest floor, which passed unappreciated by the bikers. Harry and Pietro could sometimes hear virile noises from ahead as members of the football team encouraged or jeered at one another. Eventually, after an hour and a half, when both had said three or four times that they could not go on, they came into a clearing to find that the others had stopped. They were sitting on two long tree trunks. Some were tending cuts on their legs or making adjustments to their bikes. Most were breaking open their picnics.

'Ah, les anglais!' called one. 'C'est la casse-croûte maintenant!' He made eating gestures by bringing the fingers of his right hand to a point and shoving them towards his mouth.

Pietro and Harry slumped against a fallen tree and opened their plastic carrier bag. The journey down, with the bag stuffed inside Pietro's sweater, had agitated the cheese into ripeness.

'Fait chaud, hein?' said Patrick, grinning. They agreed, as they stripped down to their shirtsleeves.

'Do you know what time it is?' said Harry. 'It's nine o'clock. It feels like we've been up for a week.'

Patrick's nephew, a lanky boy of about eighteen, brought them some wine and they began to relax. 'Hannah's not going to believe this,' said Pietro. 'This is the most ridiculous morning I've ever spent.'

He offered some of the rich cheese to Patrick, who in return held out some processed packets of La Vache qui Rit. In response to some of their sweating Provençal terrine, the goalkeeper offered a vacuum-packed piece of ham with sliced bread.

There were several photographs taken before the first signs of restlessness appeared among the young men. They started to bounce their bikes up and down impatiently and to make wine-affected challenges and bets.

Pietro looked at Harry and grimaced. 'La gloire.'

Harry pulled himself stiffly up. The football team rode slowly round the sun-latticed clearing, over the broken twigs, before one of them let out a yell and pointed his bike down an apparently vertical path. Momentarily emboldened, Harry and Pietro hurried after him.

'Fait chaud, n'est ce pas?' said Patrick's nephew, as he shot past.

AT midday, an hour after they had finished the descent, they found their hands still shaking with exertion as they began their second *demi-pression* in the square at Bédoin. At the same time some sense of achievement began to seep through them. Pietro put his feet up on a spare chair as he engaged one of the team in conversation; Harry put on his sunglasses and rolled his head back to catch the sun.

After the picnic and the wine the standard of riding had declined. Every hundred yards or so there would be someone lying by the track with a bleeding knee. This helped slow down the overall speed of the party, though it did not deter the riders themselves, who thought each cut and graze a sign of endeavour. They had taken the wrong route and, when collapse was near, had had to climb for ten arduous minutes. At last, as they navigated a dense patch of wood, there came the sudden sight of tarmac. They released the brakes and freewheeled on the flat road for a mile into the village.

Most of them hurried off from the square, pausing only for a single drink and a slice of pizza from the lorry. Pietro and Harry, who felt inclined to discuss their triumph, found themselves with only two people left to tell. Eventually they too shambled off, with hand-shaking and promises of next year.

'We're due in Uzès at one,' said Harry.

'OK.' Pietro left some coins in the plastic saucer and grimaced as he stood up. 'I think they're called the adductor muscles,' he said, putting his hand on his groin. 'I had the same thing after I'd ridden a horse once.'

Now the car was on fire. The seats burned the backs of their thighs and the steering wheel was too hot to hold. They headed off for Carpentras with the windows down and the fan blowing cold. They had rented a house outside Avignon but had driven east the night before to be near Bédoin for the early start. Patrick was the brother of the man from whom they had rented the place; he had arrived one evening to see how they were, and after a glass of pastis had told them they were expected for the ride down Mont Ventoux: there had been no invitation and no description of what was entailed, just an assumption that they would be there.

They pulled up outside the Café Univers in Carpentras to ask the way. Something like a Sunday morning *passeggiata* was happening, with a number of exactly dressed young women and men ambling through the crowded tables on the terrace.

'I'm thirsty,' said Pietro. 'What do you think?'

Harry looked at his watch. 'Better not. Not with the children.' He shrugged.

'That it should come to this.'

'I know,' said Harry.

THEY had difficulty finding the restaurant in the old part of town. Eventually the sound of Mary's crying guided them down a narrow alley to a courtyard where Hannah and Martha were pacifying three children. Mary was banging her fork repeatedly on the table, Anton was whimpering and grabbing at his mother's arm; Jonathan, Harry and Martha's fretful two-year-old, was moaning softly in a shaded pushchair.

Pietro felt so dazed by the exercise he and Harry had taken that the noise, which might have been intolerable in their house in London, was barely noticeable. No one else was outside, so there was no embarrassment about annoying the neighbours. Pietro took Anton on to his knee so Hannah could relax in the sun; Harry rocked the pushchair hopefully. The waiter brought water and a basket of bread.

Hannah began to explain to Martha and Harry how she and Pietro spent their time in London. She exaggerated elements of their day into something which would amuse them, usually at Pietro's expense. He liked it when she talked. He watched her with half an eye through his sunglasses as he whispered to Anton and bounced him up and down on his lap.

Hannah still had the commanding manner that had aroused him when he first met her; there was a bourgeois seriousness over matters of family coupled with an impatience with him if he seemed dilatory. There was also, however, a low humour which saw the pretensions in both of them, and was not above pointing out the ridiculous qualities of their closest relatives or friends. Her fringe hung girlishly over her forehead, shading the calm brown eyes which spoke of something more womanly and serene. She had well-shaped hands with long fingers that she spread when she spoke or explained; Pietro liked to watch them, contrasting in his mind their slender elegance with the comfortable shape of her hips.

'When Pietro proposed to me,' she was saying, 'he pointed out how dull Belgium was. "The most bourgeois people in the world" was one phrase he used. Wasn't it, darling? All that was going to be so different in London. Oh yes! All the theatres and the cinemas and the parties. I was rather frightened about coming. I didn't think I'd have the stamina to keep up with Pietro's social life and all the culture of the big city. Antwerp, after all, was just a little inland trading town – is that what you called it? Of course, some of the bars do stay open till four in the morning, but Pietro told me that was nothing.'

Pietro rolled his eyes and Hannah smiled. 'When was the last time we went to the theatre?' she said. 'It must have been when John Gielgud was young enough to play Hamlet. I'm not saying we're not cultured. We must have watched more

211

programmes about nature and current affairs than anyone in London.'

'I never watch television,' said Pietro, 'except the Open University.'

'Why is there so much applause during the Open University?' said Hannah. 'Who is that man with the Australian accent saying "England need another fifty to win"?'

Pietro shook his head and closed his eyes. 'Quite untrue.'

'One thing I don't quite understand,' Martha said to him. 'With all this watching television and not changing nappies and not taking Hannah to the theatre, I don't quite see where you find time to fit in any work.'

'Yes, it's curious, isn't it? She manages to describe a life of torture and injustice at my hands without once mentioning that I spend most of the day in an office.'

'Do you like being back with your own company?'

'I prefer it to working for Coleman.'

'What happened to him? Did he go out of business?'

'I doubt it. He had too many irons in the fire. But the project I was on had a lot wrong with it. He spent several thousand pounds on a Japanese version of a London A-Z before he realised it would be quite useless.'

'Why?'

'Because the street signs are not written in Japanese.'

'Didn't you stop him?'

'No. That wasn't my part of the project. I was doing maps and design, supervising photographs and colour origination. It was the printers who finally noticed. The other language versions sold very well.'

Martha laughed. 'What a ridiculous man.'

Pietro looked at her. 'Yes, he was.'

'And is that why you left? Because the Japanese project was going to fail.'

'No, not really.'

'Harry told me you had a row with him.'

'Did he? Well Harry shouldn't tell tales.'

'Really!' said Hannah. 'Martha was only asking.'

'Listen,' said Pietro, 'I do *not* want to talk about Coleman.' He had sat up in his chair, looking flushed and angry. 'We haven't come on holiday to talk about people like him. Now let's order.'

Harry raised his head quizzically and wondered what Pietro was concealing.

Pietro silenced Hannah's budding remonstrance with a look that promised later explanation.

'WHERE'S Mary?' said Hannah, putting down her empty coffee cup.

'I thought she was over there with you,' said Pietro. 'She's probably gone inside. I'll have a look and pay the bill at the same time.' He stood up and flinched at the stiffness in his legs and back. The cool, dark restaurant was empty except for a waiter sweeping up at the back by the small maroon door saying 'Toilettes'. While he added up the bill Pietro went through the door to see if Mary had locked herself in. There was a single washbasin and two doors, marked 'Hommes' and 'Femmes'. There was no sign of her in either.

'We'd better have a look round the square,' he said when he rejoined the others. He felt that if he refused to accept there was any sort of crisis then none would develop. Hannah looked alarmed already. She grabbed her bag from beside her chair and looked at him accusingly.

'I'll help,' said Harry. He turned to Martha. 'You stay and look after the boys.'

They went up the alley into the square, an open area of yellowish stone with arched cloisters at one side and a cathedral or solid church visible on another. Two people were eating ice cream under a red parasol with the sound of music from a tired radio in the background; an old man moved through the exit at one corner. Otherwise the heat had completely emptied the area. Its blank, well-preserved walls yielded nothing to their searching eyes.

Hannah looked at Pietro imploringly.

'Don't worry,' he said. 'She can't have gone far.' Why not? he asked himself. 'Let's spread out. You go that way. Harry, you go that way, and I'll go through there.'

He went down a narrow street with baskets full of lavender for sale. He began to call Mary's name.

Now that he was alone, without the need to be calm, he felt the tightening of panic. He was surprised by how quickly he became unable to control the feeling. The concern he felt on her behalf was more acute than anything he had ever felt for himself.

He asked the owner of a shop if he had seen a small girl with fair hair. The man shook his head. 'Je suis désolé, monsieur.'

Désolé, desolate. No, no, it was he who was desolate. The tension had given an unreal quality to the surroundings. What only a few minutes before had seemed a charmed holiday town was quite changed. The luminous green cross in the chemist's, the red pole on the tabac, the spindly white writing on the glass window of the food shop, were no longer small auguries of pleasure but signs of a suddenly comfortless world.

He remembered that he had not agreed where or when to rejoin the others. What if Hannah had already found Mary and his search, and his anguish, were unnecessary? By now he had emerged from the small network of back streets out on to the main circular road that ringed the town. It was flanked on either side by cafés and shops. Round it drove the inessential traffic of a Sunday afternoon – buzzing two-stroke mopeds, laden Citroen Deux Chevaux with their roofs rolled back, family cars with heavy bumpers and sleepy children in the back, light open-backed delivery trucks with fizzy drinks or barrels of butane.

Pietro began to swear and pray, cursing his bad luck, refusing yet to believe that this should happen to him, but asking also to be spared. Part of him knew that only by confronting what was going on could he deal with it; part of him just turned away. In the heightened clarity with which he saw his surroundings and in the way that the passage of time had slowed, he was aware that

214

his existence was pitched at some unwanted new level of intensity.

He saw Mary's face clearly in his mind and he saw the whole of her short life squeezed before his eyes, from the moment her head had emerged into the world, blue and bloody, face down on to the white hospital mat between Hannah's legs. He remembered the soaring of his heart when the midwife turned her over and he had finally let go of his emotions, sobbing on to Hannah's shoulder. Mary had barely yet lived except as an extension of him and Hannah, the subject of their speculation, their love and their impatience. They had constructed a character for her in their teasing but she had not yet developed her own, except as something, someone in whose safety all his happiness now lay. From the moment she had finally appeared, whole and breathing, he had seen her as an independent being, had known that no love or influence he might try to exert could finally change her; and he had respected, admired almost, that serene quality of otherness that was visible even in her baby's cries, had wondered at the innocent confidence with which she had confronted the world, another being, another attempt, undaunted, unworn-down, oblivious to the millions who had preceded her.

He found he was running through the hot Provençal town: rue Gambetta, Place de la République, names that would never be the same again. His pain was making him so mad that he wanted it to be over one way or the other, even if it meant the worst.

He paused by the edge of the road, watching the heavy traffic. He decided to seek comfort in Hannah, not to be alone, and turned back towards the centre of the town. At the end of a narrow street, just before the place became a pedestrian zone, he saw a small group of people gathered next to a lorry. He ran towards them and saw that they were looking over the body of a girl which lay on the pavement. Pushing them aside he bent down over her. It was Mary. 'C'est ma fils,' he said, wrongly. 'She's mine.' He was so relieved to see her that in some way he was not frightened by her stillness. He picked up Mary's body and kissed her face.

'Le camion . . .' muttered someone.

Pietro felt consoling hands on his shoulders. He held Mary close to him, burying his face in her neck, as he had often done before. Her body did not feel broken or limp. A nervous shiver ran along the lids of her closed eyes. He kissed her cheek and murmured her name several times. He felt her arms reach out for him. Her eyes opened.

He held Mary to him tightly, the tears of relief running from his squeezed eyes. He was shocked by how quickly he had adjusted to the idea of her death and then to her regiven life.

'Are you all right?' he said. 'Does it hurt?' He looked down at her and gently tested her thin arms and legs to see if the bones were broken. There was a long graze over her left shoulder and down the side of her back. Where her dress was torn he could see a purple swelling at the side of the ribs.

'No, it doesn't hurt.' She shook her head. She looked dazed.

Pietro thanked the people who had gathered round and set off quickly with Mary in his arms so he could find and reassure Hannah as soon as possible.

When he got back to the restaurant, Martha was sitting with the children. He left Mary cradled on Martha's lap and went running off to find Hannah.

He saw her wandering distracted at the end of the street with the lavender baskets. He shouted and waved and ran to her with his arms held up in the air. 'It's all right! It's all right!' he called, as he drew closer.

'What happened?' said Hannah.

'She was knocked down by a lorry. But she's all right. Well, she looks all right. We must take her to a hospital and have her examined.'

Hannah seemed too frozen to show her relief. 'That girl. What are we going to do with her? I would die if something happened to her, I would just *die*.' She gripped Pietro's arms. 'Do you

216

know, I feel angry with her. I feel really, blindly angry. I want to beat her until she screams, until she understands.'

'There now, it's all right.' Pietro folded his arms round her shoulders and pulled her to him.

VLADIMIRCI

Yugoslavia 1986

IT was slashing with rain when they emerged from the terminal at Belgrade airport.

'Where's this car, then?' said Coleman, holding his raincoat over his head.

'Must be over there, where the Hertz sign is,' said Pietro. 'Let's run.'

'Jesus,' said Coleman, as they pulled out of the airport complex. 'What a country.'

The car crawled through the suburbs of Belgrade where withering bursts of rain rebounded from the pavements and obscured the grey tower blocks that ringed the city. Coleman struggled with the heating control in an effort to force hot air on to the windscreen, which was clouded by their breath.

'How far is this bloody place?' he said, as a dry blast came into their eyes. He lit a cigarette.

'It's no distance at all,' said Pietro. 'You want to look out for signs to Sarajevo.'

PIETRO had begun to tire of Coleman and his company. He felt as though he had lost some freedom of his own and gone backwards in his life to a position of submission and servility. For the sake of Hannah and their two children he had decided to

218

stick with it for the duration of the contract, though there were days when his body would barely carry him down to the tube station to take the train to work.

Coleman's offices were in Clerkenwell in a Victorian building that had been modernised in the Sixties. Five other companies shared the building and could never agree on what renovations needed to be done. The central heating came on during the first week in October and could not be adjusted until April without bonuses to the maintenance staff who otherwise refused to go into the basement and wrestle with the pre-war boiler that grumbled and muttered, fatly swathed in lagging, for a humid six months. The substantial plumbing was visible as it climbed the walls that flanked the stairwell, with its metal banisters and steel-tipped linoleum steps. Two lifts operated from beside the front door, though their tendency to jam a few feet beneath each floor or to sink like a miner's cage discouraged people from using them.

A yellow reception desk, dense with styrofoam coffee cups, was manned by a chain-smoking commissionaire called Bob. Visitors were offered a book and a ballpoint pen attached to the spine by string and wound round so many times with Sellotape that it was fatter than Bob's orange finger that stabbed the page under 'Name', 'Time In' or 'Company'.

'There's a Mister . . .' Bob would pause, telephone to his shoulder, and swivel the book round so he could peer at the page curling under ballpoint pressure '. . . Smitt' or 'Brawn' he would improbably deduce, 'to see you, Mr Coleman . . . Right. Take a seat, please.'

Never having worked in an office before, Pietro was surprised by how little work was actually done. He arrived at 9.15, as requested, in time for the main meeting of the day at 9.30. Most of the secretaries and staff didn't get in before ten, and regarded the first hour as dead time, given over to traffic or television post-mortems or to speculation about the surprisingly numerous office romances. Coleman had about forty employees, though shared lavatories and canteens meant that gossip could draw on the staff of the other companies as well. Lunchtime saw the doors open and a flow of mostly young women erupt like starlings from the doorway, some to the park with their lunch in hand, some to the pubs and sandwich bars in neighbouring streets. The in-house canteen was serviced by a youngish man with greasy hair and a concentrated growth of stubble on the edges of his chin. When he bent down to pick up a catering tin of marmalade or beans from the floor, the blue-check chef's trousers sank low enough to reveal the puckered white cleft of his buttocks. His manner varied between the abusive and the merely truculent, depending on what he imagined to be the status of the customer. The sandwich fillings lay in rectangular plastic containers, illuminated by a strip light behind the glass. The mashed sardine and tuna mayonnaise glistened with a bluish sheen; the ham looked reconstructed, the winking green eyes at the joint of lean and gristle acting as rivets. On the blackboard the hot dishes of the day were abbreviated: lamb and roast pots, chilli con c, B and b pudd. The canteen, however, was the place where the best information changed hands, and experienced employees still ventured in, but bought only sealed cartons of yoghurt or thick-skinned oranges.

Pietro's office overlooked the back of an old printing works with sooted brickwork and tangled fire escapes. On a winter's afternoon it was like the view that must have met the eyes of clerks and office workers in London for a hundred years or more, from the days when the railway cuttings were first violently driven through the uprooted houses of Camden Town. He didn't mind being part of this historic pattern and he liked the way that office life made someone else responsible for all decisions. But when the twilight of November afternoons rushed in so soon after lunch and the call of schoolchildren headed for the bus reached his third-floor window, he also wondered what had happened to his independent life. He thought of the long curve of the American Atlantic coast, the clustered towers of northern Italy and regretted that he was no longer free to go there. His life had become easier; the endless

effort of his earlier years, always pushing back against the limits
of what he could do, seemed, through chance or through
circumstance, to be over.

After a heart-stopping encounter with the lift in his first week,
Pietro always took the stairs. There was an office etiquette, he
quickly discovered, about who said hello to whom. Those who
doubted the legitimacy of his project and thought it might lose
money, or those who thought he was too old or too senior,
ignored him. The others usually said something, varying from a
grunt to the full cross-examination offered by Frank in Stores.
Pietro tended to nod and smile at everyone he passed on the
stairs, introducing their first name if he knew it. One or two
seemed to be playing a longer and trickier game. Most un-
predictable was Chris Mitre, who was head of the computer
department. He was a sallow man who wore tight trousers and
coloured shoes. At the approach of Pietro his face would set into
a sneer of distaste which no amount of nodding and smiling from
Pietro could shift, until approximately every tenth encounter.
Then, just when Pietro had given up and was trying to look
away, Mitre would stop and greet him by his name. Once he
asked him and Hannah round to his house.

The person who had refined the war of greeting to its subtlest
form was Sheila, Coleman's large secretary. Her telephone
manner lacked the phrases, 'I'm afraid' or 'if you like' with which
the other secretaries smoothed their conversation. She could
never be surprised into smiling or civility. When she burst into
an office, without knocking, to deliver a message, or when she
saw someone coming down the corridor, she had clearly had
time to prepare a sullen expression or stare downwards.
Occasionally, however, she might be startled as the lift door
opened on two smiling colleagues. But her eyes flicked on and
failed to register, her mouth turned down, her broad hips
brushed past before either of the others had had time to do more
than check an unwanted greeting.

Pietro normally read the paper in his room for a few minutes
after he had got in, and drank some coffee from the machine. It

was from these tastes and details of repeated daily life that the flavour of office life was established: the dusty coffee, the steel-tipped stairs, the dense cigarette smoke that gathered as the morning meeting in Coleman's room progressed. All of them were tolerable, but it took time for Pietro to grow used to the idea that more of his time was to be spent amongst strangers than with his family. The strip-lit world of battered desks and filing cabinets, pigeonholes and piled reference books, takeaway sandwich cartons and transferred telephone calls: day after day the time there mounted, yet the longer people did it, the more they seemed able to bear it.

Hannah had given him a Toulouse-Lautrec poster and a reproduction of a coloured sixteenth-century map of the Pacific Ocean to pin to the walls of his office, which was fitted with an orange sofa and blue curtains in addition to the usual desk, chairs and shelves. Chris Mitre had the equivalent office on the other side of the building, but with the addition of an armchair. Brian Anderson, who was the financial director, had a smaller office but a full-time secretary called Deborah with whom, according to Simon Levy, the deputy sales director, he copulated athletically throughout the lunch hour. Pietro and Chris Mitre shared a secretary called Annabel. She was a very tall woman who had previously worked for the civil service in a department in Curzon Street, which she coyly but forcefully hinted had been connected with MI5. She was the recipient of Chris Mitre's unwanted advances and rewarded Pietro's self-control with a steady supply of information, some of it from Simon Levy, but most of it from the other secretaries, particularly Deborah in Brian Anderson's office and Barbara in Accounts.

Meetings in Coleman's room were regarded with anxiety by those who attended. He fostered, or at least did nothing to discourage, the rumours that moved around the office. 'I take pleasure,' he told Pietro, 'in starting an impossible rumour in the strictest confidence and then seeing how long it will take to come back to me, also, of course, in the strictest confidence.' The choice of confidants varied, however; and to be singled out for advice over a period of time was a doubtful privilege: it could be a mark of Coleman's favour or it could be the sign of an extended trial. 'This is not the soft-toy business, you know,' Coleman was fond of concluding when he was on the point of exposing or demoting someone.

Ahmed, the sales director, was by general consent the person with most to worry about. A heavily built man glistening under gold bracelets and watches with multiple functions, he wore choking aftershave and had a loud, self-confident air which Coleman enjoyed deflating. 'Tell us the underwater temperature at noon in the Bay of Bengal,' Coleman once invited him when Ahmed had appeared with a spectacular new chronometer. Usually Coleman was more subtle. He would wait for Ahmed's contribution to come almost to an end before suddenly redirecting the conversation. 'I expect you all know the story about Winston Churchill and the Russian envoy,' Ahmed began one morning. 'Forgive me for telling it again, but these reports reminded me irresistibly. Apparently the Russian ambassador was concerned that Churchill had not fully understood the importance of the Allied attacks on the Eastern front and . . .' Everyone waited as Ahmed neared the end of his story. 'So finally Churchill wrote back, saying –'

'Brian, would you mind giving us the latest costings on the A to Z project?' said Coleman.

Coleman's room was significantly larger than anyone else's with a long built-in walnut unit against one wall. This held framed photographs of his wife and two daughters, and several volumes of company reports. It was alleged that there was an extensive drinks collection in the lower part of it, though no one had had first-hand evidence.

Coleman was powerfully relaxed in his room, with Sheila on the red sofa, her shorthand notebook folded over on her round thighs, and the half-dozen men perched either on three hard seats that lived in the office or on chairs they had had to bring in. Coleman's air of being slightly out of place, which Pietro had noticed when he first met him in Evanston, was quite gone when he tipped back the black leather desk chair, and rested his feet on the edge of the blotter. He, like the walnut cabinet, might have been designed for the office.

Pietro, awkward on the backless chair he had dragged in from the corridor, watched the bemused faces. Only Sheila looked content. Brian Anderson sucked deep on Embassy kingsize cigarettes and devotedly realigned a slim gold lighter with the edge of the packet on the table as though searching for some geometrical absolute. Simon Levy tapped his foot and swivelled one of the office pens round in his fingers like a drumstick. Chris Mitre seldom raised his head, which some saurian reflex caused to sink into his body when Coleman spoke; his unblinking eyes would gaze down at the sheet of paper on his lap which he covered with drawings of gibbets and three-dimensional boxes.

THAT evening Pietro lay on the bed of his hotel room in Belgrade drinking whisky from the half-bottle he had bought at Heathrow. Various bits of paper, estimates and draft contracts from the printers at Vladimirci, were fanned out on the purple tartan bedspread. He looked over to where his case lay open on the slatted holder. The cheap fixed wardrobe and single chair were the only other items of furniture; the narrow room seemed to have been conjured from the alcove of a former dispensation. A fan roared in the sealed bathroom when he pulled on the light.

When I die, he thought, I will go to a hell that is entirely composed of hotel bathrooms. My tired face flaring into view in the mirror under the grey flicker of the strip light; the clammy embrace and uncertain smell of the plastic shower curtain; the lavatory roll, half finished, the next sheet folded into a genteel V; the tightly wrapped miniature soap; the towels that don't meet around the waist; the feeling of displacement unassuaged by false economies, dubious hygiene and cheap corporate tricks.

He could have been enjoying this expedition; in fact he had been enjoying it when they drank a bottle of slivovitz with the men at the printing works to celebrate the agreement of terms. There were only minimal guarantees of quality, but the price was spectacular. Their offer was half that made by a London printer and considerably lower than Korea's. Coleman had been pleased; perhaps that was why he had drunk freely and then, in the steamy canteen at the printers', made his move.

His thick glasses could not conceal the feral look in his eyes as he leaned over to Pietro and said, 'I want your help.'

'Help?'

'Yes. Let's talk about the business first.' Coleman was wearing a dark-blue tie with a huge knot that pushed at the sides of his striped shirt. 'Once we get this printing contract signed then we're away. They've got Japanese typefaces, the lot. Your cartographer's nearly through London isn't he?'

'He's done the grids. Now it's over to design.'

'Good. And your share of the business. Remind me.'

Pietro swallowed the last of his drink. 'What do you mean, remind you? You can't have forgotten.'

'Just spell it out for me.'

Pietro shrugged. 'The salary for two years, the percentage of profits and then the pay-off so I can return to running my own business.'

'And the share options. Don't forget them.' Coleman had a waggish tone to his voice that Pietro had never heard before.

'Sure. The share options.'

'And then when the company floats . . .' Coleman opened the palms of his hands wide. 'If it works well, we could renegotiate. I might be able to make some more options available. I'd have to consult the other directors, naturally. Would you like that?'

'Of course.' Pietro watched Coleman light a cigarette. Although he was obviously scheming something, he seemed agitated, unable to come to the point. He poured himself some more slivovitz.

He said, 'Tell me about Martha Freeman.'

'Martha? What about her? You've met her a few times, haven't you?'

'Yes. But you must know her well. Harry's your . . . best friend, isn't he?'

'Yes. But what do you want to know about Martha?'

'Come on, Pietro, you'd think I was asking for classified information.' Coleman laughed. 'What's she like? What makes her tick? What sort of girl is she?'

Pietro took what he thought was a completely straight line. 'Early thirties, American, brought up in New England some-where, capable, friendly –'

'Yes, I know all that. I could see that for myself when you all came to dinner that time. What I mean is, what is she like deep down? Is she passionate, is she . . . cold, is she romantic?'

Pietro looked closely at Coleman's eyes, which looked blood-shot behind the thick lenses of his glasses. He felt the need to respond very precisely. 'I'd say she was naturally an affectionate person, pretty well balanced. You sense that she loves Harry a lot, but she's not uncritical. She has that kind of ebullience, you know, a sort of naturalness which is checked by her manners. You'd guess her parents had spent a lot on her education.'

'Christ, you make her sound like a case history.'

'What do you want me to make her sound like?'

Coleman leaned forward, much as he had done in the rosy darkness of the restaurant in Evanston. 'I want you to tell me how to get to her, how to win her. I'm in love with her. Completely, utterly in love with her.'

He had a triumphant smile as he sat back, as though he were pleased at the daring of his declaration.

Pietro's face did not respond. 'When did this happen?'

'Over a period of months. They asked us to dinner. We asked them back. Then when Harry pulled out of the project I took her to lunch to try to get her to talk him back into it. We went to the American bar at the Savoy for a drink. Do you know it? She was so neat, so elegant. That laugh, those eyes.'

Pietro felt sick. He wasn't sure if Coleman talked in this way because he was inventing this folly or because that was the way his mind truly worked.

He said, 'I don't think you'd better tell me any more.'

Coleman put a large hand on Pietro's. 'I understand. I don't want to put you in an embarrassing position. Just give me a little clue. Just one tip. The sudden weekend in Paris? Letters? A charity ball? Would she respond to that kind of thing? Good works and so on?'

'For Christ's sake, Coleman.'

Pietro felt his hand being squeezed tighter. Coleman leaned across the table and from this range Pietro could sense how drunk he was. There was nothing in the colouring of his swarthy, closely shaved face or the obscured eyes that gave it away; just a sense of blurring at the edges of his speech and the pressure of his hand. He said, 'This business is going to be a humdinger. We're going to be rich. You're going to be rich. And with those extra options –'

'Forget the options. Let's go and –'

'No. You don't understand. This is not some game with me. This is the greatest passion of my life. I don't suppose you've ever felt anything like it. It's overpowering. I'm prepared to sacrifice anything, anything I own to have that woman.'

Pietro thought of Hannah, and of Laura. Coleman said, 'I'm not asking you to betray your friend. I just need some help. I need a way in. Once I've got that, I can do the rest for myself. But I've never met anyone like Martha before. I just can't get a grip, a toehold . . .'

'You're drunk. I'm going back to the hotel.' Pietro pushed his chair back, but Coleman hung on to his arm.

He spoke angrily. 'Don't spoil it for yourself now. This is your one and only chance. You know that, don't you? You miss this and it's back to being a journeyman snapper, a beach bum. Or a cuckold, like your friend Harry.'

'What?'

'You heard.'

'Fuck off, Coleman. You'll get my resignation tomorrow.' Pietro pulled his arm free, so that Coleman overbalanced, sprawling forward across the table, sending the bottle and the glasses rolling on to the floor.

★

227

THE day he got back to his house in London, Pietro received a letter from Laura.

DEAR Pietro, It was so nice to get your card. My dad sent it on from Lyndonville. Will you send me a photograph of your children and your wife? Your life sounds very interesting and I'm really happy for you. I knew you had great talent as a photographer. I always said you could be a professional, didn't I? Right from the beginning. Do you remember those freezing cold mornings in New York when you used to make me come on the subway with you to all those strange parts of town? We'd go all the way up to the Bronx and I'd have to stand around for hours while you checked the light and everything. Then we'd have coffee and donuts. I never knew how this fitted into the scheme for capturing the 'real' city on film. I remember in the finished pictures I always seemed to have crumbs round my mouth. And that sailboat by one of the piers downtown where we had that argument because I said boats like that were a cliché in pictures and you said something about how it was all to do with 'displacement' – was that the word you used? – and then we had to go and make it up with a huge lunch somewhere. Was that the day we went to the fish place? Or maybe that was in San Francisco, come to think of it. I'm losing my memory as I get older. Forgive me.

You say you want to catch up with all my news. I guess there's a lot to say. First of all, I got married! Richard is a lawyer. We met when I was on business in Australia and it was kind of awkward because he was getting divorced at that time. He is quite a bit older than me and he has two girls who live with their mother in New York, but they come and see us too and they're really the best. Louisa is twelve and Kelly is fourteen – very interested in boys right now, though I keep telling her it's a phase that will pass! I guess she's the age we were when we first met all those years ago. It doesn't seem possible. She's just a kid, even though she's grown-up for her age, she's still a kid. It makes me wonder what we were like then.

Richard is very kind and very attentive. He looks after me very well. We are living in Connecticut because Richard has a year-long sabbatical from his company and I had come to the end of a job. Also, I am expecting our first baby in November. This makes me feel very excited and a little scared. You will understand all about that, I expect!

Our life is therefore very quiet and we are making the most of this precious time together before the new arrival puts an end to it. We have done a house swap for our apartment in New York and we are living on the edge of town here in a lovely quiet house. I am sure you would love it. It has lots of white weatherboarding and a real wooden porch. I am trying to persuade Richard to buy me a rocking chair, so I can sit here in the evenings knitting socks for the baby. I guess he thinks that sounds a little middle-aged. He is always off playing softball in the evenings with one of the local teams. I just sit here and read, sipping long drinks from the refrigerator. So *some* things haven't changed . . .

Did I tell you about my last job? I don't remember when I last wrote. I'm afraid it was a long time ago. Anyhow, I worked for this company on Wall Street for a time and it was unbelievable. So much excitement, so much going on. We would work from six in the morning, then stay out partying till three. I certainly couldn't do that any more.

After the crash I kind of lost my interest in finance. Some of it seemed a little tacky also. I took a job with a big art dealers which was much less money but more interesting. I got to travel a good deal, mostly to the Far East. I spent some time in Japan and even learned a little Japanese. Also in Hong Kong and Australia, which is a fine country. Have you ever been there? You would like it, I think. Especially Sydney, which is where I met Richard.

My little sister Sally got married a couple of years back and she has twin boys. She lives in Los Angeles, so I don't see her as much as I would like. My dad is still not retired, though he doesn't work quite so hard. He still talks about going to live in

England, though I don't know if he ever will. My mother is very well and delighted with Sally's children. She says she doesn't mind being a grandma.

I love being married and all the trust and security it brings. I can't think why I waited such a long time. Richard is such a kind man, I know you two would really get along well together. Perhaps you'll come and visit us one day. He is mad about sports, softball and golf particularly. He gives classes once a week at a local college to kids from difficult backgrounds. He teaches simple economics and business programs.

I guess that reminds me – I must go and put the soup on for dinner. He is picky about what he eats – has to be all fresh, nothing canned. Could be worse, at least he'll eat most things, even my cooking!

We are so happy here in our little world. I dread going back to NYC at the end of the year. I could be quite content just baking cakes and rocking on the porch with a book, then slipping inside at sundown to squeeze some oranges (for R) and mix a shaker full of whiskey sours (for me).

I loved reading about your life in your note. I didn't think it strange that you didn't ask me over when you got married, so don't worry about that, please. The time we had together, all those years ago now, was something unique, nothing will ever change that, or take away the memory.

If I press my hand to my belly I can feel a little wriggling inside. Sometimes I can even see the skin move as the Beast turns over. Write to me again, or better still, come and see us. With much love always, Laura.

HE had never understood her. No one could have predicted that she would end up married to a lawyer, settled in domestic harmony. Could they? She had seemed so impulsive, so ignorant or contemptuous of the regulations and customs of people like her parents that he could only envisage her on the move and independent. He had been so dazzled by her looks that her character had always seemed to him in some way dominated by them; perhaps he had never really known her as an ordinary, vulnerable, venal human being at all.

Yet it was not quite as simple as saying that in his youthful shallowness he had liked her only for the way she looked. He had loved her properly and truly; it was just that he could more easily locate what he loved in the glow of her eyes or the slant of her mouth than in some abstract excursion into what made up her personality. It was not a question of being superficial; if you had never felt that passion for another person's body and appearance, he thought, you had not fully loved.

He looked at the letter again and he felt his heart at last close over. He saw a life that bore no relation to his own. At one point the solitary orbits they tracked in space had overlapped, and the gravity of his tiny world had shifted. Now he saw only a woman he did not understand, still liked, but did not wish to see again. She was gone.

WATSONVILLE
California USA 1974

ARKING or breakfast. You could have either but not both for the price of the hotel bedroom. They opted for breakfast and thought they'd take a chance on the hire car getting towed. The hotel was lower on Taylor Street than was desirable, and lower than Laura's credit card could have got them, but Pietro always insisted on paying. The room over-looked a patch of waste ground and the backs of other buildings. A gnarled palm tree grew up between the fire escapes.

After they had unpacked Laura said, 'I'm going for a walk now. I won't belong.'

'Sure,' said Pietro. 'See you later.'

When she had gone he realised that she couldn't really have said 'I won't belong.'

The idea of her going for a walk on her own would once have seemed absurd, but the more independently she behaved the more he hung back. After she had been gone for a few minutes he decided to go for a walk himself. He went up to the top of Powell Street and right, down into Chinatown where the rubbish was piled high on the streets. In an American café he ordered a sandwich and an orange juice. He watched the people going past the window and thought how much he would have liked San Francisco in any other circumstances. It was bright and bold but also what people called 'manageable'; to a European there was no difficulty in understanding it.

He supposed that at some point he had been too passionate. It hadn't happened at once. Laura had been so loving to him, had given him so much encouragement that in the end he must have lost some elemental piece of self-control. Now it was too late. Both seemed afflicted by inertia. Laura particularly was listless: she couldn't concentrate on anything, she seemed to have lost her ability to take the best from her surroundings.

The next day they went to Haight Ashbury. The painted houses and tranquil streets leading down to green parks, just a bus ride from the city centre, could not have been more promising. To the young men and women of the Sixties the dream of revolution must have seemed so close that they could almost touch it.

'You couldn't imagine a better place,' said Pietro. 'If only it hadn't been for the drugs.'

'I don't think they could have had much of a movement without drugs.'

'Maybe. They could have gone a long way on Anchor steam beer, I would have thought.'

Laura would not be drawn. The elegance and the courtesy of the city had no effect on her; the trams toiled unregarded up the streets, while the dockside pleasure ground, its restaurants and music, seemed like a ten-cent trick under the indifferent breezes of the Bay.

Laura had to see a friend of her mother's, so Pietro spent the following morning on his own. After he had finished lunch he decided to go back to the hotel for a bath and a sleep. As he once more climbed Powell Street he found his legs beginning to ache. The tracks of the cable car began to rattle urgently with the impact of their invisible load. He decided to stop and wait for it; he was wearing thin-soled sneakers which gave no cushioning from the pavement.

He was overcome by tiredness. Next to a garage that proclaimed itself a Certified Smog Tester, he leant against a wall, resting his head on his arms. Then there was a silence into which there suddenly came from across the street the sound of a male voice singing opera in Italian. For two years Pietro had heard no music but FM radio and car tapes, the continuous throb of pop music, the background of America. The tenor voice was as clear as ice, and in his mind there suddenly formed a picture of a track that joined two things: a broken-down barn at one end, and, at the other, a dense and slightly threatening wood. For almost twenty years he had barely given it a thought, and now he felt it pull with a vast, unaccountable force.

THEY ate dinner in a Chinese restaurant which had little in common with the one near Baker Street where, after his escape from Dorking, Pietro had first sampled soup that looked as though the waiter had blown his nose into it. Here a young man brought two plates of meat and lit a gas fire in the middle of the table, inviting them to cook their own food. Pietro drank quickly, searching to find an elusive lightness of spirit. Laura smiled stiffly over the chopsticks and the unappetising strips of raw chicken, beef and pork.

'Hey, you know one thing I regret about Lyndonville,' said Pietro brightly. 'We never did spend an afternoon in the Darling Inn apartments.'

'It stopped being a hotel a while back. It's now an old people's residence.'

After dinner they went for a walk and Laura said, 'Tell me about your mother.'

'What about her?'

'You always said you'd tell me about her properly one day.'

They had walked down to Fisherman's Wharf and had stopped for a moment between the amusement arcades. Seals were honking in the shallow water among the boats.

Pietro said, 'I told you she died, didn't I?'

'Yes. I'm sorry, Pietro. I don't know why I asked you that question. It's none of my business.'

'That's all right. There isn't much to tell when someone dies. It's not an event, it's an absence.'

'You weren't there with her?'

'No, I was told by a doctor when I got back from school. I do remember, though, about a week later this woman called Mrs Graham, who used to look after the house, she took me on one side and described it to me.'

'Why?'

'I think she knew I felt excluded. It wasn't morbid. She sat me on the sofa and she held my hand.'

Pietro stopped, but Laura's expression was intent, urging him to carry on. He drew a deep breath. He found he could remember.

'Mrs Graham said, "She was very bad during the night. I sat up with her until three and then I felt myself nodding off. When I woke up she was sitting up in bed. She said I was to go and get your father. Then she stopped me and she said, 'I haven't been a good wife to him. Tell him I knew that.' Then when I was at the door she stopped me again and said, 'Does my little boy know how ill I am?' And I said, 'No, the doctor said best not to tell him.' And she said, 'I want him to know I'm dying.' And I said, 'Don't talk such nonsense about dying now.' And I sat back on the bed with her." '

Pietro looked across to Laura's face. It was filled with concentration. It seemed he had her attention at last.

'Shall I go on?'

'Yes. Tell me exactly what happened.'

He scratched his head. His gaze swept the Bay, from bridge to bridge, over the shattered island. 'I remember that Mrs Graham was squeezing my hand all the time and I was sitting there nodding. Then she said, "I sat there with her and she talked about Italy and about her parents. She might have been a little bit feverish, I think, because she was in pain. The doctor had given her these tablets but they made her very thirsty. She told me when she was a little girl in her village she dreamed of marrying a rich man from Rome and living in a villa with a garden and lots of children. And I said she hadn't done so bad, here in Backley with Mr Russell and with you. And she began to cry a little bit and she said she knew that was true. She said it wasn't what she dreamed of, but she loved England because you were there in it." Mrs Graham was squeezing my hand so hard now that it was hurting. Then she said, "I knew she was getting very low. She lay back against the pillows and she asked me for some more tablets and some water. And I gave them to her and then I went over to the window and I drew back the curtains and I remember it was just getting light. I was looking over that way up towards the hill. And when I sat back by her bed again she was gone." ' Pietro paused. 'I don't think I realised till then, till Mrs Graham told me, that she was truly dead.'

'I suppose that was good for you,' said Laura.

'I think so. I think you're supposed to confront these things.'

Laura said, 'I'm sorry. It must have been awful.'

There was silence. Laura looked down.

He said, 'That's not what you really wanted to talk about, is it?'

Laura didn't answer, though her silence confirmed what he meant.

'I think we should give it a bit longer,' said Pietro. 'Let's finish the holiday at least.'

Laura nodded dumbly, her eyes brimming with tears.

'Don't cry, please,' said Pietro. He felt quite calm now that he had faced the subject.

'I hate this,' said Laura. 'I don't want this. I just . . .'

Her voice trailed off. She took his arm and they began to walk back towards the hotel.

Once in the room they talked about the travel arrangements and packing and paying the bill. Pietro felt as though he was bracing himself to be smacked in the solar plexus. That night he lay awake and listened for the soft sound of Laura sleeping. She was silent, and when the first light came through the curtains he saw her open eyes staring at the ceiling.

★

IN the morning they trailed through the south of the city, and eventually swung up on to Route 101 towards San José. The sun began to burn down in another day of smooth Californian weather. The local station on the car radio crowed in pleasure: 'OK, folks, we're looking at temperatures of twenty-five degrees today in the Bay area and if you're down in Carmel it's really time to get down to the beach. We're predicting a midday high of twenty-six!'

'I'm sorry I made you go through that story about your mother last night,' said Laura. 'I guess I just wanted you to slow down a bit.'

'How do you mean?'

'You've been so frantic, making jokes all the time. I wanted you to be serious.'

Pietro nodded. He manœuvred the car out past a giant truck and into the fast lane.

After a while, Laura said, 'Couldn't we stop for a swim? I'm so hot.'

'We've only just started.'

'But we don't have to get anywhere, do we?'

'I suppose not. We've come back off the coast a bit now, though. We could take that road down to Santa Cruz.'

Down on Route 1 they saw signs to Watsonville and Castroville, the 'artichoke capital of the world'.

'Let's go down there,' said Laura. 'Watsonville. I bet there's a beach there.'

Pietro turned the car off the freeway. 'What happens in Watsonville?'

'I've no idea. I never heard of it before.'

They drove through flat agricultural fields. Only an hour or so from San Francisco and the place looked impoverished.

'What's that extraordinary smell?' said Laura.

'I don't know.' Occasionally when carrying his armful of books along the colonnade to the nine o'clock lesson at Brockwood, Pietro would pass the ventilator shaft from the kitchen where the Brussels sprouts were already boiling hard for lunch. The aroma from the fields of Watsonville reminded him of it.

They were on the San Andreas Road when they came to a Stop sign. To the right was Beach Road, to the left Thurwachter. There was no one else in sight as they headed for the beach. The sea was far colder than they had expected, and they ran back over the scraggy dunes to warm up afterwards. Laura took the picnic lunch she had prepared from the back of the car and laid it on the sand.

She looked at Pietro over the rug and smiled. Her hair was still damp at the tips. She wore a navy-blue top which was half open to reveal the white skin of her chest and neck. She had black earrings beneath the tumbling, errant hair. Nothing had changed in her.

Pietro drank some beer from the bottle: Michelob, said the inscription on the label. He fingered one of the sachets of artificial sweetener Laura had produced from her handbag. He looked up into her steady brown eyes.

'I'm going to go now,' she said. 'You take the car. Take it on where you want. I'll get my bag from the back.'

'What'll you do?'

'I'll get a ride back to San Francisco, then I'll see.'

'Will you find your way?'

'It can't be more than a mile back to the interstate.'

'One day,' said Pietro, 'you'll talk to me about this and I'll understand it.'

'Yes,' said Laura, standing up. She touched his hand and went up towards the road. Pietro looked after her until she had disappeared from sight, then he looked down at the picnic on the rug. French's mustard, Hi-lo sweetener, Michelob beer. What was the point of it? What was the point of anything if you were on your own?

He sat for a long time looking over the sea. High above him an aeroplane was flying up from Los Angeles. From overhead, Watsonville was just a point among the brown hills with the little smudges of white made by the paths and roads that run along the crests. Low cloud obscured the ocean to the west; it began to sink down and cover the sea, like fog. Nearer to the shore, the water itself could be seen to sparkle. From the air the surface looked scaly and still; it was stippled and drawn like black vinyl on a car seat cover.

Pietro, invisible, sat looking towards the horizon. His throat was too constricted for him to swallow the beer. Eventually he stood up and went towards the car. As he got closer, he started running. He drove off with a squeal of rubber and chased up to the junction. Laura was gone. He turned round and looked on the back seat. She had taken her bag.

He was on the road they had come on, Thurwachter Road, though here it appeared to be called McGovern Road. Confused, he turned the car round. He followed the end of a low hill through fields of Brussels sprouts and artichokes. He came to a row of low white buildings on his right with bales of hay, piles of compost and a sign saying 'Bay View Mushroom Farm'. He was pouring sweat.

He drove faster and faster, now quite lost. Bluff Road farms. Fresh eggs. Monday thru Saturday. He turned left again and eventually found himself back on the interstate, but not at the point where they had left it that morning. He headed back towards San Francisco and eventually came to the junction with Beach Road. There was no young woman by the side of the highway.

He kept driving until he could turn the car around so it pointed south, towards Mexico. He slammed one of Laura's cassettes into the player.

Watsonville. What happens in Watsonville? he had asked. Now he knew.

XIANYANG

China

I N the first flat he owned, off the Archway Road in north London, Pietro decorated the bedroom with Michelin yellow maps of France. He began by trying to make the edges line up, so that the wall would give a continuous picture, but decided after some fiddling with Sellotape and scissors that part of the charm of them lay in their random evocation of French life, so that it didn't matter if the Pyrenees were next to Burgundy provided you could let your imagination roam the roads. They had been prepared with a care that bordered on patriotism, even in the fat red arteries leading into Rennes, the candid demarcation of the *zones industrielles* or the grim plain of Poitiers. In other areas you could almost sense the avenues of plane trees leading into the villages, you could tell what sort of bridge the road then crossed and guess at the scenery as a white track left a minor road deep in the Auvergne. Cow bells, hay rolled in circular bundles, the silence of la France profonde – a mythical place that existed in the minds of the inhabitants in all parts of the country, a place of atavistic feelings, fertility, a triumph of backwardness, where murders and lovemaking took place according to prehistoric ritual; whose inhabitants had drenched the earth with their blood at Verdun before returning to invisibility.

The names on the map still held some alphabetic secret. Vichy

240

had a hissing sound that suggested treachery. Vannes could only be a windy fishing port facing west.

Among the things his grandfather had left him, was a trunk full of army souvenirs, including a trench map of the Somme. The red line with square crenellations that marked the German trenches ran in a tangle to the west of Beaumont Hamel. A little further west, the British front-line trench was marked by a thin blue line between two places they had christened Hawthorn Ridge and the Bowery. To the south and east were Thiepval and Thiepval Wood, where the red German trenches were so thick they cast a pink haze over the map. An officer's writing noted that the map was correct to July 28 1916, well into the slaughter. The battle itself might have gone under the name of the Somme, whose muted bell-like sound had become impossible to disentangle from its associations, but in fact the British forces had fought beside the narrow river Ancre. The battle had been named by the French, whose smaller contingent was closer to the Somme. It was not even the Ancre which had the most deadly significance to the British; the men who found themselves killed in thousands, their bodies piled up, useless meat before breakfast, had died at Beaumont or Thiepval. There was no threat in those names, nothing of the cat's howl of Auschwitz, or the grim, ferrous ring of Verdun. Beaumont and Thiepval were inconsequential villages in a part of France best known for sugar beet; their names were no more than a reasonable ordering of letters to represent an identity.

Yet with what scared eyes must the private British soldier, on learning of his next destination, have scanned the letters of Thiepval. There was a suggestion of 'cheval', which by May 1916 he must have known had a friendly meaning, but after the firm capital T and the lightweight vowels, was there not an ominous downward lurch in the 'v'? It was an unstable word, which changed its nature midway through. The ordering of the letters, the shape of the ABC, had carried a destiny for the British soldier as surely as the superstitious third light carried not the longed-for Blighty wound but death.

241

The alphabet was the means by which a place became articulate. Without a name, it was no more than a collection of buildings or a natural landmark. But although places were given this access to articulacy, their single utterance was void of meaning. Even names whose derivation was clear, like Newtown, did not reveal the character of the place. A given arrangement of letters from the alphabet broke the silence, but meaning could be grasped only by some more patient human process.

RAYMOND Russell's interest in the derivation of words had led him over the years to enquire into how the words themselves were made. He had told Pietro that the letter A had first depicted an inverted ox's head. The Phoenicians, he said, had seen how signs could represent not just an idea, but a sound, and had developed Egyptian pictures so that an 's' was not only a snake but could indicate the noise made by one. Then the Greeks had taken the idea, and had presented a range of vowels and consonants whose function was not to depict objects but to replicate human sounds.

Pietro sometimes thought about this when he looked at the maps on his wall. What puzzled him were the countries whose writing systems were different. While the Greek word for Athens could be transliterated as accurately as you wanted (Athens, his father assured him was not all that close, but that was through choice), in what way could English renderings of the places in China be appropriate? Not one letter had anything to do with a Chinese ideogram. In so far as scholars in both languages had developed a way of understanding one another, this did not matter. You could find your way to Peking: it was the same place, however you wrote it down. And yet with a completely different way of rendering their idea of the place, the Chinese did see it differently; their experience of it was not the same. In your alphabet was contained the limits of your perception.

Raymond Russell, whose study of words was no more than a

hobby, could not help on this point, and Pietro himself did not feel inclined to delve further. If he felt confused by the problems of maps and language he would return to the verifiable facts. There were rivers and roads, and cities made of brick and stone. Their physical reality overrode such questions. Even Quezaltenango. You could visit them, and there they were.

SOMETIMES in Oxford, a few years earlier, when he had talked to Dr Simon, their conversations had become similarly abstract and, sometimes at least, confusing.

'Since you never say anything,' Pietro said one day, 'but leave it all to me, I could have told you a completely different set of stories and you would have formed a completely different idea of me.'

Dr Simon nodded, and smiled a little.

'I mean,' Pietro went on, 'I told you about Laura, but I didn't tell you about Gabriella, did I? I never told you about India or the week I spent in Rio.'

It was towards the end of his treatment, and Dr Simon looked pleased with the way Pietro was beginning to answer his own questions.

'I could have been lying, couldn't I?' he said. 'I could have made it all up. I haven't, of course. But suppose I had told you different things. Even at the age of twenty-six I have a choice of things to relate. Would you have reached a different diagnosis?'

Dr Simon raised an eyebrow.

Pietro said, 'I suppose you think I was bound to bring up only the most important things, that even if I'd tried to avoid them, the evasion itself would have been obvious, so we would have got there in the end.'

Dr Simon still said nothing.

Pietro, exhilarated by the knowledge that this would be one of his last visits, thought he would pursue the idea. 'I don't believe in your paradoxical view of things. I could honestly have given you a different story, without lying, just by choosing different things, and you'd never have been any the wiser.'

243

At last Dr Simon was provoked, though it was to laughter. 'There is no one grand pattern with neatly interlocking junctions, no one truth to a human personality,' she said. 'Another version would have been just as good.'

THE night before his fortieth birthday, Pietro lay in bed with Hannah, thinking fearfully of the onset of middle age. It was not exactly that he was frightened of hell or of the torment death might bring, more that he had become greedy to live; he did not want to let go, and he felt that he had reached this age without yet having started in earnest on anything he had meant to do.

This little splinter of light without practice or meaning that made up one's life on earth . . . Perhaps, he thought, shifting the weight of Hannah's head against his chest, there was some parallel world or place in which it would be more comprehensible.

He half believed so, though he had never told Hannah, because his evidence came from a dream and it was a strict rule between them that they should never tell each other their dreams, just as they would not show holiday photographs to visitors. Some things did not translate. Secretly, however, and a little shamefully, Pietro believed that one, or possibly two, of the dreams he had had in his life were significant.

He was walking along a road near Backley with his mother, aged twelve or thereabouts. With them was a child of about two – also his mother's, and therefore his own younger brother. In the emotion he experienced towards the child, the overpowering mixture of love and pride, quite free from any complicating jealousy or ambivalence, he felt that all the conflicts of his life were resolved, washed clean away. He awoke in tears of joy.

The second dream took place in a setting also drawn from his childhood, a room off a nursery school, perhaps the earliest place he could ever remember. In it, as an adult, he conducted a love affair of extraordinary physical passion. The woman was one he half recognised. She resembled someone he had known in London, but was not her. The ecstasy, the exaltation of sex, were extraordinary; but more memorable was the sense that this had actually happened, in a place or a time that were very close to the one in which he lived, removed only by the thinnest partition, which his unconscious mind, in the act of dreaming, had penetrated.

In Hong Kong, when he had gazed into China, he had known that he would never visit it. Back at the hotel he studied maps of it, pored over this primitive and beautiful country that he had seen from the border. There was a town deep in the interior called Xianyang – or at least that was how it was rendered in English. He let it become in his mind the representation of all the places he would not go, and Xianyang was the name he gave in his mind to the place or the time in which the half-remembered love affair and the healing birth had happened.

In the spring of 1980 Raymond Russell returned to Backley, to a small cottage near the house he had bought after the war. He had fallen ill with bronchitis and had retired from the Civil Service. Although he was only sixty-two his hair had gone white; he looked like his own father at the age of eighty. And like him he kept a dog, though his was a whippet called Murray.

Pietro visited him frequently in the new cottage. He took down Mary, his father's first grandchild, to see him there soon after her birth. Hannah also came down with him from time to time and was shown the nearby house in which Pietro had grown up.

Alone with the old man one winter afternoon in front of the fire, Pietro found himself asking about Francesca. His father was more forthcoming than he had been before.

'I was so worried about how it would affect you,' he said. 'I was frightened for what it might do to you. But you seemed to manage pretty well.'

'I suppose I was good at concealing what I felt,' said Pietro. 'I looked to you for a clue, but you just carried on as before. I thought I ought to do the same.'

Raymond Russell smiled. 'That's right. Soldier on. We made quite a good fist of it between us, I reckon.'

Pietro poured some tea from a pot on the low table between them. 'We never really talked about her, did we?' he said.

His father looked at him with weak eyes. 'No, we didn't. I meant to, you know. Often in the flat in the evenings I'd try to pluck up the courage. Somehow I couldn't bear it. I wasn't brave enough.'

'Not brave enough? After the trenches at Anzio?'

'Yes, it's funny, isn't it?'

Pietro felt a complicity between them. 'How different would your life have been if she'd lived?'

'Aah . . .' His father smiled. 'I've asked myself that a thousand times. I should have loved it if she'd lived. I mean, when you're married a while, if you're happy, you forget a bit who the other person is. It's just like there's a mirror there all the time. What I miss is not having anyone to share things with. When you brought little Mary down here the first time I was very pleased to see her, but all the time I was thinking: what would *she* think, what would your mother say? We had so much fun together and now I've been alone so long. I've forgotten what it's like to have someone there you can just turn to all the time and laugh with. When I think of her now I see her as a young foreign girl, younger than you. The clothes I picture her wearing are from a different era. It all seems such a very long time ago.'

Pietro looked at his father closely. He said, 'We did talk about her once, when we were on holiday. Do you remember?'

'No. Where was that?'

'I'm not sure. It was somewhere hot. I suppose it must have been that time we went to Ibiza. It was quite late in the evening and I brought the subject up. The conversation didn't last long. I was only about sixteen and I remember feeling shocked. I thought that when you were grown up you suddenly became calm and magisterial and well balanced. Something you said made me realise this wasn't so. I could see you felt the same raw, childlike emotions I did. It was depressing.'

'I don't remember. I expect you're right, though. I don't think people ever grow up in the way you've described.'

Pietro cleared the tea things away into the kitchen. He felt saddened by what his father had said, but relieved that in some way he had confided in him. When he got back into the sitting room he found his father examining the bookshelves.

'Did you ever get the full set of that encyclopaedia or whatever it was?' he said. 'You know, the one you were always chasing after?'

'The dictionary. Yes, I advertised in a magazine and I got a reply from someone in Edinburgh. The trouble was that most people only wanted to get rid of a whole set. It was a tricky way of going about it, getting one volume at a time.'

'But now you've got the lot?'

'Oh yes, I got "V to Z" years ago. I'm all set up now.'

Raymond Russell sat back in his chair again by the fire with the book he had taken from the shelf and gave a long, rattling cough.

PIETRO had met Hannah at an age when it was already impossible for them to catch up on all the details of each other's past lives. One of the first things he had done with Laura, when they were both twenty-two, was to exchange information about everything they had done, everywhere they had been before they met, so from then on it was like growing up together. Pietro had had a good memory for years and seasons, but by the time Hannah burst into the upstairs room of the flat in Ghent he had already begun to lose it. At the age of forty he quite enjoyed the sensation that there were pockets of his past that he could keep private. He wished he had forgotten less, but there were still incidents and people who arrived for no reason in his mind and brought memories that gave him pleasure. Hannah's understanding of his past life therefore came in small packages, in stories and episodes he described; there were long periods and short interludes that had never come to light.

He had been reluctant to tell her about what had happened in

Quezaltenango and afterwards, feeling that it represented some sort of self-indulgence of which he was not proud.

However, she seemed to guess. When Pietro's father died there had been an awkward party after the cremation at which friends, relatives and a few of Mr Russell's former colleagues came to drink wine and eat sausage rolls. Back in London Pietro cried for his father.

'He was a very kind man,' he said to Hannah as he sat on the sofa. 'He was very good to me all my life and I owe him a great debt for his tolerance.'

What he said struck Hannah as formal and reserved. She pressed Pietro on his feelings, but it seemed he had nothing to add. Under her gentle questioning, however, he did reveal a little more of earlier episodes. Unsettled by his grief, he was more expansive than usual.

'And what did this Doctor Simon say?'

'Nothing. She never said anything.'

'But did you find out what the matter was?'

'Not really. I think I couldn't understand why anyone should love me. I had a peculiar idea of what constituted a nice person and of what other people expected.'

'You didn't think you were worth loving?'

'No. I just wished I had been more attractive. I wished I had been nicer.'

Hannah flushed. 'Life is not about being nice!'

'No, but –'

'It's about negotiating your peace with the world, on whatever terms you can.'

'Darling!'

'I'm serious,' said Hannah.

'I know. I know you are. But I was young. I also felt that the trouble I was having made me even more unworthy. It's like the way shyness is said to be a kind of pride. This turbulence, these symptoms seemed to me like an extreme form of self-regard.'

'And therefore a mortal sin?'

'Maybe.'

'Anyway,' said Hannah. 'You no longer feel this? You can see how you could be lovable now?'

'Oh yes.' Not because I think I'm worthy or unusual, but because I now see that one can be lovable anyway, that it's not these things that decide it.'

Hannah still seemed a little on her dignity.

'And what about you, my love?' said Pietro. 'Could anyone love you?'

Hannah crossed the room to light the fire, bending down on her long, elegant legs. Her head was turned away from Pietro, the hair cut boyishly short, her slightly round, humorous face bent over the matches. There was a bump as the gas caught the flame and began to flicker round the counterfeit coals.

'Perhaps,' she said, standing quite upright in front of the fireplace. 'I don't really mind. If two people love each other then one must be the more dependent, the more giving. I don't mind if that one is me, only that you should not take advantage of it.'

YARMOUTH
England 1991

O N his way to Norwich, just before the Suffolk village of Yoxford, or thereabouts, Pietro drove past a sign for Satis House. He wondered if this was the original of Miss Havisham's dusty mansion, now restored or perhaps reinvented, complete with cobwebbed wedding cake, as a Dickens museum. Round the next corner, at the gateway to the drive was a sign reading 'Satis House Malaysian Restaurant'. He didn't pause to look, but as he drove on began to think idly about the book. The marshes and their convict hulks: backdrops to scenes that had lived static and unchanged in his mind like shapes in a night landscape that are momentarily revealed by lightning. Essex, Suffolk . . . this was not country he knew well, but hadn't the passages about the sea in *David Copperfield* been set in Yarmouth? Presumably the place where David had lived as a boy could not have been far from here if he was able to take the stagecoach up to the Peggottys' boat on the sands.

Finding his interest quicken, he followed a signpost for Southwold, the town his AA road map suggested would be large enough to have a bookshop. He passed a newsagent and stopped the car to buy a paper ('Soviet Union to cease existence'), which he tucked under his arm. The assistant directed him to a shop halfway up the main street on the left where he found what he wanted. It was a fat modern paperback, edited with notes for students. On the second page of the text it announced clearly: 'I was born at Blunderstone, in Suffolk, or "there by" as they say in Scotland.' After the word 'Blunderstone' was a small number 2, indicating a note. The editor disclosed that Dickens had written to a friend: 'I saw the name "Blunderstone" on a direction-post between it and Yarmouth, and took it from the said direction-post for the book.' The note added: 'Dickens was immensely careful in his use of names, whether for people or for places', and went on to give examples.

Pietro could not find a Blunderstone on his map, though just north of Lowestoft, on the road to Yarmouth, there was a Blundeston. It seemed too close to be a coincidence. Yet if this was the right place, why had the notes, which insisted on Dickens's precision, made no reference to the fact that he, or perhaps subsequent local authorities, had changed the village's name?

As he emerged from the clotted one-way system of Lowestoft, he saw a sign for Blundeston, and, after a mile or so of flat green fields, he found himself outside a large prison. He turned the car round and headed towards a group of houses. There was a curiously shaped church, lumpish and off-centre, with a circular Saxon tower.

The ridiculous nature of his search suddenly struck him. How was he to establish whether or not this was the village in which a fictional character was supposed to have lived? He pulled up by a low brick building – a sheep shelter, perhaps – sited on a grassy triangle at the crossroads, and walked over to the church. To his surprise he found a notice in the porch that said this was the church used by Dickens in his book; postcards and souvenirs could be obtained from the bungalow next door.

Armed with a green souvenir towel he walked down the lane to the house identified by the bungalow owner as the Rookery in the book, now called the Old Rectory. It was set back from the road. Fixed to the gate was a metal plaque with the words 'I live here' above a picture of an Alsatian. Another notice said, 'Please shut the gate'. He could see a caravan and some beehives next to an outhouse. There was a slight smell, even outside, of cats.

And yet the house was the Rookery, without any doubt. It was perfect in shape and size, in its position on the flat fields, with Mrs Copperfield's bedroom at the front and the boy's overlooking the churchyard where first his father, then his mother had been buried. For minutes he stood gazing at the front door, picturing the child being taught to read by Peggotty, his nurse, and then the interruption of his contented life by the arrival of the Murdstones.

In this house had been played out the scenes that had lived in his own mind as both the most peculiar yet most representative of childhood, with its passions and bereavements that are never surpassed by adult grief. Although he had not read the book until he was thirty, what had happened here was as real as anything that had happened to him.

The wind was blowing a thin drizzle from the fields that led down to the prison. Pietro returned to his car and began to move off. His eye was caught by a pub called the Plough, a whitewashed coaching inn with leaded lights in black-framed windows. A notice told him that 'Barkis (the carrier) . . . started from here'. And then a little down the road was the hedgerow from which Peggotty had erupted with a parcel for the boy as he was taken off in the stagecoach, away from here, to a distant place.

What uneasy feelings he must have had towards the village and the house. Imprisoned by Murdstone, who had by then married and impregnated his mother, yet anxious to return when banished on Barkis's coach to an unknown destination. His mother had stood and waved goodbye to him, the new baby in her arms the final proof to David of how she had been violated and he had been supplanted. Perhaps it was not to a place that he wished to return, but to a time.

In his car, Pietro was free, pressing the accelerator and moving away between the hedgerows back to the Yarmouth Road. Freedom of movement was the blessing he had. You could not revisit the past, but as an adult you could drive away from the present.

TWICE in the previous six months he had come close to trouble. At a party given by his parents-in-law in Antwerp to mark their fortieth wedding anniversary, he had found himself in conversation with a widow of about forty-five. Though not really, not now, much older than he was, she had seemed in her propriety to belong to a different generation; she spoke to him as though he were a boy who had just left school. She had blonde hair held back off her face with brown combs, and eyes which had a competent, friendly sparkle. He was told that she was an inspired cook and immaculate housekeeper. She wore a tight-fitting and shiny blue dress that sent confusing signals. All the women had spent time and money on their clothes; the party seemed to have a much greater significance to these normally sober people than a similar function would have had in London. Yet this woman's manner suggested something more than social *joie de vivre*.

Hannah had become absorbed in hostly duties; the children were asleep at a neighbour's house: alone and on foreign soil, Pietro found himself slipping into some old, instinctive pattern of behaviour. When the woman invited him upstairs to view the painting she had given Hannah's parents as a present, he followed eagerly, feeling not guilt or furtiveness, but something more like bravado. Her seduction, attempted in a spare room where the coats were piled on the bed, was disarmingly direct. It did not speak of loneliness or a need to be loved; it was a frank invitation to sex, so free of all the complicating factors that had helped to keep him faithful that Pietro would have found it impossible to resist, had it not been for the sound of footsteps running up the stairs. In the preliminary grappling, her tight blue dress had ridden up, and now she had to slide it down quickly, which caused it to catch on her white underwear, a momentary indignity which seemed to linger on into the embarrassment of neutral conversation and false friendliness that followed the entry of the third guest, a fat Dutch psychologist who had come looking for his coat.

The other problem had been less dramatic, but had troubled him for longer. He had developed an interest, which now threatened to become an obsession, in a young woman he had met at the photographic laboratory in Waterloo. She had dark hair that curled inward at her shoulder, where it brushed her white coat. She smiled when she saw him, an uncertain and ambiguous expression that intrigued him. His conversation with her ran on predictable lines. He asked her about her work, commented on the weather, and she replied in a slightly timid voice. Once they went to lunch in an Italian restaurant nearby. Though she was not exactly evasive, he found out little about her. When they returned to the laboratory there was a powerful charge in the air between them. As he eventually picked up his coat to leave, she looked up from the darkroom with a stricken expression.

Stephanie, her name turned out to be. There were more lunches, conversations, drinks after work. Her father had been a railway signalman. She had been brought up in Clapham. She had two brothers and both her parents were dead. She loved dancing and American pop music, though she admitted to this sheepishly, as though worried about his response. Beneath her white coat she turned out to be a dramatically fashionable dresser. She told him about the things she wore – who had designed them or whose clothes she wished she could afford. She asked him about photography, about lenses and subjects and light. He explained some of the techniques he used to get the right texture in his prints.

Pietro knew he could no longer pretend that their meetings were innocent lunch breaks, or work-related conferences that happened to continue after hours: he was entranced by her catalogues of dance records and by her modest evasions. She was annoyingly pretty, too, out in the light; her eyelashes flickered or dropped, according to whether she was enthusing or retreating. It also occurred to him that, although she had given nothing away, she would not be so eager an accomplice in their meetings if she were not drawn in some way to him.

HE finished his meeting in Norwich at four o'clock, a low time in a provincial town. Afternoon shoppers in the streets wove between each other on the pavements or queued for the car parks of the giant supermarkets. It was early December and the windows were already full of Christmas trees and tinsel, the edges of the glass sprayed with mock snow that looked like shaving foam. Tins of biscuits showed Victorian coaches on which the caped driver lashed prancing horses down a muddied road; Stilton cheeses, pots of ginger, electronic games and plastic machine guns were piled beneath plump golden stars that replicated the forgotten sky of Roman-occupied Palestine.

He had missed many years of this ritual, which had not changed since he had been born. In Cardiff, Worcester, Newbury, whichever way the compass had pointed from his parents' house, the people had kept it up. Through different governments, through wars and strikes, through brief and uncomfortable bursts of prosperity, the annual reflex had persisted. The old people had kept coming with single shopping bags, still wearing the clothes old people had worn when he was a boy, though these slow creatures taking single coins from their purses were those his boyish eyes had seen as mothers in their capable middle age and fathers only just feeling the press of their stomach at the waistband of their working suits. Now they had unthinkingly adopted the posture and habits of their parents before them, and of all the old English people in the towns and villages who had sprouted in the individual brilliance of their lives, then joined the generality of the old and dead, leaving the world no different after all.

Pietro had for a long time felt surprised that people kept to the same routines. When he left Backley and, correspondingly, he thought, his childhood, he had unreasonably felt that Christmas trees and the automatic rituals would cease. He had occasionally seen them from a distance and thought them exhausted and

pointless. Now as he moved his car down the thronged street and
out of town, he felt reconciled to what he saw, as though a great
loop that joined him to his childhood had been completed, and
the intervals of exile and effort were forgotten. The repeated
years of custom he had missed did not now seem pointless to
him, but welcome; his own children would inherit something he
had done little to preserve, and for which he was therefore
thankful.

He had intended to drive back to London the shortest way,
through Thetford and Newmarket, but Hannah was not expecting him till late. Encouraged by the success of his trip to
Blundeston, he decided to make the short detour east to
Yarmouth, a town he had never visited before.

The approach was forbidding, as the road took a long sweep
through an industrial zone that the flat, sandy landscape did
nothing to conceal. The recommended route seemed designed to
keep people from entering the town itself, which Pietro
imagined dimly to be full of fishermen's cottages and people
cooking bloaters for tea.

Eventually he found his way to the sea front, several miles of
guest houses on one side, and the sound of immeasurable water
on the other. He stopped the car and walked along the front until
he found a way down on to the sand. It was dark by now, and the
wind that came in from the sea had a sharp, penetrating sting.

Pulling his jacket around him, Pietro trod awkwardly over the
packed sand that was driven into dunes, whose tumid, grassy
shapes were visible at regular intervals. There were no upturned
boats, however, no fires emitting cheerful smoke from metal
chimneys.

He looked out towards the sea, an element whose impersonal
horror was never truly told, even in descriptions of storms. The
grey waves sucked and heaved with a pointless energy, their
motions not majestic but an overpowering demonstration,
covering two-thirds of the world for twenty-four hours of the
day, of the random and futile movements of atomic matter. It
was not only futile, it was inescapable: the waves that rolled over

Yarmouth Sands were joined to those he had seen from his window in Los Angeles, to the water by the coast road in Colombo and the currents of the Tyrrhenian Sea.

He sat down on the edge of a dune, hearing the water roll. He remembered coming to the chapter in *David Copperfield* that described the storm off Yarmouth. A ship from Spain or Portugal – some warning note had been struck in those names – was heaving off the coast and breaking up in the waves. The sea appeared to be trying to disgorge it. An old fisherman had come to knock on David's door to tell him there was a body on the beach. He went down and found it was that of his disgraced friend Steerforth – 'I saw him lying with his head upon his arm as I had often seen him lie at school.' By this time the book had been shaking in his hands.

When the mental anguish that had started in Guatemala had receded, two years later, Pietro had rashly prided himself on having found solutions. He saw the episode as an isolated illness caused by – by grief, by drink, or stress, what did it matter? – that his strength of mind had overcome. He had no wish to see it as connected with a longer passage of events. But then the symptoms had resurfaced some years later, and he had known that the causes were deeper. He had understood, bitterly, that any sense of grand enlightenment was always likely to be misleading.

He must go back to Hannah. It was in the stillness she offered, the static point of her love, that he had found his destination. He recognised how much he loved her only after they had been apart. When they were reunited he saw her anew each time, as he had seen her for the first time in the apartment in Ghent, through the haze of his unhappiness. The sweetness of her nature was apparent in her face. It welcomed him unquestioningly every time, dismissing his faults, his moods, his failures, in her guileless smile, which he saw as evidence of her dedication to their shared life. She seemed to have no suspicions of him, she held no grudges; her view of him and of herself, though not a complicated one, seemed based on infinite determination. He kept expecting it to falter, for her to see the truth of his unworthy soul, but the steady glare of her love did not weaken, and he felt it helped him somehow to be worthy of her.

How traitorous his memory was. How he had forgotten the agony of the mental crisis he had gone through. In his sick mind each minute had been filled with enough sensations for a day, so two years of illness had seemed unbearably long. If he was not careful, he found he could pretend it had not really happened. But, he thought, you needed to have a clear recollection of the details of unhappiness if you were to recognise and value what saved you from it. Other less dramatic episodes of loneliness and discontent had almost disappeared from his memory. Sometimes he felt that in the course of his life he had learned nothing. He determined that from that moment on he would never again forget what he owed to Hannah.

Yet it was not just for the sake of his own salvation that he would turn away from the sea ahead of him. He had created a need for himself in his children. Perhaps this was a harsh way of defining their dependency; he had done no more than any other man who had reproduced. But it was in fact only he who could properly calm Mary when she awoke at night, dreaming of being crushed. Although Hannah was more important to them than he was, there was a role for him too with Anton and James, whose echoing cries of welcome greeted the sound of his key in the lock. And what hidden part of him had been revealed by them? What low need had been released, then satisfied, so that now he felt redefined and augmented?

He tasted the Yarmouth wind on his face. In the gas station at the junction of Sunset Boulevard and the Pacific Coast Highway the attendant would be listening to his radio in the cabin, watching the ocean sparkle as the sun rose above the hills behind him. In Lyndonville, Jack the yard man would be deep in mid-morning snowdrifts, hacking out another car. In New York City Laura was in a meeting, the roofs of cabs on Fifth Avenue visible from the window through which the light enflamed her hair. It was raining in the foothills of the Caserta Mountains, on the farm and the orchard. It was that time in Rome when the cobbled streets were lit only by the neon of shop signs before the lights came on, so that it looked more than ever like a film set, the flower sellers at the junctions of the via Frattina making their last sales, a sinister glow on the doorways in the narrow via della Lupa. In Hong Kong there was an hour's uncommercial sleep and stillness, a truce on the rock. The sun had left the mountain in les Houches, and all the children were gathered in.

Pietro stood up and began walking back to his car. He did not cry or feel moved at the thought of the terrifying sea and the unmade journeys it contained. He put from his mind the thought of the Italian shore and his mother, young Italian girl denied the world. He opened the car door and repositioned himself in front of its familiar gadgetry. He switched on the radio and sank the key into the ignition: particular objects in an appointed place, like a knot of wood in the plank of a cabin floor. . .

He drove along the front, searching for the London signs.

ZANICA

zzzzzzzzzzzzzzzzzzzzzzzzzzzzzzzzzzzzzzzzzzzzzzzzzzzzzzzzzzzzzzzzzzzzzzzzzzzzzzzzzzzzzzzzzzzz

Italy 1970

THE album sleeve lay on the bed. It was of the drugstore surrealist school. Planets turned in Technicolor space adorned by fauns and muscular warriors with bearskin loincloths. Nymphs with low-cut bodices welcomed sunsets on purple seas.

Pietro clamped the headphones tighter over his ears as the music swelled, electric organ rolling under the guitar, which screeched and rose in anguished progression, like some simulated ecstasy. The singer's voice spewed words of torture and yearning which nevertheless, boosted by the volume of the music, seemed to Pietro to proclaim something vital. He felt inflamed by them; they aroused desires in him he could not name; they gave a shape to his frustration. At the same time, the riding cymbals, splashing over the repeating rhythm of the bass guitar, also gave some exhilarating vent to the feelings trapped in him by age and circumstance.

The windows in his bedroom were locked and the curtains drawn. Outside, the sun shone unregarded on the back wall of the mansion block; in the closed bedroom Pietro had begun to sweat into the scarlet T-shirt which he pulled from the waistband of his jeans.

There was a knock on the door and his father stuck his head

round the corner. Pietro peeled off the headphones with an embarrassed wrench. His father looked round the room and at the drawn curtains but made no comment. He said he had made a pot of tea and invited Pietro to come and have a cup in the sitting room. Pietro smiled his acceptance.

Raymond Russell wanted to know what his son's plans were. 'The world is your oyster,' he said. 'I wish I was your age again.'

'I know, I know.' Pietro lowered his head and smiled. He had never really understood the expression. Was the world fishy, expensive, or just small?

'You don't have to decide irrevocably,' said his father, lighting one of the small cigars he had taken up in place of his pipe.

'Well, I think I do really. Supposing I get a degree all right next year. I'll have to get a job then, and I'll have to find somewhere to live.'

'Then you must decide what you want to do.'

Pietro sighed. It was warm in the flat; the air was thick and undisturbed.

'That should be a privilege,' said Russell.

'I understand.'

'I envy you. I just don't want you to get it wrong. And where are you going to go this summer?'

'I'm going to Italy.'

The word caused a small *frisson* between them.

'I'm going to the north. Up to the lakes. I'll have saved enough from working.'

Raymond Russell was not listening. He was staring through Pietro. 'Which lake?'

'I thought I'd start at Como and then see what happened.'

Pietro watched his father through the smoke of the cigar. The carriage clock on the mantelpiece ticked audibly. It had a glass base through which you could see its endlessly rotating mechanism.

'Your mother and I went up to the lakes ones. It must have been the year before you were born. It was the first time she had been back to Italy since we were married. She said she had always

261

wanted to go up to the lakes for a holiday. A friend of her family lived in Milan and he lent us his car – a funny old thing. Very unreliable.'

Pietro felt a twinge of embarrassment as his father attempted to touch on some personal memory.

'We drove out of Milan, I remember. We had a little hotel booked in Como, but somehow we took the wrong turning. Your mother was not much of a navigator, I'm afraid. We ended up in Bergamo. It was getting dark and I didn't like the sound of the engine at all. We asked someone the way. It can't have been very difficult because Como was the next big town on the main road, as far as I remember. But your mother was cross with me because she thought I'd criticised her for not finding the way, so she didn't listen properly when she was given the instructions. The long and the short of it was that we took the wrong road out of Bergamo. At about eight o'clock we ended up in a little village – I can't remember what it was called – and the car was overheating. I said we ought to stop for the night, and your mother agreed. What was that village called? Wait a minute, I'm going to see if I can find it in the atlas.'

Mr Russell crossed the sitting room to the shelf that held his reference books. He returned to his chair with a selection of atlases and opened an old blue book on his lap. Pietro watched as he hoisted his glasses further up his nose and stubbed his cigar out in the bronze ashtray, which habit enabled him to find without raising his eye from the page.

'That's it. Zanica. That's what it was called.' He closed the book and put it down by the chair.

'And then what happened?' said Pietro, more out of duty than curiosity.

'Oh, I don't know. I suppose I got the cases in from the car. We stayed the night. Whatever people do.'

There was silence for a moment. Then Russell stood up quickly and gathered the books to return them to their shelf. Pietro saw that his eyes were wet.

★

In the summer term at university the students in their final year prepared for the future. Some seemed happy to move directly into jobs that were chiefly done by people twice their age. Others tried to postpone decisions by applying for further courses, more degrees, or anything that would buy them time. Pietro wanted neither to bring on middle age, nor prolong his youth, but to live in a way that fitted what he was. This seemed to mean, for some reason he could not determine, that he would have to go abroad.

It might be easier in America, he thought, though he had never been there. He pictured two different kinds of country: a brash place where children wore baseball caps and watched TV cartoons all day with sandwiches from the icebox; and somewhere eerily civilised where people like Laura and her family lived, where they read books and wore tweed jackets and behaved in a way that was like the English, only without the defeated element of Surrey lanes and south London streets. He could not imagine that they had the same crisis about work and career. He knew they made cars in Detroit, that people worked in factories and that labor unions were on strike; but from films he saw it seemed the kind of place where people of his age didn't have to tie themselves to something, but just evolved. He was entranced by the thought of travel. He was so pleased by the surface of the world that already he had begun to be afraid of dying.

Pietro lugged his backpack out of the terminal at Milan, Malpensa. It was a long walk from the compound to a suitable road. By the time he set his pack down and stuck out his thumb he was sweating. He had forgotten what hard work hitchhiking was. Once in Greece he had waited two days for a lift, twice watching the sun crawl slowly up in the sky and slowly sink as the cars ploughed on past him.

He took a swig of water from his army surplus water bottle, which he had filled at the airport. Soon he would need to reacquire the scavenging habits of the hitchhiker, picking up spare bread rolls in the breakfast basket, saving a few sheets of paper in restaurant lavatories. He planned to stay in youth hostels or guesthouses in Lecco, Como and Bergamo. There would be other people there he could talk and have dinner with, but he preferred to travel on his own.

He tried to meet the eyes of the drivers as their cars approached. Some looked embarrassed and fixed their gaze on the horizon, others looked indifferent or hostile. Several made a curious movement with their hand, pointing downwards to the ground beneath them. At first Pietro thought they were saying that they lived in Milan and were not going anywhere; later he guessed they were saying it was he who was staying put. After two hours a fruit lorry going to Bergamo pulled over and he ran up to it with his pack.

Up in front he talked to the driver, a young man not much older than himself. Pietro gave him cigarettes and explained what he was doing. The driver nodded and smoked. He talked a little about football and the teams in Milan. After a while they settled into silence and Pietro watched the road unfolding through the dull plain of Lombardy. In Bergamo the driver set him down at the railway station; he himself was going on to a depot in the outskirts. Pietro thanked him and lugged his pack over to the buffet. He decided he could afford a cappuccino.

He pulled out his maps and laid them on the café table. He had come slightly out of his way but it was a rule of hitchhiking never to refuse a lift. His father had lent him an old army map he had used during the advance from Rome, but unfortunately it did not come as far north as Bergamo. He had also bought a tourist map in London. As the waiter set down the coffee he took his bearings. He estimated that Lecco was no more than thirty miles away, so he would easily make it that evening, if he found a lift. There were plenty of other villages dotted around: Zogno, Seriate, Verdello, Zanica. Zanica. What was it his father had said about it?

He paid the bill and walked up the viale Papa Giovanni XXIII towards the centre of town. It was a handsome, open city, bursting with muscular Lombard wealth. Two of the grandest buildings were the Credito Italiano and the Banca d'Italia. A large civic statue was not of Dante or Garibaldi but of someone called Gucchi. Ahead, visible on the hilltop, was the imposing upper city, reached by funicular railway or a winding road.

My life is in front of me, Pietro thought: I can go anywhere. He had the thrill of release which the first day of travel brings. He saw a sign for the bus station and decided he would go and see when the next bus went to Lecco. Although Bergamo was impressive it also looked dauntingly expensive. From what he could make out from the bus schedule, he would have to wait for three hours. On the other hand, a battered vehicle destined for Crema, first stop Zanica, was already rocking backwards and forwards under the vibration of its engine. It was only about four miles. Why not? If the worst came to the worst he could walk back in the morning.

Zanica was a village like a hundred others, small, unfavoured, an aggregation of houses and people on some economic principle now forgotten. It had an impressive town hall in the French style with a war monument to its fallen – *ai sui caduti*. The dates of the wars were principally from the nineteenth century. The main road to Crema ran through two right angles in the village, and the traffic was heavy. Some older buildings by the roadside were flaked and burned by fumes, but back through the Piazza 11 Febraio was a grandiose church with a bell-tower and a large clock. Around the outskirts of the village were signs of intensive agriculture. A lorry full of pigs caused Pietro to step quickly back on to the pavement as it rounded one of the sharp bends. On the southern side of the village was an enormous cemetery. The shops included a butcher, a bank, a chemist and a photography shop; but although there were two cafés there was no sign of a hotel or *pensione*.

Pietro followed one of the streets westward out of Zanica. Just as it left the village there was a track leading off it called via Madonna dei Campi. It overlooked fields of fat, overgrown corn and red, turned earth bordered by clumps of trees. At the junction with the main road was a bar. Pietro left his pack outside the door, straightened his hair as much as he could with his fingers and went inside. Two men were sitting drinking at a table. There was no one behind the bar. He called out *buon giorno*, and sat down. He felt self-conscious under the men's silent gaze.

Eventually a large woman with reddish hair scraped back into a bun came up to his table.

He asked for a beer and she disappeared behind the bar, which had several coloured pennants in a row above the bottles. There were half a dozen cheap sporting trophies and a framed colour photograph of an Italian footballer.

What had his parents been doing here? Pietro could not imagine they would have come out of choice. Then he remembered. They had lost the way. His mother had been navigating. And then what? What had his father said? Nothing very much, except, it now came back to Pietro, he had seemed moved. What did they do? His father had said something about getting the cases from the car. It was the sort of detail he would think important. So they had brought the cases in. Where? Perhaps to this place. There could be nowhere else in the village.

The woman said something in a strong accent to the two men at their table. She picked up a couple of glasses and put them on top of the bar. Pietro took his drink up to the bar and asked her if there was somewhere to stay in the village.

'You want to go to Bergamo,' she said.

'I've just been there. Is there nowhere here?'

'It's just a little place. No hotels.' She began to wash the glasses.

Pietro felt determined. He said, 'About twenty years ago my parents stayed the night somewhere in this village. Was there a *pensione* here in those days?'

The woman looked at him in surprise.

'Where are you from?'

'From England. But my mother was from Italy. And they were on holiday here.'

'It's possible,' she said. 'When my father had this place he

266

sometimes used to have people to stay the night. There were two or three guest bedrooms. But we don't get many people.'

'And now?'

She shrugged. 'Now it's a bar. And we have the shop.'

Pietro said, 'Can I stay the night?'

The woman looked at him curiously. 'No. It's not possible now. You should go to Bergamo. There are plenty of places there.'

'No. It must be here. I'll pay you.'

Suddenly she laughed. 'How old are you?'

'Twenty.'

'Come with me. I'll speak to my husband.'

She led him through the shop into a tiled hallway at the end of which was a bare wooden staircase. She disappeared into a ground-floor room. Pietro could hear the sound of voices. He did not understand why he was so determined to stay, but it was too late to change his mind now.

The woman emerged, pushing back a greasy wisp of hair.

'Come along.' She led him up the stairs and on to a wooden landing with a single threadbare mat. He saw the muscles in her calves swell as she climbed in front of him. She opened a door. There was a room with a metal bedstead and an old wardrobe with carved doors.

'You can sleep here for one night if you want to,' she said.

Pietro looked around. The room was reasonably clean. The window gave a view of indifferent fields. He said he would stay.

He unpacked his clothes and took his sponge bag over to the basin. He could hear a dog barking with a strangled, howling sound. He brushed his teeth and splashed water on his face. He wondered if he should go for a walk around the village, but felt reluctant to leave his belongings unattended. There was no lock on the door. He opened the window and looked out over the cluttered yard at the back. There were some hens enclosed by wire mesh and a kennel with a chain attached but no dog visible. Beyond the fields was a horizon from which the light was beginning to drain.

He took his book out and settled on the bed to read. He could see the grain of the wood in the paper, the varied density of ink in the printed words. He could hear a thin whistle of birdsong from outside, and a door turning slowly on its hinges in the hallway below. He was finding it difficult to concentrate on the book. He looked down at his hands and removed a tiny flake of dried skin with a fingernail. When he was dead, no one would know what those hands had looked like to him, how they had shaped everything he had done. When he was dead, the tiny hairs on the backs of his knuckles would go down into nothingness, as though they had never been.

There was a cheap picture on the wall of the room that showed a house overlooking the sea. The pigmentation of the sky and the water was crude. Whoever had painted or copied or printed it had not looked at the coloured surfaces of the world.

The book was an autobiography, the story of a man's life told with emphasis on the facts. 'My maternal grandfather, on the other hand,' one chapter began. He laid down the book and took out his maps from the side pocket of his pack. His father's army map was a small-scale and therefore huge affair, folded several times. Unfortunately it petered out just north of Bologna, but his father had been keen for him to have it. On a mountain just south of the city a private in his regiment had won the VC. The troops were at the time being supplied by mules.

Pietro let his mind wander, trying to imagine his father pushing north through the terrible winter, his efforts helped by the knowledge that there was a woman who loved him. But could he have been sure of her? He must have been an unlikely suitor, and the anguish of wondering if she was faithful must have made the struggle even grimmer.

There was a knock on the door of his room. Pietro jumped and dropped the map on the counterpane. His heart thudding, he went over to open it.

A girl of about eighteen in a pinafore stood staring at him. 'My mother said you can come and have dinner with us if you want,' she said.

'Thank you.' He found himself accepting instinctively. The girl vanished. She had had staring blue eyes and, more strangely, hair so fair it was almost white. It stood up around her head like a frizzy albino hedge. He stepped on to the landing and looked both ways, but there was no sign of her.

When he got back into the room and closed the door, he found that his heart was still pounding. He felt certain that something had happened in this place and wished now that he could remember what his father had said about Zanica.

We stayed the night . . . Your mother was not much of a navigator . . . the year before you were born.

And yet it had been their summer holiday and his birthday was in May. Less than a year.

This was the place they had stayed. He was certain of it. He tried to picture what had happened. It was night time. His mother would have climbed the stairs and come into the room first while his father talked to the owner about the luggage and the rate.

They had some wine and some bread and salami downstairs in the room that was now the shop, but was then a restaurant. It was too late for dinner. Then Francesca said she was tired. She came up ahead of him. In this room she looked over the dim fields in the darkness. She opened the window and let in the warm night air and the sound of cicadas and a dog somewhere in the distance. She took off her dress and hung it in the old wardrobe by the basin. Then, in her slip, she sat down on the bed and went through the contents of the suitcase to take out her night things.

Meanwhile Russell, who had finished his cigarette downstairs, came up the stairs slowly, feeling the broad planks of wood give beneath his weight. Then he came to the landing, the single thin rug illuminated by the yellow light of the shaded bulb above. And he opened the door to the room, this room, and Francesca looked up, and because it was her habit and her nature, she smiled at him. And . . .

It was not quite like that. He could almost picture it, but not quite.

269

There came another knock at the door and Pietro sprang up. There was no one there. From downstairs he heard his name called. No, that was impossible.

He heard a call. 'Signore.' That was the sound he had heard. He was being summoned to dinner. The woman with the reddish hair in a bun, the owner, stepped out into the hallway and gestured to him to come down.

PIETRO descended the stairs slowly. The room that opened off the hallway, where the woman had earlier gone to consult her husband, contained a mahogany table with a lacy white cloth and several heavy chairs. It was very ill-lit, but Pietro could make out some sort of serving hatch at one end, and a glass door. Seated at the head of the table was a man with grey hair, wearing a blue checked shirt. He was crumbling bread between his fingers.

The woman came through the glass door with a steaming china bowl in her hands. She gestured Pietro to a chair. He sat down, uneasy at not having been introduced to the man. The woman pushed her hair back into its bun and served two bowls of pasta, giving the first to her husband, then placing Pietro's in front of him. She said nothing, but poured a glass of water from a carafe. She left them.

Pietro looked towards the man and nodded. He said nothing, but bent his head to the bowl.

'Is your wife not going to eat?' said Pietro.

The man did not reply.

'And your daughter?'

Still he said nothing, but worked his fork around the bowl in front of him. Pietro did likewise, discovering he was hungry after his journey. The sound of their forks on the china was the only noise in the room.

When the woman came to take the plates away Pietro asked if she would not eat with them. She shook her head.

'Don't talk to him,' she said, looking towards her husband. 'He never talks to strangers. He only talks to me.'

'I understand.'

Pietro looked around at the solid rustic furniture of the room. It seemed dusty and overlooked. Much of the wood was draped, as though they thought it better off concealed.

Pietro swallowed some water. He wondered if they would be offered wine. He glanced up towards his silent dining companion, who showed no interest in him. Eventually the woman returned with a flat dish on which were some pieces of meat in gravy. She also carried a bowl of salad.

Pietro again worked his way through it. When it was cleared and he had declined the offer of an orange, he asked the woman: 'What about your daughter? Has she had dinner?'

'My daughter?' The woman's voice was even.

'Yes. She came to tell me I could come and eat with you.'

The woman looked at him in a way that seemed to suggest he was lying to her.

'She's very pretty,' he went on, trying to placate her. 'Beautiful blonde hair.'

The woman let out a strange sound, somewhere between a sigh and a smothered laugh. 'Ah . . . Isabella. Yes.'

PIETRO went up to his room as soon as he could. He took up his book and began to read again in the yellow light from the bedside lamp. Through the open window came the sound of cicadas and, closer now, the barking of the dog.

He tried to lose himself in the autobiography but found when he turned the page that he had taken nothing in. He would leave early in the morning and take the bus back to Bergamo, then on to Lecco. It would be good to meet some other people on their travels.

There was the sound of running footsteps on the landing outside and a young woman's raised voice. It sounded like the girl who had knocked on his door. Isabella. He opened the door gently and looked out. There was no sign of her, though from the dining room downstairs he could hear two voices raised in anger.

Pietro went back into his room and undressed for bed. He

folded his clothes on the chair and then, for some reason, placed the back of the chair under the door handle. He turned off the light and pulled up the sheet.

He knew his parents had been here. He closed his eyes and tried once more to imagine it.

His father had pulled up outside, saying, 'This place may be able to help.' His mother, still a little put out by her inability to find the right road, had agreed quietly. They came into the bar. Francesca explained to the owner that they wanted to stay the night. She came upstairs to see the room. She had come in through the door, crossed to the window and looked out. She opened the wardrobe to see if there was space and turned back the bed to make sure the sheets were clean.

Then she went back and told her husband it was all right. They had asked for dinner but the owner had said it was too late. They ate some bread and salami which was brought to them by a sturdy young woman with red hair pushed up into a bun. She was still in her twenties then.

Francesca said she was tired and went ahead up the stairs to the room. She took off her dress and hung it up in the wardrobe. Her husband stretched and finished his wine downstairs. Then he climbed the stairs gently, feeling the treads beneath his feet. He pushed open the door and Francesca turned and smiled up at him. Then, then . . .

'THIS place may be able to help,' said Russell. The car radiator was steaming. Francesca nodded, sulking a little at his impatience with her navigation.

Once inside, she asked the owner if they could stay the night. He said they had a room at the top of the stairs and handed her a key. Francesca ran upstairs, her spirits lifting at the thought of shelter. In the bar Russell asked if they could have something to eat. The owner shrugged and said it was too late for dinner, but that he would send his daughter through with something in a minute. Russell drank a glass of red wine at the bar.

In the bedroom Francesca passed a quick eye over the furniture and the washbasin. It was simple but clean enough. She crossed to the window and opened it. There was a sound of cicadas from outside, and a single bark from a dog chained in the yard. She looked in the wardrobe and turned back the cover to check the sheets. Leaving the door open, she tripped down the stairs.

Russell took her over to a table on which a candle was stuck in a saucer. She smiled at him and he filled her glass with wine. He touched it with his own next to the candle flame.

From behind the bar a plump woman in her twenties with greasy red hair appeared with a loaf of bread and some slices of salami and olives. Francesca began to yawn before they had finished eating.

While Russell lit a cigarette and poured the rest of the bottle of wine into his glass, she kissed him on the forehead and went up to the room.

She took off her dress and hung it in the old, carved wardrobe. Then she sat on the bed and sorted through her night things in the case.

Russell finished the wine, stubbed out his cigarette and climbed the stairs, feeling the soft timber yield beneath his feet and the risen banister against his palm.

He pushed open the bedroom door and Francesca turned in mild alarm. Seeing it was him, she smiled, her head turned up towards him as though in question or surprise.

Then he looked at her and saw the narrow straps of ivory-coloured silk across her shoulders. He went and sat beside her on the bed, laying his head on her shoulder where the material cut into the white skin, pulled down by the weight of her body.

He peeled down the straps on either side, pulling gently down until her breasts were exposed, white with their dark-brown nipples, moving slightly up and down where they had just been freed.

He looked up into the almost black eyes of this dark-haired girl. She laughed, a movement which caused her hair to lift and

273

sway back from her white neck and throat. Her lips parted when he placed his own on top of them.

His hands reached down her body, fumbling with further straps and layers of underclothes until her own hand gently stopped him. She stood up, pulled down her clothes, undignified, like a child pulling down its drawers. Then she held his head against her abdomen. Her fingers ran gently over the indentation in his skin where the shrapnel had entered. He clasped at her legs, on one of which a stocking had escaped her quick undressing.

He lifted himself up and peeled off his clothes in swift, embarrassed movements. He did not relax until he was lying on top of her, feeling himself enter some reassuring warmth.

Then he was for a moment calm. He looked down at her shoulder, at the skin with its teeming cells. Three years married, he thought, as he began to move backwards and forwards into her; three years and no word about a child. He had begun to fear that this was something more sinister than chance delay.

He wanted so desperately to have a child, to see some imprint of himself and what he had believed in, something that would live on, for what it was worth, when he was dead. He thought that if he concentrated hard enough, if he willed it, then he might help the fusion happen; nothing else would make tolerable the inexplicable days of war or the random tragedies of peace.

So Russell, not an imaginative man by nature, came in the urgency of his longing to picture what was happening beneath him. He could feel the forces gathering in him, ready to be released, and when the spasm came he held it back, checking his movements, twice, three times, until he judged the force was unstoppable. And when he let it come it was with a powerful shudder and a cry not of satisfaction but of hope and urging. In his mind he saw the milky fluid spurting and charging into the rosy flesh; then somehow, as the picture became less clear, he saw the daunting journey of some brave outrider of himself. He pictured it journeying through pathways lit as if by pink candlelight, through passageways and tubes and junctions, borne on only by the momentum of his hope. Then he opened his eyes and looked down at the naked body and the face of this woman, whom he loved, and buried his head in her neck, weeping, urging the seed on, willing it home.